By Derek Sowers

A Bridge in Glass

Published by Dreamspinner Press
www.dreamspinnerpress.com

DEREK SOWERS

A BRIDGE IN GLASS

Published by

DREAMSPINNER PRESS

8219 Woodville Hwy #1245
Woodville, FL 32362 USA
www.dreamspinnerpress.com

This is a work of fiction. Names, characters, places, and incidents either are the product of author imagination or are used fictitiously, and any resemblance to actual persons, living or dead, business establishments, events, or locales is entirely coincidental.

A Bridge in Glass
© 2025 Derek Sowers

Cover Art
© 2025 Derek Sowers
www.dereksowers.com
Author Photo © Derek Sowers
Cover content is for illustrative purposes only and any person depicted on the cover is a model.

Trade Paperback ISBN: 978-1-64108-812-1
Digital ISBN: 978-1-64108-811-4
Trade Paperback published May 2025
v. 1.0

TABLE OF CONTENTS

For Miguel and Cirrus and all the bridges we've built

PART 1
ENTROPY

PROLOGUE
THE LOOP

THERE CAME a time when Aaron Hayes realized that there'd been no loop at all, even though on dozens of occasions it had appeared as if there were. He'd seen signs of a loop with his own eyes, but he'd also seen evidence to the contrary. And although this contrary evidence had presented itself only once, he believed that even a solitary exception disproved a rule. He held firm to this even when his scientific mind conjured doubt, for everything he was about to do depended on it—the nonexistence of fate, the preeminence of free will, the assured absence of a loop.

Behind him stood eighty years of a long life, much of it spent in solitude. Ahead of him: his last and greatest endeavor. Success would retroactively change his life and, with luck, erase its most tragic consequences, bringing health to sickness, knowledge to ignorance, and justice to wickedness. It would change everything.

He recalled a day from his past—the only time he'd ever felt real doubt about a decision. In that moment, he'd imagined proverbial signposts all around him, pointing in countless directions, toward a myriad of possibilities and outcomes. But as he'd looked upon those signs, he'd found only one that was decipherable. Readable. Only one he could have followed at the time.

He thought it a sign of fate.

Now, he saw how he'd been wrong.

And how his doubt had been right.

Aaron chased away the memory and looked around. He sat alone in a tidy room near the back of his home. Beside him, through a large floor-to-ceiling window, he could see the dark, gentle curve of a nearby hillside. Above glittered a clear starry night and a crescent moon, bright but waning.

He then caught his own reflection in the glass. Though he had aged, time had been kind. It had taken his youth, but it hadn't blurred his focus or dulled his acuity. His graying features betrayed his years, but at his core and in his character still lived the soul of a man half his age.

He offered his reflection a kind smile.

"You've done it, Methuselah," he said, using a playful epithet for himself that had been given to him in jest when he was young. He'd often laughed at that moniker. But it was an undeniable truth now, not just the echo of the coy flirtation of the man who'd given it to him.

Dozens of etched glass data cubes, each the size and shape of a six-sided die, lay scattered on the polished wooden desk in front of him. Above the table hung a wide computer monitor—a thin pane of opaque, shatterproof glass with polished edges, but no notable design features. The room was otherwise unembellished, for it had long served only one purpose: the study of a small, enigmatic device that Aaron called "the needle."

The needle had been the source of his angst, the leading antagonist of his life, but tonight it would be his salvation. It sat before him, resting on a compact computer tablet similar in style to the monitor, an opaque glass panel the size of his hand. The needle itself was a cylindrical object, the length and thickness of a small pen and finely tapered at both ends. It had a seamless, satiny blue skin that appeared to undulate as if a stellar nebula swirled within. Embedded on one side of the device were two small gold lights, set three centimeters apart. Flanking them were two series of numbers, broken by decimal points. The needle had an electric quality overall, its features apparently projected on its glossy surface like images on a screen, but so fine and detailed that the shapes themselves seemed real and material.

Aaron hovered over the needle with an air of victory. It had been a mystery for too long. Mastering its power had been his purpose. He'd always known its function, but *how to make it work* had eluded him. Now, after years of experimentation and revelation, he understood. All that remained was to power it up one last time and set his plan into motion.

"Embed the coordinate list, please," he said finally, breaking the silence with a measured tone.

The glass tablet, programmed as an interface, activated in response. Several rows of numerical sequences appeared on its surface in crisp white text, each series conforming to the pattern of digits and decimal points showing on the needle itself. Beneath the list appeared the words:

COORDINATES EMBEDDED.

The needle's swirling blue surface luminesced. The gold lights fluttered to life like erratic, spinning pulsars. The numbers changed to match the first row of those displayed on the tablet.

Three new messages appeared:

LATTICE MOD COMPLETE.

SERIES IN QUEUE.

GATEWAY READY.

Aaron stared at the beautiful, shimmering device and subconsciously ran a finger along the thin, rounded corner of the tablet. He felt a wave of pride, but also reticence. He'd used the needle for experiments and amusements great and small for quite some time, and with each activation he'd grown more adept and confident with the technology. But as it flickered before him now, he hesitated. His next maneuvers would be his last. They'd be transformative, compounding. And there'd be no undoing them.

He nodded to himself and nudged his whispering doubts aside. He took three of the glass data cubes—each filled with his notes and research and the experiences of this life—and pocketed them. From a small desk drawer, he also took a forty-year-old SD data storage card. Last, he collected the needle and the tablet and left the workroom. The ambient lights dimmed as he exited.

The adjacent space—his living room—reflected a comfortable home life. He lived and worked in Clarendon Heights above the Castro district, in one of the few "Eichler" homes to be found in San Francisco. It had an open architectural style featuring glass walls and post-and-beam construction, which made for a spacious living room. The entire home was warmly lit and comfortably furnished.

Mounted on the wall above a long gray couch were more than a dozen framed photographs depicting images of friends and family and treasured moments now decades past. He glanced at the well-ordered gallery, then hastily looked away with a pang of remorse.

At the far end of the room, at the back of the house, were two grand sliding glass doors, identical in size to the framed glass walls on either side. Beyond was a wide wooden deck, and in the distance, the tall, glittering skyline of the city of San Francisco.

Aaron had lived in this house since late 2001—almost sixty years now, most of his life. He'd never tired of the city view, but he ignored it this time as he crossed the room. He came to a tall bookshelf. It held numerous imposing tomes but also dozens more mementos from his past. He moved from one item to the next, fondly giving each a quiet farewell. He stopped at a large framed photograph depicting two men—one in his early fifties with slightly receding short brown hair, standing beside Aaron in his mid-twenties, with his blond locks swept back. The two men were dressed in matching black tuxedos, standing on the deck of a cruise ship, leaning toward one another with warm smiles. Their shared affection was clear. Behind them, a soft twilight horizon emerged from the open ocean, expanding into a brilliant starlit sky.

Aaron lingered on the photograph and the image of his young self. His life had possessed a manifest duality. Joy had walked with grief, age with youth, and love with loss. This one photo contained each of these contradictions, mostly unseen by anyone but him.

His emotions came upon him unexpectedly. Tears threatened to break through. He hadn't anticipated losing control so readily. He clenched his hands in an attempt to brace himself, then turned away from the photograph, the bookshelf, and his memories.

Determined to linger no further, he moved to the center of the room and at last peered out at the tall towers of the city. He thought of all the ways San Francisco had changed since his youth. The city was restless, constantly redefining itself and its values, shifting from one extreme to the next in rapid succession—rich to poor, vibrant to stagnant, lauded to maligned—then back again. In many ways Aaron's life and the city itself were kindred spirits.

"Cirrus?" he asked into the room.

"Yes, Aaron," came a soothing male voice, the disembodied manifestation of the home's embedded General Intellectual Companion. The G.I.C., while technically a form of artificial intelligence, was more than just a resource. Cirrus was a colleague, a protector—even a friend. He had aided Aaron in his work for years, becoming increasingly intuitive, learning to joke and laugh with him, and on Aaron's darkest days, offering counsel and comfort.

"Thank you for being so good to me," Aaron said with genuine warmth.

"It's all part of the job," Cirrus replied with a blend of sadness and satisfaction in his tone—a tone perhaps more cultivated by his years of interaction with Aaron than by any code programmed into him, but very human all the same.

Aaron nodded. He often reminded himself that Cirrus wasn't truly alive, but it didn't matter. Saying goodbye was painful.

Aaron stood pensively for a moment, then positioned the needle in his bare left hand so it felt balanced in his light grip. He then rolled it forward with his thumb until the two gold lights made contact with the pads of his middle and ring fingers.

The small, beautiful object fused to his fingertips. A dark sound filled his mind, like a tuning orchestra settling on a single, sustained note. He could hear it, just barely, even feel it coursing through every nerve in his body.

Then it stopped.

There was silence.

The needle's grip on his fingers loosened.

It was done.

Daylight had replaced the starry night, and the room had changed. Aaron now wore a black leather glove on his right hand, which he removed and tossed into a nearby wastepaper basket. He wiped a trace of blood from his cheek. In what seemed like the blink of an eye, half of the work had been done. His first moves were complete.

He put the weight of them from his mind and looked around.

His home was now bright with the midday sun. Some familiar items were no longer present. Others were in different places. The house even smelled different, with hints of flowers and coffee hanging in the air. This was his home as it had been fifty years earlier, and as it was now, again, in 2010.

Aaron went through the other rooms one by one, savoring the differences but touching nothing. He found a vase of tulips on the kitchen counter and a single black tuxedo hanging in an empty bedroom closet.

He returned to the living room where the photo of himself on the cruise ship now stood on a side table near the couch. In front of the photo he found a man's gold wedding band, placed atop a handwritten note. It read:

SEE YOU IN 10 YEARS.

Aaron smiled sadly as he read it, fidgeting with an identical ring on his own left hand. He took the ring from the table and slipped it into his pocket along with the needle. He left the tablet, the SD card, and the three data cubes in the ring's place, then exited the house.

Outside, he was greeted by blue skies and a brilliant sun. He took in the air, letting the world around him trigger memories and dreams—some cherished, others forgotten. He glanced back at his home, indulging his sentimentality one last time, then set off down the hill.

As he walked, he kept his attention inward and his gaze ahead, averting his eyes from passersby. Though he'd once occupied this world alongside these people, they were no longer his kin. He felt a need to avoid their glances and prevent anyone from recognizing him as their contemporary. He feared that mutual awareness—fleeting and anonymous though it might be—would pose a distraction he could not afford.

At the bottom of the hill at Castro and Market Streets, he descended into the subway and boarded a train heading downtown. He stood near the front of the car, where he had a clear view through the operator's cabin and out the front window. The dark subway tunnel extended straight ahead, softly illuminated by white lights spaced equidistant along the north wall. As the train raced forward, Aaron imagined it following not the track but those lights, connecting the dots toward his inevitable destination.

He disembarked at Powell Street and continued on foot, south into SOMA. He soon arrived at a large multi-level movie theater of modern design. Unexpected anxiety rose within him as he neared the familiar building's pristine glass doors. He knew what awaited him inside, and he was prepared to face it, but his readiness provided no relief to his mounting disquiet. Stepping over this confluence of emotion, he pulled the doors open and entered a wide, bright lobby.

Brilliant overhead lights flickered in his watering eyes.

His heart raced.

His pace slowed.

Directly ahead of him sat a man, hunched over, alone on a long bench. He had his head down, his hands loosely covering his face.

Aaron knew him and knew his grief. He knew his life and every contradiction of its own distinct duality.

He knew the choices he'd made,

The choices that had been made for him,
And the tragic course of action he was contemplating now.
He knew everything that had led him to this moment,
To his place on the bench,
And this silent, mournful despair.

But now, Aaron also knew how to save him,
To change his direction,
To turn him left where he'd once turned right.
And in so doing, save them both.

This place, this time, formed the great crossroads of Aaron's life.
This was the point to which all pasts had led and from which all
futures had sprung,
Where everything he loved had come and gone,
And everything he knew started and ended—and began again.

In his mind's eye, he could see the signposts around him once more,
Pointing in every conceivable direction.
The last time he was here, he could read only one.
Now, he could read them all.

CHAPTER 1
2020

HE FELT the arm around his neck, the pressure behind his eyes, and the veins in his face blazing hot as the chokehold took him down to his knees. He felt the cold barrel of the gun pushed hard against his temple, so hard he thought the pressure itself might kill him.

And he felt the rage bearing down on him. It assaulted him as a wailing voice, hammering his ears at point-blank range, words stacking upon one other in tone and temper to form an avalanche of deafening, paralyzing fury—a threat to his life, *should you ever try to fucking leave me.*

He felt the hollow void of unconsciousness coming for him. Desperate, he strained to speak, to find the strength to reply to that voice and defuse its wrath. He forced out a small, pathetic gurgle.

"*... please....*"

It was enough.

He was released.

He dropped to the floor.

Aaron woke from the nightmare with only a meek cry and a subconsciously restrained shudder. It was early morning. The room was dark. The disorientation came first, but when he finally realized where he was—home and safe—relief washed over him, as well as the shame.

His tears came in a torrent. The dream had not merely been the bitter product of his imagination but the memory of a real event, fifteen years in the past. The man in that dream—his former boyfriend, Grant— was gone, dead for a decade now. But the dream had come anyway, as it had many times before. And now, like then, it felt real. Even after fifteen years, it had never fully left him alone.

Aaron's current partner, Drummer, was not a light sleeper, but he still woke at Aaron's shudder. Almost by instinct, Drummer put his arms around him and held him as he cried. This was not new either.

Nightmares of this magnitude had been a regular occurrence for Aaron. They'd begun tapering off in 2018, but the ominous and tragic state of the world in 2020 had proved to be a ferocious trigger.

Aaron relaxed in Drummer's arms. He wiped his eyes and took a heavy breath. He found Drummer's hand in the dark and held it tight.

"Thank you, baby," Aaron said, his voice trembling. "It'll never go away, will it?"

"It will," Drummer answered, with a note of quiet confidence in his sturdy voice. "It's already August. The last nightmare was two months ago. And you were way more bothered by that one."

"I s'pose," Aaron said, uncertain. "His voice was so loud this time, though. I know it's not really him, but…."

"I know."

Aaron took another breath and sighed. "I can still hear him screaming," he said in a whisper. "Telling me I'm a failure. That all my successes have just been luck. Saying that every time I lose something I love…."

"That voice is wrong," Drummer insisted. "Listen to me, not him."

Aaron nodded but said nothing more.

The two men remained in each other's arms as they drifted back into a light sleep. An hour later Aaron's phone alarm popped on, playing a soft, classical tune—one he had chosen with the express hope that it would gently wake him from any slumber, troubled or otherwise.

Aaron lifted himself from Drummer's embrace and stopped the music. Then he sat up fully and dropped his feet off the edge of the bed.

Drummer rose with him. "You okay?" he asked.

"Yeah," Aaron answered somewhat truthfully. "Happy birthday to me, huh?"

Drummer sat up and kissed him on the back of the neck.

Aaron let out a soft sigh and looked over his shoulder. "What would I do without you, D?"

"You'll never have to worry about that."

Aaron held Drummer's loving gaze for a moment, then stood and rounded the bed to the bathroom. As he entered, he averted his eyes from the mirror, for he knew what he would see. It was Friday, August 7, 2020, and he was one day away from turning forty. Though Aaron had experienced good times, he had certainly seen hard times as well, and this internal conflict had begun to reveal itself in the lines around his eyes.

Drummer entered the bathroom behind him, soft concern in his smile. He was shirtless, exposing two neo-traditional full sleeve tattoos that extended from his wrists to his neck. Other tattoos of various sizes and complexity were scattered across his toned torso and back.

"Well look at that," he said, studying Aaron's reflection. He wrapped his tattooed arms around him. "Forty really is the new thirty."

Aaron permitted a small grin at the clichéd joke, though his demeanor remained subdued. "Thanks, D," he said. "It's all genetics, I guess. And maybe the gym."

"And a touch of body dysmorphia," Drummer added with a smirk. He made a small pinching motion in the air, as if tossing a bit of something into a bowl.

"Maybe," Aaron conceded. "I never saw myself facing down forty, though."

"Careful, Methuselah. I turned forty-five last week, remember? And you don't technically turn forty until tomorrow." Drummer kissed him on the cheek, then motioned to Aaron's reflection and added, "I'll leave the two of you alone. Don't be too hard on him."

Drummer left, and Aaron peered directly at his reflection, this time seeing himself the way he imagined Drummer did. Through this lens he saw a youthful gaze and even glints of the face he remembered from his early twenties, though much had changed since then.

He showered then returned to the bedroom. Drummer had already made the bed and raised the shades, allowing morning light to stream through a large picture window. Beyond it stood the tall buildings of San Francisco's SOMA district and a clear view of the Mission, the Castro, and Twin Peaks to the west.

Aaron and Drummer shared a corner condominium on the twenty-fifth floor of a high-rise, south of downtown, on the five-hundred block of Mission Street. They led a comfortable life but kept it a humble one. The master bedroom was lightly furnished, containing only a king-size bed, two side tables, and a dresser. Against one wall was a full-length mirror, and above the headboard hung a textured canvas reproduction of Van Gogh's *The Starry Night*.

Aaron sat on the bed, pausing to look at a framed photograph on the side table. It was a selfie Drummer had taken of the two of them ten years earlier, on the day they'd met. In the picture Aaron wore a blue *Star Wars* logo T-shirt. Drummer wore a tight white "A-shirt" tank top. A movie theater ticket counter could be seen behind them. Wedged into the corner of the picture frame were their ticket stubs from the film they'd seen that day, the 2010 science fiction movie *Inception*.

Aaron found Drummer in the living room, reclined on the couch. Drummer's attention was on his phone. On the wall above him was a well-ordered gallery of a dozen framed photographs, most of which had been taken during their ten years together. In one of the larger pictures, Aaron and Drummer stood on the deck of a cruise ship, dressed in matching maroon tuxedo jackets with subtle but stylish embroidery. Other photos included candid shots of friends, coworkers, and events like camping trips and vacations abroad. A second large picture had been hung central to the gallery. It was a long horizontal group portrait of Drummer, Aaron, and Aaron's family—a dozen people standing around a bench at the edge of Stow Lake in Golden Gate Park. Everyone was smiling in the photo except for Aaron, who had a preoccupied look about him. Aaron loved what the photo represented—his family, proud of him and happy to know that he was with someone like Drummer rather than the man who had harmed him years earlier. But his melancholy expression indicated what he'd been thinking about at the time—that this moment of love with his family could've come sooner if only he'd made a different choice in his youth. He deemed the positive elements of the photo more important than the negative, however, which was why it was placed so prominently on the wall.

Beside the gallery, and mounted like a trophy from some safari, was Aaron's old skateboard, lightly scuffed, with bright red wheels and an underside custom-painted with black and white geometric patterns. Beside the board was a trio of smaller pictures of Aaron's friends from back in the day. The largest was of Aaron and his former best friend, Willis, leaning against a red 1993 Acura Integra.

Aaron's gaze lingered on the skateboard. It was more important than it seemed, and not only because it was his favorite of the many boards he'd owned. Like the small photographs beside it, the board represented an important part of his past, his free-spirited youth—a youth cut short. Skateboarding had been a big part of his life until he'd started dating Grant, an experience that had brought Aaron's jovial youth to an inauspicious end.

"Jesus, the news is so panicked and apocalyptic," Drummer said with obvious frustration, sliding his phone onto the coffee table beside him. Aaron understood his disappointment. Every morning brought another manic front page, portentous headlines and indignant op-eds spewing divisive bile, and clickbait articles fighting with each other over both the coming US presidential election and the Covid-19 global pandemic.

"Triggering headlines get clicks," Aaron said. A frequent reminder. He went to the kitchen, the space separated from the living room by a long countertop. He poured himself a cup of coffee. "Why do you torture yourself with that so early?"

Drummer grumbled. "I dunno. Habit."

"It's a bad habit."

"I hear ya."

"Still going to work?" Aaron asked.

"Yeah, I'm just a little slow today. It's just me and Brian. Everyone else is home for the long haul. You're going in too, right?"

"No choice. California now considers me an 'essential worker.'"

"How about just 'essential'? That company would be dead without you."

Aaron smiled with modesty.

Drummer joined him in the kitchen. "I know you're not big on birthdays," he said, "but your coworkers care about you. Give them the chance to show it."

"I said I'm going in," Aaron protested lightly. "I could've taken the day off and hid under the bed."

"You wouldn't do that," said Drummer. "You love the attention."

"Pppth," Aaron scoffed with a grin he couldn't hide.

"They're going to kiss your smooth forty-year-old ass, and you'll love every second of it."

"Oh, stop," Aaron said with a laugh.

"And you'll *love* our lunch tomorrow," Drummer went on with an over-the-top dramatic tone. "And when it's all over you'll say, 'Drummer, you were right. Everyone loves me, and you're the best boyfriend in the whole world. Let me buy you a vintage 1965 Cadillac convertible, just like you always wanted.'"

"You don't know me," Aaron said, pushing back with that persistent grin.

Drummer laughed at him. "Mark my words." He took a sip of Aaron's coffee, winced at its lack of sweetness, then left for the bathroom to shower.

By 8:00 a.m., both men were dressed and ready to go. They left the building together before splitting off toward their respective workplaces.

Aaron was a division director for a biotech company that developed chemical reagents, many of which were used in the production of vaccines. As the coronavirus had spread, his company had come under increasing pressure to adapt. He felt great stress in his job, but to his relief and surprise, that burden felt lighter today, as he was inundated via email, text, and in person with sincere proclamations of "happy birthday" and more than a few sarcastic barbs about his age.

He was standing in the doorway of his office shortly after noon when a loud, deep voice came from behind him. "So, you're forty, huh? Fuck you, looking like that at forty."

Aaron turned to see the grinning face of his employee and friend, Martin. Though Aaron was Martin's superior, the two men shared a casual working relationship, often trading spirited insults and cursing like junior-high-school kids.

"What the fuck are you talkin' about?" Aaron retorted, drawing on his younger days for the right tone and terms.

"I'm talkin' about you, being five years older than me but looking five years younger. You, looking like *that*, and me, looking like a tub."

"Bitch, you don't look like a tub."

"Standing next to you I do."

"Then why are you standing next to me?" Aaron waved him off. "Go stand over there. Six feet at least. Social distance."

Aaron entered his office and sat at his desk, while Martin remained at the door.

"I suppose you're about to tell me age is just a number?" Martin asked with a goading smirk.

"I'll do you one better," Aaron said. "Do you think when I'm eighty and you're seventy-five, people are gonna to look at us and say, 'That one looks so much younger'? Or are they just going to see two tired old men?"

Martin raised a single brow. "Sarcasm. Nice. And point taken."

"You should get back to work," Aaron said, "but let's circle back in forty years. Maybe by then you'll have found a gym and you'll look younger than me."

Martin grinned. "Shady bitch."

"Hey, you're the one who started the conversation with 'fuck you.'"

Martin laughed and walked away.

A moment later, there was a quick knock on Aaron's open door. Taraji, one of the other division directors—a tall, slender Black woman—walked in with a large vase of colorful tulips.

"I got these for your birthday, sweetheart," she said with a fabricated southern accent, the kind one would expect to hear in an old Hollywood movie. She set the flowers on Aaron's desk, blocking his view of his computer monitor, then backed up and stood in the doorway. "I know tulips aren't the most romantic flowers, but I also know they're your favorite."

Aaron looked at the oversized vase bursting with color. He pulled the attached card toward him and read it aloud with an intentionally flat expression. "Happy birthday to my beautiful man, love, Drummer."

Taraji grunted and threw Aaron a sideways grin. She continued without the accent, "Anyone ever tell you you're no fun?"

"For thirty-nine years, no one," Aaron said. "But I'm turning forty tomorrow, so I gotta practice my old man grumble."

"Old man? What does that say about me?"

"Well, if at fifty you feel old," Aaron started in reply, "you can always take solace in the fact that you have such a young, peppy friend."

"I'm not sure 'peppy' is the word I'd choose for you."

"And I wouldn't say you're old," Aaron said.

Taraji smiled warmly. "Now that's more like it. Hardly matters anyway. To the new kids in this place, the two of us are vampires."

"Do you mean we're ancient and immortal, or just blood suckers?"

She laughed. "I guess they might see both. Two thirsty elders surrounded by so much sweet young blood."

"I dunno, Taraji. These young upstarts are surprisingly bitter."

She smiled broadly. "I'll make sure none of them learn your true tastes." She winked at him, then left the office.

Aaron looked at the tulips and thought about Drummer, then about Martin and Taraji. His two coworkers had notably different personalities, but they both held Aaron in high regard. To Martin, Aaron was a foul-mouthed friend as well as a coworker. To Taraji, he was a trusted colleague and fellow director who understood the pressures of their positions. To others in the office, he was in turn a serious scientist, a committed colleague, even an empathetic confidant. He was something different to each person he knew, but he was always himself and always genuine, even if he knew he wasn't perfect. He was proud to be that sort of man—appreciated, valued, and youthful—but it wasn't until that moment that he'd recognized how much he was loved.

TWO BLOCKS away and several floors down, Drummer sat at his own desk in his third-floor office. The space was not as large or as modern as Aaron's, but it was his own. A wide window behind him gave him a view of the newer, taller buildings that had gone up in the neighborhood in recent years. San Francisco had been in the middle of a construction boom before the coronavirus had sent everyone scrambling for cover. Now, who knew what would become of all those lofty, empty, skyscraping ambitions?

Drummer's coworker Brian leaned in to catch his attention. Brian was a muscled thirty-something former wrestler, who always came to work dressed in a button-down shirt buttoned all the way up. He'd been Drummer's close friend for most of nine years, following him from one job to the next before they'd finally landed in their current gigs. Due to pandemic concerns, Brian and Drummer were the only employees in the office at present.

"You fix Laine's VPN?" Brian asked. "She's ready to get back on the server."

"She's good to go," Drummer answered with a long sigh.

Brian nodded, the dark circles under his eyes betraying his exhaustion. "Listen," he said, "if there's nothing else, I'm going to head out. I know it's early, I'm just tired."

"Fine with me." Drummer glanced at the time on his laptop. It was precisely 2:00 p.m. "Oh shit!" He jumped up from his seat and went to a long telescope standing by the window. He trained it at one of the new buildings outside, then zoomed all the way in. Most of the floors beyond appeared empty, save for one.

"Are you guys still doing that?" Brian asked, watching him.

"Don't be jealous," said Drummer, focusing the eyepiece. Through the far, semi-mirrored windows of the building in his scope, he could see Aaron's silhouette, peering back at him through his own telescope. Their mutual views were not clear, but they were distinctive.

They waved to each other.

Aaron's silhouette did a goofy little jig.

"Ugh," Brian said in feigned disgust.

"Jealous," Drummer repeated, holding his index finger out as if to scold him. He waved at Aaron, then returned to his desk.

"He's going to be forty tomorrow, right?" Brian asked.

"Yep, at exactly two ten in the morning."

"Two ten? His poor mom."

"I know, can you imagine? She was probably having a nice Swanson's TV dinner, sipping a glass of boxed wine on her aluminum wood-grain TV tray, watching JR get shot. Then in the middle of her suburban bliss, this slimy pink gremlin suddenly starts clawing its way out of her. She misses the finale and never finds out who pulled the trigger."

"You're weird."

"I'm a wordsmith," Drummer corrected him lightheartedly. "I got a B-plus in my college creative writing class, you know."

"And a master's degree in run-on sentences," Brian added. "I'm sure Aaron's mom caught that show in reruns."

"Nah, she loves a cliffhanger," Drummer answered. "She never finishes a series. She probably thinks Jean-Luc Picard is still a Borg."

Brian shook his head. "You're such a dork."

"The proper term is 'geek,'" Drummer said. "Don't make me tell you again. Now get out of here. I'll lock up."

AARON AND Drummer returned home at roughly the same time that evening. Aaron was already in the lobby as Drummer came in, leaning against the black granite front desk, chatting with the security attendant.

"Hey, guys," Drummer said, approaching. "How's it going, Marco?"

"Hey, Drummer," Marco replied. He was a handsome man of Hispanic background, about thirty-five years old. He wore a dark blue suit jacket, part of his official uniform. "Aaron was just telling me he's an *old man,*" he added wryly.

Drummer nodded. "Yeah, I can't tell you how many times I've caught Grampa Hayes here holding up the line at the grocery store trying to write a check."

Aaron punched him lightly in the shoulder. "Scandalous lies! And don't ever call me Grampa Hayes again."

"Hey, I'm not the one sitting at the stop sign waiting for the light to change."

Aaron chuckled. He couldn't deny that he found Drummer's mocking observations amusing.

"You guys are too much," said Marco, also laughing at their exchange.

Drummer pressed the elevator button, then poked Aaron in the shoulder. "Let's go, Methuselah."

The elevator doors opened, and the two of them stepped inside.

As they ascended, Drummer leaned in. "So?" he asked, leading. "How'd it go?"

Aaron felt surprisingly calm. He was sure Drummer could sense it. "Actually," he said, "it was the best day at work I've ever had… even with the apocalypse."

Drummer was visibly relieved. "Me too. This guy I like did a little dance for me in my telescope."

"Oh?" Aaron asked, following his lead. "A secret admirer sent me flowers."

"Really? Must've been Taraji." Drummer leaned over and kissed him. "Happy birthday."

That night, they ordered dinner in. They sat on the floor of their living room with a large pizza and a bottle of sauvignon blanc and shared an indica pre-roll. And they forgot, for a time, that a pandemic raged outside their door.

"Thanks for the flowers," Aaron said, as their conversation reached a lull.

"Always," Drummer answered. "But I do it every year."

"This year, though… it was more important."

Aaron was still riding high from the events of the day and not presently bothered by his age, but a lingering concern dwelt behind his eyes.

Drummer looked at him curiously.

"What?" Aaron asked.

"I was just about to ask you the same thing."

Aaron shook his head as if it were nothing, though he knew it wasn't.

"That dream this morning," he finally said. "D, this whole week I've been feeling good. Very good. Like things are finally going the way they should. Even with the pandemic and turning forty, I feel like you and I are about to leap into a whole new life together. But that dream… and Grant… he's still in my head. Therapy's been great, but he's still there."

Drummer took Aaron's hand. "I sometimes wonder if maybe he isn't."

Aaron wasn't sure what Drummer meant.

Drummer continued, "I sometimes wonder if maybe you're just *afraid* he is, so he keeps getting pulled back in."

Aaron knew Drummer was at least partially right. Grant existed in his mind as more than just a violent former boyfriend; he was a core component of Aaron's post-traumatic stress, and on more than one occasion Aaron's fear of the nightmares had itself been responsible for bringing them on.

"Good observation," Aaron said.

"You'll get past it."

"I'd like to believe that."

"Then do."

Aaron smiled at Drummer's plain-spoken optimism. He looked up at the skateboard mounted on the wall and thought about how long it had been since he'd used it.

"God, D, I wish I'd met you first."

"I think we met at just the right time," said Drummer. He followed Aaron's eyes to the board. "You know, you can take that thing down and go for a ride whenever you want."

"At forty I might be pushing it."

"Age is just a number," Drummer said. "And I think you're right; we *are* about to start a whole new life… of sorts."

"What do you mean?"

"Well, I look at it like this: we have four lives. The first is from birth to twenty, the second goes from twenty to forty, the third from forty to sixty, and the fourth from sixty to eighty. The first one hardly counts, since it's all learning and fucking up—like falling off the skateboard doing a shuvit. And the beginning of every life lets you start over."

"What happens at eighty?"

Drummer shrugged. "Free-play? The point is, you've got two whole lives ahead of you at least, and you can do anything you want with them. You can even get back on that skateboard—or buy a new one."

"I might make it down Second Street for a block or two," Aaron envisioned aloud, "but probably no Laser Flips on Lombard."

"How do you know till you try? Besides, if you screw up, I know 911 by heart. It's '9-1-1.'"

Aaron chuckled. "You're so weird, D. I love you."

"I love you too."

Aaron looked into Drummer's pale green eyes and felt a wellspring of joyful adoration. The events of the day and the general feeling of calm gifted Aaron with a sense of near bliss, despite the lingering ghost of Grant.

"I have a question for you," Aaron asked, breaking the silence that had filled the room. The feeling of love expanded in his heart as he mused over his query.

"A question? Shoot."

"Not yet," Aaron said. He wanted to blurt it out, but he also wanted to savor the suspense. "Tomorrow. Maybe at lunch."

Drummer smiled broadly. "Are you teasing me?" He sat back and took a sip from his glass.

"Maybe a bit," Aaron said. "Like a movie teaser. Or a trailer."

Drummer nodded. "Have you ever wondered why they call it a trailer, since it actually comes *before* the movie?"

"Well, my question comes *after* us being together for ten years, so calling it a trailer still works."

The two men retired soon thereafter. The number forty remained on Aaron's mind as he drifted into sleep, but now he was imagining it as the beginning of a new life instead of the end of his old one.

He slept soundly that night, free of the worldly worries that burdened him and the phantoms of the past that had haunted him. In his dreams, he sailed upon his skateboard through the lost avenues of his youth, over smooth-rolling surfaces, with the wind at his back and the sun in his eyes. With a single jump, he set himself free of gravity, like a bird taking flight.

Grant's voice would not find him tonight.

CHAPTER 2
A TURN ON DASHIELL HAMMETT

THE NEXT day, Aaron turned forty. To Drummer, he seemed content. Aaron had slept through the night, and even woken up before his alarm. He appeared in good spirits, and though Drummer could not say for sure that Aaron's upbeat attitude would last for long, it was enough for him to hope that it might last the day.

"Hey, D?" Aaron called, stepping out of the shower. "What time are we leaving?"

Drummer leaned into the bathroom. He looked Aaron up and down and gave him a cartoonish growl. "Shaved off the scruff, I see."

Aaron patted his freshly shorn face with his towel. "Yeah, it was itchy, especially with the mask."

Drummer rubbed his own smooth jaw, glad that he had decided to shave a few weeks earlier for the same reason. "I'd like to get to Huntington Park by two," he answered.

"Got it."

Drummer showered soon after. When he was finished, he found Aaron lying on the bed, poking at his phone. Drummer teased Aaron about his choice of clothing—torn gray shorts and a black Mötley Crüe T-shirt. He'd dubbed the look Aaron's "teen delinquent style," which he not-so-secretly found arousing. Drummer threw on a pair of dark jeans and a fitted baby blue polo shirt, snug around the arms.

"Ready?" Drummer asked, finally clothed.

Aaron responded with an effortless wolf whistle.

"Yeah, I know you like the light blue," Drummer said with a coy grin.

Aaron raised his eyebrows exaggeratedly. "There's something about the snug, collared shirt paired with the tattoos that really turns me on."

"Lucky for you I have a ton of these shirts. But I can buy more."

"Or get more tattoos."

Drummer lifted his arms, looking down at himself. "Not sure there's any more room."

They stepped into a warm, sunny afternoon. The streets were busy. They walked through the downtown core, zigzagging from block to block toward their destination—a park in the center of Nob Hill, a neighborhood rich with history and built up with some of the city's most exclusive housing. It was a leisurely stroll, though it gradually got steeper as they went. They climbed the final slope by way of the tree-lined Joice Street steps, intersecting Pine Street. Landscapers were busy putting the finishing touches on the shrubbery, pruning the trees and bushes that decorated each side of the stairway. The smell of fresh clippings wafted through the area.

Two blocks farther, Aaron and Drummer arrived at Huntington Park, a picturesque retreat at the top of the hill itself, surrounded by pricey condominiums and old-world hotels. Drummer spread out a blanket on the grass and emptied the backpack he had brought with him, putting out sandwiches, cheese, and wine—the latter contained in innocuous plastic bottles.

They ate, drank, and celebrated. Drummer had his phone out much of the time, taking pictures of Aaron, despite his protestations. At one point, Aaron grabbed the phone from him and shot a few of Drummer, then some of them together.

Lastly, Drummer made a video.

"Happy birthday, Methuselah." He grinned, training the lens on Aaron.

"Careful what you say, old man," Aaron retorted. "You turned forty-five last week, you know." He peered at Drummer over the top of the phone. "But thank you. You're so good to me."

"And you to me."

Drummer turned off his phone and set it on the blanket, then looked at Aaron quizzically. "I think you have something on your shirt, babe. Stand up for a second."

"What, really?" Aaron climbed to his feet and looked down at himself, brushing at whatever crumbs or splashes of wine might be there.

At the same time, Drummer leaned forward and pulled a small box from his coat, which had been resting beside him on the blanket. He lifted himself up onto one knee.

Aaron stopped and stared at him.

"Aaron," Drummer began seriously. "We've been together a long time... ten years... the best years of my life. I know it feels like the world's falling apart around us sometimes, and the future can look bleak, but you've shown me that even in the middle of all this, there's still so much happiness to be had."

Drummer handed him the velvety little box. Aaron took it, held it in his hand for a moment, then opened it. Inside was a polished gold engagement ring. Inside the band was an engraving. "To our next life," Aaron read aloud, clearly touched.

"Remember how young you are," Drummer continued, holding back a host of emotions dominated by nervousness and giddiness. "That crazy kid is still in you. I see him every day, trying new things, dragging me along, and insisting I'll love every minute. And that kid'll be with you in every life ahead. I love who you are, Aaron, and who I am because of you. Will you marry me?"

Aaron looked down at the ring, then back into Drummer's pale green eyes. He answered. "Oh, D, you know I will."

Drummer slid the ring onto Aaron's shaking finger, then stood, kissed him, and held him close.

A few casual observers around them burst into applause, causing the two men to laugh through their pressing tears.

When the commotion settled, they sat back down.

Aaron twisted the ring around his finger.

Drummer could sense that Aaron was more than just surprised.

"It's okay to feel confused," he said in response to that turbulent ripple. "I know Grant made commitment feel like a trap. But remember, when he said, 'I love you,' he meant, 'I own you.' When I say it, I mean, 'you own me.'"

Aaron smiled again, and in that smile, Drummer could see a rush of relief.

"You think you can make it home in one piece?" Drummer added.

Aaron laughed. He looked at the ring on his hand. "You're really hammering home this 'new life' thing, D."

"I like to think I'm full of surprises."

Soon after, they collected their things and started home. They walked in contented silence until they came to the corner of Dashiell Hammett Street, a quaint residential alley named after the early twentieth century author who had once lived there. Drummer suggested they cut through.

"I feel like a debutante," Aaron said, fidgeting with the ring as they made the turn down the hill, "wanting to show all my girlfriends this big rock you gave me."

"I didn't give you a rock."

"Same thing to me. You have one for yourself?"

"A ring? Not yet. I wanted to make sure you didn't run off screaming first."

Drummer's attention was caught by a glimmer on the sidewalk a few doors from the end of the alley. "Hey, check this out," he said, moving ahead to investigate. Resting on the concrete was a small cylindrical object about the length and thickness of a short pen, each end tapered to a point. He picked it up and brought it back to Aaron. They studied it together.

The object appeared to be either metallic or glass, but even once Drummer had it in his hand, he couldn't figure out what it was made of; it seemed heavier than it ought to have been. Two series of numbers—each broken into five groups separated by decimal points—ran along one side, the series separated by a pair of glowing gold lights. The surface of the object was especially intriguing, electric blue and swirling with a liquid-like quality.

"Is it a pen?" asked Aaron.

"I don't think so. There's no ink tip. Maybe it's a stylus." Drummer rolled it over his fingers. It was impossibly smooth. He heard a deep, unusual sound, which he subconsciously interpreted as a large vehicle rolling by in the distance. At the same time, a mild electric shock stung his fingertips, causing him to jump. He laughed at his own reaction.

"The damn thing shocked me." He looked up at Aaron.

But Aaron wasn't there.

Drummer spun around, but still Aaron was nowhere to be found. He had to be hiding between a couple of parked cars, pulling a prank.

"Very funny," Drummer called out.

He waited, but Aaron did not present himself.

Drummer checked the object in his hand. The gold lights were now dim, the numbers had grown cold, and the swirling blue surface was notably duller and barely moving. He slipped it into his pocket.

"Aaron, come on," he said louder, feeling a bit foolish. He walked the remaining length of the alley, expecting to find his fiancé hiding at the corner, but he wasn't there either.

As Drummer scanned his surroundings, he had the strangest feeling that things were somehow… not right. Was it the smell in the air? The sound of traffic? The angle of the sun? He couldn't put his finger on it. There was a French restaurant on the corner he'd never seen before; he'd thought the place had been a sports bar. And a cool breeze was blowing, cooler than it had been at the top of the hill. *Microclimates*, he thought.

He retraced his steps back up the alley, checking between cars as he went. He soon noticed that none of the vehicles were newer models. He was no auto aficionado, but he knew older cars when he saw them, and these were all at least twenty years old. Even more peculiar, they looked *new*. Beside him was a mint condition Pontiac Grand Am—it even had paper plates. But Pontiac had folded years earlier, a casualty of the Great Recession of 2008.

At first Drummer attributed this to coincidence, but at the same time it struck him with a peculiar sense of displacement. He'd experienced a similar phenomenon a few years ago, sitting outside an old Dairy Queen restaurant in San Jose. A late-1970s Camaro had pulled into the parking lot, while Foreigner's song *Urgent* played on the radio. At the same time, a man and a woman in vintage clothes had been seated at the table opposite him. In that moment—in that isolated bubble of déjà vu— Drummer had imagined it could've been the early 80s. Lulled by that comforting reflection of a bygone age, at the time he'd allowed himself to enjoy the feeling. But what he was experiencing now was not the same. This didn't feel like déjà vu, and it was not isolated to one car and a cute couple in dated clothes.

He reached the mouth of the alley across from the Joice Street steps. The trees and shrubbery were all overgrown, and some branches hung all the way down to the concrete. This seemed odd to him as well, but he couldn't place why.

He took out his phone to text Aaron. A series of notifications popped onto the screen.

NO CONNECTION.

NETWORK NOT FOUND.

LOCATION SERVICES UNAVAILABLE.

He restarted the device, hoping the errors would correct themselves, but they promptly returned.

He reexamined the Joice Street steps and immediately understood the problem. The trees and bushes had been pruned earlier in the day—

he was sure of it. They'd passed the landscapers at work. But now they looked like they hadn't been touched in months.

A group of five or six people approached, chatting and carrying on. They passed him, closely enough to bump him. Not one of them was wearing a face mask or made any attempt to socially distance themselves—from him or from one another. They walked off, oblivious, leaving Drummer flummoxed.

He felt an uneasy sinking in his gut. Still, he told himself not to overreact, that the anomalies could all be explained by coincidence or misperception. He just needed to find Aaron and get home.

He walked back down Dashiell Hammett, telling himself that the strange feeling of displacement would correct itself. He recalled his experience at the Dairy Queen; the illusion had ended when a contemporary song replaced Foreigner on the radio and a newer car had pulled into the lot. Drummer was certain the same thing would happen now. He would pass someone in a face mask, he would find the sports bar on the corner of a different alley, or he'd run into Aaron. He could then chalk up the entire series of events to coincidence.

But the feeling of being out of sync persisted long after he left the alley. And when he reached Union Square, the feeling left the realm of imagination and blossomed into tangible reality.

Nothing was as it should have been. The stores were different, the billboards were different, even the streets themselves were different. Union Square had undergone an extensive, years-long remodel around 2010, but none of that work was evident now. Stockton Street had been recently repaved and its lanes redrawn, but vehicles here drove over choppy asphalt and broken lane markers. A large billboard advertisement for the movie *Meet the Parents* loomed over a Border's Bookstore on the northwest corner. And people were packed on the sidewalk, shoulder to shoulder and without masks, as if no pandemic were at play. The cool breeze had become a cold wind, and the sun had already set behind the Westin St. Francis Hotel across the square.

Drummer's heart raced as he took in his surroundings with an increasing sense of dread. Was he hallucinating? Was he having a stroke? He removed the strange object from his pocket and studied it. What the hell was it? Had it drugged him? Had the electric shock done something to his brain? Or was he simply misremembering things? None of these possibilities seemed plausible. He didn't feel mentally compromised, and to imagine whole changes to a neighborhood was exceptionally unlikely.

His anxiety grew. Whatever was happening to him, he told himself he needed to lock it down and get home as quickly as possible. He directed his gaze to the pavement and pressed on, trying not to look up at the storefronts or the signage. He hastily crossed Market Street into SOMA, turned on Mission, and walked several more blocks. He stopped at a red light to catch his breath.

Beside him, in a corner building he'd thought was vacant, was a convenience store. A magazine rack stood inside the door. On each glossy cover were the faces of famous people he hadn't seen in years, and topics that had long been retired from casual conversation. At the top of the rack was a *Time* magazine with a simple black cover, framed in red, emblazoned with the words, "The ABORTION Pill."

Confused but curious, Drummer went inside.

"Excuse me," he said to the man at the counter. He gestured toward the magazines. "Are these new?"

The man looked at him askance. "Are you kidding?"

Drummer felt stupid. Checking the rack again, he searched for a better query. "I'm just disoriented. Can you… tell me the date?"

Visibly annoyed, the man answered, "October fourteenth. Are you using? 'Cause I'm gonna ask you to get out of my store."

"No…," said Drummer, his voice trailing off. "I'm not using, but…. October? Are you sure?"

"I'm sure." The man rapped his fingers against a cheap paper calendar on the wall behind him.

Drummer read it aloud to himself in a subdued voice. "October 2000."

He looked back at the magazines, each of them spilling over with announcements of old events and the younger faces of older people. The dates on every cover matched the calendar.

"You sure you're okay?" the man asked.

Drummer looked at him but could say nothing. He truly didn't have an answer. He left the store.

Late afternoon was morphing into early evening. Despite Drummer's desire to keep his gaze on the sidewalk, he started studying his surroundings for inconsistencies. He began wandering mindlessly, taking side streets off Mission and back again, crossing intersections against traffic. He made one last turn and found himself standing before a chain-link fence. On the other side was a pile of construction equipment sitting on a vacant dirt lot. Above him, a sign read: COMING IN 2005. Beneath the words was an artist's rendering of the tower where he and Aaron had lived for the past nine years.

He stared at the rendering with wide eyes and gave a clipped, cynical laugh. *Yeah, right*, he thought. He studied the flanking buildings, then the towers behind him and the street sign swinging in the wind at the intersection at First Street. He was in the right place.

He wanted to believe there was a chemical or psychological explanation for what he was experiencing—psychosis, dementia, hysteria—but the world around him was too clear, too real. This was not déjà vu or a perverse feeling of flashback. No new car would roll up to snap him out of it; no new song would play in the distance. No outside element was about to break through the bubble of his altered state and restore the life he knew.

But what, exactly, was happening?

He thought about the calendar at the corner store and felt a sudden terror.

Panicked, he turned his phone on again and opened the photo gallery. To his relief, image thumbnails appeared. The pictures and videos from Huntington Park were there, along with those he'd taken during the first half of 2020. He also found his saved-media folder, containing the selfie from the day he and Aaron had first met, as well as hundreds of the best of the images and videos they'd taken during their ten-year history.

He brought up one of the photos from Huntington Park. Aaron's contented face smiled at him. Drummer smiled back instinctively, but tears pricked at his eyes as he considered the fantastical and dismal possibility: that the images on his phone might be all he had left of the man he loved.

He removed the small blue object from his pocket. "What have you done to me, you son of a bitch?" He clutched it so tight he thought it might snap in half, but it obstinately defied his strength.

He loosened his grip.

And breathed.

He looked around him at the city in the night, deceptive in its familiarity and confusing in its differences, and asked again, more softly, not just of the object he carried but also of himself.

"What have you done?"

LOSS AND PURPOSE

It had not been there the second time,
And Aaron still did not understand why.
But Drummer was gone now, regardless.

All things had ended.

In time, he sold the condominium,
And went home to the house on the hill.
Familiar photographs,
A flower vase in the kitchen,
The telescope still trained at the tower,
All relics of a former life.

He clung to every detail of his memories.
But of the real world, he noted only the sounds.
The rain in the spring,
The birds in the summer,
And on one cold autumn night,
A strange rattling.

It drew him to a neglected room—
Once the focus of his time and energy—
Where he found what he had lost,
And rediscovered his purpose.

And all things began again.

CHAPTER 3
ROADS ONCE TAKEN

DRUMMER STUDIED the small blue object in his hand. It seemed impossible that something so diminutive could be responsible for his extraordinary situation, but he saw no other explanation. The device had been active and electric when he found it, but it was now seemingly dormant. And everything had changed the moment it shocked him.

He didn't want to accept that his condition was anything other than psychological, for the alternative was too weird to be true. But when he took the evidence of his senses together with the magazines and the calendar at the corner store, the fantastical conclusion—as impossible as it seemed—was all that remained. In the blink of eye, in that quaint alley below Nob Hill, the small blue object had somehow sent Drummer backward to October 2000. Twenty years in the past.

He felt foolish saying it even to himself, but even if he were a fool, he still needed a plan of action. It was night. He was freezing. His condo apparently didn't yet exist. He couldn't simply stand in place and cling to the hope that the world he knew would suddenly rematerialize. He had to do something. But what?

Lacking a purposeful decision, he made an arbitrary one and returned to Market Street—this time to face it with open eyes, in hopes of finding answers to the questions he was too confused to ask. He went quickly, pausing only at the convenience store to confirm that it was still the same. Shortly, he reached the corner of Market and Fourth. He'd lived in San Francisco since college in the 1990s and had passed through this busy intersection every day. He hoped the location might spark a useful memory, and perhaps inspire a plan.

He saw a city he knew, a city of the past but one that still felt contemporary to him, defined by the Virgin Megastore on the corner, the Sephora across Stockton Street, and the empty Emporium department store just up Market. He could imagine himself as a young man walking by these old places, and as he did, his thoughts spawned an option.

If this truly was the San Francisco of his memory—if this was the actual intersection he had often crossed all those years ago—then two miles away on Hayes Street would be a small one-bedroom apartment containing all the fixtures of his youth.

He could go home.

But this didn't sit well with him. First, there was the question of what he might find. He could very well discover that he had no access to the apartment at all. Would he encounter his younger self, or had he stepped into his own previous shoes? He doubted that he'd somehow become his younger self, for he was still his own man—still covered in tattoos and clearly forty-five years old. He'd seen too many movies. Time might not be working the way he expected, but he knew it did not work like that.

Second, even if he could get in, going home would mean facing his old life and seeing it for what it really had been: not the comforting fantasy of his rewritten memories, but the cold, unforgiving reality of his wasted youth. 2000 had not been a good year for him, and he'd spent many of the subsequent years repackaging the events and redefining their meaning.

Ultimately, he was forced to accept that his immediate needs outweighed his feelings. He would go to the apartment. It could offer him resources he didn't currently have. And after all, he had nowhere else to go.

He dashed across Market to the bus-boarding island. He had no money on him, so when a Hayes Street bus pulled up, he snuck aboard through the back door. He'd seen people do the same thing every day, usually without consequence. The driver noticed him but said nothing as he took a seat.

The aging bus lurched forward, heading outbound. Drummer slumped down, entertaining the unfounded fear that the other passengers could tell he didn't belong. But they ignored him, just as they ignored each other.

It was nearly 8:00 p.m. when he arrived at the corner of Hayes and Divisadero. He got off the bus, and as it continued away without him, he took in the sights of his old neighborhood. There were differences to how the area would be in 2020, but the disparities were small enough that they would've easily gone unnoticed had he not been looking for them.

He walked a half block farther and found his old apartment building, a four-story Victorian erected in 1912. Most of its decorative trim had been stripped away in the 1950s, at a time when Victorian flourish was looked upon with derision. It had then been painted solid white, rendering the structure an architectural neuter. Drummer's landlord in 2000 had treated it with similar disregard.

Drummer stood on the sidewalk across the street from the building and peered up at the rounded second-floor bay window into the space that had been his living room. It was dark inside, but a faint light farther back indicated someone was home. Drummer didn't know what he was hoping to see in that window—or if "hoping" was even the right word—but he watched and waited nonetheless.

An untold eternity passed. Finally, a soft shadow drifted across the ceiling as whoever was in the back room came forward.

The living room light flicked on.

Drummer scanned the newly-illuminated space. He saw a bookshelf against the wall and a floor lamp that he recognized as his own. Two people entered. They appeared as gray silhouettes against the brighter backdrop, but Drummer recognized them all the same. One was his now-ex, Nate, and the other was himself, twenty years younger.

Of all the things Drummer had seen in the past couple hours, this was the most surreal. But it was also the most effective at convincing him that the world he found himself in was authentic. Storefronts and street signs could remain unchanged over the years, but the scene unfolding before him in that window was personal—a precise moment from his own past playing out exactly as he'd lived it. It could not be denied, and therefore, the world in which it existed could not be denied either.

Watching his younger self with Nate, as mundane as their actions were, all but gutted Drummer emotionally. He'd felt some nostalgia when taking in the other aspects of his surroundings, but not now. Instead he felt shame, for the scene in the window betrayed the lies he'd concocted to recontextualize these years. The young Drummer was living a life he did not value, with a man he did not love, in a manner that, when he looked at it in hindsight, he would not respect.

He hated to see it, so he looked away. He needed to get into that apartment, but it could not happen tonight.

Feeling defeated—at least for the moment—Drummer walked a few blocks away to the Panhandle of Golden Gate Park. He found a bench in the darkness and lay down. He used his backpack as a pillow and wrapped himself in the picnic blanket for warmth, though neither was adequate for their purpose.

Wind swayed the tall eucalyptus trees above him as night pressed on and the Pacific fog rushed in. He thought the chill might help keep him awake so he could come up with a plan for accessing the apartment, but his adrenaline had been pumping hard for a long time, and now that it was abating Drummer struggled to keep his eyes open. He drifted into a troubled sleep. When he dreamed, he saw his life with Aaron, but then the biting cold and the rustle of leaves would rouse him and chase the visions away.

The night dragged on.

He woke with the dawn.

Reality asserted itself.

He sat up and checked his phone. There were still no connections available, but by this point he didn't expect to find any. He shut off his phone's wireless receivers to save battery power, then opened the calendar and manually set the date. According to the man at the convenience store, it would now be October 15, 2000. A Sunday.

Sunday. Drummer thought back to his Sundays in 2000. He and Nate had both worked weekends at the time. They'd be leaving the apartment soon.

He brushed off his clothes and returned to the old building. He loitered across the street, doing his best to not appear suspicious as he glanced periodically at the second-floor windows. He saw little activity other than the living room light turning on, and then off again. Minutes later, Nate opened the front gate and stepped onto the sidewalk. The young Drummer followed a moment later, dressed in gym shorts and a white T-shirt. Only one of his arms was fully tattooed. He had a brown messenger bag slung over his shoulder.

The elder Drummer knew the contents of that bag by heart. It contained a tank top, a bag lunch, and his dress clothes for work. Nate and the young Drummer walked away, Nate keeping several steps ahead as if alone and Drummer behind him, not bothering to keep up. They boarded a Hayes Street bus heading downtown.

This was it. Drummer's old life now waited for him. He approached the front gate and rang apartment four.

"Yeah?" The intercom speaker crackled under the weight of a man's amplified voice.

"Hey, Carl, it's Drummer," he chirped, hoping to sound young and upbeat. "I forgot my keys. Can you let me in?"

"Sure, hold on."

The gate buzzed and Drummer entered.

Though the exterior of the building had been stripped of its personality, the interior was still heavily ornamented. The lobby, stairway, and landings were all lined with polished wood panels stained a dark mahogany. Each floor was lit by one dim sconce. The atmosphere was brooding but beautiful.

Drummer climbed the stairs to the front door of his old unit and waited. The smell of the place was triggering, bringing him back to evenings when he'd come home from work and stand outside that same front door, purposely fumbling with his keys to delay the inevitable—boredom, antagonism, and insults from Nate disguised as comedy. Nate wasn't an intentionally offensive guy, but he hadn't been very personable either. Drummer recalled one particular dinner party at Carl's, where Nate had insulted their host with a thoughtless, backhanded compliment. Drummer had taken it upon himself to apologize for Nate on the way out.

Carl arrived momentarily with Drummer's spare keys in hand. At this point in time he was a thirty-year-old freelance designer, but he looked more like a college kid.

Drummer smiled, surprisingly happy to see him.

"Locked out again?" Carl shot him a sideways grin.

Drummer kept his head down. He'd aged well, but he'd also changed enough that he would not present the appearance Carl might expect to see.

"Yeah, I figured I should come back and grab them before I got all the way to work," he answered.

Carl did give him a second glance, but didn't comment on any dissimilarities of voice or appearance he might have noticed. He unlocked the door and pushed it open a few inches. "There you go, man."

"Thanks."

Carl dashed back upstairs.

Drummer remained in the hallway for a moment, the door to his old life standing partially open before him. He felt renewed apprehension about going inside; the place contained emotional demons. But those demons were a thing of the past, and they could no longer harm him.

He took a breath as if preparing to jump into a deep pool, then pushed the door open.

He stepped into a world both familiar and alien, comforting and terrifying. He'd recalled the generalities of the place but had forgotten many of the details. Unforgettable were the larger items—the second-hand furniture, the sagging couch wrapped in bedsheets, and the bulky CRT television sitting atop a broken console table. Everything was old or repurposed, for buying new stuff was not yet practical. Inexpensive furniture stores were few and far between; IKEA had only just opened its first Bay Area location across the bay.

In addition to the large items in the room, there were elements that Drummer had regarded only peripherally in 2000—rumples in the carpet, stains on the wallpaper, and cracks in the ceiling. He'd forgotten these details over time, but they now returned to his conscious awareness with a rush. The old doorknob, slightly wobbly, was familiar in his grip. The smell of toast reminded him of his morning ritual. The worn carpet under his feet had a recognizable resistance. The vividness of the sense-memories fed the rise of long-forgotten irritation within him.

He closed the door behind him and moved into the living room. There were piles of papers and other junk—knickknacks, coffee table books, VHS tapes, and cheap collectibles that would one day wear out their novelty. He and Nate had been packrats, to be sure, but the sheer volume of unrestrained clutter was surprising. Drummer recalled spending a good number of years after their breakup offloading most of it.

At the same time, scattered among the heaps of future garbage were several treasured items Drummer still owned in 2020. Framed family photos, yearbooks, and a small model house that he'd built for a high school architecture class. Seeing these things gave him a refreshing and much-needed connection to the life he'd left behind, an assurance that some things remained the same.

He saw motion in the corner of his eye.

Worried someone might still be in the apartment, he stepped back toward the door. He was about to return to the hallway when a black-and-gray tabby cat trotted out from the bedroom.

Drummer's eyes popped. It was Cirrus, his beloved pet. He'd died long ago.

"Oh my God, my little baby!" Drummer exclaimed in a high-pitched "cat voice," tears suddenly welling in his eyes.

He picked up the little cat and sat with him on the couch, slipping back into his old habits. He kissed his kitty on the head, rubbed his tummy, and played with his paws. He lightly poked Cirrus's cute pink nose and rubbed his chin, eliciting a symphony of delighted purrs. For a moment Drummer forgot why he was there, and he didn't care.

He looked around the room again, this time viewing the apartment as if it were his own contemporary life, as though he himself were the true occupant, home alone on a Sunday with his precious, excitable cat. But then his gaze landed on a small wooden box, resting on a bookshelf by the bedroom door, and he remembered why he was there.

He let Cirrus hop off his lap, then went to the box. Inside was a folded wad of cash held together by a binder clip—a five-hundred-dollar emergency fund he'd shared with Nate.

He looked down at his cat, who was rubbing against his ankles. "You don't mind if I take this, right?"

Cirrus remained silent.

"You know, when they find this money's gone it'll be the end of their relationship. But it was doomed anyway, wasn't it."

Drummer pocketed the cash. He then replaced the box so it would appear undisturbed, resting perfectly in the clean spot on the dusty shelf where it lived. He felt only a small amount of guilt for taking the money, and an enormous amount of relief. The cash wouldn't solve all his problems, but it would mitigate them for a while.

"It's funny," he said to himself, "I blamed Nate for taking this, and he blamed me. Strange to find out that he was right. Or at least, he's right this time."

He went to the bathroom and cleaned himself up. Back in the bedroom, he took two plain white T-shirts from his younger self and a few pairs of underwear and socks, stuffing them into his backpack. Finally, he went to the kitchen and ate everything he could cram down. He also took several protein bars, a couple cans of soda, and two pop-top cans of beef stew.

Cirrus had been following him from room to room and became especially attentive in the kitchen.

"What do we have here?" Drummer said, teasing, as he found a bag of cat treats. "The label says, 'chicken and turkey.' You want one?"

Cirrus licked his lips.

"Sure you do. Who wouldn't want two birds blended together and molded into a bunch of meat Chicklets?"

He gave him two.

When Cirrus had gobbled them down, Drummer picked him up again. The cat purred loudly and brushed his head against him, as he always had.

"Wow," said Drummer, calmed and touched. "I'm twenty years older, but you still know me. And you still love me. I don't know why I'm surprised."

Thoughts of such enduring companionship carried him back to Aaron. *Where is he now, in 2000?* Drummer wondered. *What kind of life is he living?*

The answers were not far behind.

In late 2000, Aaron would've been twenty years old and living with a high school friend in the San Francisco suburb of Fremont. This was around the time he'd met Grant.

Drummer held that thought. Aaron's relationship with Grant had damaged him and changed him. It had led to a life of stress and defensiveness from which he'd ultimately emerged, but had never fully recovered. That relationship was happening—it was *beginning*—right now.

Drummer felt sick.

He set Cirrus down and leaned against the kitchen counter, wondering. His thoughts led him to an extraordinary notion that had previously found life only in his fantasies. But now, with the unwinding of time, the fantastical had become real. Extraordinary things had become possible.

Whether he was in 2000 by accident or by design was a question Drummer hadn't even begun to ask. But whatever the answer, he was there. Then. And as long as this held true, he could define his own purpose. A plan quickly took form: he would find Aaron, intercede in his life, and drive Grant out. Drummer would change the past to give the man he loved the peaceful future he deserved. And when Drummer returned to 2020, he might find that things had changed, but they'd be changed for the better.

Drummer reflected on the conditions that had led to his own unfortunate status in 2000, to this dead-end life with Nate. As a teenager, Drummer had been ambitious and confident, with a clear vision for his future. But he had also been lonely, and his loneliness drove him to the first man to show interest. The resulting relationship with Nate had not been nearly as abusive as Aaron's with Grant, but there were obvious parallels. Both relationships had been a hindrance. Neither had inspired growth. Even alone—without a partner of any kind—Drummer and Aaron would have each fared far better.

Drummer wondered why none of his friends at the time had told him he was making a mistake. Why hadn't they pointed out the red flags? Why had they let him make the kind of terrible choices Aaron would be making now? Drummer was convinced that if someone had said something back then he wouldn't have lost his direction, and the years that followed wouldn't have been so hard.

He wouldn't let the same thing happen to Aaron again.

He picked up Cirrus one last time, gave him a soft kiss and a long hug, then carried him to the living room. Drummer set the ball of fur on the couch where Cirrus curled up on a blanket, nestling in to sleep.

"It's time for me go, little one," Drummer said, his voice quaking. "I love you dearly. Take care of him, okay?"

Drummer choked back a confusing swell of grief. The last time he had seen Cirrus had been at the end of his life. His cat had lived a long life and died peacefully, but the farewell had been agonizing for Drummer. Now Cirrus was back, and Drummer was saying goodbye once more. The circumstances were different—perhaps better—but parting was no easier.

He collected his backpack with the pilfered items inside. He took one last look around the apartment, gazed lovingly at his sleeping kitty, and left.

In the hallway, he closed the door behind him softly, then leaned against it and cried. All at once, he felt the loss of his youth and the passing of his cat. More than that, however, he felt shame for having allowed it to unfold as it had, without challenge or question.

He left the building, vowing never to return.

His next destination: Fremont.

He caught a bus heading downtown, where he descended into the subway system and boarded a regional Bay Area Rapid Transit train leaving San Francisco. The ride took an hour, passing through Oakland then southeast into the suburbs, which grew less dense and more rural as the miles swept by.

As he rode, Drummer quietly considered strategy. One option was to confront Grant himself, but he decided instead to go directly to Aaron. He hoped to appeal to him, to convince him to avoid Grant—or end whatever stage of their relationship already existed. Drummer reminded himself not to try and anticipate Aaron's responses, but to be open-minded, respectful, and honest. Aaron had always been able to see through platitudes, especially those spoken to him by strangers.

When Drummer arrived in Fremont, he hopped in a taxi outside the BART station and sat quietly in the back seat as the car made its way through town. Fremont was notably different from San Francisco. It was a relatively new sprawling suburb packed with strip malls, oversized schools, and houses with yards of mown verdant grass and trimmed juniper hedges. Exhaustion tugged at him during the ride, and he only snapped out of it when he reached his destination: an old motel called the Mowry Motor Inn.

The quaint mid-century structure was located at the foot of the grassy east bay hills in the Niles District, near the mouth of a two-lane highway that cut through a canyon to the east. The area had once been a busy transit connection, but by 2000 it had served as little more than a reminder of Fremont's rapidly fading history of truck stops and family farms.

Drummer felt oddly comforted as he approached the small front office. He'd known about this place from a story Aaron had once told him about his senior prom, which had concluded here in bumbling, comical fashion. It seemed like the ideal spot to call home for the night—partially for the sentimentality, but also because it was out of the way and off the grid.

He paid for a room with cash and stumbled in, exhausted. The room was small and unimpressive, with cheap design elements lifted randomly from the previous five decades. He didn't care. Luxury was not on his mind. He threw his coat and backpack onto a chair. He showered, set the old alarm clock on the bedside table for noon, and lay down for a nap.

He was out in seconds.

Before he knew it the alarm was blaring.

"Damn, that was fast," he said to himself, groggily. He needed more sleep, but the nap would have to suffice. He wanted to find Aaron as quickly as possible.

He dressed. He gave his blue polo shirt the smell test—which it passed, to his relief—and put it back on. He could've worn one of the clean T-shirts, but they were small and tight on him now. And while he still looked good in tight clothes, it wasn't the look he wanted to present today. Instead, he recalled the compliment Aaron had given him yesterday on the collared shirt and his tattoos. If that sentiment still applied twenty years out of time, it might endear Aaron to him and make him more likely to listen to what Drummer had to say.

Drummer reviewed an area map at the hotel front desk and set out on foot. He crossed the old highway, cut through a large warehouse parking lot, then walked through a housing development of ranch homes constructed in the 1960s. He passed a shopping center, its concrete elements placing its origin squarely in the 1970s, then navigated a seemingly endless grid of newer tract homes which came to an end at a wide, busy thoroughfare.

Across the street stood Aaron's old apartment complex. It was comprised of a dozen two-story buildings spread out across a property covered with low-cut grass and a handful of London planetrees. A single-lane driveway made a loop through the space, and carports dotted the perimeter.

Drummer crossed the boulevard. He knew which building was Aaron's but not the specific unit. He wasn't afraid to knock on doors if he had to.

Luck was on his side, however. Outside Aaron's building, he saw a group of four men in their early twenties loitering in the guest parking lot. They stood beside an unmistakable red Acura Integra, parked diagonally across two spaces. Leaning against the driver's side door, partially obscured by his companions, was a man of about twenty. He had blond hair and a lean frame, and was dressed in loose-fitting jeans and a black AC-DC T-shirt. He held a skateboard, one with red wheels and a hand-painted geometric design on the underside.

Drummer recalled the photos of Aaron and his friends mounted over the couch back home—those tiny windows to the past, which always seemed to have so much to say but had hung in stoic silence. Now those two-dimensional cross sections of Aaron's life sprung into high relief, expanding to include the greater world around them, as well as Drummer himself.

He struggled to maintain his momentum and feared he might turn around and leave, but he didn't let himself slow down. He compelled himself forward, through the fear and awe, toward the group. His eyes stayed fixed on the blond twenty-year-old, a man he'd recognized in an instant—the living, breathing genesis of the man he loved.

That young man let out a short laugh in reaction to one of his companions. Then, as Drummer entered his line of sight, he looked past his friends and locked eyes with Drummer. His laughter cooled, and his expression hardened into a cocky half grin.

Drummer stopped just outside the group's bubble of personal space.

"Aaron Hayes?" he called.

The blond skateboarder cast a look at him that was both curious and confrontational. He lifted his chin, and with a commanding tone, the likes of which Drummer had never heard from him before, he said....

"What the hell do you want?"

REDISCOVERY

He held it in his hand, disbelieving.
It had been there the entire time.
Ten years. Idle. Waiting.

Waiting for him to come home,
As he had promised.

Those ten years,
So beautiful,
Now felt wasted.

And his life in that condominium,
With a man who had brought him love,
And had eased his pain,
Now felt like little more than a diversion….

A diversion from the life that he had left behind,
In that house on the hill,
With the man who feared being seen.

CHAPTER 4
THE SEEDS OF DOUBT

DRUMMER FELT unexpectedly self-conscious under Aaron's piercing gaze. He could see in Aaron's eyes that he was studying him, trying to determine whether he knew him from somewhere. Who was this man, this heavily tattooed older dude, dressed like some prep school, bourgeois cliché? Or so Drummer imagined Aaron's inner voice saying. And what the hell did he want, indeed?

It was now on Drummer to answer that unspoken demand and to do it in a way that both defused confrontation and invited conversation.

Drummer hadn't expected Aaron to be combative. But his first words certainly hadn't been welcoming. The young skateboarder appeared quite different from the older man he would become—in poise and manner, in his steely gaze, even in the way he held his skateboard— and this caused Drummer to wonder if he knew him well enough at all. He wondered if the only thing keeping Aaron from blowing him off completely was curiosity.

"My name's Drummer Foss," he said directly. "Can I talk to you for a second?"

"You're doing it," Aaron answered flippantly.

Aaron's friends flanked him protectively but remained silent, like a band of outlaws waiting for a signal from their boss.

Drummer grinned. The territorial show was neither forced nor false, but there was a youthful affectation in it that he found amusing.

"Privately?" he added.

"What do you want to talk about?"

Drummer straightened. "Do you know someone named Grant Zimmer?" he asked with greater volume and firmness.

Aaron lowered his chin slightly to peer directly at Drummer. He then relaxed and turned to his companions. "This'll just be a second, guys," he said.

The group stood down.

Aaron and Drummer walked out of earshot, stopping at the corner of a cut-through in the driveway.

"You know Grant?" Aaron asked, slightly less brusque this time.

"I know of him. You've met him?"

"Is he in trouble?"

"How well do you know him?" Drummer asked.

Aaron scoffed.

Drummer reassessed. He quickly realized that his curt questioning was putting Aaron on the defensive.

"Listen, dude," the young Aaron said, "don't waste my time. Say what you wanna say."

Drummer felt speechless as this young man talked him down. This arrogant twenty-year-old was still the man he knew, but his uncompromising demeanor was a radical departure from the measured calm of Aaron's older self. Drummer knew from experience that straightforward people like this guy didn't always respect deference, so rather than back down or apologize for his curt behavior, Drummer stood firm and met Aaron's assertive stance head-on.

"Fine," Drummer said. "Grant's dangerous. That's what I want to say. If you've met him, don't see him again. If you're dating him, end it."

"I'll see who I want," Aaron retorted without pause. "And I'll *stop* seeing who I want. What's it to you?"

"I don't want you to get hurt."

"I can take care of myself."

"I know that." Drummer grinned again as he recalled more than a dozen instances where an older, wiser Aaron had proudly outshone people who'd presumed themselves to be older and wiser than him. Now, here was a younger, cockier version of Aaron, facing Drummer with a greater sense of righteousness. This amused Drummer, but it also gave him confidence, for it revealed that in some ways Aaron was still the same man.

"You're a strong guy," Drummer went on. "I can see that. But with Grant you sometimes feel like you're running defense. Am I right?"

"Why do you care?" Aaron rejoined.

"Because I'm a caring guy."

"Did my parents tell you to talk to me?"

"No," said Drummer. "Don't they like him?"

"Listen, dude, don't pretend to know me," Aaron said, with a sudden increase in volume. "You have anything else, or is that it?"

Drummer searched his thoughts but found them frustratingly vacant. He hadn't expected this level of resistance. "No, I suppose that's it," he said, to his own surprise.

Wordlessly, Aaron turned to walk away.

As he did, Drummer saw in his eyes an expression only someone who knew him would recognize: well-concealed disappointment.

"Please, wait," he pleaded in response to that look.

Aaron stopped and turned partly around, glancing back over his shoulder.

Drummer did have one more thing to add. Though it was a cheap shot, it was all he had. "Grant keeps a gun next to the bed, doesn't he?" he asked. His words came out as cold as a block of ice.

Mention of the gun caused Aaron to turn around completely. "What did you say?" he asked.

"A loaded magnum. You see it every night you're at his place," said Drummer, continuing as though Aaron had said nothing. "He says it's for protection, but you don't really think that's true. During the day he moves it around, leaves it in different places. Sometimes you think he's putting it where he knows you'll see it, like he's testing your tolerance."

"Part of a relationship is learning to trust someone," Aaron answered. "And believing them when they tell you things."

"So you trust him?" asked Drummer. "You believe him? Or do you merely trust that *he* believes what he says? They're not the same thing."

Aaron averted his eyes.

Drummer stepped forward, closing the gap between them. "If Grant's given you a reason to doubt, then it doesn't matter what he says. He hasn't earned your trust."

Aaron's stalwart disposition appeared to waver. "You still haven't told me why you care."

"I told you. It's because I'm a caring guy."

"That's not an answer," Aaron shot back.

"I'm sorry," Drummer said, letting his voice soften. "I don't mean to antagonize you. I just know how much you want it—to be loved. And I know Grant seems like the right guy. He fawns over you, gives you gifts, laughs and cries with you… right? But it's a mask. The real person is the guy behind the gun. And I think you know that."

Aaron stared into Drummer's eyes for a long moment. When he finally spoke again, he did so with a notably less adversarial tone. "I hear ya. But I need to get going. You have a phone number?"

"My phone's busted," Drummer lied. "But I'm staying at the Mowry Inn on Mission Boulevard. Room 120."

Aaron nodded, dropped his skateboard to its wheels, and coasted back to his friends. He tossed his board in the car and climbed into the driver's seat. The others filed in with him.

Drummer caught Aaron's gaze one last time as he drove by, heading to the exit of the property. He hoped Aaron would see in that look something more than mere concern for another person, more than just a general call to action. He hoped Aaron would see some form of genuine recognition, a personal connection that could only be conveyed in the gaze of someone who truly cared.

Aaron pulled onto the main road with a squeal of his tires and drove off.

As the car vanished from sight, Drummer wondered if he had succeeded, if that brief conversation had been enough to change events. Or was Aaron already shrugging it off and letting the course of history ignore it entirely?

Drummer sighed, then started his walk back toward the motel. A moody afternoon haze descended over the city as he went. He stopped at the strip mall for a hot sandwich. On the last leg of his trek through the warehouse lot, he took out his phone and scrolled through the photos. He thought he might see some changes in the future because of what he'd just done—an unexpected setting, maybe a new image indicating that the flow of time had been altered—but nothing novel had appeared. His stored photos remained the same.

Once back at the Mowry Inn, he found Aaron waiting for him in the parking lot. He was leaning against the red Acura with his arms crossed. His skateboard sat on the pavement under one foot. His friends were gone.

"You took your time," Aaron said disarmingly. "You walked the whole way?"

Drummer produced a brief grin. "I stopped for food. And I didn't think you'd give me a ride if I asked."

"You're right about that. Nice ink, by the way." Aaron indicated Drummer's arms.

"Thanks, it's all mythology-themed—mostly Greek." Drummer lifted a sleeve to show the details on his shoulder. He leaned against the car, beside Aaron. In a future setting he could envision putting his arm around him and pulling him close. But in this world, Aaron was a stranger.

"You have a favorite?" Aaron asked.

"A favorite tattoo? Right now, this one's pretty relevant." Drummer showed him the inside of his left forearm. It was dominated by a tattoo of a woman's face, tragically forlorn, framed with a swirl of celestial iconography. "It's Cassandra, the priestess of Apollo. She was cursed to share true prophecies of the future, but no one would ever believe her."

"Interesting."

Drummer shrugged. "I kind of identify with her right now."

Aaron looked at him, seeming to study his expression for something. "You think I don't believe the stuff you said about Grant?"

"Well, you're here, so I'm hopeful."

Aaron pointed to the device in Drummer's hand. "What's that?"

"Oh, my phone."

"I thought you said it was broken."

"It's not connected to a network, so I can't make calls."

"Fair enough. It's a weird-looking phone. Can I see it?"

Drummer's first thought was to refuse, but he also recognized that his hesitancy was arbitrary. Letting Aaron handle the phone itself wasn't likely to do any harm, as long as Drummer kept him away from its contents. He handed it over.

Aaron examined it. "How's it work?"

Drummer leaned in and turned it on but didn't unlock it. "It's a touch screen."

Aaron appeared genuinely impressed. "I have a cell, but it's nothing like this."

"Smartphones are getting pretty smart, pretty fast." Drummer took it back and turned it off. "Have you thought about what I said?"

"Yeah."

"And?"

"And…," Aaron began slowly, like he was considering his response. "I have to say, man, it really bothered me. Couldn't understand why at first. I thought it was about the gun. Then I realized… it's actually about you."

"Me?"

"Yeah, you. What's your deal? Who are you, and why do you care if I date Grant or not?"

Drummer smiled coyly. "I told you, I'm a caring guy."

"And I told you that's not an answer. You tell me to walk away from someone I'm dating, and you use a scare tactic to do it. That's kinda fucked-up. But you're right, I hate the gun, and you make a good point about trust. How do you know him?"

"Maybe I have a friend he hurt," Drummer said. "Maybe I'm holding a grudge."

"Yeah, obviously you have a grudge. And it looks like you know a lot about him—and a lot about me. The way you were talking earlier, and the way you're looking at me right now…. It's more than just me dating someone you don't like or getting back at him for someone he hurt. It's kinda like… I dunno… like I matter to you."

Drummer heard a dramatic lilt in Aaron's final few words, perhaps even a question. He tried to remain focused in the face of it, but still he was drawn in. The man beside him might not have been the Aaron of the future, but he was still Aaron. Those blue eyes were the same, and that voice—that beautiful, steady voice—was his. When Drummer looked into young Aaron's eyes, he could see his partner of ten years looking back. And when he listened to him speak, he could hear the same man. He was finding it increasingly difficult to separate the young from the old, despite their obvious differences.

"So, do I?" asked Aaron.

"Do you what?"

"Do I matter to you?"

Drummer was cornered. Aaron's question was leading, but valid. The truthful answer was yes, but he couldn't say it so bluntly. If he did, he'd have to explain why. The quandary frustrated him. He'd wanted this—wanted Aaron to see that he cared—but he didn't think it would be its own issue. Drummer hadn't imagined that convincing Aaron to stop dating Grant would be so difficult. Wasn't reminding him of the gun enough? Didn't Aaron recognize the threat or see the madman lurking behind Grant's disarming smile?

Maybe he didn't. Maybe Grant's ability to conceal his darker nature was better-honed than Drummer had anticipated. Would merely warning Aaron of the danger *ever* be enough? His words clearly carried weight or Aaron wouldn't have come to find him at the inn, but they were still just words. And to the young Aaron, Drummer was still just a suspicious stranger.

Drummer reconsidered the phone in his hand. He thought about the media it contained—hundreds of pictures and videos, each worth a thousand words or more, each one capable of telling a story far more convincing than the meager pleas of a strange man hiding behind lies of omission. If anything could convince Aaron that he was trustworthy, Drummer suspected it would be those files. But the story they told, while compelling, would beg the question of their origin. And then Drummer would have to tell him everything, including who he really was, and where—and when—he'd come from.

"You do matter to me," Drummer said finally, quieter than intended, "but I don't think I can explain how."

"I don't stop dating people just because someone tells me to," said Aaron. "Grant's got issues, but we're all screwed up somehow. He was abused pretty bad as a kid, so I don't blame him for thinking he needs protection."

"Abused people sometimes become abusers themselves, Aaron. And when firearms come into play—"

"He's been good to me," Aaron interrupted. "And I've already said that I hate the gun. So what else do you have? Something you're not telling me? If there's something that'll convince me, then you've got my attention. If not, I'll head home and make my own choices."

Drummer's eyes locked with Aaron's.

In the young Aaron's voice, he imagined he could hear the older Aaron appealing to him from 2020. He heard his future partner begging Drummer to reveal the truth to his younger self. to tell him the hard truths about Grant and free him preemptively from the abuse he was destined to suffer. This was Drummer's last chance to save him before the young Aaron walked away and his grim future continued to roll on unchecked.

He'll believe you, he heard in his mind. The ghost of the forty-year-old Aaron pleaded with him. *You know me, D. If you tell him, and you do it right, he'll believe you.*

Drummer doubted that, but he also knew that the voice in his head was right. He knew what Aaron would accept and what he'd reject. Aaron clearly hated the gun, but he also tolerated it, and by doing so, he was choosing to overlook every other red flag that fell short of it. To break that commitment, Drummer had to show him something profound—something he couldn't dismiss. It seemed clear at this point that words alone would never be enough to break the bond that had already been made between Aaron and his future abuser.

"Okay," Drummer said, committing himself. "I can show you. But keep an open mind."

"I always do."

Drummer hesitated but then nudged himself to keep going. "I think the best way to explain why I care is to show you what I've lost," he said. "And the only way to convince you to end it with him is to show you what you'll lose because of him."

"That's a little cryptic," said Aaron, "but whatever you got."

Drummer turned on his phone and opened the gallery of saved photos. The first to appear was the first selfie that he and Aaron had ever taken together—the picture of the two of them near the movie theater ticket counter on their first date in 2010. Drummer sighed heavily, holding the phone close before finally handing it over.

Anxiety surged through Drummer as Aaron took the phone from him. Drummer already wondered if he'd made the right choice by speaking to him, never mind this, but the time for that debate had passed. With the handoff of the phone, Drummer was crossing the point of no return. He was committed now. The handful of seconds that elapsed as Aaron focused on the device in his hand felt to Drummer like they lasted a lifetime.

AARON LOOKED at the image on the screen.

Two smiling faces looked back.

One was the man standing beside him now, only younger.

The other was… someone else.

Someone who resembled himself in every way, except older.

"When you want to see another picture," Drummer explained, "put your fingertip on the screen and swipe across to the right. It'll scroll through a gallery, one image after the other."

Aaron understood and swiped to the next image. He saw the same two men as in the first, this time in a different setting and at a different time.

He swiped again.

Another photo, another place, but the same two faces.

He scanned through a dozen images before reversing direction and returning to the first.

"What am I looking at?" Aaron asked, confused but fascinated. His imagination carried him away.

"That is what I've lost," said Drummer.

"So, I remind you of this guy? That's why you're here?"

"No," Drummer said softly, glancing down at his feet, then back at Aaron. "He's not someone I *used* to know. He's someone I *will* know."

Aaron looked again at the photo on the screen, and in that familiar face he saw more than just a semblance of himself.

"Who is it?" he asked.

"Who do you think it is?"

Aaron heard a challenge in Drummer's words. It was benevolent but a challenge nonetheless, and he never backed down from one of those.

He looked even more closely at the man in the photo.

All at once, in that older face, he saw all the details of his own appearance—the small freckle on his left cheek, the scar on his jaw from a skateboarding accident, the wily eyebrow hair he never bothered to pluck, and the devilish curl of his own smile. He tried to see someone else. He tried to find any element of the man's appearance or expression that didn't align with his own, but he could not, other than the classic signs of the passing of time.

"It looks… like me."

"It is," Drummer said.

Aaron searched Drummer's expression for any sign of deceit, but in the older man's pale green eyes he saw only sincerity.

"It's both of us," Drummer added, as seriously and genuinely as he could, "ten years from now. That's why I care."

That had to be a joke. Aaron's first instinct was to reject Drummer's claim outright. On its surface the notion was ludicrous, but at the same time he couldn't easily deny what his eyes were telling him. In the photos, he didn't just see the physical resemblance, but also the elements of someone's character that couldn't be photographed—the motivation behind the expression, the temperament behind the deportment, the very core of a man's nature reflected in the face of someone who could be no one other than himself.

"And what about Grant?" he asked, much softer.

Drummer took the phone from Aaron's weakening grip. He scrolled to another photograph, then handed the phone back to him.

Aaron devoured the image. In it he and Drummer sat on a bench together, surrounded by Aaron's family on the shore of a small lake in what looked like Golden Gate Park in San Francisco. Everything in the picture insisted that the man sitting beside Drummer on that bench was Aaron—everything. Aaron's parents and siblings were there. They wore clothes he recognized. They were older, but consistently so.

"This is what Grant takes away from you," Drummer said.

"What does that mean?" Aaron asked, astonished and visibly upset. He couldn't look away from the image. It carried such weight. His entire family, together, happy, save for a peculiar look of discontentment on his own face.

"If you stay with Grant, he'll take all the good things in that photo away. He'll lie to you. He'll make you believe that your family and friends don't care about you, and that he's the only one who does. He'll gaslight you so masterfully you'll reject them all on your own."

"I don't look very happy in this picture."

"You're happy, but when we took that photo, you had a lot on your mind," said Drummer. "By that day you'll have moved on and brought people back into your life, but you'll always have moments like this one, invisible to everyone except the click of a camera that happens to capture that look at just the right time."

Aaron handed the phone back to him, then looked away from the motel, up the old highway as it disappeared into the hazy east bay hills.

The world carried on, but it rested only lightly on Aaron's senses. The cars driving by, the sound of the wind, and the chill in the air were all smothered by his thoughts of the past and the future. By visions of Grant's smile and the sound of his voice dismissing a dozen warnings that Aaron had noted but not heeded. And by the cold, hard image of the gun by the bed.

"What you're saying is ridiculous," Aaron finally said.

"I know how it sounds."

"You think I'll believe it?"

Drummer shook his head. "I'm not expecting anything. I'm just… hoping."

Aaron kept his eyes on the horizon. "If those pictures are real," he said, "and you do know me—*will* know me—then you know I can be pretty emotional sometimes. But I have a logical way of looking at things too. Put it all together, and I like to think anything's possible… even crazy shit like this."

He turned to Drummer and offered a small, uncertain smile. "You've shown me a lot. I need to think about it. Before I go, I want to ask you something."

"Of course."

"You're saying—" Aaron paused, knowing that he would feel just as ridiculous uttering his next words as Drummer's claim seemed to be. Finally, he let the rest of the sentence slip out, quietly and with a hint of audible skepticism. "—you're from the future?"

"That's right."

"Then… the other guy in those photos," Aaron continued. "The younger you. He's out there? Right now?"

Drummer nodded.

"You've seen him?"

"This morning. I didn't talk to him, but it was definitely me."

"What was he doing?"

"Just… living his life, in my old apartment in the city. Working a job at the Hyatt Regency downtown. Wasting his days. Right around now, he'll be heading home to a boyfriend he doesn't love."

"I'm sorry about that," said Aaron, imagining what it must be like to look back on one's life and see yourself make the same mistakes all over again. He didn't know what else to say. Part of him wanted to question Drummer further, but he didn't know what kind of answers he wanted to get.

He opened the car door and threw his skateboard in the back seat, ready to leave.

"Whatever you're thinking," Drummer began, "I have to ask— even beg. Please don't see Grant again."

Aaron paused. He looked into Drummer's desperate eyes without betraying a sliver of his intent and said, "I have a job interview in the morning. But if you're still here, maybe I'll come by after."

He climbed into his car, revved it up, and drove out of the lot.

DRUMMER WATCHED him go.

That red Acura, seemingly lifted straight from the small photos mounted on the living room wall back home, disappeared up the boulevard into the hazy afternoon.

Alone again, Drummer reflected on his actions. Had talking to Aaron been the best possible choice? Had he taken the right steps? Had he made the most of this fantastical situation, or was there more that he could've done? Drummer told himself he'd done the right thing. But would the right thing yield the right result?

The phone in Drummer's hand timed out and shut off, sending the photograph of his past self and Aaron's future self into darkness. The image fading out was little more than a byte of code, but in the moment, it seemed to Drummer like an omen.

INNOCULATION

The sharp tip pierced his skin and, though he barely felt it, he cried. The near-painless pinch brought a year of death and isolation to an end and allayed a future of fear.

He had overcome many hardships in his life, and he felt strong and capable despite them, but his emotions could still bring him to tears. He did not usually know what to think of this, but on this day to have felt nothing would have been the greater tragedy.

He had suffered a terrible loss. But not the loss he had expected, not the one that had been predicted. One that could have been prevented, had time simply waited.

CHAPTER 5
IMPRESSIONS

AFTER LEAVING the Mowry Inn, Aaron took a winding, aimless drive through town, burning through the hours as he contemplated Drummer's words and the images on his phone. Finally, with twilight crossing into night, he pulled into his carport. But he remained unsettled. He had yet to answer the core question: Who did he trust more? The harbinger of doom or the devil he knew?

Drummer's tale was outlandish, but Aaron also found it disturbingly plausible. Aaron's initial skepticism led him to wonder if Drummer's photos were fake, but was that even possible? There were too many of them. They were too accurate. They contained images of people Drummer couldn't possibly have known. And technologically, the photos were just too *good*. Digital photography was brand new, the resolution of even the best cameras pitiful. The images couldn't be fakes, and by extension, that phone couldn't be a product of the present.

Drummer's words rang truer with every moment.

But did Aaron *trust* him?

He didn't know. He'd seen Grant's temper flare from time to time, but he didn't think it could rage out of control. He'd certainly never imagined himself as a potential victim.

He left his car, climbed the single flight of outside stairs to the balcony door leading to his apartment, and entered.

As the door closed behind him, he found himself keenly aware of the objects and furnishings in the room. Many of them had been in some of the photos Drummer had shown him, purportedly from between ten and twenty years in the future. Seeing them now felt surreal, as if he were looking back at his present life from that distant time.

He was also struck by the difference in the quality of that life. His current apartment was a mishmash of new and old furnishings, including a second-hand couch and bookshelves made of exposed particle board. Unframed posters tacked to the wall gave the place a dorm-like feel. Conversely, though the future world in the photographs contained many of the same objects, it was neat and tidy. Pictures were framed and hung with purpose, and the furnishings were coordinated. It didn't appear to be a luxurious life, but it was certainly a comfortable and organized one.

"Hey, man," came a voice from the center of the room. It was Aaron's roommate, Willis. He was sprawled on the couch with his eyes glued to the television. Some random reality cop show garbage was on.

Willis was the same age as Aaron, physically bigger in most ways yet more childlike in his demeanor. His clothes were rattier, and his scant facial hair was blotchy and unkempt. His own skateboard, resting against the wall beside him, was a scuffed-up testament to many graceless spills. He'd been one of the guys with Aaron earlier that day when Drummer had first approached.

"Hey," Aaron responded.

"What's up?"

"Eh," he grunted. "Weird day."

"Still have your date?"

"My date?"

Willis rolled over to face him. "With Grant?" he clarified. "I thought that's where you were."

Aaron grumbled. He had forgotten.

Willis pointed to a wall clock resting on a milk crate across the room. "You have twenty minutes."

"Fuck."

"Problems?"

Aaron didn't reply. He took out his cell phone—a pocket-size Nokia with a small liquid crystal display—and called Grant.

After a few rings, Grant answered. "Hey, sexy."

"Hey, GZ," said Aaron with little enthusiasm.

"Ready for tonight?"

"Yeah, about that," said Aaron, "I know it's late notice, but I can't do tonight."

"What do you mean?" Grant asked. "We've had plans for days."

"I know. I'm sorry, it's just been a hard day."

"Right. You eat shit off that skateboard of yours again?" Grant chuckled to himself.

"No, no spills today," said Aaron, unamused. "I just need time to myself."

"Ugh, *that* line."

Aaron rolled his eyes. "Grant—"

"We've had plans forever," Grant said, interrupting, sounding more incredulous than disappointed. "Now you suddenly need time to yourself?"

"Yes," Aaron said bluntly.

"Well, what is it this time?"

"What do you mean?"

"I mean, what's more important than me *this* time?" Grant's tone contained a distinct ripple of accusation—one that was often present in his voice but that Aaron only now noticed. On previous occasions, Aaron had thought Grant sounded downtrodden, but clearly that had been a misperception.

"Ugh, nothing, GZ, it's not like that."

"I'm really disappointed," Grant continued. "And I'm getting tired of you doing this to me."

"Doing what?"

"Saying one thing, then doing another. Telling me you want to go out, then canceling at the last minute."

"I've never done that," Aaron shot back. He heard the rise in his own voice and realized he was being put on the defensive. This too was something Grant often did but that Aaron had not been aware of until Drummer called out how he might frequently feel like he's running defense.

"Then we're going out tonight," Grant concluded, one part query and three parts presumption.

"No, I said we're not." Aaron held firm. There had been a time, very recently in fact, when he would've tried to appease Grant. He'd apologize, believing himself guilty of some misdeed, then yield, if only to prove that he wasn't two-faced. But not now. No longer. The compulsion to back down still nagged at Aaron, but he was able to fight it off, for he could see the nature of the conversation much more clearly now. Grant was trying to control their talk by playing on Aaron's desire to please.

"Man, why are you being so defensive?" asked Grant. He laughed. To Aaron it sounded like mockery.

"I'm not being defensive, Grant. You're *putting* me on the defensive."

"Please," Grant scoffed. "You're the one trying to cancel at the last minute, knowing how long it takes me to get there. It's selfish."

Aaron couldn't believe that he hadn't noticed it before—Grant's accusations of deception, his implication that Aaron was a victimizer and a liar. Worst of all, Aaron could still feel his empathy being yanked left and right by Grant's phrasing and tone.

Aaron thought back over the past two months. Almost every conversation between the two of them had gone this way, beginning innocently, then ending with Aaron feeling guilty for some perceived transgression and apologizing, worried that he'd hurt Grant's feelings. But with this new clarity he could see that Grant's feelings had always been just fine. Aaron had been offering an olive branch to a carnivore.

"How about we just take it easy?" said Grant, softening his tone. "We'll order in."

Aaron sighed aloud. Grant suddenly appeared amenable to negotiation, but this, too, was a ploy. It had happened before. And each time, Aaron had fallen for it because it suggested an end to conflict and signaled an evening of tenderness and affection. Now Aaron felt shame for being so easily baited.

"Grant, you're not hearing me," he said, stripping his tone of any hint of affability.

"Oh, I am. I just don't think you know what you're saying."

"Well then how's *this* sound to you? *We're done.*"

"Done?"

"We're *done*, Grant. I'm breaking up with you."

"Bullshit," Grant spouted, suddenly irate. "I don't know what this is about, but things were great when we talked this morning. Now you're breaking up with me? I at least get to have my say. I'm already on my way over, so we're working this out."

Grant hung up.

"*Fuck!*" Aaron exclaimed.

Willis's eyebrows popped. "That didn't sound good."

"It wasn't. He's still coming over."

Willis sat up. "What's going on, man? I thought you liked this guy."

"I did," Aaron said. "But today I learned something about him I *don't* like."

"Well, if he's still coming over—"

"I can't be here."

"Well, *I'm* not dealing with him."

"No, I'll do it myself. Just not tonight."

Aaron leaned against the inside of the front door, trying to decide what to do. He jingled his keys in his hand. "Can we take off?" he asked. "I'll buy you pizza or something."

Willis bounced off the couch. "Pizza? On you? Hell yeah… if you can afford it. You got that job already?"

"My interview's tomorrow."

"But you got it?"

Aaron nodded and said with intentionally muted pride, "I'm sure I've got it."

"Nice!"

"You still need a job too. Don't slack off on me."

"I *am* working," Willis protested. "Tonight, I got myself a job as a babysitter." He laughed at his own joke.

The two young men promptly left the apartment and drove to a nearby Italian restaurant, a family business that had moved into a defunct burger joint next to an Amtrak station. It wasn't a classy location, but the food was good enough—and cheap.

Willis had a healthy appetite and stuffed his face. Aaron stared at his plate, barely eating.

"You gonna tell me what's going on?" Willis asked after a hearty swallow. "It's not just Grant, right? I can tell. This morning, you were stupid-excited about tonight."

"Yeah, I'm not excited anymore."

"Yeah."

Willis waited for Aaron to elaborate. When he didn't, he pressed him. "Is it about that guy we saw earlier?"

Aaron shrugged and looked away.

"It is," Willis concluded with an impish smile, almost as satisfied with his deduction as he was curious about the details. "So, who is he? I know you're into older guys, but dude, he's gotta be twice our age. And he's probably a little crazy too, if he's out combing parking lots for kids."

Aaron peered at him. "We're not kids. And that's not what he was after."

"How do you know? He's got years on you, dude. Who knows what someone his age is thinking?"

"What's that supposed to mean? He's not *that* old."

"Too old for you."

"Bitch, like you know me. If I want to date an eighty-year-old, that's my business."

Willis bit off another piece of pizza and spoke through it. "You wouldn't date an eighty-year-old."

"Don't talk with your mouth full."

Aaron's cell phone rang.

And continued to ring.

"You gonna answer that?" asked Willis.

"I'm sure it's Grant."

"So… no?"

"No."

Aaron muted the ringtone.

"So-o-o-o-o," Willis voiced with a lilt, "bringing it back to that guy from today…. If he wasn't a horny old man combing parking lots for unsuspecting *not-kids*, then who is he? You know him? Did he say something about Grant?"

"I don't know him," said Aaron, meeting his inquisitive stare, "but we did talk about Grant."

"And?"

"And it was private. But he told me some things that make me see Grant differently now."

"Sounds like the guy's either a diplomat or a manipulator."

"At the very least," said Aaron, "he's good with words."

Once they were finished with dinner, Aaron drove them home. They arrived to find the apartment complex bathed in red-and-blue police lights. Several emergency vehicles were parked in the driveway, including a firetruck, an ambulance, and several squad cars. At least two dozen residents were gathered on the lawn, the night illuminated by the emergency lights.

Aaron pulled his car to the side, ahead of the commotion.

"What the hell's this?" Willis asked haltingly.

Aaron watched as two police officers emerged from between apartment buildings, escorting a tall, imposing man—handcuffed—away from the crowd. The officers put him in the back seat of a squad car.

"Holy shit, is that Grant?" Willis looked to Aaron for confirmation.

Aaron—his eyes surely betraying his dismay—merely stared.

"I don't know what this is about, dude," Willis continued, "but I think you just dodged a bullet."

The squad car drove past with Grant in the back seat. Aaron sank down as if to hide, forgetting how obvious his red car really was. Only after the police car had left the complex did he feel comfortable sitting back up.

Willis stepped out of the car and walked toward the crowd and the remaining first responders.

Reluctantly, Aaron followed.

A lanky older woman saw the two approaching and intercepted them. "Aaron," she said. "There you are." She sounded exhausted.

"Jackie, what happened?"

"Some psycho was out here screaming and yelling," she said, "banging on your door. Ray was in the office and came out, told him to back off or he'd call the cops. Your friend didn't like that, so he got a bat out of his trunk and started swinging."

"What…?" Aaron murmured.

"He hit Ray in the head. Sent him to the hospital. A couple other people got hit too, taking the guy down. They're over there talking to the cops." She motioned to a small group standing on the grass and speaking to two officers.

"Is Ray okay?"

"I dunno, hon. They drove off a few minutes ago. You'll have to ask Mitch. But he's not real happy with you right now."

"Shit," Aaron said under his breath. It was clear that if he and Willis had been home, they would've been the ones on the receiving end of all this. He felt responsible.

"I'm glad you're okay, Jackie," he said.

"Thanks, but I'm thinking *I* should be the one who's glad *you're* okay."

Aaron nodded with gratitude; then he and Willis went over to the group giving statements to the police. "Hey," he said as he approached, apprehension clear in his voice. "Everyone okay here?"

A man in a black tank top stepped forward, a small, bleeding wound on his forehead. He was visibly angry, but also fighting back tears. He jabbed his index finger into Aaron's chest. "Your fucking boyfriend went all psycho on us. He put my dad in the fucking hospital!"

"I... I'm sorry, Mitch," said Aaron. "Is he all right?"

Aaron's concern was evident, which calmed Mitch down.

"Yeah... yeah, he should be," he replied, pacing anxiously. "But that guy you're dating is a fuckin' animal, Aaron. I don't want to see him around here again."

"Do you know him, sir?" asked one of the officers.

Aaron suddenly felt put on the spot, as everyone in the group looked at him for a response. "You mean the guy you just drove out of here?" he asked. "Yeah, I do."

One of his neighbors interjected, "They were just asking if we wanted to press charges, Aaron. We really don't know."

Aaron thought about it. He thought about what might have happened, had he been home. He thought about the warning from Drummer. He thought about the gun.

He sniffed, wiping a loose tear from his eye.

"Do it," he said.

"Fuck, *really*?" Willis exclaimed.

"Yes, really," Aaron insisted. "After this, he needs a formal record... if he doesn't already have one."

"It would be helpful if you could answer a few questions," the officer added.

Aaron recalled one of the photos Drummer had shown him—of the two of them on the bench in Golden Gate Park, surrounded by his family. He no longer questioned its validity. He knew it was real. And the thought of losing his family and everyone he loved in the pursuit of a relationship with a violent man—it made him sick. He looked at the officer, straightened, and said with conviction, "Just tell me what you need to know."

AARON AWOKE the next morning with the unsettling feeling that his life had dramatically changed direction. His landlord had spent the night in the hospital; Grant had spent the night in jail and would certainly face serious charges.

Aaron was astonished that the situation had deteriorated so rapidly, but upon reflection, the outcome now seemed inevitable. Over the two months that he and Grant had been dating, Aaron had unwittingly given him the impression that his commitment was strong and that he was willing to accept a more passive role in the relationship. Then Aaron had hit Grant with the words "We're done," which must've seemed to come out of nowhere. Over the phone, Grant had revealed himself to be controlling and angry; Aaron should've expected a controlling and angry response.

As Aaron lay in bed, he peered up at the wall above his headboard, where he'd hung a reproduction of *The Starry Night*—an expensive gift from a relative for Aaron's high school graduation. Aaron often saw the world through the lens of Impressionist style, where detail and meaning could be conveyed or discerned through a seemingly random arrangement of mottled color. When viewed up close, *The Starry Night* was a canvas smeared with blue and yellow paint blots. But when seen from farther back, those blots coalesced into a magnificent nighttime scene, abundant with mystery, light, and life.

He now reflected on Grant using the same filter. Before meeting Drummer, Aaron had focused only on the vibrant colors of Grant's personality—his decisiveness, attentiveness, and dominance. But Aaron had been standing too close to see much more. Drummer's arrival had forced him to step back and examine the man in his entirety. Now he saw the complete portrait that those vibrant colors composed, and it was hideous.

He threw off the blankets and sat up, letting the cool air hit his bare skin, hoping it might shock him from his distraction. He couldn't lie there and contemplate Grant any longer. In two hours, he was expected in downtown San Francisco for a job interview. Even if the direction of his personal life was begging for reassessment, his professional trajectory remained unaltered and demanded his concentration.

He showered, then put on his interview clothes—expensive dark blue jeans paired with a crisp, fitted dress shirt, a stylish tie, and a sport coat. He stood before the bathroom mirror to evaluate himself. He wasn't accustomed to dressing so neatly, but he was impressed with what he saw. His reflection even reminded him of the images he'd seen of his supposed older self.

"Turning into your dad, I see," Willis teased as Aaron entered the living room.

Aaron shook his head with a lighthearted grin. It was clear to him that the jab had been planned. "You try," said Aaron, "but you know it's not funny."

"Whatever, dude," Willis replied with a shrug. "It's early, and that's all I've got."

Aaron sat beside him on the couch and flashed a cocky smile. "You know I look good."

"Yeah, good enough for traffic court."

"Better than a funeral. Last night coulda been a lot worse."

Willis tugged on Aaron's sport coat. "You'd never let yourself get buried in this. You've probably got a ripped-up Metallica shirt under all that, I bet."

"This isn't high school graduation."

"It's still all pomp and circumstance."

Aaron gave him a sideways glance. "Pomp and circumstance? You a lit major now?"

"I heard it on TV."

"And you remembered it. Bravo."

"Yeah, yeah," Willis said dismissively. "Mitch left a message, by the way. Says his dad's gonna be okay, in case you care. You heard from Grant?"

"Nope."

"I guess you aren't his one phone call, then."

"I'd rather pay for your babysitting than his bail."

Willis winked at him wryly. "You know what, kid? You're smarter than you look."

Aaron's mood became more serious. The weight of responsibility for the previous night still hung about his neck. "You sleep all right?" he asked. "It was a lot to come home to."

"Didn't sleep at all," said Willis, "but it's okay."

"It's not okay. I should've seen it coming."

"Don't do that to yourself. You can't always see through people, especially assholes like Grant. Hell, I didn't even see it, and I'm a jaded bitch."

"Not gonna argue with that."

"Ready for your interview?"

"Yeah, I'm going to eat something, then go. You'll be all right here on your own?"

Eyes smiling, Willis lifted a leftover piece of the previous night's pizza from a paper plate on his lap. "I'm fed… I'm good. Turns out I'm a pretty skilled babysitter."

"You need to raise your standards," said Aaron. "Being a fed babysitter is a low bar."

"Whatever, Dad."

"On the other hand, I might need more babysitting tonight. Assuming there's someone out there dumb enough to bail out GZ."

"Tell you what," said Willis, "I'll raise my standards when you stop using that nickname for that asshole."

Aaron checked himself and replied, "Done."

After a quick breakfast not consisting of leftover pizza, Aaron drove to the Fremont BART station and boarded a train to San Francisco, unknowingly taking the same line Drummer had ridden to Fremont the previous morning. He arrived in the city shortly before 11:00 a.m. and got off at Embarcadero Station—the first stop near the waterfront. The technology startup was only a block away, headquartered in Embarcadero Center 4, one of the towers closest to the bay. The lobby had an enviable view of the water, Coit Tower, the Transamerica Pyramid, and the neighborhood of North Beach. It was impressive and intimidating.

Aaron had already jumped through numerous pre-interview hoops, and at this point it was his job to lose. He still felt some nervousness upon arrival, for he'd been told by the company's human resources manager to prepare for a panel interview with three executives. But the department director who greeted him in the lobby was casually dressed in jeans and a *Buffy the Vampire Slayer* T-shirt and couldn't have been more than ten years older than him, which immediately put him at ease. As she brought him through the office, he was further relieved to see that many of the employees were near his age—in fact, the age range didn't appear to skew much older or younger. Aaron laughed inwardly at himself as he sat down with the two other executives, each of them similarly dressed and casually reclined. He looked down at himself and wondered if a Metallica T-shirt wouldn't have been a better choice after all.

The interview went well, despite his nerves. Aaron's charm won them over, and his understanding of the job impressed them. With a slight hint of cockiness, he added that he was on track to finish his bachelor's degree in under four years; his schooling wouldn't interfere with his job for longer than another two semesters. He rarely boasted about his accomplishments, but if he were ever to do it, now was the time.

The interview came to an end with an offer, and Aaron left the building securely employed. He was proud of the way he was taking control of his life at such a young age. Few of his friends could see their own paths so clearly.

He walked out onto the brick plaza separating Embarcadero Center from the waterfront and took a moment to soak in the scene around him. It was a beautiful day in an idyllic town. Ferries sailed across the bay. The nearby Ferry Building clock tower chimed twice. People were everywhere. Aaron cast his eyes skyward at the tall downtown towers, imagining himself working and living among them. For the first time, he felt real contentment. Rewarded. He'd grown accustomed to being challenged by others through most of his life so far—classmates or other skateboarders who tried to compete with him and teachers who prejudged him. No one had thought this young, fair-haired skater punk might also have a brain. As a result, he always felt pushed to prove himself. To fight. To compete. To win. Now he had earned a coveted job on his own merits. None of the hecklers from his past were there to witness it, but he savored his victory all the same.

It was then that he noticed the Hyatt Regency Hotel, standing right beside Embarcadero Center 4. Somehow it had escaped his notice earlier in the day, even as he'd walked right past it on the way to his interview. Drummer had told him he'd once worked there—that his younger self *now* worked there. Aaron wondered if that other version of Drummer might be inside at this very moment. The thought gave him a chill.

He tried to put it out of his mind, but as he walked toward the subway, a small voice inside him suggested that he go into the building to see if the younger Drummer truly was there. He rejected the thought almost immediately. After all, what would be gained by doing that?

On the other hand, what was there to lose?

As Aaron debated with himself, external forces interrupted, drawing his attention. From among the hundreds of anonymous people walking by, a surprisingly well-defined individual came into sight. It was a man in his mid-twenties, wearing a white T-shirt and black slacks. Slung over his shoulder was a brown messenger bag. A neo-traditional sleeve tattoo covered his entire right arm. His left arm appeared bare. Accompanying him were two women of about the same age.

Aaron didn't know any of them, but something about the man was familiar. He looked like a younger Drummer, though there were subtle differences between the two. This younger man had a slightly leaner face and less muscular body, and he carried himself more casually and with less poise. In some ways, he didn't look the way Aaron would have expected a younger Drummer to look. But could it be anyone else?

Subconsciously Aaron slowed his pace, and in his mind, time slowed with him as the man came closer. His surroundings seemed to recede. The bright blue sky, the masonry towers, and the sounds of the crowd all faded into a mottled amalgam of color and noise. It was like an Impressionist painting come to life in Aaron's mind, a world reduced to streaks, blots, chimes, and echoes. And in the middle of it all was this man.

Aaron kept his gaze transfixed on the group as they passed, paying him no attention. He questioned his eyes and ears. Was it indeed Drummer, or just a convincing doppelganger?

Compelled, he followed them as they rounded the hotel. He stayed several steps behind, studying the man as closely as he could. Their similarities were many. They had the same bone structure and the same build. The same smile, the same voice, and the same laugh. Aaron could even imagine the transition—the evolution of the younger into the older over time. Still, the differences led him to question.

The group stopped outside the hotel's employee entrance.

Aaron leaned against a concrete planter by the door, hoping to appear nonchalant as he studied the man more closely. He scrutinized his every detail, every inch of his skin, every line and shade of the tattoos on his right arm. He wished he could remember exactly what tattoos Drummer himself wore on that arm, but he could not.

Only then did Aaron notice the fresh outline of a new tattoo on the inside of the man's left forearm. The face of a woman. Celestial imagery. Cassandra, the priestess of Apollo.

The sight of it struck Aaron broadside. *Holy hell, that's impossible*, he thought. He was so distracted by the tattoo that he failed to notice that the man had become aware of him standing in his personal space. Aaron had gone too far and had waited too long. But even as he realized what he'd done, he couldn't step away. He couldn't even look away. The seconds grew even longer, expanding to the point of almost stopping, until the tattooed man faced him head-on.

Pale green eyes locked on to him.

Time stopped.

There was no doubt who he was.

Aaron was rendered mute and immobile by the possibility and impossibility that someone could exist twice in the same time. He didn't realize that he'd continued to cling to his doubt until this very moment.

The young Drummer smiled at him. It was not a smile of recognition, just a flirtatious hello from one stranger to another.

Aaron tried to smile back, but he could only stare. He tried to speak, but no words came.

Clearly disappointed, the younger Drummer broke eye contact. He turned, entered the hotel with his companions, and disappeared down a darkened hall. The heavy metal door shut behind them with a resonant thud.

Aaron barely moved. Nothing he understood about the universe could explain what had just occurred, other than what an older Drummer had shown him the previous day.

He looked around himself as his Impressionist vision dissolved into the hard-edged details of reality. Time resumed its normal pace. The sounds of the city returned. The blue sky floated above. Nothing had changed. But just as Aaron's view of Grant had been permanently altered, so too was his view of the world.

THE MESSENGER

He ruminated on his purpose and realized that it was no longer singular. No longer a simple connection between two dots. No longer a return to a crossroads where all things came and went. Time had passed and his purpose had evolved.

He'd already accepted that his motivations for going home were not the same as they'd once been and that his role would now be that of a messenger, not a participant. But it was becoming clear that neither was he held to this narrow destiny. He could do more.

At that place and time, where all things started and ended,
He could also be a harbinger.
A bringer of knowledge to ignorance,
Health to sickness,
And justice to wickedness.

CHAPTER 6
REFLECTIONS OF THE FUTURE

AARON STOOD outside Drummer's hotel room, his thoughts in fragments. Even after the hour-long train ride back from San Francisco and the subsequent drive to the Mowry Inn, he hadn't been able to reconcile everything he'd seen with everything he'd believed.

These past two days had shown him that life was painted on an even larger canvas than he'd imagined, enriched by layers of previously hidden color. That had been revealed by the photographs Drummer had shown him, by Grant's unmasking and the discovery of Drummer's contemporary counterpart. But even with these revelations, this particular canvas was still too broad for Aaron to view in its entirety. He needed clarity, and he needed it from Drummer.

He knocked on the door.

Drummer opened it, regarding Aaron with some surprise.

Aaron looked back at him, studying his face, seeing the younger man outside the Hyatt reflected in the older man's lines. Finally, Aaron spoke. "Can I come in?" he asked. There was no dimension to his delivery, just the simple question.

Drummer nodded and made way for him.

Aaron entered, went to the foot of the bed, and sat.

Drummer joined him.

Muted afternoon light fell upon them through the red curtains, giving the room a soft glow. The room was quiet, save for the whispers of distant traffic.

Aaron's eyes rested, unfocused, on the old carpet beneath their feet. His rational mind was in conflict, battling two contradicting realities— the predictable one he'd thought existed in a rigid, linear universe, and the chaotic one sitting beside him on the bed, throwing everything into question.

When he spoke, he did so softly.

"I broke up with Grant last night," he said. "It was… messy."

Drummer listened. And waited.

"You were right about him," Aaron continued. "And I can't stop thinking about those pictures you showed me. And today, something else just…."

He stopped himself, then looked into Drummer's eyes. "The things you say, and the things I've seen… I need you to tell me they're real. And how. And why. Why are you here? Is it really just about me and Grant?"

Drummer held his gaze for a moment, then removed the pen-like device from his pocket. He held it in his lap where Aaron could see it.

"This thing," Drummer started talking, his voice low. "Two days ago, this thing brought me here. But I don't know how and I don't know why. I'm not even sure there is a reason."

He handed it over.

"This little thing?" said Aaron, more as a statement of curiosity than a question. "The ends are sharp."

"I've been calling it a needle," said Drummer. "The blue reminds me of one of my mom's old knitting needles."

"How's it work?"

"No clue."

"You don't know? Then you didn't come here on purpose?"

"Nope."

"Huh." Aaron studied the needle's exotic qualities: the undulating swirls on the surface, the gray numbers, the faint gold lights. It was beautiful.

"What happened?" he asked.

"You mean, like, how I got it?" said Drummer.

"I mean, like, anything you want to share."

Drummer half shrugged. "Found it on the sidewalk. It was August 2020. You and I were celebrating your fortieth birthday in Huntington Park—Nob Hill. On the way home, we cut through this cute little one-block alley—Dashiell Hammett—right near Union Square. I saw that thing just lying there. It was bright and beautiful, like a vial of electric liquid. I picked it up, I felt a small shock, and somehow it sent me here. Back in time twenty years. I didn't believe it at first. Sometimes I still don't."

"It's actually very cool-looking," Aaron observed. "Heavier than it looks. It was just sitting there?"

"Yeah."

"Maybe someone left it on purpose."

Drummer smiled. "I'm not that special. Whoever left it there—or lost it—I don't think they intended for some random guy like me to find it."

"Maybe it was left for somebody else, and you just got there first."

"Maybe. It's a moot point now. I'm here, they aren't."

"Fair enough. So, you picked it up and it sent you here and...." Aaron hovered over the moment, connecting the dots. "And you decided to take the chance to get me away from Grant."

Drummer nodded. "Your relationship with him was a nightmare, Aaron. So I figured: *I'm here. I should do something about it.*"

"That's real sweet," said Aaron, his heart warming at the notion. "And after last night, I can understand why you did it."

Drummer looked at him with suddenly hopeful eyes. "Then… you really broke up with him? For good?"

Aaron nodded, not wanting to voice his decision aloud.

Drummer reached out and seized Aaron's hand. "Oh God, thank you!" he said. He then stopped himself and let go.

But Aaron didn't flinch or pull away. It was a wondrous feeling, to be the recipient of such genuine adoration and to have his own well-being stand at the center of another man's attention.

"I should be the one thanking you," Aaron said. He handed the device back. "What are you going to do now?"

Drummer wiped his eyes. "You mean, with Grant out of the picture?"

"Yeah."

"I hadn't thought that far ahead. I guess I should try to figure out how this thing works so I can get home. I can't leave you standing in the alley like that in 2020… abandoned."

Aaron could see the grief and guilt reflected in Drummer's eyes. He wished he could relieve him of that pain, but he didn't know how.

"This'll sound weird," said Aaron, "but can you show me more of those pictures?"

Drummer raised his brow. "You're not afraid of what you'll see?"

"I'm not *afraid* of anything. Besides, you weren't afraid of what I'd see yesterday."

"Things were different yesterday."

"And today they're different again. So, can I?"

Drummer obliged. He slipped the needle into his pocket, pushed himself up on the bed, and leaned against the headboard. He picked up his phone, turned it on, and after it had successfully started, he opened the image gallery.

Aaron shuffled up beside him.

You want me to tell you about any of them?" asked Drummer.

"I think I just want to look, if that's okay."

Drummer nodded and handed him the phone.

Aaron held it in his lap, preparing himself for anything. When he was ready, he swiped through the first group of photographs, those he'd already seen. He then ventured into those he'd not seen before, carefully perusing each one and nudging his thoughts around any skepticism that bubbled up, allowing himself to perceive the love and companionship that the images revealed.

Vacations. Holidays with family. Moments at home.

Contentment. Peace. Joy.

His older self, living a life with Drummer—a complete life.

And an enviable one.

There were several videos. He played them all. As he watched, the last traces of his denial faded away, one frame at a time. He saw his own family, his friends, and his belongings in the condo he shared with Drummer. And he saw himself. It was more than convincing; it was also exciting and intoxicating to realize that this enviable life would, one day, be his own.

As he explored, he fell into occasional bouts of delighted laughter. His relationship with Drummer appeared to be something fun, goofy, and romantic. Aaron could also see how it had matured him and brought out the best in him. In each photo and video, he saw in himself a man who knew who he was and where he was going—a man who made decisions with a broader perspective. His future self, in his eyes, was quite simply… better.

Drummer eventually fell asleep, but Aaron continued browsing through the galleries. He opened the camera roll and viewed the images and videos taken in 2020—among them, those shot in Huntington Park. Drummer had the same clothes with him now that he was wearing in those pictures—the same pants, the same shoes, and the same light blue polo, presently thrown over the back of a chair.

Aaron played the last video. It was of his forty-year-old self being recorded by Drummer, who seemed to be seated behind the camera.

"Happy birthday, Methuselah," came Drummer's voice.

"Careful what you say, old man," the older Aaron replied. "You turned forty-five last week, you know." He peered at Drummer over the top of the phone. "But thank you. You're so good to me."

"And you to me."

The video ended.

There was no more.

The soft hum of distant traffic returned as the phone fell silent. Aaron reflected on the entirety of what he'd just witnessed, and alongside the contented satisfaction about his future, he felt a profound sadness for Drummer. The man sleeping beside him had lost everything he loved.

The phone screen flashed a warning:

LOW BATTERY. 10%. CHARGE NOW.

"Hey," said Aaron, touching Drummer's leg to wake him. "Sorry, I guess I used up the battery."

Drummer glanced at the display.

"Can you charge it?" Aaron asked.

"No, it's got a new kind of cable connection, and I don't have the charger on me."

Aaron flipped the phone over in his hand, inspecting the buttons and ports. He pointed to a slot at the base. "Is this it?" he asked. "If it charges with USB, I might be able to jury-rig a connector from something I already have. Do you know what kind of battery it is?"

"Lithium ion, I think," said Drummer. "And yeah, it's USB, so if you think you can figure it out, you're welcome to try."

"I just have to get it open and take a look at the pinout. Since it's USB it probably follows the same principles as my Nokia, with a ground and power connector and one for data transfer."

"If anyone can figure it out, it's you," said Drummer. "Give it back for a second." He sat up and took the phone, shut it down, then popped open a slot on the side. He removed a thin plastic chip the size of a fingernail.

"This is a micro-SD storage card," he said, holding it up. "It's got 256 gigs of memory, if you can believe it, and it contains all those pics and videos you just saw." He pocketed the chip and handed the phone back to Aaron.

"Tell me something," Aaron said as he turned the phone over in his hands. "If that's really coming—everything in those pictures—when does it happen? I mean, what should I look for?"

Drummer flashed him a smile intended to charm. "I thought you said you just wanted to look."

"It might be good to know *some* things," Aaron said almost defensively. "You know, major events. Like, how do we meet? Was it good?"

"It was unexpected," said Drummer, with a warm smile.

"And?"

Drummer peered at him. "Only if you're sure."

"I'm sure."

"Okay, then. It was—will be—August, ten years from now. I was home alone, bored. I got online and saw your profile on a social media site. I saw your pictures. And that smile. I thought you were so beautiful.

"You also looked familiar, which is when I realized I'd seen you before, years earlier, near work—or at least I thought I had. So, when I saw your profile, I told myself, *I've got to meet this guy.* I tried to write a cool, casual message, but everything sounded so stupid. I finally sent just one word—'beautiful'—but even that seemed dumb in hindsight. I thought you'd ignore me."

"But I didn't?"

"No, you wrote back. We talked for a couple weeks; then on Labor Day weekend we finally met and saw a movie called *Inception*. A lot of people leave the city for the holiday, so it felt like we had the whole world to ourselves. We took that picture you saw of us at the ticket counter. It went from there."

"Sounds really nice," said Aaron.

"It was the best day of my life. So in August 2010, remember to check your messages."

"Got it," Aaron replied with a smirk.

"One more thing," said Drummer, "don't give up skateboarding. You always said it was like therapy, time when you could just be yourself. In my timeline, Grant made you feel childish for it and you gave it up. But it's not childish. It's important."

"Thanks."

"And from what I've been told," Drummer added, "you can do a hardflip sex change back lip like it's a fuckin' video game trick."

Aaron laughed aloud, caught off-guard by this middle-aged man uttering skateboard jargon like a teenager.

"Sorry for laughing," he said, "but hearing you talk like that is fuckin' funny."

"That's the point," Drummer admitted. "But honestly, I've never seen you skate, and I want to finally see you land this infamous tre-bomb I've heard so much about. Without you eating shit like a bitch, of course."

Aaron's laughter grew even louder. "You've got that jargon down."

Drummer attempted a mock bow. "I might be older, but I'm no old man. At least I like to think I'm not."

"You've got a young heart," said Aaron. "The ink helps too."

Drummer showed off his heavily tattooed arms. "I suppose they do add an aura of impudent rebelliousness. Actually, I didn't have half of these until I was over thirty, and most of the biggest ones until I was over forty. If you ask my parents, I looked way more respectable in my twenties."

"How old are you now?"

"Forty-five."

"You wouldn't know it, with that potty mouth of yours."

"Well, that's just how I talk with you."

Aaron appreciated Drummer's flattery, but more so, he was grateful for his respect. Normally when older people spoke kindly of Aaron, they did so in a way that made him feel patronized or objectified. But this wasn't the case with Drummer. In each of their interactions so far, Aaron had felt admired and seen.

"You wanna get outta here?" Aaron asked. "I'm having prom flashbacks in this place."

"Oh, right, this hotel," said Drummer. "You told me about that. Or, you will tell me. Where do you want to go?"

"Have you eaten?"

"I had a protein bar and a can of cold beef stew for breakfast, but nothing else."

"Gross," said Aaron. He glanced at a clock on the bedside table. "It's not too late. If we drive to San Francisco, we can get dinner early."

"Didn't you just come from the city?"

"I don't mind the drive."

"In that case, sure," Drummer said. "Would you do something for me first?"

"Shoot."

"Do some skate tricks. Just a few things out in the parking lot. I'd really like to see."

Aaron scampered off the bed and moved toward the door. "After what you showed me, how can I say no?"

"Here," Drummer called after him. He reached into his backpack, took out a white T-shirt, and tossed it to him. "You should change first."

"I've got clothes in the trunk," said Aaron, catching the shirt against his chest. "But if you wanna be T-shirt twins, I'll wear it." Eagerly, he removed his tie and peeled off the dress shirt, revealing a lean and muscular torso.

Drummer gawked, which Aaron noticed—and appreciated—without comment.

The two men wandered into the parking lot, where Aaron popped the trunk of his car, took out a much looser pair of jeans than the ones he already wore and, unashamed, changed into them right there. He grabbed his skateboard from the back seat, and in a swift, fluid movement, dropped it to the pavement, hopped on, and did a wide loop through the lot. When he swung back around, he asked Drummer, "What do you want to see?"

"Anything," Drummer replied brightly. "Just don't break your legs."

"No promises."

Aaron performed several skate tricks, excitedly describing each one in detail so Drummer wouldn't miss a single kick or flip. He loved being on that skateboard, and he loved being the center of attention while using it. When he was done, he rolled up to Drummer and kicked the board up into his hands.

"Your turn," Aaron joked.

Drummer laughed as he fumbled and caught it. "That would end badly," he said. "Besides, the owner of this place has been eyeing us. I think we're about to be chased off."

Aaron glanced at the motel front office. Standing outside the door was a man of about sixty years, clad in a dirty T-shirt and frumpy shorts. He was scowling, with his arms crossed.

"He's a real charmer, isn't he?" Aaron observed sarcastically.

"Looks like he also cleans the rooms."

"That would explain his face. You know what people do here, right?"

"Well, I know what *you* did here."

"Don't talk like you know me," Aaron said with a chortle. "But you're right, we should get outta here. I've seen that look before. And I don't want my *hooliganism* to get you kicked out of this truck stop." Aaron made sure the word "hooliganism" carried loudly across the lot.

Drummer picked up on his playful cynicism and rolled with it. "And I should probably stop enabling you and your *delinquency*," he said. "Shame on me."

"Yeah, *shame* on you," Aaron went on, with overplayed scorn. "Look at you… coming here, corrupting sweet twenty-year-old innocents like me… making me wear your clothes. *That's just sick.* You're a grown man, for Christ's sake."

"You know perfectly well that dirty old men do questionable things!" Drummer retorted, jabbing his finger at him in the air. He handed Aaron his skateboard.

They held each other's gaze, holding back their laughter as they climbed into Aaron's car. Then, as they drove off together, they let it fly.

LATE AFTERNOON gave way to evening as Aaron and Drummer made their way to San Francisco. Their conversation was bright and enthusiastic. They spoke only fleetingly of the needle and of the future and instead kept their focus on lighter subjects that would not lead them down dark rabbit holes.

Drummer was entranced by this younger Aaron, especially when he spoke about his professional goals and the job he'd just been offered. He didn't appear to view anything as an obstacle to his ambition. The future Aaron was no less impressive, but the younger's brashness and lack of restraint made him that much more provocative.

At dinner, Drummer ate enough Thai food to make up for two days of barely sated hunger and twenty years of time travel, while Aaron made up for the many slices of pizza he'd ceded to Willis. The two men were uncomfortably full by the end of the meal, but that didn't put a damper on their energy. Aaron's ebullient nature appeared limitless, and in his presence, Drummer felt younger than he had in years.

In the quiet lull that followed, Drummer considered how his worldview had dulled as he'd aged. He was still a kid at heart, but the part of him that had once seen life as an endless vista of opportunity had vanished along the way. The man sitting across from him now was like a mirror reflection of the man he used to be. He missed it, and seeing it in Aaron, he envied it.

With their dinner finished and the bill paid, the two men walked to a gay bar on Castro Street.

At the door, Aaron flashed an ID that Drummer knew couldn't have been his own, for he wasn't yet twenty-one. After some reticence, Drummer showed his own. He wasn't worried that he'd be refused entry—he was clearly old enough—but his driver's license had been issued in 2018. It had to look fake. To his relief, he was waved inside with barely a glance.

The place was packed with wall-to-wall muscle and testosterone. The music was loud, the patrons were handsy, and the smell of booze, breath, and soggy bar towels hung heavy in the air. Aaron and Drummer ordered drinks at the bar, then squeezed through the hairy-shouldered crowd toward a raised level in the back, where they grabbed two stools against the wall. Their conversation continued, though they had to shout occasionally to be heard over the noise. After some time, their vivacious interaction reached a natural pause.

Drummer took in the surroundings. He'd been in this bar before, many times between 2000 and 2020. It wouldn't change much over those two decades. On the other hand, the behavior of this era's patrons was notably different. In the absence of touchscreen cell phones, nearly everyone was engaged in conversation or making out with strangers in dark corners prior to stumbling off to "my place or yours."

"What are you thinking about?" Aaron asked.

"I was just thinking what a shame it is that I'd forgotten what innocence looks like," Drummer said with a soft smile.

"Innocence? In a gay bar?" Aaron chuckled.

"Touché," said Drummer. "It's just, the world gets real different in twenty years. In some ways you'd never know it. People still go to their jobs and raise families, and drunk locals still try to pick up the bartender—or at least try to score a free shot of tequila. Hell, even this bar's still here. It looks exactly the same. It just has a different name. What I mean is… on the outside you could be tricked into thinking it's the same world. But on the inside, a lot of people are unhappy, scared, and angry—way more than they are now. People are poorer, even if they're more privileged."

"Wow," Aaron said in a small voice. "And here I was all excited about the future."

Drummer shook his head at his own doom and gloom. "Don't worry, the world doesn't come to an end, but the future isn't all robots and flying cars. In fact, it's neither. Well, maybe it's drones. And you manage to keep me focused on the good things. I like to think I do the same for you."

Aaron set his drink on a small shelf against the wall. "I'm sure you do."

Drummer smiled at him and wondered about their future together. Was there more he could do to improve it, given his future knowledge? And could he change the world at large? Could he avert disasters—even the greatest of them—by warning the right people?

Then he recalled the tattoo on his left forearm, the one of Cassandra. The ancient myth said that with her power of prophecy came great misery and frustration, as the people rejected her and deemed her a liar. Drummer could imagine the same thing happening to him, or to whoever he chose as his mouthpiece. The people who pulled the levers of power would certainly be skeptics, while those who believed him would be conspiracy theorists. Despite his desire to build a better world, he feared he would be more likely to spoil it.

"You care a lot, don't you?" Aaron asked.

"What's that?" He had drifted off with his thoughts.

"You care about people," Aaron clarified. He waved out at the crowd. "About all these people."

Drummer looked out at them again. "Yeah, I guess," he said. "But these people feel kinda like ghosts. I look around and I see a world I used to know. It's like going back to the street you grew up on and everything feels smaller, and you ask yourself, 'Was it always like this?'"

"Like you said, things change. Just like you and me."

"Cheers to that." Drummer tapped his glass against Aaron's and took a hearty swig. He set it down and let out a long breath. "I shouldn't be here. Out at a bar, I mean."

"Afraid you'll run into yourself?" Aaron asked.

"Not really. But I could run into someone I used to know. I might be twenty years older, but my tattoos are the same, my face is mostly the same. I'd probably be recognized."

Aaron looked at him with a sweet, broadening grin.

"What?" Drummer asked, feeling those eyes sizing him up.

"I think," Aaron began, "that if the future really is like you say, with everyone unhappy, scared, and angry, then you should enjoy this innocence for what it is. And when you get home, bring some of that joy with you. I'm sure the version of me waiting for you would like that."

"That's a mature attitude for a skater punk," said Drummer. He laughed lightly, meaning it as a compliment. "Don't worry, I'm very happy in the future, but you've always been the reason for it. God, you sound so much like him. You look so much like him. You *are* him, but… you're not. You've really surprised me."

Aaron hopped off his stool and held his arms out.

"What are you doing?" asked Drummer.

"Dance with me."

"I'm an awful dancer," he replied quickly, "and there's no room. Besides, this isn't a dance club."

"We'll slow dance."

"Slow dance to this?" Drummer pointed into the air. The song playing was the 1991 release of P.M. Dawn's *Set Adrift on Memory Bliss*, a moody ballad constructed atop samples of Spandau Ballet's breathy 1983 standard, *True*. It was not a slow dance song by any measure.

"Why not?" Aaron asked. "We have space right here." He pushed his stool aside and pulled Drummer to his feet.

A clearly drunk man hopped onto one of the discarded seats, claiming it for himself.

"See?" Aaron said, indicating him. "Now we can't sit back down, so we have to dance." He reached out and put his arms around Drummer.

Though Drummer dithered, he did reciprocate. As he held Aaron, rocking slowly back and forth, he considered their conversation and Aaron's insistence that he enjoy himself. Drummer had been so focused on getting rid of Grant that he'd failed to realize he was enjoying himself already. His world had been turned upside down, and yet here he was, having drinks in a bar in San Francisco with the love of his life—albeit a different iteration of him. Drummer relaxed with this thought and held Aaron even closer, imagining for a time that he was home.

The song ended.

Gently, they released each other.

"Thank you for that," said Drummer, looking into Aaron's eyes with gratitude. "And for trusting me."

"What kind of boyfriend would I be if I didn't?"

"That was fucking *adorable*," said the drunk guy who'd taken one of their stools. He'd been watching the entire time.

Aaron and Drummer glanced briefly at him, neither recognizing him.

"I need to walk off this drink before we head back, D," said Aaron. "You want to see the neighborhood? How things used to be? Maybe we can get you to see people as more than just ghosts."

Drummer smiled. "You just called me D," he pointed out.

Aaron let out a small, self-aware chuckle. "Sorry, I do that without thinking. Is it okay?"

"Yeah," said Drummer with a forgiving nod. "Perfectly. And I think a walk's a good idea. I'm obviously not getting home tonight. But after this I shouldn't be out and about, not in this town. I need to focus on how to get back. I hope you understand."

"I do," said Aaron. "One more thing, though...."

"What's that?"

"Will you stay with me tonight?"

Drummer was not prepared for that question.

"Before you say no," Aaron added, "that hotel you're in is a dump. But more than that, I'd really like you to stay with me... just because."

"Aaron, I'm not sure."

"Why not? I'm *him*, aren't I?"

"Of course you are. But you're also *not* him. And you need to understand, I saw him only two days ago, and...."

"It would feel like cheating?"

Drummer hadn't identified the discomfort that specifically, but Aaron's guess brought it to the forefront.

"Yeah, in a way."

"Then if it makes it easier on you, think of it this way: when you get back, I'm going to remember tonight. And I'll be *real* disappointed you didn't take the opportunity with me when you had the chance."

Drummer grinned. The logic was compelling.

"So," Aaron went on, "since I'm him… treat me like him."

"I'm not sure I can do that."

"Okay then, what if you stay with me and all we do is sleep?"

Drummer returned a small smile. He knew Aaron's determined nature quite well, and he'd rarely been able to resist it. He could sense that he'd fare no better tonight than he had on any other occasion. "I suppose I can do that," Drummer said at last.

"Great!" Aaron chirped. "Let's get out of here."

They left the bar and walked the block, taking in the sights. Drummer noted the landmarks that never seemed to change, like the Castro Theatre and Twin Peaks Bar, but the differences were many and stark.

"I forgot how narrow the sidewalks used to be," he said as he and Aaron squeezed past a group of people loitering about. "They widened them a few years ago. Well, a few years for me."

"Anything else different?" Aaron asked.

"It's less colorful now than it will be. The city added rainbow crosswalks and colored LED lights up and down the block. And that store on the corner across from Walgreens—that'll turn over about a hundred times before it finally decides to be a gyro place."

"You recognize anyone?"

"No," Drummer admitted with relief.

"Good. Next question…. I'm curious, how'd you get a name like 'Drummer'?"

"Oh yeah," Drummer exclaimed lightly, "I forget that you don't know yet. I got it from my parents when I was five or six. They used to take me along to a lot of drive-in movies and put me in the back seat, thinking I'd fall asleep while they got all kissy-kissy. But I never did. I saw a lot of movies kids that age shouldn't see—horror movies and everything. Scarred me pretty good. One night we saw *Xanadu*."

"*Xanadu* scarred you?"

"No," Drummer said with a laugh. "I *loved* it. And I loved the music. I played virtual drums in the back seat the whole time. My parents were pissed. After that, they teased me by calling me a drummer. They weren't mean about it, and they even bought me a drum set because they thought I wanted it. I took up guitar instead, but 'Drummer' stuck."

"In the words of the drunk guy back at the bar, that's fucking adorable."

"I was obnoxious. My real name's Dante, if you can believe that."

"I like that too," said Aaron. "But it's a bit medieval. Drummer suits you better."

"Thanks. It feels more like me. My ex, Nate, never liked it. He introduced me to his family as Dante, and they stuck with it, even when I asked them to call me Drummer. He could be an ass sometimes."

"Why were you with him?"

"I was lonely. Desperate. I thought I had the rest of my life all figured out, but doing it alone felt pretty miserable. Nate was the first person to show interest in me, and being with him made me feel like an adult. I got instant respect for being in a relationship. I didn't think twice when he asked me to delay my education and my career. I took that job at the hotel and sidelined myself. I hardly noticed that I was passing up opportunities just so I wouldn't lose him, and in the end, I had nothing. I felt cheated. He walked away better. I walked away worse. It took me a decade to climb out of that hole and finally figure out what I really wanted."

"And what's that?" asked Aaron.

"I think you know," said Drummer with a sparkle in his eye. "A sweet guy with a roguish side. Someone I wouldn't have to apologize for on the way out of a dinner party. Someone I'd be proud to be with, and who'd be proud to be with me."

"That sounds...."

"Familiar?"

"Maybe," Aaron admitted. "But I can't say no one's ever had to apologize for me after a party."

"I didn't say what kind of behavior needed an apology." Drummer stopped and put his hands in his coat pockets. He looked around, feeling ironically out of place in a neighborhood he knew well.

"Right now, that other version of me is doing everything I once did," he said. "I haven't figured out whether to pity him or envy him. His life sucks, but he's still got a life. I've got nothing." He looked at Aaron and smiled. "At least that's what I thought, until tonight."

"What do you mean by that?" Aaron asked.

"A few things. First, I haven't lost you, not completely, since here you are. But also, I like to think that the things I have aren't just possessions or a job... they're the things I have to offer others. Comfort.

Support. Love. I still have something like that to offer you. Something no one else in the world has."

"What is it?"

A snake-like grin crept across Drummer's face. "I know all the right stocks to buy for the next twenty years. I know the winner of every Superbowl. And I know the outcome of every election—God help us. So, if I can figure out that needle and get myself home, in twenty years we can cash in."

"That's either brilliant planning or straight-up cheating."

"I'll think of it as making the most of the resources at hand," said Drummer with a smirk. "Knowledge is power."

"And profit. That would sure make the future easier."

"A lot easier."

"Doesn't help the present, though," Aaron said. "And if that needle's half as complicated as your phone, I really hate to say it, but you'll probably be stuck here longer than you think. And while you're here you'll need to be able to get around, buy things, and drive. I saw how you tried to hide your ID going into that bar. I'm sorry I didn't stop to think it might be out of place."

Drummer brushed it off. "They let me in. It's okay."

"It won't always be okay. You need a fake ID at least. Maybe even a whole new identity."

Drummer deflated a bit. Aaron was right. He was very likely not returning to 2020 any time soon, and the close call at the bar could've gone very wrong. He couldn't risk using his real driver's license again.

"I can help," said Aaron. "With the ID and the needle and whatever else. For as long as you're here."

"You don't have to do that."

"I think I do," said Aaron. "I owe you way more than just a phone charger. And if I'm really waiting for you in that alley, isn't it in my own best interest to help you get back?"

Drummer shrugged. "I suppose, but I won't hold you to it in the morning. I have this policy: never send an email when you're drunk, and never make promises when you're high."

"I'm not drunk or high."

Drummer looked at him with an insightful glint in his eye.

"Okay, fine," Aaron admitted, "maybe after that dance and all the stuff you showed me on your phone, I might be a *little* high. But it's a natural high, and you can't blame me. If all those things are waiting for me, and you saved me from a fucked-up, abusive relationship in between, then I owe you."

There was a long silence between them as Aaron's expression sobered further. "Can you tell me about it?" he asked. "My—his—relationship with Grant."

Drummer felt a sudden sickness in his gut.

"I'm not going back to him," Aaron added, "and you said being with him was a nightmare. I just want to know how."

"You really don't want to know."

"Okay, well, maybe I *need* to know. You helped me make a choice, but it was an emotional choice. I'm an emotional guy, but I also need information to be sure. Details make a difference."

Drummer studied Aaron's dogged expression. Drummer had always avoided discussing Grant's abuse directly, training himself to dance around the details, speak in euphemisms so he wouldn't insult Aaron's pride or trigger a nightmare. He'd always let Aaron lead the conversation if he needed to talk about Grant. But now Drummer was being asked to reveal the details clearly, not knowing what the younger Aaron's reaction might be.

"It's ugly," Drummer said, feeling the need to offer a qualifier.

Aaron looked at him through clear blue eyes. "I'm sure it is."

"And it's hard for me to talk about. Where do I even start?"

"How about the gun?"

Drummer swallowed hard. The gun. The day Grant had used it for the first time. The day that sent Aaron into a downward spiral, burying him deep in despair. The day that would continue to haunt him at night, fifteen years after the fact.

Drummer took a deep breath. "Okay," he said slowly. "The gun." He cleared his throat and began, speaking as plainly and unemotionally as he could. "In the last year of your relationship, he used it against you. He knew you were going to leave him. One night he attacked you, put you in a choke hold, and demanded you quit your job. You tried to fight back, but he's a big guy. He put the gun to your head and..."

He stopped mid-sentence, the heartache rising to consume him as the retelling unearthed the pain he felt whenever Aaron had awakened with that memory. Drummer could barely believe that he was describing it in such candid terms—or that he was discussing it at all. Maybe the answer was in the younger Aaron's eyes, where Drummer saw no signs of upset. He continued, though he struggled to tamp down on his own emotional tempest.

"He put the loaded gun to your head and threatened to kill you if you ever left him," Drummer said. "He raped you with the gun pressed against your temple. And he kept doing it for ten more months. Every time he looked at you, he saw betrayal. He imagined contempt in every word you spoke. He took your phone and only let you use it when he was around. He listened to every call you made, read every email and every text you sent. He didn't let you have friends or a job. And he tortured you mentally, saying he'd kill himself if you ever left… after he killed you, your parents, and anyone else he thought you cared about. He'd already made you believe they'd abandoned you. But you stepped back from them even further on your own."

Aaron had looked away as Drummer spoke, but he was obviously still listening. Drummer understood why, for he knew how Aaron had reacted during the relationship with Grant. Hearing about it had to bring on some form of shame, even if the relationship and its fallout were now averted.

"How'd it end?" Aaron asked.

"Grant lost control in a very public place," said Drummer. "You were at a restaurant. Something set him off. He punched you in the face and broke your nose in front of everyone. Two off-duty police officers were at the next table. They restrained him. You were in such pain, and afraid for your life, but you still managed to tell them you needed help.

"That was a huge moment for you. You had internalized all these feelings of self-loathing and blame. But when he punched you and you tasted your blood, saw it as it ran all over the table… that did something. It woke you up. And seeing Grant held down on the floor by those two cops—prone, kicking his feet like a fucking baby—you suddenly saw how cowardly and ugly he really was. He broke the law—first at home and then right in front of everyone. Assault with a deadly weapon. False imprisonment. Battery. Rape. He had no security cameras—he didn't want any of his actions recorded—but you can never entirely remove bloodstains, and your story was corroborated by every trace of that evidence he thought he'd erased. You pressed charges and let the prosecutors turn that motherfucker inside out."

Aaron was quiet for several moments. He sniffed, then lifted his gaze and wiped his eyes. "Thank you for telling me."

Drummer nodded sympathetically.

"You probably don't know this," Aaron went on, "but Grant was arrested last night. After I broke up with him, I went out with my roommate to get dinner. While we were gone, Grant came looking for me. He attacked my landlord with a bat, and some of my neighbors. I talked to two cops afterwards…. Maybe they were the same ones from the restaurant in your timeline. Wouldn't that be something?"

"Sounds like fate," said Drummer, "if you believe in that."

"I'm beginning to wonder. Willis—my roommate—said I dodged a bullet. His words sounded prophetic."

"Grant will end up right where he belongs," Drummer said, sounding utterly certain. "You wouldn't have been the first person he used that gun on. And your neighbors weren't the first people he hurt. If they're pressing charges, people are gonna come out of the woodwork to take him down."

Aaron nodded and gave Drummer a small, grateful smile. "Thank you, D, for saving me from that."

"What kind of boyfriend would I be if I didn't?"

Aaron smiled more broadly. "Good one."

"I learn from the best."

OUTSIDE OF TIME

On the outside, the world carried on, and it carried him with it. He lived, and he appeared to be one of them.

But on the inside, he stood apart, his mind always elsewhere, in another place and another time.

Though everything was familiar and everyone was the same, he no longer belonged. He stood outside the present and the past, a stranger in both, but with a task to complete in each.

CHAPTER 7
MOMENTUM

DRUMMER WOKE in the middle of the night. His dreams continued to reflect his life in 2020, but the cast of characters had changed. This confused him greatly and roused him often. To his subconscious mind, his life in 2020 was still the "real world," but waking up beside a much younger Aaron in 2000 forced him to accept a new truth: real was relative.

He sat up. He thought about his phone and wondered how long it might take for Aaron to build a charger. A week? Two? Drummer had no doubt Aaron could do it; it was just a matter of time. But what about the needle? The task of deciphering a time machine would undoubtedly take far longer than building a cell phone charger. But how long, exactly?

"Years," Drummer said to himself in a hopeless whisper. "Twenty years?"

For the first time, he considered the probability that the only way he might ever get home would be to ride out time, week by week, month by month, and year by year.

He climbed out of bed, careful not to wake Aaron. He stepped into the hallway, heading to the bathroom, and ran into Willis, who was himself lumbering to bed. Willis had been asleep on the couch when Aaron and Drummer had returned from San Francisco.

"Holy shit!" Willis exclaimed at the sight of Drummer, half-naked in the hall. "You're that dude from the other day!"

Drummer jumped, not having expected to be intercepted. "Sorry," he said, trying to keep his voice down. "I didn't mean to wake you."

Willis made no attempt to remain quiet. "I was already up. What the hell is this? Who the hell are you?"

"My name's Drummer. Be quiet, you'll wake him."

"I don't give a *damn*."

Aaron's bedroom door swung open, and Aaron stepped into the hall. "What's going on out here?" he demanded, visibly groggy but more annoyed than anything else.

"What's going on?" Willis fumed. He pointed at Drummer. "He's in our place!"

Aaron reached out and turned on the hall light; Willis and Drummer both shielded their eyes from the sudden brightness. "I invited him," said Aaron, with similar temper.

"You *invited* him?" said Willis. "Do I have to remind you that you just had Grant hauled off by the cops? Now *this* guy's here?"

"Willis, relax," said Drummer, hoping to de-escalate the situation.

Willis glared back at him. "Whoever the fuck you are, we're *not* on a first name basis." He returned his steely gaze to Aaron. "You told him my name? This guy doesn't have a baseball bat in his trunk, I hope."

Wearily, Aaron rubbed his forehead, then made perfunctory introductions. "Willis, this is Drummer. Drummer, Willis."

Drummer extended his hand. Willis stared at it for an infinite few seconds, then gave it a curt, obligatory shake. He returned his attention to Aaron, peering at him with demanding eyes. "You gonna tell me what's going on?" he asked.

"In the morning," Aaron sighed, clearly exasperated. "Drummer, can we go back to bed?"

"I really have to pee," Drummer replied. He looked at Willis, who stood in his way.

Aaron trained his eyes on his roommate and asked flatly, "Willis, would you please let my friend, *who I invited over*, get by so he can use the bathroom?"

Willis's eyes darted between his roommate and the older stranger. Eventually he conceded and stepped aside.

When Drummer returned, he was surprised to see the two of them still standing there.

"Everything okay, guys?" he asked.

"Everything's fine," said Aaron. "My roommate just thinks he's my mom."

He led Drummer back to his room.

"Hey…," Willis called after him.

"In the morning, Willis," said Aaron, shutting him down. He closed the door behind him.

"Sorry about that," said Aaron as he and Drummer climbed back into bed.

"He's just looking out for you," said Drummer. It was clear to him that Willis had only the best intentions, even if he slipped into cynicism rather easily. "He's very funny."

"I'm glad you think so," Aaron said. "Actually, the two of you are a lot alike. A little protective. But he's a good friend."

"He clearly is," Drummer agreed.

"Wait a second," said Aaron, rolling onto his side to face Drummer. "You're not afraid of him."

"Afraid of Willis? Of course not. Why would I be?"

"No, I mean, you're not afraid of him seeing you. Or recognizing you."

Drummer hadn't consciously considered this, but subconsciously he had apparently taken for granted that none of Aaron's skater friends would be a threat to his anonymity. The most he knew of them was in the tiny photographs mounted on the wall in the condo in another life.

"Do I still know him in the future?" Aaron asked, sounding worried.

Drummer didn't know how to reply. On one hand, the answer was yes. On the other, no.

"I don't, do I?" asked Aaron. "And that's why you don't care if he sees you. Because you don't know him, either. What happens to him, D?"

Drummer couldn't dance around the answer. He had to be direct. "Nothing happens," he insisted, hoping to ease Aaron's fears. "He just… moves away."

"He moves?"

"Yeah."

"To where?"

"To Boston."

"Boston? Why would he move to Boston?"

"Well… for a job."

Aaron did a double take. "He gets a job?"

"Yes," Drummer answered, chuckling lightly at Aaron's obvious surprise.

"But he has to go all the way to Boston for it?"

"He does very well for himself, Aaron."

"But he moves away. And I lose touch."

Drummer felt uneasy about the direction of the conversation, leading him to reveal past choices that might not happen now in the same way. Was he interfering in Willis's fate simply by talking about it? Or had his interference in Aaron's life already effected that change?

"Yeah, you lose touch," Drummer admitted delicately. "But you still talk, and you visit. And, yeah, I've never met him."

"When does he leave?" Aaron pressed.

"Do you really want to know all this?"

Aaron rolled onto his back and sighed. "I don't know."

"You said you wanted to know the big things—and maybe this is one of them—but what about the next time you want me to fill in the blanks? I don't want you to make choices just because you made them once already."

Aaron nodded. "I guess," he began, "for most things, I probably shouldn't know. Like you said, I don't want to get caught repeating myself. But if you say Willis has a good life in Boston, then this time, I probably *should* know. I don't want to screw up something that worked for him."

"I understand," said Drummer. "The way it went before, Willis moved out right after you moved to Grant's house on Potrero Hill in San Francisco."

"Makes sense," said Aaron. "But what a mess. Now there's no Grant, and I won't move in with him. And Willis won't move to Boston, and he won't have that life."

"How do you know?" asked Drummer, hoping to not influence Aaron's decision-making. "Because I don't. He might get a call from Boston in the morning, for all we know."

"Nah, that won't happen," said Aaron. "I know him. If he moves, it'll be because he's forced to. I've always been the breadwinner. I've been the master tenant, the administrator, the cook… even the maid. I've been enabling him and keeping him from growing. I can't do that anymore."

Drummer remained silent as Aaron put the pieces together for himself.

"Have you ever read *The Metamorphosis*?" Aaron inquired after a quiet moment.

"Kafka?" Drummer asked. "What does that have to do with Willis?"

"I read it for school. The message I got from it is if we don't let other people do their own thing, they'll always let someone else do it for them and they won't grow or change. If Willis can get a job in Boston and do something with his life, then I need to get out of the way." He looked at Drummer through serious eyes. "I'll talk to him tomorrow."

"About what?"

"About me moving out."

"Why?"

"Because that's the only way. If I moved in with Grant in that other timeline and Willis immediately got a job and left town, then he doesn't really need me anymore. But you do need me. You need somewhere to live. You need resources so you can study the needle. Without help, you'll never get those things, and you'll never get home."

"But Aaron—"

"Don't argue about it. It's gotta be this way. Besides, over these past two days you've changed my life. You showed me things I never thought were possible. I tried to deny them, but now I don't see anything else. And I want Willis to be happy, and you too… even that younger version of you in the city.

"Drummer," he said, softly but intently, looking back up at the ceiling, "you said you saw me once, near work, years before we actually met."

"Yeah, I'm pretty sure I did."

"You did. That moment happened today."

Drummer felt a chill. For him the encounter had always been a memory independent of time, an island sitting in the expansive memorial waters of his past. He'd never been able to assign it to a specific date. Had it really happened today of all days?

"It was after my interview," Aaron continued, with wonderment and confusion in his voice. "I saw you and followed you. You were with your coworkers outside the Hyatt, standing only a few feet away by the employee entrance. You turned around and looked right at me, straight into my eyes.

"I don't know why I followed you. But if you remember it—if you remember seeing me standing there—then… are we just fulfilling a destiny right now? Stuck in a loop? And if that's the case, how come I'm not still with Grant?"

"I don't know," Drummer answered, himself bewildered.

"I don't like thinking I'm not making my own choices," Aaron said. "Maybe I followed you today for a different reason than before. Like, maybe last time I just thought you were cute."

"You think I'm cute?" Drummer asked with a coy smile.

"You know what I mean," Aaron said. "Regardless, the life you've shown me and what I saw today… I want it badly, even if I have to wait ten years. And I want to help you get back to it. What I'm saying in a roundabout way is, I *need* to move out of here like I did before, let Willis do what he's gonna do, and find my own place—a place with you."

Drummer didn't want to argue, but Aaron was proposing a massive commitment. The weight of it sat on his chest.

"That's a big sacrifice," Drummer said.

"It's no sacrifice, D. It's a choice. It's a purpose. When you got here you found a purpose for yourself—to save me from Grant. Now, my purpose is to send you home, back to me."

Drummer started to speak, to protest, even as he knew he shouldn't.

"We have work to do," said Aaron, cutting him off before he could say another word. "Let's get power to your phone and reconnect you to your memories. Then we'll get a look inside that needle—with an X-ray, a CT scan, whatever we can get our hands on. If we can see what's inside, it can help us figure out how it works."

"I don't want you to feel obligated," Drummer pleaded. "I didn't come here to completely redirect your life. I just wanted to get Grant out of it."

"I know, D. But isn't it my choice now?"

Drummer felt Aaron take his hand under the sheets and hold it tight.

"You showed me what could've happened," Aaron went on, "and you gave me something amazing to look forward to. How many people get a gift like that?"

The two men fell into silence. Drummer gazed up at *The Starry Night* on the wall above him. He peered into the resplendent nighttime scene, finding depths in it he had never noticed before. Nothing about the painting had changed since he last lay beneath it in the condo in 2020, but for whatever reason, it now seemed brighter.

THE NEXT morning, Aaron and Drummer returned to the Mowry Inn for the last time. They collected Drummer's bag, paid the bill, and checked out. They then drove to San Francisco, where Aaron reviewed and signed the offer letter outlining the terms of his employment. They spent the rest of the day apartment hunting. They weren't looking for anything grandiose or exceptional, just a private spot in the city where the two of them could live and work—and hopefully avoid crossing paths with Drummer's younger self or any of his old acquaintances.

Ultimately, they settled on a two-bedroom apartment on Tenth Avenue in the Richmond district, half a block from Golden Gate Park. It was an area of town that Drummer had rarely visited in 2000, so he felt confident that he'd be relatively hidden there. It was also close enough to the heart of the city for Aaron to maintain connections with coworkers and friends.

The two men returned to Fremont that evening. Aaron dropped off Drummer at a nearby grocery store to pick up a few things, then returned alone to the apartment he shared with Willis. He entered the kitchen to find Willis leaning into the refrigerator, clutching a bag of Cheetos in one hand and digging around in a container of unidentified take-out with the other.

"Hey," Aaron said, "can I talk to you?"

"You're doing it," said Willis, continuing to rummage without looking up.

Aaron urged the refrigerator door closed, nudging his friend's hand out of the way.

"Ow," said Willis as the refrigerator door grazed his head.

"Please, that didn't even hit you," Aaron said with a grin.

Willis rubbed his head anyway. "What you wanna talk about?"

Aaron's little smile faded. He knew his next words would not be well received, so he didn't beat around the bush. "I'm moving out," he said plainly.

"You're what?"

"I'm moving out. I'm moving in with Drummer."

Willis laughed. He clearly thought it was a joke. "I think you hit my head harder than you thought. Say that again."

"You heard me."

Willis's laughter trailed off. He stared at Aaron blankly. "You're still gonna have to say it again, because what I heard is you're running off with a dude you just met—like, *immediately* after almost getting your brains bashed in by your psycho ex."

Aaron groaned. "Not in those words, but yeah."

"But what…." Willis stammered. "Wait, really?"

"Yes, really."

Willis's blank stare twisted into abrupt petulance. "Well, that's fucked. What the fuck, man? I don't know what this guy's done to you, but—"

"He hasn't done anything to me," Aaron interrupted.

Willis's expression grew incredulous. "How can you say that? It's only been two days!"

"He's a good guy."

"How do you know?"

"Because I know," said Aaron, trying to remain calm in the face of Willis's contentious annoyance. "It's hard to explain."

"*Try!*" Willis stopped. He took a breath and continued. "I'm sorry," he said, calmer. "Date whoever you want. But dude, you've gotta be smart, and this looks *really* stupid."

Aaron leaned against the wall. He had expected pushback from Willis, but he didn't think it would be so acute. He pointed at one of the kitchen chairs. "Sit down."

Willis scoffed at the order, but he pulled up the chair and sat regardless.

"First of all," Aaron went on, "he's not Grant. Second, I know how it looks, but me and Drummer aren't dating and a lot's happened over the past couple days. There're things I need to do with him."

"You can do *things* with him without moving in with him."

"Actually, I can't."

Willis appeared to toss the development back and forth in his mind. "Wait a second," he said. "Are you in love with this guy… *already*?"

Aaron grumbled. "I just said we're not dating, and that's not the point. He's shown me things. Crazy things I never thought were possible. And dude, he got rid of Grant, saving me from a mistake that would've destroyed my life. You said I dodged a bullet, and you're right. That bullet missed me because of Drummer."

Willis nodded, seeming to take it in. "So you feel like you owe him?"

Aaron shrugged.

"That's a shitty reason. That's how guys control you."

"He didn't ask me for anything," Aaron insisted. "He's not taking anything. This is my choice."

"Is it, or did he just make you believe it is?"

"I'm not answering that," Aaron said, having had enough of Willis's indignation.

"Fine. But did you ever stop to think about what this does to *me*? I mean, look at me—I'm a mess. I need you, dude."

"Actually, you aren't and you don't," said Aaron. "You called yourself a babysitter. You're way better than that. And I wouldn't live with you if you were a mess. You might be a reactionary jackass, but you're dependable and supportive, and all the things a good friend should be. And despite half-assing everything, you get shit done."

"Well… thank you, I suppose," said Willis, standing down. "You're really moving out?"

"Yes," Aaron answered with finality.

"And you're moving in with that guy?"

"His name's Drummer, and yes."

"Okay then, when?"

"Tomorrow."

"Tomorrow?" Willis exclaimed, his incredulity spiking again. "You drop this bomb on me and then say it's happening *tomorrow*? I need to get a new roommate first and clean out all the shit from the couch, and…."

"And get a job?" Aaron interjected with a grin.

"Yes… and get a job."

"Don't worry," said Aaron. "I'll cover your rent for a few months. David's ready to get out of his parents' basement. You could ask him to move in. He'd kill to get away from his mom. And *he* has a job."

Willis considered it. "Yeah. David. Yeah, that's cool. That works. Three months, huh? They pay you that much at your new gig?"

"I have savings, and this place is cheap. I can cover it."

"Damn."

Aaron laughed. "It's not that hard."

"Says the genius."

"Willis, you're not stupid. And you're no babysitter. Get your head out of that bag of chips and take your life seriously."

Willis laughed and threw a Cheeto at him. "Asshole. You're not gonna disappear on me, are you? Where are you moving to?"

"San Francisco."

"Fuck, dude. That's, like, a whole bridge away."

"I'm not disappearing," Aaron assured him. "I'll be back on weekends, and we can go skateboarding and talk shit and all that."

"You'd better."

Aaron's phone rang. He answered. "Hey, D… yeah, come on up."

"D?" Willis asked as Aaron hung up the phone. "You're calling him D already? Doesn't look good when you called Grant GZ."

"Like I care how I look. And Drummer's staying the night again, so play nice."

"I can play nice," said Willis defensively.

"Yeah, you were real nice last night when he nearly pissed his pants trying to get around you."

Willis crossed his arms. "Sarcasm doesn't work for you, bro."

"Sorry, I didn't mean to steal your look."

There was a knock at the door. Aaron threw the Cheeto back at Willis, then left the kitchen. Willis hustled into the living room behind him.

"Hey," Aaron said, greeting Drummer at the door as he came in.

"What's up, *D*?" Willis asked. He leaned against the wall with exaggerated coolness, popped a Cheeto into his mouth, and chewed it loudly with a wiseass grin.

Drummer returned a confused smile. "How's it going, Willis?"

"Just great," Willis said with conspicuous sarcasm. Then, with mock lust, he added, "Aaron says you've shown him things he didn't think were even possible."

Aaron groaned, took Drummer by the wrist, and led him to the bedroom.

"What was that about?" asked Drummer, closing the bedroom door behind him.

"I told him I'm moving out and he's ribbing me. It's just part of my punishment."

"He'll be fine."

"Yeah, I know."

"You don't sound sure."

"No, I *know* he'll be fine," Aaron protested lightly. "And us too. I feel good. I have a lot of confidence lately. I'm even sure I'll be able to build a charger for your phone in a couple of days."

"A couple days? That's great news!"

"Isn't it? Small potatoes compared to that needle of yours, though. We pretty much know what's inside a phone, but what if we look inside that crazy time machine and we don't recognize anything? What do we do then?"

Drummer gave him a quick smirk.

"What are you grinning at?" Aaron asked.

"Just something I never thought I'd see in a young version of you."

"I'm afraid to ask what it is."

"Just… worry."

"Worry?" Aaron asked, mildly taken aback. "I don't think it's worry. It's more like… doubt."

"Nah, it's worry," said Drummer. "I saw it in an older version of you, but just once. It was the weekend you turned forty. You were worried you weren't the man you thought you were anymore. Worried that people would treat you differently, like you'd suddenly turned into some doddering old fool they didn't have to listen to anymore. But you went to work and realized that nothing had actually changed, and you were fine. Now I see that same look on your face. You're worried that you won't know what to do with the needle. But it's too soon for worry. We haven't crossed that bridge yet."

"Still feels like doubt to me."

Drummer shook his head. "It'll only be doubt if we open that thing up and identify everything inside, but we still can't make it work. Doubt, for you, comes *after* you've got all the info and still don't know what to do."

"Fair enough," said Aaron. "How do *you* feel about it? Worried? Doubtful?"

"Neither," said Drummer. "You just told me you could build a phone charger in two days, which means you'll probably pull it off in one. With confidence like that, I have no reason to worry at all."

Aaron smiled broadly. For the first time, he felt truly *seen*. He wasn't always comfortable receiving compliments, but Drummer had a knack for expressing his flattery with observations that seemed almost scientific—provable and factual. How could Aaron refute a compliment rooted in truth?

Aaron's musings unexpectedly conjured thoughts of Grant. Grant and Drummer were polar opposites. How many times had Grant seized on some aspect of Aaron's insecurity, however insignificant, to conflate his worry, feed his doubt, and diminish his ego? Drummer seemed incapable of such duplicity.

Aaron felt a chill at the thought of life with Grant, but it was quickly chased away by a comforting relief. That old life with Grant had been averted and a new one was beginning. Aaron had indeed dodged a proverbial bullet—many, in fact—with Drummer to thank for it.

THE MACHINE

When he first returned home, he had found it a tomb.
A year later, it was a machine.

A contrivance of glass and crystal,
A window on five dimensions,
A mirror for his guilt,
And a focus for his grief.

The abstract and the absolute,
The inevitable and the immemorial,
The past, the future, and the present,
All converging in a crucible of electromagnetic alchemy,
A gravity well that drew into it all other concerns,
And let nothing—not even light—escape.

CHAPTER 8
SECOND LIVES

WILLIS STOOD by the open front door to the apartment he had shared with Aaron for two years, watching in wordless resignation as a pair of burly movers boxed up the fixtures of his life and hauled them away. He was surprised that it took them less than an hour to carry it all out. In the end, the only things remaining were a smelly old couch, the scant contents of his own bedroom, and a half-eaten bag of Cheetos. Aaron owned everything else.

Willis stepped outside onto the balcony. He pulled a joint from his pocket and lit up. As he smoked, he leaned against the railing in thought, looking out at the well-tended suburban property of grassy knolls and decorative boulders. Someone was splashing around in the gated pool across the way, though he couldn't see them through the trees lining the concrete path below.

Willis sensed someone approach from behind, but he didn't turn around. He knew who it was. "Looks like you're getting what you want… D." He exhaled with a puff of cynicism.

Drummer stopped against the railing beside him. "Wasn't my decision," he said with neutral calm.

"Wasn't it?" asked Willis. "Grant could've learned from you. He tried to land Aaron for months. You did it in a day."

"'Landing Aaron' isn't what's happening here."

"Yeah. Aaron says the same thing."

Willis held out the joint, which Drummer took, puffed on twice, and handed back. "So if you guys aren't dating, what's the deal?"

"More than I can say," said Drummer. "I don't mean to be mysterious, it's just private. Don't worry, he'll be okay, and so will you. I promise."

"Don't talk to me like you know me," Willis said sharply. He turned around and pointed into the apartment through the open door. "And don't you fuckin' hurt him. I don't want to get a call saying you turned out to be an asshole or that you ditched him in the city, 'cause that'd really piss me off."

"That won't happen."

Willis took another hit from the joint and offered it again.

Drummer accepted once more, then reached out to hand it back.

"Keep it," Willis insisted, refusing the joint. "I need to get my shit together… and you look like you could use it."

He left Drummer on the balcony and returned to the apartment just as the movers were carrying away the last of Aaron's belongings. "So that's it, huh?" he asked his friend, who was stepping out of his empty bedroom. "Your boyfriend's waiting outside."

"He's not my boyfriend," said Aaron.

"Well, whatever he is."

"I ordered Chinese for you tonight," Aaron added. "I don't want you starving."

Willis sighed and said, with obvious sarcasm, "Yeah… like a fine wine, Chinese will pair well with my pride."

Aaron raised his brow at him.

"Sorry," said Willis, seeing the guilt in Aaron's eyes. "I don't mean to be a jerk."

"I'm kinda leaving you in the lurch," Aaron admitted.

"Yeah, whatever, I shouldn't be a bitch about it." Willis looked around the empty apartment. "Seeing the place like this makes me feel like a real loser."

"Why?"

"All that stuff was yours, man. And I was just…."

"You were just waiting for me to get out of your way," said Aaron.

"If you say so," said Willis. "You'll be back, right? I'm not going skating with those assholes without you."

"If you promise to visit."

"How do I do that?"

"The train leaves every hour," said Aaron. "And you've got a phone. Use it."

Willis nodded and smiled. "Pushy bitch."

"I just know what's important. Speaking of which, sorry I'm taking the PlayStation."

"Yeah, it's okay. I was only using it so I wouldn't have to listen to you talk on the phone with Grant."

"Ouch," Aaron said. "But deserved. Before I go, promise me something."

"Don't worry, I won't tell Grant where you are."

"I'm not worried about that. I'm not even going to follow his court case. I know where he's going. No, what I was going to say is, don't disappear on me, either. Whatever happens, you're my best friend."

"Well, you've guilted me enough with dinner and rent, you'll never get rid of me."

The two of them chuckled together. Aaron wrapped his arms around his longtime friend and held him tight.

Willis responded in kind, his eyes welling up unexpectedly.

At the conclusion of their embrace, Willis stepped back. Aaron smiled at him, and in that expression Willis saw something he'd never seen in his best friend's eyes before. It was like the look of a parent seeing their child all grown up, watching them move out of the house. A blend of hope and sadness—and pride. Willis took great comfort in that unexpected look, and for the first time he imagined himself not as a needy dependent but as the capable man Aaron had always insisted he was.

Willis felt a sudden rush of self-confidence. He wanted to tell Aaron not to worry about him.

But he knew better.

Because Aaron never worried.

THAT NIGHT, illuminated by a single table lamp propped up on a stack of paperbacks and surrounded by piles of unopened moving boxes, Aaron and Drummer sat on the floor of their new apartment and shared a large pizza. They ate directly from the delivery box and washed down the carb-heavy meal with a bottle of wine poured into small juice glasses—the only pieces of glassware they could find after the hasty move.

They traded the needle back and forth between them, hypothesizing about its composition, features, and function. They had a lot of work ahead of them. It seemed daunting but also exciting, for it promised a new life of shared discovery and mutual purpose—for as long as it lasted.

"You think Willis is scarfing down his delivery order right now?" Drummer asked. He took a sip of wine from the small glass and imagined Aaron drinking Kool-Aid from it as a kid.

"He already ate it. He called an hour ago. Said he picked it up early. Then he nagged our friends for some free stuff. Right now he's kicking back with a new couch, a TV, and a DVD player. Well, new *old* stuff, I guess."

"He sounds resourceful."

"And all I had to do was empty the living room," Aaron said with a cheeky grin.

Drummer nodded, pleased to see that telling smile. He looked around their new home. Nothing was in order; the movers had brought in the boxes and furniture and set them down in any available space.

"This happened so fast," he said.

"I know," Aaron said in agreement. "It's weird. Three days ago I was thinking about moving in with Grant. I haven't even talked to my parents yet."

"What are you going to say to them?"

"It's not a stretch to say I got a job in the city and moved in with a friend."

"That's a good way to put it," said Drummer. "Ambiguous. I know your parents in the future, and they'd be shocked if you told them you're shacked up with a forty-five-year-old guy right now."

"I know," Aaron agreed. "My dad would probably drive over here and try to drag me out."

"Have you heard from Grant?"

Aaron leaned against the back of a bulky upholstered chair and sighed. He held his glass in his lap. "No," he said. "Willis told me that if he hears from him, he'll say that I moved back to my parents' house to save money. I don't think Grant'll show up there."

"Your dad had no patience for him," said Drummer, recalling multiple stories of arguments between the two.

"My dad has a knack for seeing through bullshit," Aaron elaborated in agreement. "I thought I was more like him. But I didn't see the real Grant at all."

"It's not your fault," said Drummer. "He's a master manipulator. On top of that, love can blind us. When I first got together with Nate, I didn't see what I was giving up. But I gave up everything just for some form of companionship. I was happy to have a partner and glad for the respect I got for it, and as sad as this sounds, I was happy to be able to complain about his behavior. My need for love made me a dupe."

"Couldn't have been all bad."

"No, not all of it. It was the first time I had my own place rather than a spot on someone's couch. And I learned to be self-sufficient. But emotionally I was naïve. I made dumb choices. After we split up, I took a long, hard look at myself, and I didn't see someone I liked."

Aaron swirled the wine around in his glass. "I've been thinking about that."

"What do you mean?"

"Well… at the Mowry Inn, when I was looking at the pictures on your phone—the pictures of me—I saw someone different than the guy I see in the mirror. I saw a damaged person, but he was wise. I was someone who learned from life. Someone better than who I am right now. Maybe I needed to be with Grant to turn me into that guy."

"Never say that," said Drummer, wagging a finger in his direction. "There's nothing you needed from that relationship. Grant took from you and played on your empathy. The same way being with Nate rendered me dependent, rudderless, and angry, being with Grant would destroy your confidence, isolate you, and toss you into a spiral of perpetual self-doubt. The worst of all worlds for you."

Aaron nodded, then held up his glass. "Then here's to making better choices," he said in a toast.

"We made a good choice already by being here," said Drummer, raising his glass in kind. "So, here's to making more of them."

They drank.

"Speaking of choices," Aaron went on, "have you talked to anyone else since you got here? Like, anyone you used to know?"

"Only my former neighbor," Drummer said. "And that was just to get in my old place."

"You think about calling your parents?"

"Why would I do that?"

"Why *wouldn't* you? Didn't you get along?"

"We did."

"Then I don't get it. Why wouldn't you want to talk to them?"

"I hadn't really thought about it," said Drummer. "It just doesn't feel right."

"Well, I think talking to them might be a good thing. You have to feel kinda isolated right now, right? And you don't have to see them in person. You can just be a voice on the phone."

Drummer's brow furrowed at the uncomfortable thought. Though he'd already changed Aaron's personal history by removing Grant from the mix, contacting anyone else could introduce an unknown element to his younger counterpart's life. It was frightening to think that he could somehow trigger a sort of Butterfly Effect, which could disrupt their meeting in 2010. The future life he'd already lived with Aaron was of absolute importance to him, and he wanted to make sure it wasn't derailed.

"So?" Aaron prodded.

Drummer set his glass aside and held his hands together in his lap, sorting his thoughts. Finally he replied in a carefully measured tone. "I don't think so."

Aaron looked disappointed.

"Okay then," Drummer said in response to that look, "let's say I do call them. And I talk to my mom. She'll tell me everything she's been up to, and she'll want to know the same about me. What do I say? I don't remember exactly what I was doing tonight, twenty years ago."

"Just be honest," said Aaron. "Tell her you traveled back in time and now you're forty-five, and you want to know how many packs of adult diapers you're going to need over the next decade."

"Bitch," Drummer said with a chortle.

Aaron laughed with him before giving him a nudge. "Seriously, you don't have to give up any details, so why not?"

"For lots of reasons."

"Name one."

"Okay, fine. Plainly stated, I'm an intruder here. Anything I do or say is an intrusion into the timeline. Speaking with my parents wouldn't be a benign act. There'd be consequences."

"I don't think so, D. We're not that important, remember?"

Drummer grinned in partial agreement. "Okay, then… another reason. I'll use an analogy I know you'll understand. Remember the *Star Trek: Deep Space Nine* episode, *The Sound of Her Voice*?"

"I don't usually remember titles."

"Well, I know you've seen it. So, in the episode, the crew receives an audio distress call from a woman who's crashed on a distant planet.

They fly out to rescue her, and as they get closer, they're talking to her, learning more about her, hoping to keep her spirits up before she loses consciousness in the alien atmosphere and dies. But when they get there, they find that the planet's surrounded by a sort of time barrier and it's been sending her messages to them from the past, and theirs to her from the future. It turns out she crashed a long time ago, and she's been dead for years.

"Calling my family would feel like I was the woman on that planet, sending a message to them from a place they can't reach. There'd be no way to visit, no birthdays to plan, no holidays… no rescue. It would just be a cold call from the future. Just the sound of my voice."

"I remember that episode," Aaron said with a sympathetic nod. "That's a pretty dismal comparison. I don't mean it's pathetic. It's just kinda sad."

Drummer considered that word… sad. He didn't want his life to be defined that way. "Hand me your phone," he said.

Aaron looked at him quizzically. "You sure?"

"You listened to me about Grant, I'll listen to you now. I can always hang up."

Aaron tossed his phone to him.

Drummer caught it and held it in his lap for a moment, debating. Were there truly any consequences worth considering? Perhaps Aaron was right and there were none. He flipped open the old device and dialed, surprised that he remembered the phone number. After a few rings, his mother picked up.

"Hello?"

"Hey, Mom, it's Drummer," he said, stunned to hear her voice, knowing he was speaking to a version of her who was barely five years older than he was now.

"Hey, Drummer, how are you?" she asked.

Drummer could detect the subtle differences in her tone—a slightly younger, more vibrant cadence in her otherwise familiar voice.

"I'm good, Mom," said Drummer, afraid to say much more. "I just wanted to call and check in."

"Well, your father and I are doing fine. Are you sure you're okay? You sound a little upset."

"No, I'm fine," he said. There was a slight tremble in his voice, which he tried to conceal. "It's just been a long day. Nate and I are about to make some food."

"Sounds like a nice night in," she said. "We're about to head to that raffle dinner I told you about. I think we bought too many tickets, but maybe after a few glasses of wine I won't care." She laughed.

Drummer forced a chuckle in response. "Okay, Mom, I'll let you go, then," he said. "Have fun tonight. Say hi to Dad for me."

"I will. Love you, son."

"I love you too, Mom."

Drummer closed the phone and held it in thought as he absorbed the details of the brief call. He cleared his head and handed the device back to Aaron. When Drummer continued speaking, he did so dryly, with his emotions neatly tucked away. "My mom said they're about to go to a raffle dinner. I remember talking to her the week after that. She doesn't know it yet, but tonight they're going to win a TV."

Drummer leaned back. "Surreal," he said softly to himself.

"I'm sorry," said Aaron.

"Don't apologize," Drummer added. "I suppose I *am* glad I talked to her, but this isn't my time, and that voice I just heard… that's not *my* mother, it's *his*. I can't call again."

In a display of penance and understanding, Aaron raised the wine bottle, offering to refill Drummer's glass.

Drummer accepted.

Together the two men quickly drank what remained, with little interest in savoring it.

"You want more pizza?" asked Aaron.

"Nah, I'm full."

As Aaron reached out to close the box, Drummer took his hand. "Thank you again," he said, "for everything you've done."

"You don't have to keep thanking me," Aaron replied. "Especially if I keep pushing you to make bad decisions."

"The call wasn't a bad decision," said Drummer. "It just had an unpredictable outcome. What about *your* parents? You want to call them tonight? Tell them you're shacked up with a self-pitying, middle-aged time-traveler?"

"I think we should limit ourselves to one unpredictable outcome per day."

"Cheers to that."

"But…," said Aaron, leading into a different subject, "we *could* do something with a very clear and *predictable* outcome."

"Such as?"

Aaron reached into a backpack sitting nearby and pulled out a pen and a pad of paper. He handed them to Drummer. "You can tell me all the right stocks to buy," he said.

Drummer burst into laughter.

"And you can tell me all the Superbowl winners. And the outcome of every election."

As Drummer took the pad and pen, Aaron forced his expression into a comical deadpan and added, "I'm serious. Do it fast before you get sucked into some vortex back to 2020 and I'm left alone paying rent on a pricey two-bedroom in this expensive fucking town."

"You might not want to know who wins *every* election," said Drummer as he wrote, "but I promise you one thing: what I'm putting on this paper is not a joke."

AT THE end of the night, Aaron and Drummer put the needle and the notepad in a fireproof safe in the second bedroom, which they designated as a workroom. Then they discussed their plan for the week. Drummer's tasks would include unpacking the boxes and organizing Aaron's belongings, while Aaron would begin building a charger for Drummer's phone. Where the needle was concerned, it would be Aaron's responsibility to get access to any tech at school and work that might allow him to peer inside it, while Drummer searched the year-2000 internet for relevant news about imaging technology and any theories related to space-time.

It all felt so very sci-fi.

They showered. Separately.

Drummer put on a pair of Aaron's boxer shorts and one of his oversized T-shirts. The clothes fit him clumsily—too large around the waist and too narrow in the shoulders—and he wasn't used to wearing boxers, but at least the clothes were clean. When he was dressed, he went to the bedroom, where he found Aaron sitting in bed, naked.

"Joining me?" Aaron patted the empty space on the mattress beside him.

Drummer sat. "Can we talk for a second?"

"Course."

"You know I'm conflicted about this." Drummer indicated the two of them on the bed.

"I know, D, and I get it."

"No, Aaron, I don't think you do. It's about more than just you and me, together right now. You see, whenever you talk to me… I hear *him*. And whenever you smile at me, I see his smile. You *are* him, but I also know you're not.

"This might sound weird, but I need to keep the two of you separate in my head. I can't let myself relax into thinking that I'm already back there with you. I need to focus on getting home to that *other* you. Also… because I'm not the man you're going to fall in love with. The other version of me is. And he needs to find you available when the time comes. I don't want to screw things up by getting too close."

"And what about me?" asked Aaron. "You just referred to the future me, the other you, and yourself. What about the things *I* want?"

Drummer was afraid to ask Aaron to elaborate, for what probably lay down that road was exactly what made him so uncomfortable.

"I know you won't ask," said Aaron, "so I'll just tell you. I want to have sex. That's it."

"That's it?"

"Yep, that's it. I don't want to start anything or complicate anything. I've got a job and school to deal with. And now we've got the needle too. That's plenty. But we're still more than just roommates, so we don't have to live like lifeless mannequins. How's that sound?"

"Sounds like something I can work with," said Drummer, surprised and relieved to hear such a rational perspective.

"Great," said Aaron. "And next time, D, instead of just deciding on your own—or asking those two other people in your head what they think—ask me first."

Drummer smiled warmly. "Deal."

"Now…," Aaron started with a devilish grin, sweeping the serious conversation away, "take those clothes off and get in my bed, Methuselah."

Drummer laughed, reminded of how he'd used the name himself just a few days ago to taunt an older Aaron in their other life, and Aaron's use of it in return. It was a pleasant thought, to draw that direct connection between the two versions of the man he loved, while so many abstract connections already blurred the boundaries between them.

They had sex that night. It was exhilarating and rewarding, and though it took the form of an impulsive act of lust, there was real and growing affection in their unspoken exchange. It was not love, but neither was it empty of love.

They slept well.

The next day, Aaron left early for his morning classes while Drummer stayed home, unpacking boxes and arranging the furniture. As he sorted Aaron's belongings, he came across a lot of items that he remembered from the future—a bedside lamp, an old clock, and Aaron's high school yearbooks. They were all the same pieces he'd come to know years ago. Seeing them fueled swells of melancholy but also brought calm. He might have been twenty years removed from his own time, but he was comforted to find himself surrounded by familiar elements nevertheless.

Aaron returned home after lunch and immediately began working on Drummer's phone. Drummer watched intently as he carefully pried open the case and deftly identified the power and ground connectors on the USB port. Drummer was pleased to learn that Aaron could indeed cannibalize parts from his own spare cables. By nightfall, he'd fashioned an interconnector, splicing the chain of wiring into the future port. When he was done, he connected it to a surge-protected power strip and looked to Drummer for the okay.

"Ready?" Aaron asked.

Drummer nodded, feeling a brief spike of fear. What if it didn't work? What if it burnt out the entire device?

Aaron switched it on.

For a few seconds, during which Aaron kept his finger poised over the glowing red Off switch, nothing happened. Then the phone screen flickered, the battery icon lit up, and the device began charging.

The two men let out a simultaneous cheer, then laughed as Aaron threw his hands in the air in celebration, nearly hitting Drummer in the face.

Late that night, they dropped into bed together. Lost in their individual thoughts, their minds wandered even as they both looked up at the painting hanging above the headboard. The swirls of gold and blue in *The Starry Night* suggested multiple layers of contrast—illumination and darkness, sound and silence, excitement and tranquility. Aaron and Drummer were distracted by diverging thoughts, but they were lost in that sky together.

THE DAY after that, Aaron started his new job. In the silence that followed his departure, Drummer felt an immediate sense of unease. This would be his first full day alone in a week. He had a few boxes left to unpack and a couple of pieces of furniture to move, but the stillness of the apartment drained him of any desire to tend to those chores. This new life, in this new place, in an old version of a city he used to know, had drawn him in so quickly. He needed a break from it, even just a brief one, a moment to step back and reflect. He picked up his fully charged phone and left the building.

He walked the half block up Tenth Avenue to Golden Gate Park, an ideal place for a retreat. He wandered aimlessly but not mindlessly along a winding path, surrounded by towering eucalyptus and Monterey cypress trees that blocked the view of the surrounding neighborhood. The isolation created the illusion of a timeless environment, one that was especially peaceful.

But the delightful sense of calm took flight as he emerged into a clearing at the edge of a man-made lake. The fantasy of being lost in space and time disappeared. He suddenly knew exactly where he was. He'd stumbled onto Stow Lake in the center of the park, where he and a future Aaron had previously spent a great deal of time. Or was the correct wording "would eventually" spend a great deal of time? The semantics irritated him.

He walked around the lake until he came to a bench on the southeastern shore, one where he and Aaron had frequently stopped to enjoy the view and where they'd taken a photo with his family a few years back—or forward. He sat there alone now, disturbed at first by the familiarity of the setting. But he soon decided it might actually be a good place to find retreat after all. He even questioned if he hadn't led himself to the lake on purpose.

Drummer took out his phone and turned it on, making sure to keep the device hidden from casual passersby. He opened the image gallery and found one of the last photos he'd taken of Aaron in Huntington Park. For Drummer, that day had only been one week in the past and still existed vividly in his mind. He imagined it as a moment frozen in time, where the older Aaron was currently standing in the alley, suddenly abandoned, waiting for Drummer to return. Drummer's memories had ambushed him when he arrived at the lake. Now a feeling of guilt walked alongside them.

"I'm doing what I can to get home, baby," he said to the image of Aaron, smiling back at him from the tiny screen. "And you'll never guess who's helping me. On the other hand, I suppose you might already know."

Drummer continued swiping through the photos until he came to an image from an even earlier time—a brilliant summer day in 2012. Or had it been 2014? He didn't recall exactly. Aaron had been in his early thirties, at least. Behind him was a silver single-prop airplane sitting on a short runway. Beside the runway, lying in a grassy field, was a rumpled red parachute.

Drummer replayed that wonderful day in his mind. Aaron had coaxed him into a tandem skydive on the Marin peninsula north of San Francisco. It had been his first skydiving experience, exhilarating and life-changing. He couldn't have imagined sharing that moment with anyone else.

Anyone.

"What I'd give to live that day again," Drummer said to himself, before realizing that he was drifting off into sorrow.

He put the phone away.

For a short while longer he sat in silence, listening to the tranquil lapping of the water on the shore. Memories came and went. He smiled at some and held back tears at others, before they all finally retreated into the bucolic chronicles of his mind.

He returned home.

While the walk to the park hadn't gone as he'd expected, it did give him the break he'd needed. He arranged the last pieces of furniture and unpacked the rest of Aaron's belongings.

For the remainder of the morning and into the early afternoon, Drummer saw to a task that Aaron had suggested for him: establishing a new identity. There was a lot of information available online, but none of it gave him confidence. He had no identification paperwork that could be believed, other than a useless driver's license from the future, and this led him to the frustrating conclusion that he had no legal options.

He'd be forced to take the same risks as other stateless, undocumented immigrants. He could get a fake ID for everyday needs, and possibly resort to bribes if necessary, but he wouldn't be able to hold a satisfying job, or fly, or even drive. He felt cut off at the knees, but keeping his anonymity was paramount, so the limitations to his freedom would have to stand.

Aaron came home that evening with two shopping bags of new clothes for Drummer. He also handed him a list of companies he'd purchased stock in. Drummer was only somewhat surprised that Aaron had put most of his savings into his choices, because it was a good deal of money. The wholesale flurry of investment showed a great deal of trust in Drummer on Aaron's part, which touched him in ways he hadn't expected.

The two men had sex again that night. It was exciting but devoid of emotional bonding and clearly established that their connection, but while affectionate, had finite depth. There was trust, understanding, and all the things that traditionally defined love, except for romance and familiarity. They had an enigmatic link, bound to a common goal in a paradoxical situation. But beyond the shared circumstances, there remained much for them to learn about one another.

"D?" Aaron asked as they lay in bed in the dark. "What's your favorite color?"

"Red," he said quietly.

"Really?" Aaron asked. "For some reason I thought it'd be blue."

"I can understand why," said Drummer, smiling in the dark. "But I wore that blue polo for you."

TIME BREAKS

He compared the two photographs. They were identical, taken at the same time in the same place, with eucalyptus and Monterey cypress trees behind them, a blue sky above, and family all around.

Aaron did not appear happy in either. But was he joyless or merely reflective?

In the first image, in the click of that photograph, he'd been thinking back to Grant. In the second, back to Drummer.

Two identical photographs of one moment in time, repeated and replicated perfectly, but with two different meanings. Was it coincidence, synchronicity, or fate?

PART 2
DUALITY

CHAPTER 9
A YEAR IN A DAY

"Now is not the time," they said to themselves and to each other. And they believed it. And they were right. It was not the time for love. It was time to focus and to plan.

The week that had brought Drummer to the year 2000, then led him to Aaron, and finally delivered them both to San Francisco, seemed to last a lifetime. But the ten months that followed went by in a blink. It was as if an entire year passed them by in a day, even though some days felt as though they themselves lasted a year.

After the first week in their new apartment they established a routine, one that brought a tidal shift in priorities for them both. Aaron's focus changed from school to his career. He continued his education with the goal of graduating, but it wouldn't dominate his time as profoundly as it had before. Concurrently, Drummer was consigned to domestic life, deprived of employment for the first time in decades.

During the quiet daylight hours, Drummer searched the internet and academic journals for information related to industrial scanning technology and high-speed computing. Most of his information came from print materials, given the low quality of internet databases in 2000. He studied theories related to quantum mechanics and time travel and fell into more than a few metaphysical and astrological rabbit holes, but he always managed to dig himself out and make his way back to the science.

Unfortunately, if not predictably, his research quickly reached a limit. Technology was advancing at its own pace, not his, and there was only so much information out there to find. His early flurry of discovery came to an end as he found himself reading the same news articles about the same breakthroughs and the same hypotheses again and again.

Aaron's own probing into the needle traced a similar curve of early excitement and later disappointment. His first act was to use machinery readily available on the commercial market to scan for an electric field or magnetic field generated by the device. But even on the most sensitive equipment his measurements yielded nothing—the needle wasn't producing electrical or magnetic force at all. This was shocking considering that, while relatively dormant, the needle was clearly exhibiting signs of activity in the dim lights and its undulating, nebulous blue skin.

Aaron then gained access to an electron microscope from a coworker and used it to search the needle's exterior for any seams or access ports. But the imagery revealed the surface of the needle to be perfectly smooth, with no breaks or perforations at all. There also appeared to be no molecular differentiation between the lights, the numbers, and the swirling blue pattern.

Visibly and invisibly, the needle appeared self-contained, its surface uniform and its status inert. Stymied, Aaron set his sights on penetrative scanners like X-rays, hoping to get a look inside the needle without physically opening it. But access to this technology was blocked by layers of protocol and access restrictions far above his menial role.

DRUMMER CONTINUED to make daily visits to Stow Lake. He walked around the shoreline and sometimes rented a rowboat for an hour, just to be on the water. He'd often find himself sitting on the bench that he'd once shared with Aaron, throwing feed pellets to the ducks. It was a macabre and lonely routine, and he came to wonder if his visits weren't becoming more like trips to a cemetery to pray over the grave of a lost loved one, rather than meditative respites from a confusing, inanimate life.

A FULL month went by.

DRUMMER'S DAYS seemed to grow longer. He became desperate for distraction. The outside world was reintroducing him to past tragedies that he could do nothing to change, like the 2000 presidential election and its embarrassing fallout. He found these events uniquely exhausting.

To cope, in addition to visiting Stow Lake, he committed his spare time to other ventures. One was cooking. In his old life he had been an admittedly terrible cook, but he now found himself with the means and minutes to invest in learning. He discovered his strengths and experimented with more challenging recipes. Many of his attempts crashed and burned, both figuratively and literally. But he quickly got the hang of it and was surprised to find that cooking brought him pleasure, especially when his efforts didn't end with the shriek of a smoke alarm.

TWO MONTHS passed and the holiday season came. Aaron was invited to several parties, hosted by people he knew from school and work. He went to a few of them, but he went alone. In each case, he faced questions about his career goals and his family and fielded the inevitable inquiries into his love life. Was he dating anyone? Did he want to? How about that guy Greg—you know, the one in accounting?

He deflected.

Whenever he left one of these parties, upon returning home he'd climb into bed beside Drummer and fall asleep while contemplating the next ten years. He sometimes wondered—if he sent Drummer back to 2020 tomorrow, would it be out of the question to date someone in the meantime, knowing that whatever came of the intervening relationship would—or should—end by 2010? Aaron wasn't lonely, not for the moment, not with Drummer around. But ongoing long-term companionship was not a guarantee, not if they achieved their goals.

NEW YEAR'S Eve came, and with it the dawn of 2001. Aaron and Drummer stayed home. The ringing-in of a new year just didn't feel celebratory to them, not while they were at an impasse with the needle. They shared some take-out, toasted to the future, and called it a night.

IN FEBRUARY was Aaron's parents' wedding anniversary. He celebrated with them alone in Fremont and spoke only of school and work, as if he had no other burdens or interests. He avoided any mention of Drummer, which felt uncomfortably deceptive but necessary. His parents would meet Drummer one day, and Aaron didn't want to be responsible for the outcome, whether disastrous or humorous.

WITH MARCH, Drummer dwelt upon the date he and Nate had split up. He recalled the heated accusations they'd leveled at one another in his old apartment—presumably taking place again at that very moment— with blame over the missing money adding fuel to the fire.

After, and for the better, Drummer envisioned life moving forward for his young counterpart. That man would take his cat and the many pieces of junk he viewed as mementos, leave the place on Hayes Street, and take his first steps toward becoming the man he was destined to be— the man he believed Aaron would one day fall in love with.

ALL OF these events, for Aaron and for Drummer, together and separately— holidays, parties, anniversaries, breakups—were uniquely conspicuous. They both loudly marked the passing of time and brought the uneasy feeling that time itself was slipping away. The two men noted this inwardly, shrugged it off outwardly, and told themselves that they were still making progress on the needle. Even when it was clear that they were not.

SIX MONTHS passed.

AARON RECEIVED a call from Willis and learned he'd been offered a job in Boston. Though Aaron hadn't doubted Drummer's prediction, seeing it come true gave him a chill. A week later Willis was across the country, immersed in the future Drummer had said he'd pursue. Aaron was happy for him, but he mourned the fact that his relationship with his best friend would apparently now remain distant for decades to come.

SIX MONTHS became seven.

DRUMMER FELT himself losing time. Seven months were gone—seven months of his life, stolen by the past and that damned needle. His hours of rumination in the park grew bleaker. His memories of the future Aaron became more tenuous, more reliant on the photographs and videos on his phone. Drummer was forced to accept that he was no longer visiting the lake to find peace. Rather, he was doing it to hold on to his memories, to package the years between 2010 and 2020 as though they were somehow containable, like sealing an entire world in a snow globe he could carry in his pocket.

He was also still trying to draw separation between the young Aaron and the old, and to tell himself that the two iterations were in fact different people. This was necessary, he believed, to keep his feelings in check and his focus on the future, so if he *were* suddenly able to jump back to 2020, he could look upon the forty-year-old Aaron waiting there as the *true* Aaron, and leave the younger Aaron in the past, as part of history—not as a man he cared about but then abandoned. Time could then resume as intended, in a neat and orderly fashion. But the truth was, despite Drummer's intentions, he could never quite do it. Whenever he looked at the young Aaron, he still saw the older one looking back. And in his voice, he still heard the elder's charm.

Drummer had trapped himself in a revolving, unresolving pattern. Every day he'd sit by the water, mourn his loss, and tell himself that the older and younger Aarons were as different as the lives they led. Then he'd scold himself for the indulgence and return home with no more peace of mind than he'd had the day before. Aaron would come back that night, and once again, in Drummer's mind, the young and the old would fuse into one.

WHILE DRUMMER was struggling with this conflict, Aaron himself was sinking into his own emotional nadir. He had made no headway in his attempts to look inside the needle. With condescending regret from professional and academic acquaintances alike, he was repeatedly denied access to advanced tools and technology. After seven months, the last of his leads had dried up.

He felt guilt.

Personal disappointment.

Looming failure.

Compounding this feeling, Aaron could see Drummer's despondency growing with each day. He could hear it in his voice and feel it in his touch at night. Some days would pass with the two of them saying nothing to each other. Aaron told himself that he couldn't let an entire year go by with nothing to show for it. His pride, as well as Drummer's fate, depended on him making some measure of progress in the next few months.

If he wanted to get a look inside the needle, he would have to take greater risks. He would have to bend his own rules and possibly break them. He'd have to seek out the corruptible opportunists in his circle, and if he found none, he'd have to expand his circle to include them. Then he'd use his savvy to manipulate them. He hated this approach, for he'd always taken pride in his ability to succeed without cheating. It also reminded him of Grant and the man's corrupted and selfish behavior, and Aaron didn't like the prospect of seeing that face in the mirror.

Grant.

Aaron hadn't thought of him in months.

No word from the courts or lawyers.

But also no desire to look into it and possibly find something he didn't want to see.

Aaron put Grant out of his mind.

Time raced.

Progress halted.

So....

In May 2001, with seven months of defeat in his pocket, Aaron did what he'd thought he would never do—he compromised himself. He started to use his natural charisma and his quick wit to pursue avenues he'd previously rejected as unpalatable. He had never intended to compromise himself that way, but he did it all the same. He told himself that compromising did not make him a compromised individual; he was simply using all his resources to make progress, just as anyone else would. Whenever he did something that felt shameful, he reminded himself of the nobility of his purpose. He didn't have a choice. He wasn't doing any of this for money or fame. He was doing it to repay a debt and to return a wonderful man to a wonderful future that just happened to include himself. What better incentive to do the wrong thing, than for love?

Love.

Aaron reminded himself that what he had with Drummer was *not* love.

Even after all these months, as the two of them built a real connection, their relationship remained rooted in emotionally sterile soil. It imitated a marriage-like partnership—it was sexual, thoughtful, even flirtatious—but it was also disciplined and cautious. That was where their intimacy ended. For as they had told themselves at the beginning, reminded themselves often, and as Aaron repeated in his mind at night while Drummer's hand rested in his... "Now is not the time."

CHAPTER 10
ALL THINGS BLACK AND WHITE

ON THURSDAY, July 5, 2001, one month before Aaron's twenty-first birthday, he came home from work with a new lead. A coworker had offered to pass the needle through a computed tomography scanner at an offsite lab. Aaron could get three small, sectional scans made of the object, potentially revealing its composition.

There were two conditions.

First, Aaron would have to allow his coworker to take the needle to the lab himself, meaning it would be out of Aaron's immediate control for half a day at least.

Second, Aaron would have to have sex with him.

While Aaron and Drummer had exchanged no romantic vows, this didn't mean that the second condition was of no concern. Aaron felt a pang of guilt for merely mentioning the proposition, and he could sense from Drummer's silence that he was none too fond of it either. But ultimately, they agreed that they couldn't pass up the opportunity.

The following day, Aaron brought the needle to work, secured in a hard-sided, velvet-lined pen box. He gripped it especially tight as he stood outside the office of the man with the scanner access. He knocked on the door.

Long seconds passed. He could hear the faint sounds of a telephone call inside. As Aaron waited, he questioned his commitment to his choice. Was he truly willing to give himself to this person for a night, just for a glimpse inside the needle?

Was his dignity really that negotiable?

Over the course of the preceding two months, he'd crossed many lines in pursuit of technology that might give him a look inside the device. He'd lied repeatedly, all the while refusing to acknowledge the many ways he was damaging his integrity. This opportunity today was the first, best chance he had for any kind of result.

His dignity could wait.

The door opened and the man leaned out. He was not unattractive, but neither were his looks remarkable. On a regular day he'd be as unnoticed by the general public as any other regular person going about their regular business. His name was Olson, and even this was often misremembered.

"Aaron, come on in," he said. He left the door open as he went back to his desk.

Aaron followed, closing the door behind him.

Olson's office was cluttered and underwhelming. It was located on the inside of the building and had no window to the outside world. Two heaps of office equipment stood precariously in one corner. Olson's desk was a mess, with barely enough surface space for a keyboard, a mouse, two oversized monitors, and what Aaron hoped were the previous day's fast-food wrappers.

"Let's see whatcha got," Olson said, flopping onto his chair.

Aaron handed him the box with the needle inside.

Olson opened it and let out an impressed whistle. "Damn, this is nice," he said. "What is it?"

"I'm just curious what it's made of," Aaron said, choosing to avoid the question.

"It's heavy. Could be metal or glass, I guess. Is this one of those top-secret things you guys steal from other companies and reverse engineer?"

"I'd rather not say," Aaron replied with a small grin, allowing Olson to cling to his theory.

"I'll keep your secret safe." Olson put it back in the case and set it on his desk.

"Don't lose that, please," said Aaron nervously.

"Don't worry, man. I take good care of things. I'm heading to the lab in about ten minutes. I'll have the scans for you at my place tonight. How's ten sound?"

"Ten's fine."

"Oh, and I don't have one of those shower fixture clean-out things," Olson added. "So take care of that before you come over."

Aaron nodded. He was feeling dirtier by the second, especially when Olson mentioned the shower. Aaron knew exactly what he was referring to, but hearing it described so crudely made him feel like a farm animal about to be inspected at a county fair.

"Don't worry, I'll be good to go," Aaron assured him.

"Great." Olson sat up. "You know, I always thought you were one of the hottest guys here. Never thought I'd actually have you."

"I'm full of surprises today," Aaron said, trying to appear at ease.

"And tonight, I hope," added Olson. "See you at ten."

Aaron left, feeling as if he'd just sold his soul. Worse, he felt as if he'd sold it out from under Drummer, as if his soul were a shared commodity and not his alone to bargain with.

IN THE early morning hours, with the fruits of his labor in hand and his feelings in check, Aaron returned home. He found Drummer awake on the couch in the living room, his laptop open to a news website he'd likely already read many times.

Aaron placed a large manila envelope on the coffee table.

"You okay?" Drummer asked gingerly, sitting up and putting the computer aside.

Aaron kept his eyes on the envelope, for although his pragmatism was currently in control, his hold on his emotions was tenuous. He felt weak, like an unfortified dam stood within him, straining to hold back a rain-swelled body of water.

"I'm fine," he said.

"You don't look fine."

"Well, I am," he countered, in as much of an attempt to convince himself as to end the line of questioning. He glanced at a clock on the wall and saw it was 3:00 a.m.

"You didn't have to wait up, D."

"What kind of boyfriend would I be if I didn't?"

Aaron managed a meager smile in response. "You know we're not boyfriends."

"Doesn't mean I don't care. Was it… enjoyable, at all?"

Aaron paused before answering, his shame hovering behind his eyes. He wanted to tell him. He wanted to crumple on the couch, lean into Drummer's shoulder, and cry that shame away, but the relationship they shared wasn't that kind of relationship. Or so he told himself.

"I was hopeful," he replied, "but no. He wanted me to do things I normally wouldn't—except maybe with you. And he made me shower at his place after I got there, even though he stank like a dog."

Drummer started to stand, clearly intending to comfort him.

"Don't get up," Aaron insisted, rejecting the offered sympathy. His voice cracked just a bit as the dam within struggled to contain that weighty body of water.

Drummer obliged. Instead, he leaned toward the envelope. "Have you looked at them?"

"Not yet. I guess I just don't feel…." Aaron stopped himself. He knew what he wanted to say, but he also knew that if he spoke his feelings aloud, he'd hear their effect in his voice. He took the needle from the inside pocket of his coat and handed it to Drummer.

Drummer took it and set it carefully on the table, keeping his eyes on Aaron. "You don't feel like you *deserve* to look at them, do you."

Aaron stared at him. Drummer's concern was frustratingly obvious. Aaron had hoped to return home with confidence, share the contents of the envelope with a feeling of accomplishment, and congratulate himself on his victory, with Drummer's thanks. But his feelings betrayed him despite his attempts to conceal them. Drummer was reacting to the obvious: the dam inside Aaron was failing, and everything he wanted to hide was starting to show.

"I feel like I cheated on you, D," he finally admitted, hoping to bleed off some of the pressure with a small concession. "Like I betrayed you to get these."

"You know you didn't."

"Doesn't mean I feel good about it."

"I understand. But *cheating*? Aaron, you know you couldn't possibly cheat on me. So I'm wondering if it's not more about feeling like you're just… cheating in general."

The proverbial body of water expanded suddenly. He hated cheating. And he hated when people saw him do it. He tried to ignore the comment. "There're three printed scans in the envelope," he said, deflecting, "one vertically, tip-to-tip; one perpendicular, across one of the gold lights; and one at a thirty-degree angle through the center. Just like we said. Olson said he'll give me the digital files on Monday."

Drummer took his hand.

Their eyes met.

"Sit with me," Drummer insisted. He motioned to the space beside him on the couch and then collected the envelope. When Aaron was seated, Drummer uncoiled the string fastener, reached inside, and pulled out three black-and-white acrylic sheets—prints of the computed tomography scans Aaron had asked for.

Drummer set two of the scans on the table and held the third up to the light. The image was clean, and the outline of the needle was sharp. Indeed, the focus was perfect. But what the scan revealed was unexpected. According to the image, the inside of the needle had no detail. It was merely a white silhouette set against a black background. The other two scans showed the same thing.

"I don't believe it," Drummer said, aghast. "The needle... it's empty."

Aaron took the sheets from him. "It's not empty, D. It's... *solid*."

"Solid? Solid what?"

Aaron shrugged, trying to interpret the images. "I don't know," he said. "But in this kind of scan, black indicates voids and white indicates solids. The needle is solid white."

"No voids? How's that possible?"

Aaron had no idea, but the images didn't lie.

"The pictures I took with the electron microscope indicated that the surface was made of some type of crystal," he said, thinking aloud. "It might be the same inside. There's no empty space, no gaps, nothing to indicate other materials."

"No processors or wires or chips?"

"No, nothing."

"What about the lights and the numbers?"

Aaron glanced at the needle on the table. "I know they look like they have depth, but I'm betting they don't. I don't know how it's possible, D, but the whole thing seems to be one piece of solid glass."

Aaron spread all three scans out on the table and viewed them together, bewildered and crushed. He felt as though the images were laughing at him, mocking him for his sacrifices and compromises, especially the sexual humiliation he'd just put himself through. The dam within him could hold no longer. It broke open, and an ocean of despondency crashed through his formerly noble pragmatism. "I... I'm so sorry, Drummer," he said, unable to conceal the anguish in his voice.

Drummer took his hand again and held it tight. "Aaron, it's okay," he said. "This is the first look we've had. Even if it's not what we thought, it's still something useful."

But Aaron barely heard him. All he could hear was the blood-curdling victory cry of his shame standing atop the ruins of his dignity. He could still smell Olson's sweat on his clothes. He could feel his selfish touch on his body and the sweat dripping onto his back. He could smell Olson's vile breath. He hated him. And he hated himself.

"It's not okay!" he snapped. "After everything, this is all I've got, *and it's not okay*."

Drummer put his arm around Aaron and drew him close. He took Aaron's free hand into his. "Oh, baby," he said, consoling Aaron as he wept. "I'm sorry."

That term of endearment—"baby"—was not something Aaron had heard Drummer use with him before. And the great tenderness and affection in Drummer's tone was unmistakable. Was it truly meant for *him*? Had Drummer been holding that in reserve all this time, for the older Aaron he'd left behind in 2020? What did it mean that he'd used it now?

Unanswered questions aside, Aaron clung to that endearment. It was like a fortuitously placed sea wall, containing the spilled waters of his broken resilience. He closed his eyes and repeated it himself with the same tenderness Drummer had shown. "Thank you, baby."

Drummer kissed him on the cheek.

The two men looked down at their hands, now tightly entwined, then gazed into each other's eyes and saw… something. But they said nothing, each waiting for the other to make that perilous identification.

"So…," Drummer started quietly, "you feel better?"

Aaron shrugged noncommittally. "I suppose. I still feel like I failed."

"The emotional side of you feels like you have, but the logical side of you—even if it doesn't see it yet—knows you haven't."

Aaron glanced at the acrylic sheets on the table. "Those scans don't agree."

"I don't think they've spoken their truth yet," Drummer replied. "They look like they have no answers, but sometimes 'no answer' *is* an answer. And that'll lead to the right questions."

"You're just trying to make me feel better."

"Obviously. But I also want you to see that this is still a win."

Aaron allowed a small, appreciative smile, but he just didn't feel as though he'd won anything.

"There's something I want you to know," Drummer said with a slight tonal shift that indicated a change of subject. "You know how you said last year that when you looked at pictures of your older self you saw someone better than you are today?"

Aaron nodded slowly.

"That's not true," Drummer said. "And it's always upset me to think you believe it."

"He's got so much on me, D," Aaron said, almost defensive.

"He's got nothing on you, Aaron. Every day when you're at work, I go to Stow Lake and I… think about him. I think about all the things we did and the places we went. I think about how he was always there for me and how many times I screwed up and needed his help. I've been trying to hold on to him—separate from you—and convince myself that the two of you are two different people. You know that. I've been doing this to keep from getting too close to you, because one way or another, in 2010, I'll have to leave.

"But every night you come home and I see the look on your face as you tell me about the work you're doing. I see the pride you feel at your success. And I see *him*… so clearly. It reminds me how wrong I've been to think I can completely separate the two of you. There are some things between us that simply can't be, but despite those things, I can't deny that he's still with me, every day, in you. And every day I feel the same pride at having you beside me as I did at having *him* beside me.

"Aaron, he's not better than you. He *is* you. There's just a twenty-year road between the two of you that you're still walking."

Aaron's eyes spilled over again. "You're too sweet, D," he said. Drummer's words meant more to him than he understood himself.

Drummer smiled with him and continued, "You know, I've been thinking about that night in the bar last year, when you told me I should enjoy myself while I'm here. I haven't been doing that. I've been cooking, cleaning, doing laundry. At the same time, you're doing the hard work, taking risks, putting yourself through nights like tonight. We're both hurting ourselves, and neither of us is having any fun."

"Yeah," Aaron said in agreement.

"But we should," Drummer said. "We should enjoy our lives. I shouldn't just be sitting here, sorting socks and giving you stock tips. And you shouldn't be torturing yourself trying to make heads or tails of the needle. What kind of life is that for us?"

Aaron grinned through bloodshot eyes. "We're making a lot of money off your stock tips."

"But aside from that, what are we doing?" Drummer gave him a long, gentle stare. "I feel like I have no purpose, Aaron. I sit in the park, looking back and looking ahead, but I look at right now and I feel like I'm wasting time. Wasting *your* time, especially. I don't know what made me think we could figure out the needle so fast, and I'm sorry I put pressure on you. It'll obviously take a while. And since it will, I need to find a new purpose for myself, one that acknowledges you and supports you and what you're doing for me. Reflecting on what you said in the bar, I think I know what it is."

"And what's that, D?"

"Our life in the pictures and videos I showed you," Drummer started, "it was all because of you. It was your condo. It was your money, your ideas. Before I met you, I had a career and friends, but every day felt like a series of boring, tedious tasks. Meeting you gave my life dimension. We did things I never would've done alone. And you did it all with a smile on your face, never demanding that I give more than I could and not once letting your past with Grant turn you cold. Now, what? Here I am with everything your older self gave me—all the joy and experiences we had together—and I haven't done a damn thing with them.

"I want to give some of that joy back to you, so that as long as I'm here we aren't just sitting in this place, killing time, waiting for the right tech to come along. Aaron, in 2010 you'll lift me up from an unfulfilling life. Until then, will you let me show you the beautiful world that you first showed to me?"

Aaron gazed at him. The question was not a simple one. It carried weight. It suggested that the year behind them had possessed meaning beyond their working relationship, and that the time ahead was theirs to define. It also implied commitment without fear, even knowing that it could all end tomorrow. Most importantly, it acknowledged the affection that already existed between them, even though it was confined by circumstance—even if Drummer's younger counterpart would eventually be the one to claim that affection as love.

Love.

Aaron reminded himself that what he had with Drummer was not love. And yet he was proposing to introduce a layer of emotional connection that might complicate everything.

"Wouldn't it be a distraction?" Aaron asked.

Drummer shook his head. "We need a little distraction so we don't go crazy. And if that's not enough to convince you, then I want you to consider the words of a wise young man who I'm getting to know better each day. He reminded me that I'm going to have to answer to you when I get back, and you're going to have to answer to me. And I don't want either of us to ask ourselves why we didn't enjoy this time when we had the chance."

Aaron smiled broadly. The waters behind his shattered dam had settled, leaving behind renewed perspective. For the better part of a year, he'd focused his attention on work, school, and the needle, denying himself rest and reflection. He and Drummer had sex often, and were caring and supportive of one another, but enjoying their companionship hadn't been in the cards.

But Drummer was right—it should be.

Uninvited, Drummer leaned in and kissed Aaron on the forehead. He sat back and motioned to a far corner of the room where Aaron's skateboard was propped up against the wall. "That board's getting dusty over there, don't you think?"

Aaron looked over at it. He hadn't gone skateboarding in months. He'd convinced himself that he was saving it as a reward for the day he made progress on the needle, but in truth, he'd been holding off as punishment for his *lack* of progress.

"I'm gonna make us something to eat," said Drummer. "Why don't you put this out of your mind and go kick that board around for a while?"

"It's 3:00 a.m."

"So? You'll have the streets to yourself. You'll appreciate that."

Aaron felt an unexpected excitement cut through his exhaustion. He knew he didn't need Drummer's permission to go skateboarding, but getting it had a way of countering his self-imposed prohibition. And the dark, empty streets held a lot of appeal.

He looked into Drummer's pale green eyes and saw more than just understanding there. He saw forgiveness—the forgiveness he'd been unwilling to give himself. Forgiveness that offered healing to his wounded pride without having to say anything aloud.

Aaron dashed to the bathroom and showered. As the water rushed over him, washing away the humiliating evidence of the previous hours, his anticipation grew, cleansing him of the guilt he'd felt upon arriving home.

He dried, put on a pair of jeans and a T-shirt, then found Drummer at the kitchen counter preparing a rather elaborate meal for so early an hour. He kissed Drummer on the back of the neck, then went for the front door, snatching up his skateboard along the way.

Outside, the moon was bright. The air was crisp. Stars dotted a cobalt sky. Aaron hopped onto his board and set off down the gentle slope of Tenth Avenue, with Golden Gate Park behind him and the tree-lined silhouette of the Presidio's forested hills ahead.

It was like redemption, like a prayer being heard and answered, as he coasted through the hush of the early morning. He reveled in the sensation of speed, the Pacific wind against his face, and the sound of his skateboard's wheels rolling over the pavement.

He felt absolved of all guilt. His shame receded, and in the resulting absence of thought emerged a sublime new feeling. It came to him as a whisper, words that stirred the air and excited the stars above, lighting them afire like the vibrant swirls of gold and sapphire in *The Starry Night*.

It was the comforting echo of Drummer's voice reaching out to him, soothing his grief, and calling him "baby."

TWO WORLDS

The skateboard on the wall told a story. It was a bridge between two worlds, between Aaron's youth and his adulthood. It existed in both, and for the same purpose, but with a different role in each.

The photos beside the board told a story as well. They, too, were bridges between two worlds—between the same life lived twice, experienced in different ways, but with the same milestones, the same signposts, and the same outcome.

The question was: Could he change one without ruining the other?

CHAPTER 11
GRAVITY

AARON AWOKE in the early afternoon. It was dark and quiet, save for a sliver of sunlight breaking through the window shades and the faint sound of children playing in the yard next door. He was alone. He checked the clock. It was 2:00 p.m.

He got up and found Drummer in the kitchen, leaning over the counter with the three CT scans spread out before him. He appeared deep in thought.

"Thanks for letting me sleep," said Aaron, breaking the silence.

"I could tell you needed it." Drummer straightened up fully. "How are you feeling?"

Aaron shrugged. "I'm waking up at 2:00 p.m. on a Saturday with regrets."

"Sounds like my twenties," Drummer said with a grin. "You look less… wrecked."

"Thanks for rushing in with the bandages and Bactine."

"I know what's important to a skater," Drummer joked lightly. He picked up one of the scans and handed it to Aaron. "I have a couple of ideas. I thought about what you said, about the needle being solid. I don't think it is."

"Why not?"

Drummer picked up his touchscreen phone from the counter, where it had been lying beside the scans. He turned it over in his hands. "The tech in this thing is really dense. It's not solid, but there's almost no unused space. What if the needle's the same way? What if it's not solid, just packed together really tightly?"

Aaron glanced at the acrylic sheet in his hand.

"It's possible," he said, "but computed tomography's really sensitive, D. Even if the parts are packed together like Tetris pieces, we'd still see dark areas where they fit together, and probably shades of gray showing areas of different density for the different materials. Everything here is solid white."

"That doesn't mean the needle's solid. Maybe it's made of just one material, or multiple parts with the same density. As for gaps, what if they're only a few microns wide? Would we see them in these scans?"

"In a print like this, probably not. But with no grays or voids showing, I'd still bet it's all one substance."

"Then let's work with that," suggested Drummer. "If it's one material, densely packed, what could it be?"

"It's so early, and I'm tired," Aaron said in protest.

"Tell me anyway," said Drummer. "You've got a clear head right now."

Aaron relented and broke down the details in his mind. "Okay. Well, whatever it's made of would have to be conductive. It would also have to work as a power source, or at least be able to hold a charge. It would also have to be interactive, like a touchscreen."

"Anything like that exist right now?"

"Nothing I know of."

"What about glass?"

"Glass isn't conductive, D."

"Maybe a glass compound?"

Aaron rested against the counter. "I can tell you're trying to lead me into something," he said.

Drummer conceded with a nod and a shrug. "In 2020, I read an article about how tech companies were looking at glass as a data storage medium. I don't know if it's something they'd really made or just speculation, but the idea was that you could microscopically save information inside a block of glass, using lasers to 'etch' it in multiple dimensions—they called it '5-D optical storage.' It wouldn't deteriorate. It couldn't be corrupted or erased. Make it shatterproof and it could last for a million years. Take that one step further, and imagine if glass could also run software and hold a charge. As a transparent material, it can already be etched on more than just the typical X, Y, and Z axes. Imagine using power and software with this same multidimensionality? And... it would be solid."

Aaron peered at the acrylic sheet, searching for answers he knew he wouldn't see.

"A quantum computer in glass," he wondered aloud. "But even if it *could* be that, it's still just a guess."

"Isn't reverse engineering mostly guessing?"

"Yeah, but it has to start with a known. You need at least one recognizable point of reference, like the USB pinout when I made the cable for your phone. Even a solder or a wire, or a micron-wide gap, would give us a hint about where to start, but these images give us nothing."

"What if we can identify the material?"

"I don't think we can, not without breaking it down chemically, and that could destroy it. Another CT scan might show more, but until we know why *these* scans show nothing, I wouldn't know what to calibrate for."

"What about other kinds of imaging?"

Aaron shook his head. "The CT scan's the best we've got." He dropped the acrylic sheet on the counter.

"What about something theoretical?" Drummer asked. "Is there anything in the works out there in the industry?"

Aaron groaned loudly. "I appreciate what you're trying to do, D," he said. "There might be a way, but it's a long shot."

"Long shots are worth three points," Drummer replied, using a basketball reference he hoped Aaron would understand. "What is it?"

"My company focuses mostly on hard tech—chip design, that kind of thing. We've been talking about getting into biotech—making chemical reagents for medicine and vaccines, stuff like that. There's profit in it, but we're already established in the computing market. From what you've shown me about the future of phones, I think our best bet is to stay where we are. Pivoting into biotech wouldn't hurt us, but I'm convinced the big profits are in that touchscreen warlock of yours.

"I've been talking to some of my closer coworkers about holding our course, and a lot of them agree with me. We already have a big R&D budget and a production site outside Sacramento to build prototypes. We think we should expand on that, stop focusing on components and start making complete devices."

"How does that help us?" asked Drummer.

"There's a government contract for a penetrative scanner sitting on my boss's desk. The idea is that it could be used to detect miniscule threats—bomb-making materials embedded in dental work or triggers hidden in micro-electronic devices. Theoretically it could see through materials that block other kinds of scans. It could even parse out voids missed by X-rays and CTs."

"Sounds ideal."

"Doesn't it?" Aaron's tone sank a half-step. "There're two problems. We've never bid on a contract like this before. It would be ambitious considering our resources. Worse, if we couldn't build the thing and we had to give the project to someone else, it would destroy our credibility. And personally, the second problem is… one of the people with influence in making the decision is… Olson, the guy I hung out with last night."

Drummer leaned against the counter with a slight grimace, thinking. He let slip a curt exhalation.

Aaron met his eyes.

"No," Drummer said. "We'll find another way."

Aaron smiled, relieved by Drummer's reply. But he felt more than just relief—he felt joy. He knew Drummer wouldn't ask him to compromise himself again; Drummer's respect for him was clear, and it had been since day one. But to be shown such respect when the alternative path could potentially unlock the needle's secrets signaled something more: that Drummer's empathy was immutable. His concern for the younger Aaron would never be trumped by his desire to get back to the older.

"I'll keep my eye on the project," Aaron said, feeling unexpectedly energized. "Whoever gets the contract will have to work with us for components, so we won't be out of the loop. And I know how to avoid dealing with Olson again."

Drummer smiled. "You always have a plan."

"I try to think ahead," Aaron said, smiling back. "And I never do anything without a reason."

"I like that about you." Drummer stacked the scans into a short pile and pushed himself away from the counter. "It's nice outside. Let's take a walk."

THE TWO men left the apartment and strolled up the street to Golden Gate Park. There they followed a wandering path, saying little as they enjoyed the scenery. Aaron was appreciative of the quiet aimlessness.

He often felt the need to fill silence with conversation, but today he just wanted to feel like a part of his surroundings.

He and Drummer emerged from a dense throng of tree ferns at the edge of a moderately sized body of water. They continued walking around the shore.

"Stow Lake?" Aaron asked, already knowing.

"I take this walk instinctively now," said Drummer. "I know it seemed like we were just roaming around, but I wanted to bring you here to give you a surprise."

"A surprise?" Aaron asked.

"A *big* surprise."

Aaron grinned. "Well, don't hold back, D, or I'll start calling you a tease."

Drummer laughed brightly, then let his jovial expression fade. "Listen, Aaron," he said, speaking more seriously, "I meant what I said last night. I'm tired of moping around like a broken man, baking cookies. Going through my photos a while back, I was reminded of something we did together once—more than once, actually. I think it'd be fun to do it again."

"What is it?"

"Skydive."

"Uh…."

"Hear me out, because something like that… I think you'd love it, maybe even need it."

Aaron looked at Drummer askance, unsure if he should be excited or worried. "Right now? Is that your official prescription, Doctor?"

"Maybe just a shock to the system."

"Shock therapy. Even worse."

Drummer grinned. "I didn't mean to be your shrink last night, sorry. Or today for that matter. It's just… I can't ignore it when I see something hurting you. I hope I didn't come across as lecturing."

"Course not," Aaron said, dismissing Drummer's worry. He studied his expression and could see that Drummer still had quite a lot on his mind. "So, you brought us out here," Aaron prompted with a coy little nod. "You obviously have more to say. Spill it. I'm a big boy."

"All right," Drummer began with a big breath. "At the risk of 'talking like I know you,' you have this voice inside you. It tells you to compete and to win, and it compels you to be perfect at everything. The older and younger versions of you aren't too different in that respect."

Aaron chuckled lightly. "I'm a perfectionist. I can't deny something that sounds like a compliment."

"Yeah, it's a compliment. But the voice isn't always encouraging, is it? Sometimes it's an asshole. The scans you brought home last night helped us form a theory, but you still think that the way you got them was cheating."

"We don't have a theory yet," Aaron reminded him. "We have ideas. And yeah, I took it hard last night. But I'm just pushing myself like I always do."

"Nah, last night was different," Drummer said. "Everything was. That voice is usually a cheerleader. It lifts you up, and it helps you over setbacks. But last night it did exactly the opposite."

Aaron digested Drummer's words. He felt somewhat psychoanalyzed, but he also felt understood, for Drummer was hitting the mark.

"A cheerleader, huh?" Aaron asked, his coy demeanor fading as he looked inward. "How would you describe the voice now?"

"I'd say it's an angry dad at a Little League game," he said.

"Ouch."

"He's yelling at you to do more but still anticipating that you'll accomplish less. Expecting you to fail. It's a voice I've seen in you before."

"Hm," said Aaron, musing. He looked out over the lake at the boats on the water and the people walking together on the opposite shore. They seemed to have no worries in the world. Aaron wasn't sure about the voice Drummer referred to, but he couldn't deny that he often held himself to a high standard. At times he wished he weren't so driven, so he could live like the people he saw across the lake, laughing and enjoying the day without his troubles nagging him in the background of his mind. But that kind of life also seemed to lack focus.

"An angry dad," Aaron thought aloud. "So you think if you push the angry dad out of a plane, he'll stick the landing and turn back into a cheerleader?"

Drummer laughed. "You're a terrible patient. No, not exactly. But skydiving had a big impact on you once, even before I was around to dish out unrequested therapy. You did it for the first time after leaving Grant.

From what you told me once, you hated yourself for that relationship, and you were looking for ways to punish yourself for what it did to you—what you thought you *let him* do to you. You thought throwing yourself out of a plane would be a guaranteed failure. You could land on your face, or break your legs, or even get killed. You didn't even want to enjoy it. You just wanted to terrorize yourself."

"Sounds like a very angry dad," Aaron admitted, feeling a bit ashamed for the version of himself in Drummer's story. "I assume I came out of it okay?"

"You did. Because there was no Little League game after all. Nothing to actually yell at yourself for. No competition. Nothing to win. When you were up in that plane you realized, *this is just an experience*. Grant wasn't there anymore. It was just you. Skydiving could be something to lose yourself in—and maybe find yourself as well."

"What does that mean?"

"*That*," said Drummer with a touch of mystery in his tone, "is for you to find out tomorrow."

Aaron looked over at him. "Tomorrow?"

"No time like the present."

"Skydiving it is, then." Aaron winked at him. "You have a real way with words, Doctor. Has anyone ever told you that?"

"Once or twice."

THE NEXT morning, Aaron and Drummer drove north out of San Francisco, leaving the city for the first time since moving there ten months earlier. They crossed the Golden Gate Bridge, passed through the forested Marin peninsula into Napa County, and wound their way through the trellised hills of wine country. The air was clear and warm, the perfect conditions.

Off the main highway, they came to a small regional airfield at the end of a semirural, tree-lined road, situated in a wide valley open to the north and south and flanked by short, grassy foothills to the east and west. To have called the facility an "airport" would've been an overstatement, for its services were minimal. There were no terminals, no check-in counters, and no security lines. Furthermore, with only one narrow runway and a single hangar, it could clearly accommodate only the smallest of aircraft.

Aaron stopped his car in a graveled area beside a chain-link fence, beneath a sign that read, PARK HERE. He shut off the engine, but he didn't get out.

Drummer gave him an inquisitive glance.

"This place is really small," Aaron said before Drummer could speak a word.

"It's no United Airlines hub," Drummer agreed. "What were you expecting?"

"I don't know. I guess I just thought it would be… bigger. Maybe a paved parking lot. Without that 'park here' sign, I probably would've driven right out onto the tarmac. And is that the only hangar?"

Drummer laughed lightly. "This isn't the kind of place with moving sidewalks and priority boarding. I know it looks rustic, but they pretty much just do skydiving here." He reached out and mussed Aaron's blond hair, adding, "Let's go, scaredy-cat."

Drummer left the car, followed by a hesitant Aaron. They crossed the gravel lot to the hangar.

Inside was a small desk and a makeshift seating area for about six people. Behind it was the bulk of the hangar, reserved for aircraft maintenance and storage. Several people—experienced skydivers, presumably—milled about in conversation.

"Morning, gentlemen!" came a deep, jovial voice.

A tall, sturdy man in his early thirties entered the hangar and rounded the desk. His prematurely graying beard framed a large, natural smile.

Drummer gave Aaron a nudge with his elbow.

"We're checking in," said Aaron. "The reservation should be under Aaron Hayes."

The man found their names on a printout tacked to a corkboard on the wall. "Aaron and Drummer for a tandem jump?"

"That's us."

"Welcome," he said, shaking their hands. "I'm Vin. You're a little early, but no problem. I'll be one of the instructors taking you up, and Reg over there in the yellow shirt, he'll be the other one." He pointed to a similarly built man chatting with the group in the hangar.

"If you want to go early," Vin continued, "the pilot's here, and Reg and I are good to go anytime. There's a safety video to watch, some paperwork to fill out. We'll do some one-on-one instruction. And when we go up, we'll talk you through the entire jump so you know what to expect. It's a lot of fun."

"I think we're ready," said Aaron. He took a big breath, trying to psych himself up.

"Great!" Vin chirped, clapping his large hands. He handed Drummer and Aaron a clipboard each and a packet of papers, which included a description of the flight up, the responsibilities and expectations of tandem jumpers, and a series of liability waivers containing some very scary words.

Aaron and Drummer reviewed them, watched the video, put pen to paper, and returned to Vin.

"Good to go?" he asked.

"Haven't scared us off," Aaron said.

Aaron handed him the clipboards and their identification. While Drummer's ID was fake, it was convincing. Vin glanced at it to confirm his name and age, then returned it without question.

With the formalities complete, Vin led the two men to a grassy field outside the hangar to wait for the arrival of their aircraft, where Reg joined them to help conduct their preflight training. Aaron and Drummer were fitted with tight, heavy harnesses that wrapped completely around them, over their shoulders and between their legs, but didn't restrict their movement. Aaron felt it oddly comforting, like being swaddled in a security blanket.

"You holding yourself together?" Drummer asked.

Aaron was being unusually quiet. He looked over at Drummer and saw a look of calm expectation in his eyes. It was like the gaze of a father figure, hopeful and excited for the experience to come. But there was something else nestled within that look of platonic pride.

Unable to identify it, Aaron merely smiled back. "I'm okay, D. Thanks."

The sound of a thrumming propeller caught their attention. A small silver airplane was rolling toward them on the tarmac. It was a single-prop craft with top-mounted swings, which looked like it could seat a maximum of four passengers. A top-hinged door on the side of the fuselage was open, flush against the wing's underside.

Vin and Reg connected their parachuted harnesses to Aaron's and Drummer's at each of their four attachment points. Then, once the plane had come to a stop, the four men climbed aboard.

There were no seats for passengers, only the one for the pilot. Behind him, the cabin space was literally empty—a flat metal floor with no embellishment. Vin and Aaron shuffled to the back on their butts and sat down, facing forward. Drummer and Reg climbed in afterward, closed the door, and sat facing backward, directly behind the pilot. They all did their best to find room for their legs. It seemed like a rather makeshift setup to Aaron, but he tried to relax.

The plane taxied to the runway, and with nary a pause the engine raged, throwing the propeller into a nearly invisible spin. The aircraft raced forward and took off within seconds. The engine was loud inside the unpressurized, uninsulated cabin, and as the plane ascended, a light breeze whistled through gaps in the window seals. The air grew steadily colder.

Aaron felt like he was in an old convertible sedan tearing down a highway at a hundred miles per hour, rattling and vibrating, nearly shaking itself apart. He craned his neck, trying to get a look out the windows, but from his seated position on the floor, he could see little more than the sky. He caught a glimpse of the horizon whenever the plane made a turn, but it didn't help to calm him.

Maybe it's for the best, he thought, *not knowing exactly how high we are.*

He caught Drummer staring at him. This time in those pale green eyes he saw tranquil contemplation, an extension of the fatherly gaze he'd noticed on the ground. It didn't chase away Aaron's worry, but it did provide him with much-needed comfort. It was enough to know that he wasn't doing this alone.

He gazed back at Drummer.

Drummer's soothing expression expanded into a wide, delighted smile.

Soon, far sooner than Aaron had anticipated, the plane reached its target altitude of 12,000 feet. Aaron had told himself he'd be braced and ready when the time came, but now that it had, he wasn't sure.

There was no time to dither. Drummer and Reg were already climbing to their feet. Reg flipped open the fuselage door, and a torrent of wind fought its way into the cabin. If the plane had been that old convertible in Aaron's mind, the fabric top had suddenly ripped clean off.

Drummer and Reg teetered at the doorway's edge, readying for their jump. Drummer looked over at Aaron one last time, gave him a wink and a curt salute, and after a short countdown with Reg, he jumped from the plane.

Aaron felt a wellspring of excitement at seeing Drummer leap into the abyss. But that feeling was quickly sidelined by a new, unidentifiable sensation—he was numb and unable to move. The time to jump had come, but with Drummer no longer on the plane, he felt uncertain and alone.

His mind jumped back unexpectedly to a specific summer day when he had been seven years old—the day he'd first picked up a skateboard. With no one to supervise or bear witness at the time, he'd shakily rolled down the long, steep twenty-yard driveway of his childhood home. He'd been terrified but also committed to the act.

The same conditions presented themselves now.

That's when he realized what he felt.

Fear.

For the first time in ages, he was feeling real fear.

But what am I afraid of? he asked himself, struggling to find an answer. *Am I afraid of dying? I don't think so. Am I afraid of landing flat on my face? I don't care about that.*

As he debated with himself, he heard Drummer's reminders in his mind. He wasn't in competition with anyone here, no prize to win. This skydive was just an experience, something to lose himself in—and perhaps find himself as well.

Then what am I afraid of? he wondered again.

The answer came to him as he recalled that first precipitous ride on his skateboard. There had been no competition that time, either. His goal had been merely to make it to the bottom of the driveway—just to try, just to get there, even if he broke a leg. He'd committed himself, and he'd leaned on that commitment, using it to help him climb on the board, push himself forward, and let go.

He had no memory of the ride down the driveway, of trusting his instincts to carry him along. But he did recall picking himself up off the ground when it was done, turning around and looking back at where he'd been, and hearing himself roar with joy and pride at the realization that he'd made it. And now, aboard this loud, hollowed-out little plane, he understood himself better.

He didn't fear the jump at all, or even the landing. He wasn't afraid of throwing himself out the door, or of breaking himself on the ground at the end. What he feared was the space in between. He feared that long driveway—now 12,000 feet high—that unknown, shaky ride, and the untethered fall to earth.

He feared the letting go.

Letting go of control.

Letting go of his expectations.

Letting go of the promise he'd made to himself to save Drummer singlehandedly.

Maybe Drummer knew this already, he thought. *Maybe this is why he brought me here. To put me face-to-face with the part of myself that can't allow mistakes—the angry dad at a baseball game—and silence him.*

Aaron had always told himself that he had no fear, that his ambition and confidence could carry him through any challenge. But he now saw this boast for the lie that it had become. His ambition and his confidence had both faltered in the face of his months-long stagnation, leading to self-recrimination and bad judgment. And it had all been out of fear.

Fear of disappointing himself.

Fear of letting Drummer down.

Fear of not being able to do everything on his own.

Aaron forced himself to his feet. He moved with Vin toward the open door and stood at the edge. Nothing lay between himself and the ground but the crystal-clear vastness of the sky.

Aaron looked down.

Just fall. Leave your fears on the plane and just fall. When you land—even if you land on your face—you can look back up at where you were and know that you did it. And after that, you'll know that you can do anything. You can convince your company to build the scanner. You can decipher the needle. You can send Drummer home. And you can do it all without competition or compromise.

His countdown with Vin was brief.

With the image of his seven-year-old self in his mind, tearing down the driveway with the wheels of his skateboard spinning and rattling beneath his feet, Aaron leaped into the sky.

A fury of wind hit him with a loud, disorienting rush. He was surrounded by everything and nothing as the entirety of the world tumbled around him, howling in his ears and spinning in his eyes. Vin steadied them, then flipped them over, facing skyward, and held that pose.

Aaron stared wide-eyed at the plane as it sailed away above him. He didn't feel like he was falling, but that view of the plane receding demonstrated quite clearly that he was plummeting at incredible speed.

"Oh wow," he gasped, watching the plane—the top of the driveway—shrinking away. His anxiety flew off with it, leaving only awe in its wake.

Vin rolled the two of them over and eased them into a slight forward tilt, bringing the world into view. A massive swath of California spread out beneath them, bathed in brilliant sunlight. Clear blue skies craned over the Pacific Ocean to the west. Billowing clouds hovered over the Sierra Nevada mountain range to the east. Far to the north, the snow-capped peak of Mount Lassen could be seen brushing the sky, while to the south, rising from the earth, were the tall towers of San Francisco. Surrounding the city, the bay and ocean waters glittered in the light like silver mercury.

Aaron lost himself in that view, falling into the resplendent ether like he'd been hurled into a living, breathing work of art. Green, cultivated hills. Trees in rows, crisscrossing countless vineyards. A dark, forested ridgeline separating the valley from the coast. Clouds, mist, fog, and haze. And directly beneath him—clear and distinct—the airstrip, the nearby highway, his bright red car, and all the other tangible elements of his modern life, reduced to near nothingness in size and importance.

The entire world unfolded beneath him in expansive miniature as he careened through the sky, seeming to not grow any closer to the ground at all. He took it in, let it fill him, and as he did, he felt an unexpected unshackling. Tears welled up in his eyes, and he laughed aloud.

Restrained by nothing.

Concerned with nothing.

Fearing nothing.

He was utterly free.

Every burden he'd ever put upon himself, every expectation, everything he clung to, and everything that clung to him—the stresses that followed him from the hour of waking to the moment of sleep—disappeared, replaced by this visceral, overwhelming confluence of sight and sound.

He could've lived in that state of heightened exhilaration forever, but it was already time to open the parachute. He'd thought the experience would be finished once that happened, but he was mistaken. It would merely evolve.

He felt a strong tug on the harness as the chute flew open, which brought home just how fast he'd been falling. The howling, audible rush disappeared, replaced by a sublime silence. The thrill of free fall shifted into a sudden peace as the parachute carried him over the wind. None of the sounds of the earth could reach him, for he was still nowhere near the ground.

Aaron laughed again and kept laughing as Vin pulled on the steering lines. The two of them cut through the sky, sweeping and weaving, literally flying. He could see the top of Drummer's parachute below, a bright red, billowy rectangle swooping over the landscape, nearing the grassy field beside the airstrip where they had started.

Then Vin allowed Aaron to take control. As he gripped the lines in his hands and turned the chute himself, he remembered the day after his first skateboard ride down the driveway. By the end of that second day, he'd learned to stop at the sidewalk without falling. He'd found control, vanquished his fear. The birth of his seemingly unshakable confidence had not been far behind.

He returned the lines to Vin, who then brought the two men into one last wide turn, angling toward the grassy field beside the runway.

Now much closer to the ground, coming in for their landing, Aaron became acutely aware of their incredible speed. The sounds of the world came rushing back as he neared the surface—the wind in the trees, the birds seemingly everywhere, the vehicles whispering on the highway beyond, and the voices of people outside the hangar.

Vin told him to raise his legs in case they needed to land on their butts, but then they slowed and reared back, like a bird stopping in midair just before touching down. Aaron was told he could lower his feet, and before he knew it, he was standing on the ground.

A perfect landing.

Aaron laughed again as Vin disconnected his harness. He wiped his eyes, still chuckling. The world hummed. He could feel the warm wind on his tingling face and the rapid beat of his heart in his chest. He had returned to Earth, right back where he started, but everything was different now.

Drummer hurried toward him with an enormous smile. It was the same look Aaron had seen before the jump, but now it was imbued with hope—hope that Drummer had done right by him. In Drummer's eyes Aaron could see the proud father figure, as well as the insightful therapist of the day before and the caring companion of two nights prior. He could also see—unmistakably—a man he loved.

Aaron continued to laugh, tenderly and tellingly, as Drummer wrapped his arms around him. Though words were evasive, he held Drummer close. Graced by the gentle breeze and grateful for this exhilarating experience, he felt a sense of shared devotion and an unexpected yearning.

Soon after, they drove home.

On the road, Aaron said little. His thoughts were not empty, but rather clear and open, without prejudice. It was a state of mind that he'd never known before. He'd always coexisted with some form of self-judgment, the voice in his head that Drummer had spoken about simultaneously encouraging and biting. But now he merely existed with his thoughts.

He drove for several miles before he felt inclined to say anything. And even then, he held back. At one point he opened his mouth, preparing to speak, but stopped, smiled, let out a subdued laugh, and said nothing.

"What's on your mind?" Drummer asked with a knowing grin.

Aaron shook his head with mild embarrassment. "I'm just thinking about what you said yesterday."

"Oh? What was that?"

"You know what I mean."

"I have an idea," said Drummer. "I saw the smile on your face when you landed… and the tears on your cheeks."

"Yeah," Aaron admitted quietly. He cleared his throat and continued. "I started to laugh on the way down. But we're talking goofy, stupid laughter, not nervous, scared laughter. I was scared on the plane, but during freefall I felt kinda… liberated. I'm usually confident, but I guess that confidence isn't absolute. Deep down I know I'm not perfect, but I still try to be. I'm always aware of eyes on me. But up there, I didn't care how I looked or how I sounded. And I just laughed."

"You never have to care about what people think of you," Drummer reminded him.

"I've never found it easy to *not* care," Aaron answered. "I'm ambitious, and my ambition demands my loyalty—'do what I say or you won't succeed,' it tells me. And a lot of that means keeping up appearances. I go to extremes to impress people. I was the 'alpha' with my skater friends, to use a term I hate. They did whatever I said. Hell, I don't even listen to Metallica, but I wear the shirt. I play the part. At work, sometimes I say too much, explain too much, defend myself too much—all to demonstrate that I know what I'm talking about before anyone can challenge me. But I think it's catching up to me, because at some point during the past year, my ambition… well. I guess it decided I wasn't being loyal enough."

"For what it's worth," said Drummer, "I've always been impressed by your ambition. It's benevolent, and for the most part you do a good job at keeping it from leading you to dark places."

"For the most part, yeah," Aaron agreed tentatively. "You know, last month we hired a new woman named Taraji. She's only thirty, but she's so smart, so calm, so direct and to the point. Our field is heavily dominated by men, but she's got something no one else has. She's kind and personable, but still strong and professional. She'll sit in a meeting, quietly taking it all in, and then she'll say something that puts everything in perspective. When she's silent, people make an extra effort to get her attention. Then, when she speaks, they listen. She's perfectly effective. Do you know why?"

Drummer didn't answer. He merely shook his head and allowed Aaron to continue.

"She's effective because confidence is quiet," Aaron said. "Confidence doesn't need reassurance from others. And Taraji doesn't need their approval when she already approves of herself. As for me, well… cockiness is loud. And all my life I've been very, very loud."

"You still know your stuff," Drummer assured him. "That's why they value you."

"Value's great, D. But respect… that's something else. Taraji had a hard time her first week. Some people talked behind her back and didn't even try to get to know her. But her decisions have been smart and spot-on. She and I have different life experiences, and in a lot of ways, hers have been harder. But her confidence is much more genuine. I respect that, and the people I work with who can look past their biases… they respect it too. I want people to see me like that, not like some arrogant kid with a dozen gold medals around his neck, but as a confident contributor they can't live without."

"That's an interesting take," said Drummer. "I'm impressed to hear it coming from you."

Aaron smiled inwardly, grateful for Drummer's acknowledgment. "Thanks. But I have a feeling you knew what you were doing today, pushing me out of that plane."

Drummer grinned. "I didn't push you at all. You took that leap all by yourself."

UPON THEIR return to San Francisco, Aaron saw the vistas of his life through clearer eyes. He sensed two parallel paths taking shape ahead of him—one at work and the other at home. He intended to follow them both.

At work, he took a cue from Taraji to refine his professional voice. He listened to people more and spoke less, and in doing so, he found that he understood them better and judged them less often. As a result, he appeared wiser and older, and his coworkers started to see him not only worthy of praise, but also attention.

To Taraji, this demonstrated Aaron's capacity for growth, and it put him at the top of her list of trusted colleagues. It also gave rise to a prosperous collaboration between them as they petitioned the company together to win the government contract for the scanner. This had the added effect of reducing Olson's influence in the decision and eliminating his importance to Aaron's goals.

On the home front, Aaron suggested to Drummer that they buy a house. It would give them greater control over their environment, but more importantly, it would enable Aaron to live the role of the man he now saw himself becoming—a man with an eye on his future and with a plan to get there. He'd already been researching home ownership prior to the skydive, so the venture progressed quickly. Escrow closed in only two months.

The house he chose was a sleek, low-profile California Modern "Eichler" house—a design style featuring glass walls and post-and-beam construction. It stood in the upscale Clarendon Heights neighborhood just below Sutro Tower, with a striking view of downtown and the bay. It was not a large home, and despite the affluent location, it wasn't ostentatious. It was big enough for two people, with a workroom for the needle, and offered privacy. It stood on its own lot, flanked by narrow side yards and tall juniper trees. A spacious deck ran the length of the back of the house outside the living room, a feature that Drummer expressed a great love for.

By the time the two men had moved into the house, Aaron was satisfied with his choices, and with his life's new direction. He hadn't entirely lost his loud cockiness, but it was taking a back seat to his quiet confidence. At home, he developed a greater sense of partnership with Drummer. He no longer saw himself as the younger version of an older man, but as his own person—someone who might one day become that older ideal.

He still felt some guilt over the length of time he was taking to deconstruct the needle, but he also vowed to face his failures and celebrate his successes with Drummer as they came. The angry Little League dad never came back. In fact, the proverbial games ended, replaced by less competitive adult pursuits.

On the first night in their new home, with their belongings moved in but hardly unpacked, Aaron and Drummer lay in bed, sharing the familiarity of each other's warmth. Though their original romantic relationship wouldn't officially start for many years yet, at times like this, Aaron felt as if it already had. Immediately after the skydive, when he'd held Drummer on the airfield, he'd felt love for the first time. The feeling had risen in him suddenly and powerfully, and it had not waned in the weeks that followed.

Now, with their hands clasped loosely together beneath the sheets, Aaron tried to find the words to express what he was feeling. He wanted Drummer to know that he saw their relationship as more than just an intimate, cooperative enterprise. There was more to it for him than just sex, friendship, and a common goal—and he believed, or hoped, that Drummer might feel the same way.

But he worried about the consequences of saying any of it.

What if I say something and then we decipher the needle tomorrow?

In such an eventuality, Drummer would return to the future with eight years to go before 2010. And though Aaron would meet Drummer's counterpart then, the Drummer he knew today would not become himself for another decade. Cumulatively, that was eighteen years in the future. Was it wise to introduce a deeper layer of connection now, knowing that this version of their relationship could end at any time?

Aaron silenced his anxieties and focused on the peace he'd found. With this in mind, and braced for any reaction, he decided to say what he wanted to say.

"I love you, D," he whispered tenderly into the darkness.

Drummer's chest rose with his breath.

Aaron thought for a moment that he was about to reply.

But as Drummer exhaled with a rough, subtle snore, it was clear to Aaron that he'd fallen asleep.

Aaron felt sadness at this, but also relief. He'd said what he wanted to say, and he was proud of himself for it, but when it came down to things, he knew full well that his relationship with Drummer didn't need more complications. There was already something wonderful between them, and though it lacked mutual expression—beyond flirtatious, wordless glances and sexual adventure that teased at lovemaking without calling it by name—Aaron deemed it sufficiently reciprocated.

He also wondered if his need to express himself tonight might've been a side effect of his knowledge of pending world events. Drummer had warned him that hard times were on the horizon, after all. It wasn't so impossible to believe that—like a man five minutes before closing time desperately looking for someone to go home with, Aaron was grasping for a deeper connection before the world changed for the worse.

He closed his eyes, trying to excise Drummer's warnings of coming tragedy from his thoughts. He slipped into a semi-doze but never quite found sleep. Instead, his mind conjured ghosts. They haunted him through the night, until he awoke the next day on September eleventh, 2001, to an empty bed, the sound of urgent voices emanating from the living room television, and a sad awareness that not only had those hard times suddenly come, but the opportunity to express himself had passed.

He found Drummer in tears in the living room.

And their lives changed.

MIDDLE AGE

Middle age should have come for him, but he did not notice, for it did not notice him. With this he was content, until the day that time forcibly manifested itself around his eyes and in the eyes of those that looked at him, and in the words they used when they spoke to him, and in the actions they took when they thought of him.

Those who'd known him when he was young were gone. And the effortless charm of his youth receded beneath a middle-aged shell.

He was not old, nor was he young, but suspended somewhere in between, carried along by time's indifferent current. This unyielding forward motion terrified him, for he now had fewer years ahead than behind and more knowledge undiscovered than brought to light.

But he also had experience, and the poise needed to further his goals through taking and not asking, and by ignoring the very people who judged him. They were only workers now, and the more they regarded him as outside their circle, the more they unwittingly permitted him to become their master.

CHAPTER 12
THE ABSTRACT AND THE ABSOLUTE

TIME IS an abstract but also an absolute. It is intangible yet measurable. It is a variable but a constant. We cannot touch it, but we know it touches us by the marks it leaves: an aged face, a changed house, and sometimes, a dream made real.

Time is an abstract—"then."

And it's an absolute—"now."

This is how ordinary people live.

Aaron and Drummer were not ordinary people. For them, the abstract and the absolute—the then and now—were synonymous. They were places they'd been and places they would yet be. They were memories to be made, and in Drummer's case, remade. They were destinations, crossroads, and dots to be connected. They were tragedies and triumphs, feared although expected. Hindsight was foresight, while somehow lacking insight.

Time touched the men and left its mark. Drummer acclimated. Aaron calmed. And from each other, they learned. Drummer discovered a youthfulness he thought he'd lost, and Aaron embraced a maturity he'd never known he had. They met somewhere in the middle, living with shared spontaneity and responsibility and a connection best described as devotion, but purposefully suspended somewhere short of something else.

The needle, meanwhile, remained a mystery. An MRI scan revealed nothing new. Additional CT scans presented the same results. The device stayed a stubborn enigma, committed to obstruction, as if consciously aware of their attempts to dissect it. Locked in a safe most of the time, it brooded and waited to be brought out periodically for study, revealing nothing before being returned to its dark sanctuary.

Aaron and Drummer's agreement to "not get too close" solidified. It manifested as an invisible wall between them, a durable, semipermeable membrane that allowed the free passage of flirtation, admiration, and sexual exploration, but filtered out infatuation, passion, and love. They cared for each other. But the wall they erected demanded that they avoid the language that gave that care meaning.

The seasons came and went.
Time touched the world,
And the world changed.
Aaron and Drummer watched,
And worked,
And lived,
And the wall stood firm,
As "then" became "now,"
And the abstract became the absolute.

IT WAS early morning on a midsummer Saturday in 2005 when Drummer stood in the living room, staring out the window at downtown San Francisco. He peered through a telescope at the skyline. Many new buildings had sprung up recently, including one hauntingly familiar structure: the condominium tower south of Market Street where he had lived with Aaron for nine years, ending so abruptly in 2020.

By daylight the building appeared finished, with every concrete floor poured and the glass façade in place. One could be forgiven for thinking the building inhabited, until nightfall when the dark windows revealed the structure to still be empty.

Whether illuminated by daylight or moonlight, the shimmering addition to the expanding skyline was a disquieting sight for Drummer. Over the past four years as the structure had gone up—day by day and week by week—he'd felt more and more keenly that the life he'd left behind was racing ever faster toward him. Eventually the world of the future would catch up with him, and Aaron would leave him to become part of it.

It was a disturbing thought, but the details remaking the outside world offered some comfort. Each new building, each new movie, and every global event demonstrated that the past and the present were conforming to his memories of the future, that his journey backward in time had not significantly altered history. This gave him confidence that when his counterpart contacted Aaron in another five years, everything would be as it should—whether Drummer himself had returned to 2020 or not.

"Looking out there again, I see," said Aaron, entering the room. He'd been on a call with his parents and now set his phone on the coffee table.

Drummer stepped back from the telescope. "Just checking out the view," he said.

He was not a good liar.

"We still have five years. That life out there will wait."

"I know," said Drummer, shrugging off a subtle malaise. "It's just weird seeing the condo go up."

Aaron stepped around him and peered through the telescope. "What bothers you about it?" he asked. "That it's a beginning of something, or an end?"

"Maybe it's just a deadline," said Drummer.

Aaron grunted. "Can you tell me which unit's ours?"

"The actual condo? Twenty-fifth floor. Northwest corner."

Aaron trained the telescope on the said location. "A corner? Fancy."

"It's simple, but we make it nice."

"I've seen the pics, remember?" Aaron stood and swung the telescope away, then sat on the arm of the couch. "I know what you're thinking," he said gently.

"You do?" Drummer asked.

"I do. You're thinking that in five years I'll leave. And you'll still be here, looking at that condo out there, wondering what I'm up to."

Drummer shifted his gaze away from the tower but said nothing.

"I'm sending you home," Aaron insisted.

"I haven't given up."

"I know. I just don't like seeing you without hope. Because your hope is what keeps me going."

"There it is again," said Drummer. "That charming, benevolent ambition couched in a cliché."

Aaron smiled at the compliment. "I have good news," he said. "I was going to save it until we were on the ship, but I think you'll want to hear it now."

"What is it?"

"You remember the patent cases stalled in the courts? The last one was just dismissed. We've been given the green light to start." Aaron spoke his last few words with barely contained excitement. Construction on the scanner had been approved three years earlier, but patent disputes had prevented development from moving forward.

"You can build it now?" asked Drummer, brightening considerably. "How long will it take?"

"That's the rub, D. A couple of years."

"Still, it's great news. Thanks for telling me."

"I could see you needed it. The advisory committee will meet in a few weeks to talk about next steps. I'll do what I can to speed things up."

"Thanks, Aaron. You really amaze me."

Aaron feigned a cartoon-like shyness and added, "Aww, shucks, you so crazy."

The two men laughed together and shared a smile. They held each other's gaze, which happened often but wasn't something they ever spoke about. Drummer looked away just as that gaze was about to become uncomfortable, as it threatened to put pressure on the emotional wall they'd erected between them.

"Are we ready?" Aaron asked, standing.

Drummer indicated a lineup of suitcases on the floor near the hallway. "All packed," he said. "Fourteen days… this'll be the longest I've ever been away from the house."

"Me too," said Aaron. "I'm glad you suggested this trip; I hate the thought of you being here alone all the time. A question, though. When you did this in 2015 with the other me, did you make the same plans?"

Drummer made a hand gesture that mimicked a tipping scale. "Yes and no. We're taking the same route to Hawaii and back, but we're on a different cruise line, and we're going on different excursions. Ah, that reminds me…." He reached into his coat pocket and pulled out a blue Canadian passport. "Thank you for this," Drummer said, flipping through its blank sheets. He studied the data page containing his photograph and personal information. Half of the details, including his birthday and middle name, were necessarily altered, but the document itself looked legitimate.

"It's surprisingly genuine-looking," he added.

"That's because it *is* genuine, D. Don't ask me what I had to do to get it. Just remember… when that's in your pocket, you're a Canadian citizen."

"Duly noted," he said, putting it away.

Aaron and Drummer collected their suitcases and called a taxi, which carried them through town and dropped them off at Pier 35 on the Embarcadero waterfront. The pier housed a minimalist cruise terminal desperately in need of an upgrade. In the coming years it would be replaced by a larger modern terminal at Pier 27, from where Aaron would take this same cruise with Drummer's counterpart in 2015. Drummer studied the older structure, committing it to memory, aware that it would soon be replaced. He pulled out a digital camera and took a few pictures for posterity.

The two men breezed through check-in. Drummer's passport cleared inspection, and they quickly found their way to their stateroom— number D520 on the Dolphin Deck, level nine.

"That was easier than I thought," said Drummer.

"It was," said Aaron. "But for a second, when you held out that passport, I thought you were about to blurt out, 'Leeloo Dallas, Multipass.'"

Drummer snickered. "I wasn't that nervous, you little shit." He grabbed a pillow from the bed and lightly swatted him with it.

Aaron laughed in retreat. He opened the sliding glass door at the far end of the room and stepped onto the small, sunlit balcony. Drummer came out behind him and put his arms around him. The view was spectacular. All of downtown was visible, including Aaron's office and the Hyatt Regency farther on. Drummer's counterpart surely no longer worked there; the breakup with Nate had been a turning point in many ways, personal and professional.

"This is real nice," Aaron said.

"Only the best for my rich, smart, hot, future boyfriend," Drummer said. He felt Aaron slump ever so slightly and immediately regretted it. He rarely spoke of the future Aaron anymore, and bringing him up now felt insensitive, as if he were somehow drawing a comparison with the younger Aaron in his arms. Drummer vowed not to bring up Aaron's future self again.

With the coming of late afternoon, the cruise ship pushed away from the Port of San Francisco and began its journey through the bay toward the ocean. From the water, San Francisco had the appearance of a seaside utopia—forty-nine square miles of parks and monuments laid out over rolling hills, nestled in a dense grid of old-world Victorian charm. As the ship rounded the wharf, the towers of downtown disappeared behind Telegraph Hill. Then came Fort Mason, followed by the Marina Green, the Palace of Fine Arts, and finally the forested hills of the Presidio.

Drummer and Aaron stood at the railing on their balcony, watching the view roll by.

"It's a shame we don't get to see the city like this more often," Drummer mused.

Aaron didn't answer. He merely reached out and took Drummer's hand. "What time's dinner?"

"Seven thirty," said Drummer. "I'm actually looking forward to this—sitting with other people."

"Dinner with four strangers," said Aaron with lighthearted foreboding. "What if we're put at a table with people we hate? Or worse, people you know?"

"I doubt that'll happen," said Drummer, "but I've got a fake moustache in my bag, just in case."

"No, you don't!"

"Of course I do," said Drummer, playing it up. "I've also got a trench coat and a big fat wig, all tousled and ratty. And the backstory! You want to hear it? Sure you do. Get this: I go door-to-door in Calgary selling hot tubs. Priceless, right? Canada's cold, buddy. I make a killing."

Aaron covered his face with his hands and laughed. "I hope you're kidding," he said.

"Hey, it's a good job," Drummer insisted.

The ship passed beneath the Golden Gate Bridge and headed out to sea. The city settled into the horizon, and before long, open ocean surrounded the vessel in every direction. The air cooled, and Aaron and Drummer went inside.

A couple of hours remained before dinner, so the two men used the time to explore the massive ship. It consisted of thirteen decks with a capacity of 2700 passengers and over a thousand crew. There were two giant theaters inside, several swimming pools on the top levels, three dance clubs, and a grand five-story atrium at the ship's heart. Aaron and Drummer got lost once or twice but found their way back to their stateroom in time to prepare for dinner.

Drummer was excited for this adventure, to say the least. He and Aaron had taken a dozen short trips together, but this was the first time they'd enjoy two solid weeks of uninterrupted retreat. Aaron had had matching tuxedos fitted for them both, especially for the occasion.

"This is really doing something hot and sparkly for my ego," said Drummer, standing before a mirror in his crisp black-and-white attire. "I've gotten used to tank tops and cargo shorts."

"Maybe it's time to step up your wardrobe."

Drummer turned to find Aaron standing beside him dressed in the same style of tuxedo, but somehow wearing it better.

"Oh, wow," said Drummer. "You look amazing."

"Aww, thanks, ya big lug."

"No, I mean it. Where's the red carpet?"

"You seem flustered, D," Aaron said. "Maybe you should lie down."

"I think I can hold myself together," Drummer said with a wink, "but you're going to have everyone in that dining room calling you Chippendale by the end of the night."

SOON AFTER, Aaron and Drummer made their way to a large banquet-style restaurant near the front of the ship. The tables were configured for groups of six to eight people, in a setup known as "traditional dining," where passengers were seated at the same tables and at the same time each night, with the same waiters and the same tablemates for the duration of the cruise. Aaron had no idea how this would turn out. He was a bit concerned for Drummer's comfort level around so many people, but Drummer had insisted that he couldn't pass up the opportunity for a little unpredictability in his otherwise predictable world.

The restaurant host greeted them at the door and led them through the room toward their table. As they approached, they saw that two of their tablemates had already arrived—a woman in her mid-to-late sixties and a man who was perhaps seventy. She wore a cream-colored lacy dress reminiscent of the early twentieth century Edwardian style, but with updated lines. The man beside her wore a well-cut tan suit with a stylish dark brown tie. They looked like they belonged together, and the timeless appearance of their outfits evoked a bygone age.

When it was clear to the woman that Aaron and Drummer were to be their tablemates, she smiled broadly and clapped her hands in rapid little pats. "Oh, I'm so glad!" she chirped as the two men approached. She waved her hands at the closest of the four empty chairs, looking excited enough to burst. "Please, sit! When I saw the two of you come in, I said to my husband, 'look at those two, I hope they're at our table.' And now here you are!"

The man sitting beside her leaned forward, raising his eyebrows exaggeratedly. "We've both had a lot of coffee."

Aaron didn't know what to make of the couple's enthusiasm, but it was welcoming, if heavily caffeinated.

"Well," he replied with bright eyes, "I hope we're entertaining."

"Oh, I have no doubt," said the woman. "We go on about three cruises a year, and so far, the people we've been seated with have been *so boring*. We're dying to have a conversation with someone who doesn't talk about their terrible relatives or their ungrateful children. And you two already look like something else."

"I suppose we have no choice but to take that as a compliment," Drummer said.

"As you should, because it is! I'm Lorraine, by the way. This is my husband, Francis, and before we go any further, let's talk about *this*!"

Lorraine made a wide, circling hand gesture in Aaron and Drummer's direction and added, "The two of you, in your matching tuxes… adorable!"

Aaron lightly nudged Drummer, feeling validated for the choice of formalwear.

"How about we introduce ourselves first," he suggested.

"Oh, my goodness, of course," said Lorraine. "My apologies."

"My name's Aaron."

"Aaron," Lorraine said, pondering the sound of it. "Yes, you look like an Aaron." She turned to Drummer. "And who's your dashing companion?"

"This is Drummer."

She tapped her chin, appearing to roll the name over in her head. "Hm, you don't look like a Drummer to me. You look like… lead guitar."

"Groovy bass," Francis insisted.

"I don't think there's such a thing as groovy bass, dear."

"Tell that to Marvin Gaye."

"*Anyhow*," Lorraine continued, "I know people say, 'never apologize in advance,' but you'll have to excuse Francis and me tonight. We're bored, lonely, and we feel like we've been on a go-nowhere treadmill since we retired in '98, so we're probably going to talk a lot and ask too many questions."

"I'm fine with questions," said Aaron. "But this big guy next to me may be a bit tight-lipped."

"No, I'm okay with it," said Drummer. "I'll just dance around anything I find too probing. And I can always lie."

Lorraine's eyes popped with intrigue. "Just promise me that if you do lie, you'll make it *absolutely titillating*."

"A promise I can keep," he replied spiritedly.

"Great!" she exclaimed, clasping her hands together. "Now, let's get back to the two of you, your tuxedos, and what we're all doing here. I hope this doesn't come across as too nosy, but are the two of you… *together*, or is this a father-son sort of trip?"

"Uh," sputtered Aaron. Already, one of the very first questions of the night was one of the hardest to answer. "You could say we're together, I suppose."

"You suppose? Well, either you are or you aren't, my handsome young friend."

Aaron looked to Drummer.

"We *are*… together," said Drummer, a little stilted, "but this is our first time on a trip like this. We don't get out much."

Aaron breathed an inward sigh of relief. Drummer's answer was sufficiently deflective without seeming evasive.

Lorraine nodded. "I get it. Some couples are social butterflies, but others prefer their own company. You two give me the latter impression, and the matching tuxes put an exclamation point on it. Now, if only Francis here would wear a matching outfit with me sometime."

Francis leaned in. "I keep telling her I've already tried on that dress and it's too loose on me." He laughed.

Aaron laughed aloud in response. Francis's facial expressions were exaggerated but clearly intentional, which Aaron found entirely amusing. As Aaron's grandmother might've said had she been there, "This man's a *hoot*."

"Obviously that's why the waist is all stretched out," said Lorraine, lightly mocking him as she tugged at her dress.

"Speaking of clothing," said Francis, "is this an anniversary for you two? We don't see many tuxedos. You look like you're celebrating."

"Well, we've been… together for five years," said Drummer. "I'm also turning fifty. And Aaron's turning twenty-five this year."

Somehow, Lorraine's expression brightened even more.

"That's so sweet!" she said. "An anniversary and two noteworthy birthdays. And twenty-five years between you… that's a big difference. I hope people don't give you trouble for it."

"We haven't run into anyone who had anything to say," Aaron said.

"I'm glad to hear that. I have a friend back east—he's forty-two and his partner's twenty-six. People can be vocal about the age difference, as if they're entitled to judge. Some people think that by being with a younger man my friend's displaying some desperate need to cling to his youth, but the truth is, he just wants to explore the world with another vibrant soul, rather than sit around, getting old, watching reruns of sitcoms he's seen a hundred times."

Drummer nodded. "What about you two?" he asked. "You're both impeccably dressed."

"Thank you," said Lorraine. "We don't really take dressing up all that seriously—it's just fun. I used to teach middle school English class, so I'm partial to practical clothes. But I also respect the rules, which means no sweatpants or Christmas sweaters for formal dining on cruise ships."

"Despite the tuxes, we're pretty casual too," said Aaron. "Drummer mostly packed tank tops and cargo shorts."

"And Aaron's got a beat-up skateboard back in the room," Drummer added. "I think he expects one of our excursions is going to be to a skate park."

"Gotta be prepared," said Aaron. He leaned into Drummer's shoulder to nudge him again.

He met Drummer's gaze and grinned.

Lorraine glanced back and forth between them, seemingly endeared by their effortless nonverbal interaction. "You two already fascinate me," she said. "I love when people are more than they appear."

Aaron looked over at Drummer and raised his eyebrows with a telling smile, one that communicated a thought that didn't need to be spoken aloud.

Drummer shrugged in response to his look. "It could be fun," he said, answering an unvoiced suggestion.

Aaron returned his attention to Lorraine and Francis to explain the exchange.

"We have this game," he said. "At the beginning of the year, we randomly choose six days each, that we use as a sort of April Fool's Day. On those days we can tell one big lie, but it can't be blunt or mean. So, we make up a story, pretend it's the truth, and lead each other on.

"Eventually…," he said, working the suspense, "we pull the rug out. The word 'dalmatian' is our usual code word to indicate that what we were just saying was a con. And then we cross our fingers and hope we don't get swatted for it.

"So, if you two are game," Aaron went on, "we can do the same thing here, tonight."

"Oh, I *love* that idea," said Lorraine, rising in her seat.

"But it can't be obvious," Drummer interjected, "and you have to let us in on it at the end."

"Yes, of course, of course. Francis, you're playing too. But if you lie about me, be kind."

"No promises."

"I do have one question," Lorraine asked. "Why 'dalmatian'?"

"There no specific meaning behind it," Aaron said. "It's just a word we wouldn't accidentally use."

"I see." She appeared to give this some thought before continuing. "May I propose a change?"

"Sure, I don't see why not."

"How about a butterfly?"

"A butterfly? Why a butterfly?"

"Well, lies often require more lies to sustain them," Lorraine said. "One falsehood added to another, each new lie piling on the rest just to support the first, until the end result is something much bigger than originally intended. It's like the butterfly effect—the idea that one small change now can lead to exponentially greater change in the future. One tiny lie, leading to more lies just to keep the first one alive. In the end…."

"In the end that one lie can change everything," Aaron said. Lorraine had been looking directly at him. He couldn't help but hear double meaning in her suggestion. As he exchanged glances with Drummer, it was clear that he had heard it too. One small change, indeed. How many small changes had they already made? And how many lies had Aaron told to himself about his feelings?

"Butterfly it is," he said.

Lorraine's attention was drawn away at that moment. She looked over Drummer's shoulder at the restaurant host, who was escorting a man and a woman to their table and the last two empty chairs.

The two sat but did not address anyone. They looked to be around thirty, with matching sour expressions.

As the host turned to leave, the man snapped his fingers in the air. "Bourbon on the rocks, before you go," he said bluntly. His female companion also shouted out a drink order. The couple then began a private conversation at a low volume.

Aaron, Drummer, Lorraine, and Francis exchanged telling looks, silently sharing the same not-so-flattering sentiments about their newly arrived companions.

In time the dining room filled, orders were placed, and dinner was served.

LORRAINE AND Francis proved to be a true breath of fresh air. Aaron rarely spent time with others outside of the office, and he felt bad for Drummer, who was typically stuck at home and unable to make friends. Now they were part of an ensemble, getting to know new people, with their commitments and concerns out of sight and out of mind.

The late-arriving couple never did engage with the rest of the group. They offered only obligatory hellos after receiving their drinks, then spoke between themselves for the duration, steadily getting drunker before finally staggering off before dessert.

"Do we have to sit with those two bricked phones for the rest of the trip?" asked Drummer once they were gone.

Lorraine rested her hand on his forearm. "Only for dinner, if they even come back. I promise they won't spoil your breakfast."

Aaron let out a small laugh. "That reminds me of a camping trip we took last year," he said. "We showed up at the campsite, and there was this pile of breakfast cereal left behind in the dirt by one of the trees."

Drummer sniggered quietly under his breath.

Aaron glanced at him and continued. "We told ourselves we should clean it up before it got dark so no animals would be attracted to it. But after we pitched our tent we took a walk and forgot all about the cereal.

"So, in the middle of the night, here we are lying in the tent and we hear this hideous eating sound. I swear, it was like some *creature* was out there gobbling up everything—the cereal, the dirt, the rocks—all of it together. We just laid there in terror, wondering if we'd be next. Thank God the thing eventually wandered off."

"Did you ever find out what it was?" asked Lorraine.

"Oh, it was definitely Apple Jacks," Aaron answered plainly.

She chuckled. "I meant the animal."

"Oh yes, that." He turned to Drummer and asked, "What was it after all?"

"We found a small local wildlife museum the next day and asked them," Drummer said. "They said it could've been a fox or a mountain lion… but ultimately we figured it had to be a butterfly."

Lorraine looked at Drummer with a flat expression. Then to Aaron. "*You…*," she said after a moment, pointing at him. "I can't believe I walked right into that."

Aaron laughed, leaning against Drummer's shoulder. Drummer shook his head, grinning.

"You two are going to get it tomorrow," Lorraine added with a broad smile.

"And it won't be a small, believable lie like that one," Francis interjected. He then added with his best hillbilly drawl, "She'll be comin' fer ya."

"Did either of you actually go on a camping trip at all?" Lorraine asked.

"Nah, I'm just devious," Aaron said.

"And a good liar," Drummer remarked. "He used the same story on me once."

Drummer looked at Aaron with a glowing expression Aaron had seen increasingly often in recent months. It was the same look from several years back on the airstrip after their skydiving excursion. Drummer appeared excited. Even proud.

Aaron's own grin broadened as he thought about his camping story—a moment from their own past. Not an event from another time or a tale about another version of an older or younger counterpart, but a memory of a game they'd made up all on their own.

And he felt love.

And he felt the wall push back.

So he looked away.

"You know," Lorraine went on, "this whole night, I don't think I've asked you how you met."

Aaron and Drummer's mutual grin eased into a shared sentimentality.

"Go ahead," Aaron urged him. He knew the story of how they would meet, of course, but it felt inappropriate for him to tell it himself. Drummer had been the one present in 2010, after all, so it seemed like his story to share.

But to Aaron's surprise, that was not the story Drummer told.

"It was October 2000," Drummer began. "I was in the suburbs, and I saw this guy in the parking lot of some apartment complex with his skater friends."

Aaron listened with a swelling sense of serenity as he realized that Drummer was telling the story of *their* meeting, not the meeting still to come.

"He wasn't bothering anyone," Drummer continued, "but his car was parked across two spaces, which I just hate. So I thought I'd go over there with something to say. But then when I was standing there, and he was looking at me, I was struck by how much he reminded me of someone I used to know. Someone I used to love very much. I was suddenly terrified. Then this guy raised his chin with this cocky smile, and he said to me, 'What the hell do you want?' I was so taken. And confused and excited. I was looking into a face I thought I knew, but looking back at me was this completely different guy, this utterly compelling personality.

"The next night, we had dinner and went to a bar and talked. It was unlike anything I'd ever experienced. This person—this guy right here— chased all my fears away. In just twenty-four hours, he changed my life. I might even say he saved it."

Lorraine looked back and forth between them, her expression almost tearful. "That's very sweet," she said.

Francis picked up his napkin and dabbed his eyes, sniffling.

"Oh, this one," said Lorraine, prodding him with her elbow. "He's a bigger baby than me."

"I just enjoy love stories," he said with childlike defensiveness. "And the coffee's worn off, so I'm emotional."

"Francis, you know that's the wine." She looked back at Aaron and Drummer. "Thank you for sharing."

"My pleasure," said Drummer.

Aaron pulled himself together and checked his watch. "I think it's time for us to go. We're going to that huge bar in the back of the ship if you want to join us. Karaoke."

"You two could sing a duet," Drummer added. "Islands in the Stream?"

Lorraine chuckled. "Judging by my husband's emotional state, I don't think we'll be up for karaoke, but I'm sure he'll sing it in the shower."

"I need to use the restroom first," Aaron interjected.

"Me too," added Francis.

"Then we'll meet you boys outside," Lorraine said with a wink.

The group gathered their belongings and left the table.

As Aaron and Francis walked to the restroom, Drummer and Lorraine left the dining room together through a side door. They stepped onto the deck on the starboard side of the ship into a warm, dark night. There was no moon above them, and the ship was far from shore, so the Milky Way shone brightly.

They crossed the walkway to the railing, where Lorraine paused and gazed out at the pitch-black ocean. Her excitable disposition from earlier in the evening had set sail, leaving in its wake a satisfied calm. "Would you look at that," she said, pointing out over the water to the north, where the Big Dipper constellation was brilliantly visible. "I've never seen it so bright," she added. "The constellations have always fascinated me—how we connect dots to form images where none exist. And we see gods in the night sky looking down on us."

Drummer was put at ease by the sound of Lorraine's voice. She was one of the most complex people he'd ever met—self-aware, humble, educated, casual, and sentimental. She was everything he'd always strived to be.

"I've been on this same cruise three times," she continued. "The water's never been this peaceful, or the company so enjoyable. Thank you for an entertaining dinner, Drummer. And for putting up with my husband and me."

"It really was our pleasure," he said.

"No, it was ours," she corrected him politely, leaving no room for debate. "Most of our friends are gone, and we don't have much of a social life. Trips like this give us an excuse to accost strangers at dinner and force them to talk to us."

"We didn't feel accosted," he assured her. "It's been a long time since we've shared such good company ourselves."

"You're very gracious," she said. "And if I may add, you two really are quite handsome together."

"The matching tuxedos help."

"They certainly don't hurt. But it's not just how you look together. I can clearly see how much Aaron loves you. And I can see how much you love him. But what confuses me is that I can also tell that neither of you has said it yet. At least, not to each other."

Drummer's gaze fell slightly, but he didn't look away. Lorraine was right. The wall he and Aaron had put up between them still held them apart.

"It's been five years, Drummer," she said. "What are you waiting for?"

"What do you mean?"

"I mean you look at each other, but you don't look into each other's eyes for very long before you look away. It's like you're afraid to see his love looking back at you, and he's exactly the same. I have to assume you're waiting for something."

Drummer didn't answer, but he hadn't stopped listening, and Lorraine continued.

"I don't know what it is," she said, inquiringly. "Why do you keep him at arm's length? Is it about your age difference? A fear of dying and leaving him behind, or a fear of being left for someone younger and stronger when you're old? Don't concern yourself with those things. I see nothing but devotion in his eyes."

"I'm not worried about that," Drummer insisted.

"Then what is it? What are you waiting for?"

Drummer still had no answer. He didn't feel like he was waiting *for* anything. His reason for keeping Aaron at arm's length had always been the same: he didn't want to complicate the present in a way that might sabotage their future. Their "first" meeting in 2010 would be the most important moment of their lives—the moment when time itself came full circle and the loop that had been created when Drummer was sent back to 2000 would begin to close. An emotional entanglement today could spoil it. It could get in the way of deciphering the needle and might even undo that meeting entirely, sending the original Aaron back to a terrible life with a volatile man and a traumatic destiny.

But Drummer couldn't tell any of that to Lorraine. So he concocted an answer that he hoped would satisfy her and still stay true to what he believed. "I suppose," he said, "I've always told myself Aaron and I weren't meant to be truly together. Maybe in the future, but not right now."

"Drummer," said Lorraine, with a deep, caring softness in her eyes, "you have something wonderful with that beautiful young man *right now*. Waiting for the future just seems like wasting time."

Drummer understood her perspective and how he and Aaron must've appeared to her, but he also knew that Lorraine was not like them. She lived like ordinary people, with the present always moving forward and with only educated guesses to guide her through the days and years to come. The natural abstractness of "tomorrow" was an absolute to him, and he didn't want to risk the possibility that his actions today might undermine it.

"Maybe…," he heard himself add, his tone becoming unexpectedly serious, "I'm just worried I might do the wrong thing. I might make the wrong move and wreck everything."

"It's not hard for me to see that you're afraid you'll lose him," she said. "But there is something worse than doing the wrong thing, and that's doing *nothing*. Inaction never saved anyone or gave them a good life. And it never took two people meant for each other and brought them together. These are actions that must be *taken*, not avoided."

As Drummer listened, he thought about the previous five years and all the actions he'd taken to change Aaron's life: removing Grant, moving into the house in Clarendon Heights, the skydive and every shared experience since then, including this very cruise. In each of these cases, he had acted without fear—without worrying that he was doing something to damage the future. The only thing that restrained him was the emotional divide between them. He'd been selective about his choices, arbitrarily so. And now he began to question why he'd put that wall up in the first place.

Certainly he'd always seen the absolute and abstract qualities of time as interchangeable and fragile. But was it possible that they weren't? The two of them had made many changes to the world, but the future was still unfolding as he remembered it. Was it possible that there *was* no real butterfly effect? Would their meeting in 2010 happen no matter what he did? And could he really live like Lorraine and Francis—like ordinary people—and enjoy his time with Aaron without fear? Care for him and love him? Was it possible that the barrier he and Aaron kept between them served no purpose other than to deprive them of joy?

"Hey, D, are we ready?"

Drummer turned to find Aaron approaching with Francis. "Uh, yeah," he answered, flustered.

"Personally," said Francis, "I'm ready for bed."

"And that settles it," said Lorraine. "Drummer, Aaron… good night. And thank you both. We'll see you at dinner tomorrow, if not sooner."

Lorraine took her husband by the arm, and the two of them walked off together. Drummer watched them depart at a leisurely pace, with their love on full display.

And he felt envy.

He turned his attention to Aaron, who looked at him with an inquisitive grin. It conveyed more than just a question. It conveyed… expectation. Hope. Love. Had the younger Aaron always looked at him that way—the same way the older Aaron had?

"Are you ready to sing?" Aaron asked.

Drummer held his gaze and smiled. "I'm ready."

The wall between them still stood, but now it seemed remarkably flimsy.

THE DANCE club on the highest level ran the full width of the ship. Picture windows lined the entire room, with tables all around the perimeter. There was a dance floor in the center and a long bar against the inside wall. Aaron and Drummer found a table overlooking the vessel's stern, with a view of the curling wake disappearing into a dark, watery horizon.

Karaoke was still in progress, but the host announced that it would continue for only another thirty minutes. Drummer put in his song request, while Aaron went to the bar and ordered drinks before returning to their table.

"A martini for me," he said, sitting, "and a rum and Coke for the handsome gentleman." Aaron handed Drummer his glass. "Cheers!" They toasted, relaxed in their chairs, and took in the space.

"This trip was a great idea, D. Thank you."

"You're paying for it," said Drummer. "So, thank *you.*"

"Paying with money you made for me and the memories you've shared. So, thanks to us both. What song are you singing, by the way?"

Drummer smirked. "'All Over the World,' by ELO."

"Oh my God, 'Xanadu'!" Aaron laughed. "I should've known. Are you sure you can handle it? That's a *big* song."

Choosing not to acknowledge Aaron's words of warning, Drummer casually took off his coat and tie and laid them over the back of his chair. "I can't wear these, though," he said, fully committed to his choice. He opened the top three buttons of his tuxedo shirt, exposing his tattooed cleavage.

"You want a gold medallion with your zodiac sign on it for that scandalously exposed, middle-aged chest?" asked Aaron.

Drummer stared at him flatly as he reached into his coat pocket and pulled out a 1-inch round medallion on a gold chain, exactly as Aaron had described. He put it on and held his arms out, as if presenting a costume.

"You come prepared," Aaron admitted.

"Fuck yeah, I do!" said Drummer, mocking himself. "And worry not, young padawan, I've been singing this song for forty years. I've got it. But what about you? What are you *pretending* to sing tonight?"

"Well," said Aaron, straightening his bow tie, "I thought about doing a Frank Sinatra number, since I'm all gussied up. But instead, I'm gonna go country. The question is, do I sing Patsy Cline or Tammy Wynette?"

"Country?" Drummer asked, surprised. "That I'd like to see. Whatever you choose, I promise to stand by you, no matter how many tomatoes the audience throws."

Aaron reacted with an excited grin. "Thanks, D, you just made my choice for me."

Drummer wasn't sure what that meant, but he was intrigued.

Aaron ran up to the karaoke host and made his request.

The next several songs were belted out by drunken guests both on- and off-key and with and without finesse. The club was full, and the sheer number of people in the room made for an energetic audience.

Finally, Drummer's name was called. He took a swig from his glass and crossed the room to the small stage beside the bar as the room applauded.

"Let's give a big hand to Drummer," announced the karaoke host in exaggerated radio-announcer fashion. "He'll be singing Electric Light Orchestra's 'All Over the World'!"

The ridiculously upbeat music began. The song's lyrics appeared on a screen suspended over the stage, but Drummer knew the song well enough that he rarely looked up. He sang with gusto, his performance inspiring more than a few people to clap along and bounce in their seats, even if he wandered off pitch here and there. He felt almost no nervousness, which he took notice of. Only a few years earlier, singing karaoke would've tapped into a rarely seen anxiety.

The song ended, and a sweaty, overextended Drummer basked in his well-earned applause. He handed the microphone to the host and returned to the table.

"Well done," said Aaron, with an impressed but patronizing clap. "And all without needing a defibrillator."

Drummer tugged on his shirt to pull the air inside. "I'm fifty, not dead. But a few whorish paramedics in roller skates really would've made the show. By the way, the lights up there are hotter than you think. Are you going to wear that whole tux?"

"I'm making it part of the act," said Aaron, "like your popped buttons and sweaty sex medallion. And I've been under hot lights before, so I'll be fine."

"You have?" Drummer asked, his curiosity piqued. "Hiding a stint on Broadway from me?"

The microphone crackled, and the host's voice boomed over the speakers. "This'll be our last performance for the night before I hand it back to the DJ," he announced. "I think it'll be an entertaining way to wrap it up. Would Aaron H. come on up, please? Aaron will be singing Tammy Wynette's classic, 'Stand by Your Man.'"

Drummer's eyebrows popped. "Now *that* is a choice."

Aaron tightened his bow tie and gave Drummer a smug wink and a nod before leaving the table.

The room was instantly abuzz as Aaron took the stage and held the microphone with the casual flair of a jazz singer. In his perfectly fitted attire, he looked like a Rat Pack crooner, a resemblance he exaggerated by producing a pouty, seductive grin.

"Evening, y'all," he said with a charming smile and a subtle, respectful southern accent. "This one goes out to all the ladies in the room living with a man doing things they just don't understand."

The music began.

Drummer watched, rapt.

Somehow Aaron's roguish personality seemed to effortlessly melt away, replaced by a cultivated southern charm. If Drummer hadn't already known him, he would've been certain that Aaron was a legitimate country singer, his professionalism showing when he found himself standing under a spotlight.

Aaron's voice was smooth and mellow. He unfurled one line of the song after another about standing by the one you love. Even if the one you love is imperfect. Even if you don't always understand him. Even when being with him hurts.

Aaron sang with concise pacing and genuine feeling, reaching out to Drummer with his eyes from time to time. At these moments Drummer knew that Aaron wasn't just singing to the room. He was singing to *him*. And Aaron wasn't just repeating the words of a song; he was sharing how he truly felt.

As Aaron rounded off the final lines, Drummer found himself emotionally overcome. Aaron had stood by him for five years, taking him at his word that they'd one day be together, saying things and doing things he didn't fully understand but trusted in all the same.

This wasn't just a song. It was a promise. Like a solemn pledge. Or a wedding vow.

Drummer laughed lightly as a small tear rolled down his cheek. He thought back to Aaron's description of his skydive—of simultaneously laughing and crying as he fell, finding himself free of the ties that bound him. Drummer knew intellectually that Aaron had needed that experience, and now he felt it for himself.

Never in Drummer's life had Aaron moved him in such a way. Someone new had emerged on that stage—an almost fantastical personality, and someone Drummer had never seen before—in this

Aaron, or in the other. Drummer would never be able to look at him the same way again.

The room erupted into applause.

The host announced that karaoke was over for the night as the DJ stepped up and began playing recorded music.

Aaron returned to the table. "Are you feeling all right, D?" he joked. He could clearly see the tear. "You want me to call those roller-skating paramedics?"

Drummer was a trifle embarrassed by the reverence he knew his stunned expression betrayed. He wiped the teardrop from his cheek. "I think I'll survive," he said, "but wow, you could've warned me."

"Warned you?" He casually finished off his drink. "About what?"

"About *what*?" Drummer asked, almost incredulous. "About that song. And that voice! I've never heard you sing like that."

"I sing in the shower all the time," Aaron said humbly.

"I know. It's nice, but… it's never like *that*."

"There's no audience in the shower, so why go all out?"

"Some people do."

"Yeah, but here, D, it's a *performance*. It's like doing a skateboard trick in front of a younger kid who sees you as a god—or in front of an older man. You didn't know? I mean, my mom made me join the church choir when I was a kid. I wasn't really into the church part, but I loved singing and wowing people. They even had me do a few solos. Didn't the other me ever do karaoke?"

To Drummer's dismay, he realized that the Aaron he once knew had never sung a note—not at karaoke, not in the shower, not anywhere.

"No, he didn't," he admitted. "In fact, he never sang at all."

"I'm sorry to hear that," said Aaron.

"Why be sorry?"

Aaron shrugged. "I guess it's just sad that he never felt like singing," he said. "But also, because now you'll never be able to ask him why."

This hadn't occurred to Drummer, but it was true. He could never ask the future Aaron why he never sang, or why showering had been a rote, silent routine for him. He could never ask why they never went to karaoke together, or why he never even hummed a tune to himself. Why? Because the version of Aaron that knew the answer would not be the version Drummer ultimately returned to.

Drummer looked at Aaron, and as he studied his puzzled expression, he began to understand exactly why the barriers he'd placed between them now seemed so pointless. It was because he no longer saw the older Aaron in the younger Aaron's face, nor could he hear him in his voice. The two versions of Aaron—once inseparable in Drummer's mind—had become two different people after all.

More shocking still, Drummer realized that at some point over the past five years, the worst of all things had occurred: he'd let the older Aaron go. All that remained was the man sitting before him now. Drummer sat in stunned silence as he absorbed the meaning and consequence of this realization. Finally, he spoke. "You're right," he said, almost mournful. "I'll never know. Because he's gone, isn't he."

"Oh, D," said Aaron, "he's not gone. He's right here. He's *me*."

Drummer knew, technically, that Aaron was right, but he also saw an undeniable truth: that the Aaron who sat with him on this ship tonight was not the same Aaron as the first, and he never would be. Instead, he'd evolved into the man Drummer had hoped he'd become when he'd first driven Grant out of his life—someone joyful and at peace with himself.

Someone who felt like singing.

This was the future he wanted, right now, but it had come at a cost. For the Aaron that he'd *previously* known—the damaged soul with a troubled past, the man he'd fallen in love with in 2010—no longer existed. And for all intents and purposes, that man was no longer waiting for Drummer in the alley in 2020.

"I'm sorry, D," Aaron said again. "I didn't mean to—"

"No," Drummer interrupted, forcing his emotions down. "It's a good thing. It's a very good thing. It's just not something I'd thought about."

Drummer sat back in his chair.

"I'm going to get another drink," Aaron said finally. "You want me to bring you something?"

"Uh, yeah," Drummer answered, barely audible. "Rum and Coke. Please."

Aaron hesitated only briefly, then stepped away toward the bar.

Drummer continued to ruminate on his revelation. This new, youthful Aaron truly was happy, and while Drummer was sad for his intangible loss, he was glad for the change. The outcome of his efforts had proved so positive and so profound that an idea once entirely abstract—an Aaron free of Grant's violent legacy—had become real and absolute.

And as he considered all this, he also realized something else.

He was in love with this Aaron.

Deeply.

Undeniably.

Without regard for the older Aaron he used to know.

He heard Lorraine's voice in his head, asking him what he was waiting for. Now he knew. He had been waiting for himself to recognize the truth—that the wall between himself and Aaron had never mattered, because there was always only one Aaron. And that the time they had together was their own, whether the years they spent together were consecutive or not.

"Rum and Coke...."

Drummer looked up from his chair as Aaron handed him the glass. He took it and set it on the table. "Thank you, baby."

No sooner had the words come out of Drummer's mouth than he recognized what he'd said. That term of endearment—"baby"—was something he'd been unconsciously holding in reserve for the older Aaron. He hadn't used it since that time a few years ago, the night the younger Aaron had come home from a difficult experience and fallen apart at his side. But the term had come out naturally then, as it did again now.

The current song ended.

A new one began.

It was P.M. Dawn's, "Set Adrift on Memory Bliss," the same song that had played in the bar on Castro Street in October 2000.

Hearing it, Drummer knew what he had to do. He stood, took Aaron's drink from him, and set it on the table. He then reached out and took Aaron's hand, looking deep into his eyes as they stood face-to-face.

Aaron glanced away. Drummer knew now that it was a reflexive action, just as it had been for himself.

"Will you dance with me?" Drummer asked, calling back to the very question Aaron had posed to him five years earlier.

Aaron looked back at Drummer. "I'm a terrible dancer," he answered.

Drummer smiled broadly, tears welling in his eyes. "I know better than that."

He wrapped his arms around Aaron, and Aaron embraced him in return. They rocked slowly to the song together as all notion of time sailed away. Whether it was 2005, 2000, or 2020—they didn't care. They were together, and nothing else mattered.

Their gentle rocking came to an easy, natural stop, even as the song continued. They stood together, savoring each other's touch.

Without letting go, Drummer leaned back and looked into Aaron's eyes once more.

And neither of them looked away.

Drummer kissed him. And Aaron kissed him back.

Drummer was on the verge of tears. He managed to summon the strength to hold them back long enough to say what he needed to say.

"No more butterflies," he began, his voice shaking. "I've been lying long enough. To myself and to you. Aaron, I love you."

Aaron's expression broadened to a limitless smile. He let out a laugh and a joyful cry. "Oh, D, I love you too."

They kissed again and held each other tight, crying into each other's shoulders with shared and unbridled affection. Relief and elation swelled within them, and together—wordlessly and with mutual understanding—they allowed the wall that had existed between them for five years to fall to dust.

MEANING IN FRAGMENTS

The Starry Night hung above him. He thought back to the cruise, the Milky Way, and the Big Dipper suspended in the northern sky.

He thought of all the ways human beings connect dots and see meaning in fragments—like finding shapes in the clouds, images in Impressionism, or as Lorraine had often said, "gods in the night sky." In each case, we fill in the blanks to paint a picture, see what we want to see, or take us where we want to go. These dots we connect become the signposts of our lives, putting clarity on the moments that we deem most important—like photographs with meaning, words with profundity, music with passion, and dreams made real.

The dots define us.

But as he lay there, he wondered if, in this case, the answer to his dilemma would not be found in the dots themselves. Perhaps, instead, it lingered in the voids between them—in the memories forgotten, photographs untaken, words unspoken, and dreams unimagined.

Chapter 13
I Will Come Home

By their second day at sea, Aaron and Drummer were changed men. They no longer averted their eyes when they met each other's gaze, nor did they concede to the illusion of an emotional divide between them. They embraced their connection and reveled in it, loving each other for who they were and not for who they had been, who they would be, or who they *imagined* they might become. For two weeks aboard their floating paradise beside the islands of Hawaii they lived like ordinary people, with ordinary lives and an undefined future. They lived in the now—in the absolute—and savored every minute of it.

Though much had changed between them, they couldn't ignore the fact that other things had not. Specifically, the year 2010 and all it represented was still ahead, and unavoidable. It was five years away, but five years had already passed. This made them keenly aware of exactly how much—and how little—time they had remaining before they would be forced to make a choice.

After two weeks at sea, they returned to San Francisco.

It had been a transformative odyssey.

It had also been exhausting.

They took a taxi home from the pier, in comfortable silence. The evening air was warm, and the muted sounds of people on the streets seemed somehow surreal. San Francisco had carried on in their absence and appeared to pay them no mind as they returned. But once the two men were back in the house, that feeling of isolated bliss dissipated.

They were greeted by familiar sounds, familiar silences, and familiar sights and smells. The telescope, the neatly-made bed, a shirt draped over a chair—these things had waited, frozen, for an entire two weeks. Returning to them felt like visiting an old relative whose view of others never altered; as though the house itself had a soul and had kept everything the way they'd left it, expecting them to return from their trip unchanged as well and ready to resume their lives from that static point.

Aaron and Drummer clumsily hauled their suitcases inside, tossed them into a corner, and in ways that echoed fate more than free will, they obliged the house by returning to their routine.

Aaron showered.

Drummer checked the mail.

Soon, Aaron went to bed. He fell asleep almost immediately.

Drummer wasn't quite ready to turn in. He closed the bedroom door so he wouldn't disturb Aaron, then went to the living room, turned on a single floor lamp, sat back in a large armchair, and took in the warm, inviting space.

He saw the house in a new light now—as a haven and a refuge. It was beautiful, peaceful. And he hoped going forward that his future would be the same. But he was aware that lasting change didn't always come quickly. He still heard loud echoes of what the house—and his daily life—had said to him every day before the cruise: *don't get too close... don't forget the future.*

The emotional wall between Drummer and Aaron had fallen, and Drummer was glad for this, but he realized, sitting in this chair, in this house, that the feeling of having abandoned the Aaron of 2020 had not fully vanished after all. Being on the ship was, in a way, akin to being in rehab, detached from one's familiar surroundings and the triggers of one's pain. Returning to those surroundings brings the risk of relapse, just as returning to the house called up that echoing voice in Drummer's mind.

He peered out at the skyline, glittering in the twilight. The windows in his past-future condo were still mostly dark, but one floor was now brightly lit with staged units for prospective buyers. Drummer noted this development, but his thoughts did not linger on the tower.

He turned away and pulled a messenger bag from the bundle of suitcases. Inside, he found the digital camera he'd taken on the cruise. He clicked it on and jumped to a photo Lorraine had taken of Aaron and Drummer just before dinner on their last night on the ship. In the picture the two men stood on the deck, leaning into one another with bright smiles, their affection for one another clear. Behind them, a soft twilight horizon emerged from the open ocean, expanding into a brilliant starlit sky.

There was no doubt from their appearances in the photograph that Aaron and Drummer had changed—both for the better by almost any measure. But for Drummer there'd also been a loss, and while it hadn't intruded on him much during their trip, it came calling to him now. That echoing voice refused to be silent.

IN THE bedroom, Aaron woke. It was dark and silent, and the door was closed. He reached over, expecting to find Drummer asleep beside him, but he hadn't yet come to bed. A faint light crept in beneath the bedroom door.

Quietly, he stepped into the hallway. The floor lamp in the living room was the only light turned on in the house. Drummer sat in the armchair beside the lamp, facing the city, silent and still. Aaron drew closer, noticing the camera in Drummer's lap as he did so, though he couldn't make out the image on the screen.

He stopped when he heard Drummer begin to speak, apparently to himself. Aaron remained concealed in the dark and listened.

"I KNOW he's you," Drummer said softly, speaking through time to the forty-year-old Aaron he remembered, unaware that the younger lingered nearby. "I *know* he is. But I can't help but think that I've betrayed you with him. And that you're gone now, because of something I've done.

"I tried to separate the two of you in my mind at first—to see the young you and the older you as different people, to preserve you and the life we had. I finally accepted that I couldn't do it, but I thought it would be okay because I saw you in him, and it made me feel like I hadn't really lost you. All I had to do was get back to Dashiell Hammett, and there you'd be—the same guy, smiling at me. But you'd be a happier man without Grant in your past and with a few new memories instead.

"But at some point," Drummer continued to himself, "I started seeing you as different people anyway. Part of me wants to believe it's because of the differences in our relationship—because he's so much younger than you were, and I'm so much older. But it's not just that. The real reason is because he's living a completely different life now, and it's changed him. It's changed him so much that I'm afraid—I'm so afraid— that now he's *not* you and he never will be."

Drummer scrolled through a few of the other photos, most of them of Aaron.

"He looks more and more like you every day," he went on. "A few weeks ago, he bought that shirt I remember you wearing the day we met. I didn't say anything about it. Moments like that are hard because they remind me that the end is coming, but they're also beautiful, because they remind me that the future is coming back."

He turned off the camera.

"It's been five years, and we still don't understand the needle, but all the progress we've made has been because of him. He's so much better than me at this, but in a few years, if we haven't figured it out, he'll be gone—out there."

Drummer glanced at the condo standing tall in the darkness, then took out his old phone. He swiped through the image gallery until he came to a photo of himself with the older Aaron in 2015, standing on the deck of the cruise ship. They'd taken the cruise to Hawaii in celebration of Drummer's fortieth birthday and Aaron's thirty-fifth. "What a beautiful moment," he said, allowing his memory to take him back. "But what have I done to it?"

He shut off the phone and set it on the coffee table beside the camera—two idle pieces of technology that defined two separate lives.

"When I first got here, I thought I could save you from Grant and help give you a better life. Looks like I've done that—but what if it's at the cost of all the memories I have and the person you were? I try to remind myself that the things we did are still coming. And I look at that phone and I see the photos are still there, and that gives me hope that my actions didn't wipe them—us—out. But... what if I did? What if those are just empty images now? What does that say about the choices I've made?

"All this time I've been patting myself on the back, thinking I've been selfless by rescuing him from Grant. By putting an end to the nightmares, the PTSD, and everything else. But I can't help but wonder if this whole thing, from the moment I approached him outside his apartment, hasn't been the most selfish choice I've ever made."

AARON REMAINED in the hallway for a moment, aware that Drummer was done talking to himself but still hoping more words would come.

Words that wouldn't leave Aaron feeling so helpless. Drummer's internal conflict was understandable, and his sentiments were moving. They proved how much Aaron meant to him—in the past, the present, and the future—and that made him feel more loved than ever. But they also made him feel utterly powerless to help.

Aaron returned to the bedroom without letting on that he was there. Doing it was difficult, for Drummer had begun to cry quietly to himself. Aaron wanted to go to him, to comfort him, but he knew he shouldn't. This moment was Drummer's alone—a time to grieve the loss of his old life and the loss of a version of Aaron he believed had vanished with it.

Aaron climbed into bed and settled between the soft, cool sheets. He stared up at *The Starry Night* and thought back to Drummer's first evening with him in Fremont. Five years had gone by since then, and Aaron had come to accept that *this* life was the real one, even though the photos and videos on Drummer's phone proved he'd once lived a different one.

That other Aaron, in that other life, was only now walking away from his relationship with Grant, and he would be doing it a damaged man. Aaron had always understood this, but only after listening to Drummer speak directly to the Aaron of 2020 did he appreciate that his personal salvation had come at the cost of Drummer's joy. Aaron had apparently lived two lives, but he only knew the good one. Drummer had lived two lives as well, but he had known them both.

Aaron could only imagine Drummer's burden, as every day he'd experienced since 2000 had to invite comparison. Every day must remind him of the same day twenty years earlier, as well as any pain the days brought along with them—like experiencing the events of 9/11 all over again. And just as reliving the past five years had added new joys and sorrows, so too would the days still to come. And each of them would demand that Drummer find a way to reconcile their outcomes with everything that he'd done in the meantime.

Would Drummer continue to blame himself for the things he'd done or failed to do? Would he go on carrying the burden alone, believing himself responsible for the preservation of two separate lives? Aaron feared he might. So he vowed to relieve Drummer of this burden, to bridge the gap between those two lives and bring them together. So that with each future day, and every action or inaction Drummer ever questioned, he would know that he was not alone and that he'd made the right choices.

Eventually, Drummer came to bed.

Aaron rolled over as if stirring from sleep, though he'd been awake the entire time.

"Don't get up," Drummer said softly, kissing him on the cheek.

Aaron wrapped his arms around him, and the two of them drifted off together.

THE FOLLOWING week continued their return to routine. Aaron went back to work and Drummer to his research.

Drummer also had several photos from the cruise printed, including the picture Lorraine had taken of them on the ship. He had it framed and placed it on a side table in the living room.

That Friday, Aaron returned home late in the evening.

Drummer had fallen asleep on the couch a few hours earlier, and he woke as Aaron came in the front door.

"Hey," Drummer said, sitting up, greeting him.

"Don't tell me you've been asleep all day," Aaron said with a smirk.

"I did a little work," Drummer replied, "but less than I wanted. I was going to watch TV, but I guess I fell asleep." He glanced out the large windows overlooking the city. It was dark outside. "You're later than usual."

"Yeah, well… I had to pick something up," said Aaron haltingly. He held a long, small box wrapped in shiny gold paper and topped with a gold bow.

"Is that for me?" Drummer inquired.

"It is," said Aaron. He hesitated, then pulled an ottoman closer to the couch and sat, facing Drummer. He held the wrapped box on his lap. "I was going to say something profound about it, but now I'm at a loss."

"Lucky for you I'm the one who's supposed to be good with words, right?"

Aaron smiled shyly. "D, I have something to ask you."

"Is everything okay?"

"Yes, fine. Better than fine."

Aaron took a breath, held it, then relaxed with a long exhalation before finally continuing. "Drummer," he said steadily, "after the cruise I realized something. I know I'm *him*—that older Aaron you left behind—but I also know I'm not him. Not yet."

Drummer's casual curiosity about the gift became serious, for in Aaron's eyes he saw a swirl of emotions, none of them casual.

"I can only imagine how hard this has been on you, D… to see him in me and to see shades of the two of you in the two of us. To see two lives—and to *live* two lives—and hope you did the right thing when those two lives eventually reunite.

"I want you to know that you *have* done the right thing by rescuing me and by being with me all this time. I know you're afraid that you've been selfish, that you've erased him, and that the version of me you used to know is gone. But he isn't. He's right here. He's with you every day. And he's *so grateful* for what you've done for him."

Drummer's eyes began to water, Aaron's words reaching right into his heart. But he held his composure and kept his silence, allowing the nervous young man seated before him to say what he needed to say. It seemed quite likely that it was also something Drummer needed to hear.

"I have to believe that in five years I'll still be the guy you met in 2010," said Aaron, "and in fifteen years I'll be the guy you knew in 2020. And I want you to believe it too. You don't have to feel guilty or regret any of the changes you've made—the changes *we've* made—because it was always the right thing to do."

"Thank you for saying that," Drummer replied.

"There's one more thing," Aaron added. "You might look back on that day when you picked up the needle and wonder if you left me in the alley with nothing—no goodbyes and no way to tell me how much you loved me. But that's not true, not anymore. Because when that day comes again and you pick up the needle for the first time *again*, that Aaron and the one sitting in front of you right now will be the same person. And this time he'll know how you found him in 2000 and stopped him from making a huge mistake. He'll also know exactly how much you've missed him and how hard you've tried to get back to him.

"But more than this—and I want you to hear this clearly—he'll forgive you for embracing the younger me. Because the truth is, by coming back here and changing my life and my future, and by giving me all the love you gave to him, you won't have left me with nothing. You'll have given me back everything Grant ever took from me."

Aaron handed him the gift.

Drummer's hands shook as he received it. He held the package for a moment, fearing tears might come if he opened it hastily. Then he slowly, meticulously removed the paper. Inside was a long, flat jewelry box, and inside that box, resting on black velvet, were two gold wedding bands. Drummer's heart raced at the sight of them. The tears behind his eyes threatened to break through.

"I don't know if we ever got this far before," said Aaron. "I've seen every picture and video on your phone, but none of them show either of us wearing a ring. So, whatever happened or didn't happen then, I want it to happen now."

Aaron sat forward, compelling Drummer to lift his gaze to meet Aaron's. "D… I am him. At all times, in all places, *I am him*. And wherever I am, he is. And wherever you are, that's where I want to be."

This wasn't a moment Drummer had imagined he'd ever see. There had indeed been no photographs of Aaron wearing the ring in 2020; they hadn't taken any after the proposal, and Drummer had never spoken of it.

Drummer realized that, in an attempt to preserve his composure, he was holding his breath. Reflexively he inhaled, deeply and unsteadily. The pressure behind his eyes increased. He held his hand out over the rings, hesitating. He knew that the moment he touched one of them, Aaron's proposal would no longer be an unimaginable event; it would be a true reflection of the tangible life they shared.

"The rings are identical," Aaron said, "one for you and one for me. But the one on the left will fit you better."

Drummer wiped his eyes as the tears started. With a trembling hand, he took the ring. He could see something engraved inside, so he tilted it and read the inscription aloud, his voice cracking.

"I will come home."

Aaron smiled, his own tears rolling down his cheeks. "I love you, Drummer. If we can't figure out how to send you forward and I find myself standing alone in that alley in fifteen years, then I promise… I'll come home. To you, here, to this house."

Aaron gently took the ring from Drummer's hand and slid it onto his finger.

Drummer, still shaking, took the second ring and slid it onto Aaron's.

"But baby…," Drummer started, struggling to find the words.

"Yes, I know," Aaron interjected. "You're about to tell me that you'll be sixty-five and I'll only be forty. But you should know by now that your age has never mattered to me."

Overwhelmed and relieved, Drummer kissed him deeply and passionately, and Aaron kissed him back.

"I never thought I'd see this," said Drummer.

"And I never imagined it *wouldn't* happen," said Aaron.

The two of them laughed.

"The inscription inside both rings is the same," Aaron went on. "As a reminder of my promise."

"And my promise to you too," Drummer added. "I'll be in that alley when he's gone. Holding the needle or not, fifty years old or sixty-five, I'll be there."

He leaned forward again, and with love and gratitude too great to be contained in his enormous heart, he wrapped his arms around Aaron and cried, openly and freely. It was the first time in his adult life that Drummer put no restraint on his feelings. After five years of uncertainty, he could at last accept that he'd done the right thing—for Aaron and for himself. His grief and his joy, his loss and his gain, in his current life and in his old one, were all brought together, symbolized by that one little ring engraved with those four little words: *I will come home*.

TWO LIVES

He held both rings in his hand, one inscribed with a message of hope and the other with a promise—a promise neither of them had been able to keep.

Those two rings symbolized two distinct lives and everything they had built during them. Two loves, two futures, two shared histories. Similar in many ways, but distinct and separate.

Now, as he worked and as time passed, he was becoming increasingly certain that he could bring those two lives together. That he could still go home—if only to send *him* home—and turn their message of hope and their mutual promise into a single dream made real.

CHAPTER 14
RELATIVITY

WASTING TIME. While living in the Richmond District, Drummer had said that he'd felt like he was wasting time by not taking the initiative to enjoy life with Aaron. Lorraine had used the same words four years later to describe his hesitancy in defining their relationship. Now, with both concerns resolved and no further excuses, Aaron and Drummer were done wasting time. They began to focus more on the life that they currently shared and less on the future years when they would be apart. Though Drummer still spent most of his time at the house, they now traveled when they could.

They also stopped second-guessing the impacts their actions would have on the future. They concluded that as long as Aaron met Drummer's counterpart on Labor Day weekend in 2010, the decade that followed would not be markedly different from Drummer's own experience. The photographs on his phone hadn't changed, and they chose to see that as a sign that their actions hadn't triggered any meaningful kind of butterfly effect. Instead, they speculated that the opposite might be true: that when time was broken and events changed, time would instead seek to heal itself and still point toward a similar, stable future.

Aaron and Drummer enjoyed their life together, but a metaphorical ticking clock still loomed over them, urging them forward without regard for their relationship or their research progress on the needle. They faced moments of doubt, but when these arose, the pair buoyed one another so neither would sink into despair. And when they were alone, they had in their hands the comfort of the promise they'd made to one another—that even if time outran them and they found themselves parted, they would each, one day, come home.

Externally, the world continued to transform into the one Drummer remembered. Movies, television, and advertising all resurfaced with no obvious changes. World events repeated themselves, Aaron's company relocated its headquarters to the skyscraper in SOMA, and scientific papers began to make mention of five-dimensional optical storage on glass.

Concurrent with these developments came the rise of a new technological phenomenon: social media. Social media websites had existed since the early years of the web itself but had been regarded by much of adult society as little more than a fixation for impatient and self-obsessed youth. Now they were becoming a force that could no longer be ignored. The most compelling entity was Facebook, a site that Drummer knew would change the world in ways more profound and alarming than anyone in those early days could imagine.

On a cold November morning in 2008, Aaron sat at the kitchen table with his laptop. He swiped idly at the trackpad. A Facebook page scrolled up the screen. Image after image, post after post—it appeared as if it could go on forever.

Drummer came in and glanced over his shoulder. "You're back on that site?" he asked.

"Yeah, this is Eric's feed," answered Aaron, his eyes fixed on the screen. "I'm lurking, but I shouldn't. It looks sorta fun, but I can see getting obsessed over this."

"Planning to make a profile?"

"I don't know," said Aaron, uneasy. He knew from Drummer's stories that Facebook would serve as their initial means of contact in two years' time, but he wasn't necessarily looking forward to getting that ball rolling.

Drummer sat beside him. "Society's going to demand that you to have a profile sooner rather than later."

"You think I should do it."

"I think it's about time. If you start now, you'll have a lot of your own posts and pics on there by 2010. And trust me, the more he sees of you, the harder he'll fall for you. Share the fun things you do. Movies you love. Trips you've taken."

"But I can't mention you."

"No," said Drummer. "But you don't have to mention me to be true to yourself."

"Don't I?" Aaron asked. "We don't exist independently, D. You're a part of me—the biggest part. I wish I could tell people about you."

"We've told people."

"Yeah, safe people," said Aaron. "People who don't ask questions. People we've vetted. And now, with Lorraine and Francis gone…." He stopped himself, feeling a familiar wistfulness. Lorraine and Francis had moved away from San Francisco a few months earlier, presumably to Ohio to be with Lorraine's remaining family. They stayed in touch, but daily contact with them had ended.

"They're the only people who really know us, you know?" Aaron continued, wiping his eyes. "People who know *us*… you and me, together. I wish the whole world could know us like they do."

Aaron looked back down at the laptop. "I mean, look at this," he said, pointing. "Pictures of happy couples, parties, and vacations. I'd love to post that photo of us on the cruise, but I can't show it to anyone."

"You can still talk about the things we've done and where we've been," said Drummer.

"And how would that read?" asked Aaron, trying not to sound cynical. "'Here I am on the best trip of my life, with the most amazing man in the world, who I can't name or describe,' and the picture would be of me and you, with your face blurred out?"

"I'm sorry, Aaron," said Drummer. "You have every right to be upset. That website connects people, but being with me kinda sidelines it for you, doesn't it."

Aaron sighed, grateful that Drummer understood but still feeling glum. He tapped at the keyboard. "I wasn't able to find you on here. Yes, I looked. Just… curious."

"My counterpart won't have a profile till 2010."

"Why?"

"He doesn't feel like he's part of it, really. He spent a big chunk of his life feeling judged, and Facebook looks like a playground for sociopaths to him."

"But he makes one later. What happens?"

"A lot," Drummer answered. "Over the next couple years his cat will pass away, and he'll lose a close friend to an abusive spouse. It'll be hard. But because of those things he'll realize he can't do it alone anymore. He can't just shrink into himself and tolerate life. It doesn't work like that. He'll learn how to trust people again, revitalize his career, reject toxicity. And he'll find out just how much strength he has and the empathy he's capable of."

"He sounds pretty great."

"He'll go back to being the guy he was before Nate. The kind of guy *you're* looking for."

"It's hard to believe he's not that guy already."

"Maybe," Drummer conceded. "And maybe my hindsight is tainted, but I was always glad we met when we did."

Aaron smiled. "Don't you think it's ironic that now we've met ten years sooner?"

Drummer stood and returned Aaron's grin. "I guess it just depends on who you ask." He tapped the laptop screen. "You should do it. Connect with people—Eric, maybe Willis. Just don't post photos of the house or me. I'll stay hidden, and it'll be fine." Drummer kissed him on the forehead and left the room.

Aaron pulled the laptop closer and began. He browsed Eric's friends' pages for ideas, then created his own profile. Building a virtual representation of himself and curating it so that it exposed only what he wanted others to see was a curious exercise in duplicity. Excluding Drummer from the diorama made him profoundly uncomfortable. He chose not to reveal a relationship status.

As a result of signing up on Facebook, Aaron saw a dramatic expansion of his social circles in a matter of days. He connected with family and friends and was bombarded by requests from long-lost high school acquaintances.

He connected with Willis in Boston and followed that up with a two-hour phone call. Drummer came up in the conversation, which gave Aaron pause, but Willis barely remembered him—not even his name, only that Aaron had called him "D." It turned out that Willis's dominant memory of the man was as an older guy who'd shared a joint with him on the balcony of their apartment eight years ago and told him to move on.

"What about that asshole, Grant?" Willis asked. "You ever hear from him?"

"No," Aaron answered flatly. He didn't want to talk about Grant at all.

"Last I heard, he was on his way to prison," Willis said.

"Really?" Aaron asked, only partially curious.

"A few counts of assault, I think. I never heard more. It was a long time ago. But if anyone deserved to get put away, it was him."

Aaron considered that possible fate for Grant, and he felt strangely sorry for the man. Grant had been abused as a child, and while it was not an excuse for abusive behavior as an adult, Aaron regretted that Grant had become so irredeemable.

"So, how about them Red Sox?" said Aaron, lamely trying to change the subject.

"Eh, I don't follow 'em," said Willis, taking the bait. "But they won the World Series last year, so I made bank in the office pool. I might bet on them again."

"A word of advice…," Aaron offered with a mock whisper, "save the big bets for 2013."

AS AARON added more friends to his profile, the degrees of separation between himself and others narrowed, and he found himself contacted by an increasing number of individuals he barely knew. Friends of friends. Friends of coworkers. Family members of friends of coworkers that he'd once met "… at that holiday party back in 2002. You were so funny! Hey, are you still single?"

The requests poured in, and Aaron could already see that Facebook would become a burden if he didn't set some limits. So he stopped accepting new friends, except for people he knew in the real world. It slowed the influx, but it didn't stop it. Despite his best attempts to ward off new connections, social media continued to demonstrate a sinister ability to pry open and seep into the cracks of his life, no matter how tightly he tried to seal them.

A few days later, a new friend request arrived.

Aaron stared at it on his screen.

Grant Zimmer.

There was no message. Just the request.

Aaron viewed the accompanying profile. He saw pictures of Grant out and about, on the street, at the beach, at the park with friends. In every photo—whether Grant was smiling, laughing, or stoic—Aaron imagined the police lights flashing at his old apartment. He thought back to his neighbors, bruised and shaken. He recalled visiting his former landlord and the gruesome sight of a four-inch row of stitches across his forehead. And he heard Drummer's voice, warning him about it all.

Aaron had never thought he'd hear from Grant again, and he'd felt particularly free of him after speaking to Willis. Now, though, it seemed as if the man he thought he'd escaped from was standing right outside his door with a baseball bat in hand, like no time had passed.

Aaron blocked Grant's Facebook profile and hoped that would be the end of it. He prayed Grant would accept the lack of reply and move on. It had been eight years, after all. What could he possibly expect after so much time?

The next day, while sitting at lunch in an empty breakroom, Aaron received a text message.

"This is Grant. Is this still your number? I sent you a request on Facebook, but I don't see your profile anymore."

Aaron lost his appetite immediately. He buried his head in his hands, cursing himself for not changing his cell phone number years ago.

Another message followed a moment later.

"Think I saw you at the gym the other day. Didn't know you'd moved to SF."

Aaron deleted the texts. He threw away the rest of his lunch.

He returned to his desk and opened Facebook again. He studied Grant's profile, searching the photos for clues about where he lived. Looking at his news feed showed him familiar faces, names, and places. To his dismay, he and Grant appeared to be only a few degrees of separation from each other. Worse still, Grant had evidently never moved out of his house on Potrero Hill. Which meant he'd been right there, living in San Francisco, the entire time.

Aaron went home early. He said little that night and slept even less.

The next day, there was another text from Grant.

"Saw you again this morning leaving the gym. Hit me up."

Then again at lunch.

"I'm sure you're getting my messages. Don't know why you don't reply."

And on his way home.

"My friend Eric says he knows you. I know this is the right number."

Aaron arrived at the house, holding back his panic. He wanted to tell Drummer about the messages, but he was afraid. Should he respond to them, block Grant's phone number, or what? The texts could be read as perfectly innocent, but Aaron imagined a threat in every single one.

"What's wrong, babe?" Drummer asked over dinner. Aaron had been unusually quiet.

Unsure of what to say, he tripped over his own thoughts. Finally, he spat it out. "I heard from Grant."

Drummer stopped eating. He put his fork down.

"I thought he was gone," Aaron continued, staring at the table. His voice quavered. "But he sent me a friend request on Facebook. And he's been texting me for the last two days."

"Two days?" Drummer asked, alarmed. "What's he been saying?"

Aaron tried to play it off. "Nothing, really. I guess he just wants to reconnect."

"Have you replied?"

"No."

"Good. This is what you do." Drummer sat up. His tone was firm and serious. "You tell him you don't want to hear from him again, that you've moved on, and you wish him luck. Be emotionless and direct, and don't apologize for anything. Most important: don't engage him in conversation *at all*. Don't ask questions. Don't answer questions. Doing anything more than just telling him to leave you alone will enable him."

Aaron had never felt such passionate concern from Drummer before. Those typically contented pale green eyes were on fire.

Drummer took a breath and continued with a lighter tone. "Aaron, I want you to understand this: Grant will see any contact from you as an opening. Don't give him one. He might try to woo you or antagonize you, anything to get a reaction out of you, even a negative one. But remember, everything he does is a baited hook."

Aaron heard him and understood. Wordlessly, he nodded.

"I'm sorry," Drummer went on, much calmer. "I don't mean to scare you. But people like Grant don't let go easily, and time passing means nothing to them. If anything, he'd use it as an excuse. He'd say he's changed, that he's been to therapy or whatever. But time doesn't make psychopaths any kinder."

"He knows Eric," Aaron added.

"He does? Are you saying Grant's still here, in San Francisco?"

"He is."

"But he's not supposed to be here," said Drummer, clearly puzzled and outraged.

"Where's he supposed to be?" Aaron asked.

"He's supposed to be in prison," said Drummer firmly. "What he did to you in that other life was so criminal that he was sentenced to ten years in a federal penitentiary. In late 2010 he's supposed to be killed in a prison riot. What he did to your landlord and your neighbors might not have been quite as bad, but at the very least it was aggravated assault—against multiple people. He can't possibly have gone the past eight years without being held accountable. Why isn't he in prison where he belongs?"

"I don't know," said Aaron, shaken. "But he still lives on Potrero Hill. He goes to my gym. He shares my friends. What am I supposed to do? Did we do this?"

Aaron felt crushed by a stampede of confusion. He'd never expected to hear from Grant again. To compound the problem, if Grant lived in town, Aaron and Drummer couldn't easily keep hiding from him. 2010 was coming fast, and when it arrived Aaron would already have to be living in the SOMA condo if the future was to carry on as it was supposed to do. If Aaron didn't live in that tower, then Drummer's counterpart wouldn't come home with him after their first date, and the entire preamble to their relationship—the easy days and nights spent there together, learning about one another, sharing their respective pasts, falling in love—would be rewritten, if not erased entirely.

"Call Eric right now," Drummer insisted, "and tell him to stop saying anything to Grant about you. Emphasize that you don't want it to look like he's passing a message along, or that you've told him to avoid Grant. Just tell Eric to stop. Tell him Grant was an abusive boyfriend and that you want nothing more to do with him. If Eric wants to be his friend, fine, but he needs to know where you stand.

"Then reply to Grant like I said, block him on your phone so he can't respond, and change your phone number. And change gyms."

"Can't I just ignore him?" Aaron asked, not wanting to go through all those steps.

"No," Drummer insisted. "Right now, he thinks the door is open, and if you don't actually close it, he'll keep looking for a way in. If you run into him on the street without saying something to get rid of him first, you're cornered. And it sounds like he already knows where to find you, so you don't have a lot of time."

Aaron stared blankly at his food. His appetite had been scant for the past two days, but now he had none at all. In eight years, how had he never run into Grant? Then he realized: Drummer's isolation had passively isolated Aaron as well. But Grant had always been out there, and now social media was forcing open doors he never even knew existed.

"Hey," Drummer said gently, taking Aaron's hand. "It'll be okay. I'm sorry to be so forceful, but I know that man. He isn't reaching out just to catch up."

Aaron sensed the same thing. "I know. Everything he ever said to me was a ploy. There's no reason to believe him now."

He looked into Drummer's eyes and saw the empathy and strength that Drummer had said his younger counterpart was only now developing. It was clear to Aaron why his other self would've fallen for him. After Grant, he no doubt would've needed someone like Drummer, a man with obvious integrity, to earn his trust.

That night in bed, Drummer told Aaron Grant's full history with his other self. Grant had used his charms to confuse and brainwash the other Aaron into believing every manner of deception. He'd woven sob stories to garner Aaron's sympathy. He'd used gaslighting, guilt trips, and victim complexes to manipulate him and keep him under control, and when those tactics wore themselves out, he'd used threats of violence—against Aaron, his friends, and his family. He'd even threatened to implicate Aaron in criminal activity if he ever tried to leave. When Grant had finally been incarcerated, even more sinister truths had come out. Old romantic partners came forward. Ex-friends. Family members he'd assaulted. The picture it all painted of Grant was of a relentless, resourceful psychopath who'd hacked his way through the lives of a dozen other people without a shred of conscience.

To the core, he was insidious.

The stories chilled Aaron to the bone, but he felt protected, for Drummer appeared to know Grant thoroughly and understand the best way to manage him.

Comforted, Aaron fell asleep.

The next morning he skipped the gym and went directly to work. He replied to Grant's texts with conviction and a kind farewell, then immediately blocked his phone number. At lunch, he changed his own number and enrolled at a new gym. He also opened Grant's Facebook page one last time, noting any mutual acquaintances that he should avoid.

Though Aaron did everything necessary and felt safe in Drummer's presence, he felt vulnerable when he was alone. Whenever a text message appeared on his phone, his adrenaline spiked. None were from Grant, but this did not prevent him from worrying that, at any moment, one of them would be.

On his way home, he stopped in the Castro to buy groceries. This was an errand he had always done without much conscious thought, but it now gave him the jitters. As he walked through the neighborhood, the overcast sky seemed to emphasize the darkness in the windows of the buildings he passed. In every shaded pane, where blinds had been left open or drapes were pulled back—even just slightly—he imagined Grant standing there and watching him from the shadows.

Aaron did his shopping hastily, checking each aisle and every corner for Grant's face.

In the check-out line he texted Drummer.

"Can't wait to be home."

Drummer replied immediately. *"I understand. Sorry I freaked you out."*

"It's okay," Aaron replied. *"Still better than the alternative."*

"Let's go out tonight," Drummer's text continued. *"The café down the hill has a good dinner."*

"You sure?" Aaron replied. *"Not worried about being seen?"*

"It's okay. I'm feeling stir crazy. I'll wear long sleeves. Maybe that wig and fake mustache I've been threatening you with."

Aaron returned home with the groceries.

Drummer met him at the front door with a long, much-needed hug.

Aaron chuckled a bit in his arms, more from the release of stress than from finding anything amusing. "I love you, D," he said, giving him a kiss on the neck before letting go. "I've been freaked out today. I keep seeing him everywhere."

"He can only be in one place at a time," Drummer assured him. "And the man's gotta shit just like the rest of us, so just imagine he's on the toilet."

Aaron laughed genuinely. "Is that how you deal with stress? You just imagine your nemesis taking a crap?"

"It works," Drummer said. "And sometimes I like to think he's got an awful flu and he's lying on the bathroom floor twitching, shitting his pants, while *also* barfing his brains out into a dirty, piss-soaked toilet while some poor 911 dispatcher yells at him for his address through his cell phone."

Aaron continued to laugh. "Then that's how I'll see him too."

THEY PUT their groceries away.

Drummer quietly considered his next steps, the first of which involved dinner tonight.

He knew he'd be a fool to believe that he had any time to waste. Grant wouldn't simply walk away just because Aaron had blocked him. Grant knew where to find him—through his friends for sure, and possibly even at work—so he would come for him. He might even know where Aaron lived and had already taken to trolling the neighborhood, seeking the right circumstances to run into him—accidentally.

The more Drummer had considered this over the past twenty-four hours, the more sure he was of it.

And the more he counted on it.

With their groceries stowed and the house locked up, Drummer and Aaron took a cab down the hill to a small corner café on Eighteenth Street, several blocks up from Castro. It was out of the way but convenient for those who didn't want to venture into the thick of the neighborhood.

Aaron usually popped into the place only long enough to pick up a take-out order, but Drummer intentionally made this dinner a longer affair. They lingered over soup, a main course, and dessert, and Drummer insisted on slowly sipping several cups of coffee.

Outside, strangers passed on the sidewalk. Most of them paid no attention to the place or the diners inside, but one man glanced in. He stopped, appeared to read the menu taped to the window, then haltingly moved on.

Drummer watched him the entire time but pretended not to notice him. He'd spent eight years avoiding the eyes of those who might recognize him, and he'd become quite the master of passive disguise—knowing how and when to look away or glance down so his features would not be recognized. But tonight he remained in place, in full view, so the man outside could get a good, clear look. Aaron appeared none the wiser.

"Ready to go?" Drummer asked a few minutes later.

"Yeah," said Aaron. "Dinner's been great, but it's been a long day. I can't wait to cuddle."

"Lucky for you that's my plan too."

They returned home.

The next day—and every day following, while Aaron was at work—Drummer returned to the café. He spent several hours there each time, working on a laptop, eating breakfast or lunch, or just hovering over a large cup of coffee. He kept his tattoos hidden and his wedding ring in his pocket, but he always chose the same table, facing the door. If he thought he saw someone he recognized, he casually slipped into his chameleon-like behavior and disappeared into the woodwork.

Finally, on Friday afternoon—Drummer's fourth day alone in the café—the man who had passed by several days earlier entered the sparsely populated dining room. Presumptuously, he sat in the chair opposite Drummer.

"This table's taken," said Drummer, delivering his words with disconnected calm. He did not look up.

"I know who you are," the man said smugly, also keeping his volume low.

Drummer lifted his gaze and met the man's eyes with iron stoicism.

It was Grant.

"I want you to get away from my boyfriend," Grant said. He spoke with a featureless monotone.

"And you are?"

"You don't need to know. Just get away from him."

"Funny," said Drummer, "he never mentioned a boyfriend to me. You must not be very memorable."

"We've been out of touch, but I'm back, and he's not going to want you around anymore."

"How long have you been 'out of touch'?" Drummer asked. He looked back down at his laptop, giving the impression that he didn't really care. "Must've been a long time."

"Doesn't matter how long," said Grant, his voice rising as he took Drummer's bait. "The point is, he doesn't belong to you. I know guys like you—desperate old fossils who've got their claws in a hot young thing and think it's love." Grant leaned across the table and added, "Time to snap out of the delusion. It's best for everyone."

"It's best for everyone," Drummer parroted dismissively. "Those sound like words you've used before. Do you think they're a sufficient threat?"

Without answering, Grant got up to leave.

"*Grant Abraham Zimmer*," Drummer said clearly, his volume rising.

Startled at being identified, Grant stopped before he was even a foot away from the table.

"Yes, I know who you are too," said Drummer. "I've known for a *long* time. I also know that you're carrying a gift for Aaron, aren't you. You're not very creative, you know. I know you've been scouring the neighborhood, hoping to run into him and give it to him, and tell him how you've changed. Well, I have a gift for you too."

Drummer closed his laptop, reached into the messenger bag on the chair beside him, and pulled out a stack of papers. The pile was a couple inches thick and tightly bound, looking very much like a court filing. He set it on top of the closed computer.

"Is that supposed to scare me?" Grant asked.

"It should. It's your record." Drummer allowed a few silent seconds to pass, to let Grant tangle with his own interpretation of what his "record" might include. Drummer had done his research, much of it recalled from his other life, and had used it to dredge up court filings of Grant's criminal history and other public information smeared with Grant's ugly name. Much of it was in that stack of papers.

"Suspension from Saratoga Prep in 1991 for assaulting a professor," Drummer continued, his voice ringing with equal parts judgment and statement of fact. "Harassment of a classmate in '93. Expulsion from Stanford in '95, and an arrest for misdemeanor assault. Multiple run-ins with law enforcement in 1996, followed by a civil lawsuit in '98. But most egregious of all, felony assault on residents of an apartment building in 2000, this time with multiple charges pressed against you—which it turns out were dropped, unfortunately."

Drummer placed his hand on the bound papers.

"There are many other people in here that you've harmed since," he said, "but who haven't confronted you—probably out of fear. But I'm sure they'd all find it very enlightening to learn about one another. And your bosses at Foster Bay Distribution would certainly be interested to hear what you've been up to all these years."

Drummer looked directly into his eyes. "Let me be plain, Mister Zimmer," he said. "You will leave *my* boyfriend alone. You'll go back to the festering cistern you crawled out of, and you'll never—*ever*—bother him, or me, again. Is that clear?"

Grant paused. Drummer suspected that he wasn't accustomed to being confronted, let alone being given an ultimatum. The court papers Drummer had seen regarding Grant's transgressions described a man who, when facing a challenge, always responded with greater force, until his opponent buckled under the barrage and either retreated or surrendered. Grant had overpowered his victims with that tactic time and time again.

Drummer imagined he could actually see the thought processes playing out in Grant's shifting expression—this volatile man trying to read his opponent, then readying his habitual ammunition and taking aim.

Drummer beat him to the proverbial punch. He stood and took up a position inches from Grant's face. He then spoke, with a dark, even tone, words that would chill even Grant Zimmer to the bone:

"Listen closely. You do not know me or what I'm capable of. And this pile of papers is not just a threat. In fact, it's *nothing* compared to the sour heaps of shit I have on you. Now, you will leave, and you will never bother us again, or I will not hesitate to do what I must to put you out of our lives. Even if that means I have to hunt you down… *and kill you.*"

Drummer held his piercing gaze steady. He showed no weakness, nor any indication that he was anything other than deadly serious. Ice cold, he concluded, "Is that clear?"

Grant peered into Drummer's concrete eyes. He glanced at the workers behind the counter and the few people seated around the room, all oblivious.

This was the moment Drummer had gambled on. The brink of real confrontation. Would Grant retreat or attack?

Several seconds passed. Grant said nothing.

And Drummer had his answer.

"Good," Drummer said. "And remember… I'll be watching."

With no further word, Grant walked out of the café.

Drummer kept his eyes on Grant as he went. Once the man was gone, he sat back down.

His head spun. It was hard for him to be confrontational, even with evil people—but Grant wasn't just any evil person, and Drummer was not naïve. Drummer had long ago learned how to deal with him—when to fight fire with fire and when to overwhelm it with a conflagration.

He hoped his targeted inferno had chased Grant away for good, but he couldn't be sure. And though Drummer would not rest easy for quite some time, the quiet weeks and months that followed suggested that he had succeeded. But Grant would not stay away indefinitely, he knew. Drummer understood bullies. They might back down at first if they feared they'd met a match, but they'd never accept defeat. Grant would bide his time, recalculate, and regroup.

And when his anger and need for dominance finally overcame his feelings of humiliation, he'd be back.

TIME HEALS

They had changed the world, and they had looked to the photographs for signs of their changes and found none. Now, years later, alone, he looked again.

The selfie at the ticket counter in 2010.
The photograph on the ship in 2015.
The video at the picnic lunch in 2020.

On the outside, the world appeared identical; the images and videos remained the same. But on the inside, the changes were notable. It was clear to him that although time had healed, it had done so imperfectly; for the meaning in those photographs and videos—and many others— had been drastically altered.

Chapter 15
Causality

THE YEAR came to a close with no further word from Grant.

Aaron visited his parents for the Christmas holiday—alone, as he had every year for the past nine—while Drummer remained at home. Though the two men were apart for yet another family celebration, they didn't suffer each other's absence as acutely as they had in the past. Grant's sudden silence was a comfort to them both.

Drummer had not told Aaron about the confrontation at the café, and he was not planning to. He believed that Grant would rear his ugly head again eventually, and when he did, he would be ready. Until then, Drummer didn't want to worry Aaron about something that might never happen.

The two men spent another quiet New Year's Eve at home. While the holiday had once given them the feeling that they were losing time, they had since reclaimed it, turning it into an intimate date night—an evening to revel in another year spent together, to tell stories of a future yet to come, and make hopeful plans for the distant tomorrow—for life beyond 2020.

Aaron and Drummer slept well that night.

And 2009 appeared bright.

And for many months, it was.

In January, Aaron learned that the scanner had entered the final stages of development and the team projected that they would have a prototype by summer. He could hardly contain himself when he got the news. He checked on the progress daily, reviewing assembly reports and stress tests. He felt like he was watching the future build itself right in front of him, the same way Drummer had watched the condo tower rise from the dirt, but without the lingering feelings of weariness and trepidation. In fact, Aaron felt confident, even a little cocky, and more like himself than he had in years. Soon the device he'd helped construct would also help him to deconstruct the needle. And once that happened, he believed anything could be possible.

Lorraine and Francis visited in the early spring. It was a pleasant time for everyone, but especially for Aaron, who longed desperately to share his loving life with Drummer with others. Lorraine and Francis didn't stay long, but their brief visit would stand tall and glorious in all of their memories.

The day after Lorraine and Francis departed, Aaron and Drummer laughed and cried, intermittently and at unexpected times, celebrating the fact that their love had witnesses. They framed a photo of the four of them together and put it on the wall above the couch with the rest of the gallery.

In August, Aaron turned twenty-nine and Drummer fifty-four. Their physical differences were clear, but the numbers that described them felt at odds with their self-perceptions. Drummer had once found himself playing the role of father figure, but this rarely occurred anymore. In many ways, he now looked to Aaron for guidance. At the same time, Aaron had matured far beyond the nine years he and Drummer had spent together. He now relied on his own judgment and made his own choices, only occasionally looking outward for affirmation and advice. The two men owned themselves, admired each other for it, and saw each other as equals, despite the disparity in their ages.

In this, they rejoiced.

And life felt complete.

Then, in October, the long-awaited day arrived. After several delays, the scanner was finally in prototype, and testing of the scanning beam began on both solid objects and cadavers. The resolution was extraordinary—it revealed details down to the atomic level—but there were unforeseen side effects. No one had predicted the machine would be a radiological hazard or a chemical biohazard, but somehow it produced a waveform that caused cellular damage to organic material. On inert objects the effects were less deleterious, but the waveform still altered some molecular bonds, inexplicably and inconsistently. The only materials that appeared unaffected by the beam were those with a face-centered cubic lattice, like a diamond—the hardest known crystalline material.

The department head and project leads debated putting the entire enterprise on hold to conduct a prolonged analysis of the data, but Aaron knew that such a review might shelve the project indefinitely. He needed that scanner operational, and he needed it *right now*.

The problem was, he had no access. At least not officially. But he had learned in many cases—particularly in those where the need was dire—that it was better to ask forgiveness than permission. So, ignoring his better judgment, he brought the needle to work one weekend and covertly made several detailed scans on his own. He made physical prints for closer examination and brought them home.

He and Drummer studied them all.

The scans revealed—as Drummer had originally surmised—that the needle was not perfectly solid after all. Rather, it was composed of a single, microscopically thin diamond filament, which twisted and bent around itself in a manner so mathematically complex that it left no empty space whatsoever. In the center of the needle was a small sphere the size of a pinhead, encased in a diamond node, with two clear connections to the filament. The skin of the needle—revealed to be less than a micron thick—bore hints of a haptic touch-sensitive layer that could not be fully resolved. Lastly, the device's tensile strength appeared unmeasurable. This suggested that the needle could never be broken by conventional means.

Aaron marveled at the engineering required to fashion a substance as complex as the filament. Diamond was the hardest known crystalline material, and yet somehow, someone, at some time, had learned to manipulate its ductility and toy with it like spaghetti. Unless the material was not diamond after all, but an entirely new substance…. The molecular composition certainly looked like diamond, but there were inconsistencies in the lattice constant that led Aaron to wonder. In two of its three dimensions the constant was nonvariable, as he had expected. But in the third dimension it appeared random, and yet somehow those inconsistencies didn't compromise the material's integrity.

Further research was necessary, but Aaron was excited nonetheless. He'd found his starting point—his solder, his pinout—and it was a good one. It hinted at answers to questions he had held since the beginning. The first: Where was the software? He and Drummer had once speculated that programming might be etched into the material that comprised the needle—like data stored in glass—but the scans revealed this not to be the case. The filament was only a few atoms thick, and it was perfectly smooth and clear, so the programming—if that term was even appropriate—had to exist in some other form. That didn't help immediately, but it did eliminate other questions.

The scans also revealed that the tips of the filament touched the haptic skin in two conspicuous places—at each of the gold lights. Aaron speculated that these ends were contacts of some sort, like the exposed tips of an open electrical circuit. More than likely, they were the point of human interface that acted as the needle's trigger.

As for a power source, the node in the center was the obvious candidate, but for all intents and purposes its properties were unreadable. Theoretically the prototype scanner could detect the smallest details down to the atomic level, but the node in the center of the needle appeared so dense that even at maximum magnification, the scanner revealed no differentiation. The node didn't seem to lend itself to any conventional means of energy storage or delivery, but since it also didn't appear to be capable of data storage, what else could it be but some kind of battery?

"Maybe it's a heat sink," Drummer suggested, slumping backward into the couch.

"This has to be the power source," Aaron maintained. He reclined beside him, feeling just as tired as Drummer looked. Aaron pointed to one of the scans displayed on the laptop sitting on the coffee table. "The numbers on the side of the needle—they're clearly coordinates, maybe a way to designate a target time. The lights are the contacts that close the circuit and trigger the action. That core has to be a power supply."

"But how?" Drummer asked. "If it's just a metal ball, the only kind of energy it could hold is heat."

Aaron shook his head. "The needle interfaces with a human being through skin contact, so it should be electrical. But I scanned for EM radiation, and there was none. No electrical activity at all. But that doesn't mean it isn't shielded. I'd still bet it's there. That means this core has to be more than just a metal ball."

"Then how can something the size of a pinhead hold enough electrical charge to send someone twenty years through time?" Drummer asked. "And *backwards*, at that? No one would invent a time machine that could only go one direction, so that battery has to hold at least two charges so it can bring the person back to wherever they came from."

"Maybe the amount of charge isn't the point. Maybe the needle doesn't need that much power. It could be low voltage, with high energy conservation and insulation."

"Baby, that sounds like grasping," Drummer said.

"So? We're looking for a solution to something we *think* is complex—time travel. We tell ourselves that it needs a freaking DeLorean with a flux capacitor and 1.21 gigawatts of power to work. *Star Trek* says it's a slingshot around the sun. But what if all these big answers are wrong? What if it's so simple, so small, we can't even see it?"

"Okay," said Drummer, sitting up. "Simplicity. How about a singularity? It bends time and space. It's infinitely small. It's exactly what you're talking about."

"You're mocking me," Aaron noted.

"Not at all. Think about it."

"My brain's fried. How 'bout you tell me. How would a singularity work?"

"Well," said Drummer, accepting Aaron's challenge, "a singularity is basically a black hole, right, warping time and space. It's also constantly exerting gravitational force on matter around it. What if the needle is somehow converting that force into usable energy?"

"That's a nice, simple explanation, D," Aaron said. "I like your use of the word 'somehow' to skip over the whole science part. But remember, a singularity and a black hole aren't actually the same thing. A singularity is that point at the *center* of a black hole, inside the event horizon, where the density and gravitational field are supposed to be *infinite*. If there was a singularity in the needle, it would literally suck the entire earth into it.

"On the other hand," Aaron added, following his own train of thought, "there *is* that crystalline casing around the core with a lattice structure I've never seen before. But I just don't think it could be strong enough to contain something as powerful as a singularity. It would still just rip the whole thing to pieces."

Drummer shrugged. "You just said you wanted to think simply. If it *were* a singularity, it would explain the needle's tensile strength and its ability to tinker with time and space. Maybe it's more than just crystal and wouldn't collapse like you think."

"Maybe," said Aaron, "but that just feels like a shortcut, D, not simplicity. And the needle's dormant… right? Since a singularity's gravitational pull is basically 'always on,' if that was the power source, it wouldn't need charging. So why isn't it revved up and ready to go right now, vibrant and electric, like you said it was when you picked it up?"

"Maybe the casing around it works like a power gateway," Drummer suggested, "opening only when the user programs it to."

Aaron grunted. "A power gateway. It's a good idea. And yeah, it would work with all kinds of energy sources. But I still think we're dealing with something conventional, like a mini matter-antimatter reactor, a fusion reactor… something like that. Because the tech required to construct or capture, and then contain and harness a singularity, would be far bigger than us. Even forming a working theory about it is generations away."

"Does it matter what powers it?" asked Drummer, shifting gears. "I mean, understanding *how* it works might not be important. Maybe we should be focusing on how to *make* it work. We can drive a car without needing to know how to build an engine, right?"

"Fair enough," Aaron conceded. "But that brings us back to the programming. If the core is the power source and the lights are the trigger, then the road from one to the other is still that filament."

"But the filament holds no data," said Drummer, completing Aaron's assessment with a sigh of defeat. He yawned. "I do love how passionate you are, and I love this Scooby Doo mystery-solving, but I'm falling asleep. And frankly, I feel like I'm bowling with mittens on."

Aaron chuckled. "I see it. Go to bed, D. I'll stay up for a while."

"With that fried brain?"

Aaron shrugged with a cocky grin. "It's weird, but I'm suddenly feeling overclocked."

Drummer kissed him on the cheek and lumbered off to the bedroom.

Aaron remained. He collected the printed scans from the coffee table and took them with the laptop to the workroom, where he spent the rest of the night.

Morning came.

It was a Sunday.

Drummer roused, surprised to find that Aaron had not come to bed. He found him in the workroom, hovered over the needle on the table.

"You've been at this the whole time?" Drummer asked. "It's 10:00 a.m."

"Yeah, yeah I know," said Aaron slowly, leaning back in his chair.

"You want to go to bed?"

"Nah, I need to clear my head or all I'll do is dream about this thing. Can we get some air?"

"Sure, let's take a walk."

They stepped into a cool, sunny morning, where wisps of high fog grazed the tips of the trees. They walked up the winding two-lane road leading to Vista Point on Twin Peaks and sat on the short stone wall facing downtown. The view was spectacular; they could see everything from Castro Street all the way down Market Street, to the Ferry Building at the waterfront and beyond.

Drummer put his arm around Aaron and pulled him close. They sat in silence, listening to the wind and the sounds of the city echoing below.

"I don't think those scans will be any help," Aaron said after a while.

Drummer could hear the clear pangs of regret in his voice.

"D, we only have ten months left."

"I know, baby," Drummer said softly. He'd been dwelling on the fact all morning.

"And even if that ball thing is a battery," Aaron went on, "I wouldn't know where to start with it. For the first time, I feel… real doubt."

Drummer's gaze lowered. The scans revealed a lot of detail, but he feared that those details pointed to a solution beyond his expertise. And if Aaron himself was doubting….

"Do you think we can still do it?" Aaron asked quietly, interrupting Drummer's musing.

Drummer already had an answer. He'd known from the very beginning, from the moment he'd appeared in 2000. The needle was beyond their understanding and always had been. Possibly always would be.

"D?"

Drummer held off on his reply. He wanted to lie and give Aaron hope that they could still fast-track their progress. Because he knew that acknowledging the truth meant defeat, and defeat meant failure, the worst of all Aaron's fears. And Drummer didn't want to give him that answer.

But it already hung in the air.

"No," Drummer finally said, steady and with no outward emotion, though he felt torn apart inside.

The two men's eyes met. They said nothing more, communicating without speaking. Confirming what they already knew. Yes, they'd keep trying until the last possible minute. And when that minute had elapsed and Aaron was gone, Drummer would carry on alone until 2020. When that time came, if there was still no solution in reach, Aaron would return home and they'd be together again.

Drummer took some comfort in the prospect of this future reunion, but he was troubled by the lost time and the likelihood that Aaron would spend it blaming himself for breaking his word and their inability to decipher the needle.

Subdued and wistful, they returned home.

But as they approached the house, it became obvious that something was amiss. The front door sat partially open, though they were certain they'd locked it. They stepped cautiously up the front walk, growing more apprehensive with each step.

"I'm calling 911," said Aaron. "Wait outside with me, D."

But Drummer insisted on going in.

At the door, he found the lock had been forced. He pushed the door open and entered.

Aaron followed close behind.

They moved through the house, one slow step at a time.

The foyer was a disaster. A large mirror had been shattered. Coats, keys, wrecked picture frames, and the shards of a crushed souvenir mug littered the floor. The front room and the bedroom were likewise demolished, large holes punched in the walls. The bathroom mirror was smashed like the one in the foyer. Splintered glass crunched under their shoes as they continued toward the back of the house. The windows had all been thrown open. The smell of bleach filled the air.

They reached the living room and the kitchen. Tables had been overturned, the television smashed. The stereo was turned up to full volume and blared Phillip Glass's frenetic composition, "Floe," adding to the sense of savage pandemonium.

But most upsetting was a message left behind, spelled out in blood-red spray paint. Large capital letters were drawn on the wall above the couch, defiling the gallery of framed photographs from Aaron and Drummer's life together.

It was only three words, but they were terrifying: I'VE BEEN WATCHING.

Drummer turned the message over in his mind and remembered his final statement to Grant in the café a year earlier—they were almost the exact same words.

It had to be him.

Drummer reached out to the stereo receiver and turned the volume all the way down. A miserable silence filled the house, even as the message in red continued to scream. A drop of paint slowly rolled down the wall, the wet streak an indicator that Grant had been there very recently.

Aaron, who'd been following Drummer slowly through the house, immediately pushed past him, almost knocking him over. He went directly to the workroom, kicking broken items out of the way as he went.

Drummer heard Aaron's cry. He rushed to the workroom and stopped in the doorway. The computer was in pieces. The printed scans were scattered everywhere, some crumpled. The tray that had held the needle was empty.

Aaron had already begun searching.

"We forgot to put it away," Drummer said to himself, in a state of shock.

"I know!" Aaron screamed back as he checked the room. He pushed past Drummer again, returning to the living room, where his search became more frantic, more scattered, more reactive, and more destructive.

Even as Drummer struggled with his own emotional paralysis, he called out to Aaron, hoping to calm him.

Aaron threw a decorative glass bowl against the wall in a burst of rage. It shattered into hundreds of splintered shards, glass exploding outward and raining down on the floor from one corner of the room to the other.

Both men stopped. Silently, they looked around, taking in the disfigured wreck their sanctuary had become. The couch was soaked with bleach. Many of their photos were ruined. Aaron's books had been ripped in half.

Their eyes met.

And Drummer saw something utterly horrifying.

Aaron's expression revealed more than just feelings of defeat and failure, more than the palpable cries of his doubt and anger. It exposed the anguish of a man who'd been viciously assaulted, with no way to defend himself. A man who previously believed he'd escaped the venomous bite of his abuser but had, once again, become his victim.

WHEN THE police arrived, Aaron spoke with them alone. The house was in his name, and Drummer—with his Canadian passport but no US documentation—couldn't risk being questioned. Aaron filed a police report and gave the officers Grant's name, but implicating Grant in the break-and-enter would not be so simple. The man hadn't shown himself to them in over a year, and without evidence of harassment or a tangible sign that he was the perpetrator, it was unlikely that a case could be brought against him. There was no security camera footage, no evidence of theft aside from the needle—which Aaron did not divulge—and there was no clear motive. The words painted on the wall were the only things pointing to Grant. But as incriminating as they seemed, in the eyes of the law they were circumstantial.

SEVERAL BLOCKS away at Kite Hill, Drummer waited on a bench, alone with his thoughts. Years earlier, he'd sought to save Aaron from Grant, and he'd believed himself successful. But he wondered now if he'd merely delayed the inevitable. Was his interference in 2000 to blame for Grant walking free today? Since he would obviously no longer die in a prison riot in 2010, would he instead continue to harass Aaron from afar?

The possibilities tormented Drummer, and for a while, he wallowed in them.

But if he knew one thing about himself, it was that he never gave up. He might despair at first, but he'd soon remind himself of the mantra he'd adopted years ago—"there's always a way"—and he'd snap out of it.

And there *was* a way.

There was still a way to keep Grant from wreaking havoc and a way to preserve the future. But it would take great personal sacrifice on Drummer's part.

Grant was not the negotiating type. He was not the kind of man to cut a deal or take a bribe or accept compromise. Drummer suspected that he might have to follow through with the threat he'd made a year earlier.

He might have to kill Grant.

Drummer had given occasional thought to how it might be done. The best option was also the most gruesome: a fire. It wasn't about causing pain or the degree of violence involved as much as the hope that it would eliminate the most evidence. There would be no confrontation. No public scene. Just a straightforward bullet to the head from Grant's own gun, followed by a house fire.

It was a clean plan and would destroy the most evidence, but it had a glaring flaw: in the event of Grant's killing, Aaron would immediately become the primary suspect. After all, he had the motive and the means. He had history with Grant. He was being harassed. His home had been vandalized and his career had been threatened. And he'd shared this information with the police and professional colleagues. Unless a different assailant could be pinpointed, Grant's death could cause greater harm to Aaron's future than his survival.

Drummer barely hesitated to identify this hypothetical assailant.

"It has to be me," he said under his breath. "There's no one else."

And he would do it.

But only if he had to.

BACK AT the house, the police concluded their interview with Aaron. They were sensitive and understanding, and they insisted that they'd do what they could for him, but their assurances came with the admission that the perpetrator would likely not be caught. Such cases rarely resolved in an arrest unless the crime was repeated and generated additional evidence. This case would likely now be one for the insurance companies.

The officers left.

Aaron did a desperate sweep of each room, looking for the needle, but it was nowhere to be found. He nailed the front door shut from the inside and left the house through the garage, then drove to Kite Hill, where he found Drummer.

Aaron took Drummer's hand and lifted him up from the bench. He'd found some semblance of composure on the drive over, but Drummer still appeared quite disturbed.

"I locked up the house as well as I could," said Aaron, his voice empty. "I didn't see the needle anywhere."

"It's gone," said Drummer, conclusively. "It looked important, so of course he'd take it."

"Maybe he still has it."

"He wouldn't keep a souvenir," Drummer said. "Aside from that gun, he's always been averse to the existence of hard evidence. If he took the needle, he threw it away to make sure we wouldn't have it."

"What do we do now?" asked Aaron.

Drummer looked at him, and in his eyes he saw the same loss of purpose he felt himself. The needle was gone, and with it, their motivation. Drummer would never be able to make the jump forward to the moment he had vanished in the alley, and Aaron would not be able to send him there.

Drummer answered the question by taking Aaron into his arms. "Now we make the most of the time we have left."

That night, they stayed in a hotel. And though they hurt inside, they made love with an intensity unlike anything they'd shared before. They kept their defeat to themselves and gave everything else they had to one another. They laughed together, cried together, held and explored each other. They repeated the words *I love you* in every conceivable iteration. To be together was all they wanted now, to reveal every part of themselves to one another, for as long as time would allow.

The future was stable, and time would go on. But Aaron knew that the two of them as a couple, Drummer now fifty-four and Aaron twenty-nine, would come to an end in ten months. The encroaching deadline pressed upon him like a weight, but it also offered him a peculiar release, the freedom to fully focus on his life with Drummer in what remained of the present.

ORIGINS

As time passed, the aging scientist's goal became clearer and the road toward it smoother. He learned to act swiftly and strategically, seeking avenues of advancement wherever possible, but always with a finger on the pulse of his pride.

He soon had enough sway to affect mergers and acquisitions and used that capital to direct the absorption of a competitor that had long been in his crosshairs. This single takeover yielded answers to many questions and solved a mystery that had vexed him for years. The company's patent filings described two intriguing inventions: The first was a quantum-strength crystal lattice—a physical containment cell meant to replace the traditional donut-shaped tokamak design of fusion reactor cores. The second was a machine that could theoretically transport an individual from one location to another instantaneously. Neither device yet existed, but the mathematics that gave strength to the crystal lattice appeared sound, as did the quantum parameters of the transit device.

Moreover, from these proposed inventions he was able to find confirmation of his own theories. He identified the power source that would function inside the containment cell. It wasn't a fusion reactor after all—such a machine would press outward in an effort to expand, ultimately blowing the chamber apart. Instead, it was a power source that exerted *inward* force, holding the chamber—and the power gateway—closed until triggered. A singularity.

Furthermore, the plans for the transit device introduced a new form of spatial coordinates to the scientific community—five numerical sets, separated by decimal points. The scientist recognized this sequence as the same pattern they'd found on the side of the needle. This discovery confirmed what he'd long suspected: they too represented a target, a physical destination. Not a fixed set of coordinates, but ones relative to the needle itself—move the needle north and the destination moved north with it, even as the numbers stayed the same.

It was easy enough to conclude that the second set of numbers on the needle represented not a location in space, but time. And like the geographical location, that time was also not defined by human metrics—a year, a day, an hour—but was relative to the existing time of the needle, determined by the ever-moving nature of the here and now.

Though many gaps still existed between theory and reality, proposal and invention, the scientist could see the road ahead. The needle's components were being imagined and invented before his eyes. The coordinate system. The triggering mechanism. The crystalline containment cell. And the singularity at its heart.

One day, a future generation would put them all together. New patents would be filed, old ethics would be debated, and the race to construct the needle would begin.

CHAPTER 16
NEED

ON THE first of January 2010, Aaron and Drummer sat down together, looked into one another's eyes, and saw the previous nine years looking back.

They could no longer trick themselves into believing that time was on their side, using deceptive terms like "next year" or "someday." September fifth, 2010—the day when the loose end of one loop of time would meet its tether and tie its knot—was fast approaching. The finality of that coming moment was clear.

Evening fell.

Aaron went to bed.

Drummer remained awake.

Much of the house had been repaired in the two months since the break-in. They had replaced broken items, reprinted and reframed photographs. They'd painted over the three ugly words over the couch, though Drummer knew they remained under those obscuring layers.

The house appeared as it had before, though now it contained invisible scars.

Drummer lay back on the couch with his laptop, buried in the news. He was fixated on the ongoing H1N1 influenza pandemic, reading every article he could find about it. He recalled being twenty years younger and how the country's paranoid reaction to the outbreak had amused him. But now, having experienced the rapid spread of Covid-19 in 2020, the H1N1 event took on new urgency. It loomed in his mind like the Grim Reaper standing on a not-so-distant hilltop, sending a warning to the world that would sadly go unheeded.

He didn't know what he was looking for in the H1N1 news—an answer to the question of what to do about the coronavirus, perhaps? That was something he still hadn't told Aaron about.

He shut off the laptop, forcing himself away from the headlines, and looked out at the nighttime skyline. San Francisco was a beautiful city, and he'd now lived in it most of his life. But as he took in the view, he realized that he had few recent experiences with it. He and Aaron had traveled quite a bit over the years, but their excursions had always led them out of town. They had done almost nothing within the city limits, save for the occasional escape into a darkened theater. But even this they did with no other companions.

Oftentimes, Drummer felt as if his life in San Francisco was like that of a hermit living in a cave, venturing out briefly to interpret and deliver prophecy, then skulk back into the darkness. But he was not a hermit. He was a human being with certain social needs unfulfilled. With time running out, he found himself reconsidering his isolation.

When morning came, he suggested to Aaron that they spend the weekend out in the city. He would cover his tattoos with a long-sleeved shirt but make no other attempt to disguise himself. He needed to experience the city once more as a man unafraid to explore its streets—a man who truly *lived* there—and he needed to do it with Aaron.

Aaron didn't need much convincing. Aaron had adopted a sympathetic isolation alongside him—Drummer hadn't been blind to that—and the thought of setting it all aside excited him.

They set out after breakfast on Saturday morning, and together they had the kind of weekend that Drummer remembered having all the time in his former life. He and Aaron walked through crowds without concern. They strolled along the Embarcadero waterfront, mere yards from the Hyatt Regency and Aaron's old workplace, without fear that any of their friends or former acquaintances would recognize them. They made the city their own.

As Saturday blurred into Sunday, Drummer recognized something in Aaron that he'd failed to see in all their years together: need. Aaron needed to get out and be social, with Drummer at his side. He needed to have no fear of running into people he knew. He needed to share his life in this city with the man he loved. And he needed to be able to stand up and proclaim to everyone that he was married to the most amazing person in the world, even if their marriage wasn't official. Aaron had voiced this need in the past, but Drummer had failed to understand its true depth. Now he saw it, and he took great pleasure in satisfying it.

It was a wonderful weekend, but as Sunday afternoon came and Drummer's excitement mellowed with his waning energy, he found himself troubled. He wanted to spend the next several months with Aaron like this, but he knew he couldn't. Though they hadn't crossed paths with anyone they knew over the past two days, they'd merely been lucky. They couldn't rely on their current good fortune to carry them through even the next day, never mind the days following. Drummer's need for anonymity persisted, despite Aaron's need to be known.

This led Drummer to a sad revelation: that the opposite would be true for his counterpart. The younger version of himself could—and would—satisfy all of Aaron's social needs, not just for a weekend but for every day over the next ten years. There was a beautiful relationship ahead for Aaron, where he'd live freely and openly, share the entirety of his life with his friends and acquaintances, and where he might, at times, even forget about the man cowering in the dark in the house on the hill.

ON SUNDAY night, Aaron and Drummer staggered home, drunk, cursing like sailors and laughing like kids. Aaron didn't care if he stumbled into work the next morning with a hangover. The weekend with Drummer had been worth it—giving him a tour of his office, walking with him on the beach, dining downtown, and finally returning to the Castro Street bar they'd visited in 2000. Which, as Drummer had predicted, appeared the same but now had a different name.

Aaron cared about nothing but the happiness he and Drummer shared as they fell into bed that night. They had wild, drunken sex, then lay beside one another in each other's sweat. In the afterglow, Aaron rested his head on Drummer's chest, thrilled at having been able to share such a carefree weekend.

That was the moment when he truly recognized the outgoing social personality that Drummer possessed, but that, by necessity, had been suppressed. The weekend wasn't just something Drummer had enjoyed; it had been something he'd *needed*. Aaron was thrilled that he'd been able to satisfy this need, and he hoped they'd be able to repeat it soon—though he was unaware that Drummer had already decided that they would not.

THE NEXT day Aaron did indeed bring a hangover with him to work, but it was worth it, he told himself. The weekend had been amazing. He threw back a few ibuprofen and chased them down with a cup of coffee when he arrived at the office, committing himself to a day of half-capacity and hoping that his bloodshot eyes would not betray his foggy mind. He set his sights on simple tasks, avoiding the complicated situations he often juggled.

But complicated situations didn't wait for hangovers to abate. He was immediately summoned to his supervisor's office without warning, an unusual and worrying development.

His company's new headquarters were large and modern, situated on a high floor with views of the city all around. His supervisor's office was spacious, with a broad picture window facing east with a view of the bay, the city of Oakland, and beyond. The sun was rising over the east bay hills, casting light into Aaron's eyes as he came in.

Before him was a wide glass desk, clean and tidy save for a polished silver laptop, a glossy white touchscreen phone, and a few personal items, including a clutch of metal keys that glimmered in the sunlight. He approached and sat. In the chair behind the desk, dressed in a pristine white suit, sat his boss, Taraji.

"Hey, T, what's going on?" Aaron asked, attempting to lean on the casual relationship they'd nurtured over the years.

Typically Taraji would have looked at him with the welcoming eyes of a friend and close colleague. Today, she looked at him with disappointment. "Aaron," she said, greeting him as he sat. "Yesterday I got something in the mail. It was addressed to me, the CEO, and the head of R&D. It came anonymously, with no return address. Can you tell me what this is?"

She placed an eight-by-ten-inch acrylic sheet on the glass desk. It was one of the scans he had taken of the needle, presumably stolen by Grant during the break-in at the house. Aaron stared at it, feeling like the floor had suddenly dropped out from under him.

"It looks like a scan from the imager," he said, clinging to a stoicism he hoped wouldn't expose his culpability.

"It is," said Taraji. "It has our watermark. Included with the scan was a letter, accusing you—by name—of using this experimental equipment for personal purposes."

She put the letter on the table. "Can you answer to this accusation?" she asked.

Aaron heard no hint of the friend or colleague he knew in Taraji's voice as she posed her question. At this moment, she was his superior.

"You said these came anonymously?" He struggled to form a response as he stared at the letter and the scan. The letter was professionally formatted and printed, like a form letter from a politician.

"I did," she said, "but it doesn't matter where they came from. Access to the imager is tightly restricted. Your fob logged in and out of the lab after hours. Twenty-eight scans were taken. And after reviewing the logs, it's obvious this scan was one of them."

Aaron choked. "I don't know what to say."

"I don't know what to say either. Unapproved use of that machine could cost us our funding—or worse. Aaron, you're one of the best people we've got, and I've been on your side from the beginning. What's going on?"

Aaron felt a desperate need to defend himself, but he was lost in fragmented thoughts. Taraji was his boss, but she was still his friend. Even as she bore down on him with the requisite professionalism, he wanted to believe that he could trust her and appeal to that friendship.

"Taraji," he said, his vulnerability showing, "there's someone out there—someone I used to know. He would've destroyed my life if I hadn't gotten away from him. It's been almost a decade. but now he's back, and I think he's trying to ruin me. He wrecked my house last year—you know about that—and now this. I don't know what to do."

"I hear you," she said, "but whether this person's responsible for sending this or not is beside the point. Did you make this scan?"

Aaron swallowed hard. He stared at the letter on the desk, straining to read it without picking it up, but the words all blurred together.

"Aaron."

He looked up at her, wanting to explain, but he was lost in a new dread that every aspect of his world might now become victims of Grant's sabotage.

Taraji leaned back in her chair. Her expression softened.

"Look," she said carefully, "I don't know what this thing is or why you used the imager on it, but I can't ignore the fact that you used company resources on a personal project. At the same time, I'd be a fool to think this company would be here today without you. Winning this contract, and the pressure you put on us to pursue at least eight others, lifted us out of obscurity. *We're here today because of you.* But these scans represent a serious breach of protocol and demonstrate a willful abuse of responsibility. In an hour, I'll be meeting with Corinne and Argo to discuss the letter and your future with this institution.

"What I need is this: give me something I can take into that meeting. I don't care what you tell me as long as it explains your actions and I can say it with a straight face."

Aaron's mind spun at the speed of a computer. Nervously, he looked around the room, the morning sunlight glinting off everything—the polished laptop, the silver keys, and the perfectly smooth glass desk.

And he had an epiphany.

"You'll laugh," he said finally, settling on an answer.

"Then it better be funny."

Aaron found his center and put his emotions away. He assumed the straightest game face he had, looked directly into Taraji's eyes, and lied. "It's a Christmas ornament," he said. "A crystal Christmas ornament."

Taraji raised her eyebrows, unamused. "That is funny," she said, "but I'm not laughing. A Christmas ornament? Why would you—"

"I wanted to see the potential level of detail for myself," Aaron said, interrupting her with quiet confidence—a measured tone he knew she'd respect. "As a proof of concept. I suspected that Corinne and Argo wouldn't let me try, so I did it myself."

"Why?" she asked. "You put everything you've done here on the line."

Aaron leaned forward in his chair and answered, allowing his confidence to draw from his cockiness and infuse his words with passion.

"Taraji, there's a future for information storage on glass," he said, "on a manufactured, face-centered cubic lattice strong enough to last a million years—we both know that. But I don't think it ends there. I think we can harness and transmit both power and information through similar modified crystal lattices, highly compressed, with no negative space and no energy loss. No heat, no vibration, no moving parts. I'm talking about the power and speed of a quantum computer, capable of billions of transactions in a millisecond, all contained in a device the size of a ballpoint pen with the tensile strength of a metal beam two feet thick."

Aaron held her gaze.

"How do you imagine this working?" she asked, intrigued.

"We've seen how the scanning beam sometimes causes molecular changes in the object being scanned," he said. "Cellular damage to organic material. Altered molecular bonds in certain metals. And we've never been able to figure out why. As a result, I know we're about to shelve this project. But I've started to think that these problems might be the beginning of a solution to a different puzzle. I believe we can use the scanner to make *intentional* modifications to an object—specifically, a crystal lattice designed to harness and transmit energy and data together, at the same time, on the same stream. The scanner could be the key to building a viable, scalable quantum computer unlike anything currently theorized."

Taraji sat up. "Modifying a lattice structure and still preserving its integrity is pretty out there, Aaron. On the other hand, if the beam didn't outright shatter that ornament you put into it… then I suppose it's at least conceivable."

She picked up the acrylic sheet and studied it. "I'll admit I don't know what you see when you look at this," she said. "But your ideas always seem to bear fruit."

She set the scan down, then looked directly at him and smiled.

"Thank you," she said, "for saving *both* our asses. Send me a quick summary of what you just told me when you get back to your desk. Corinne is going to lose her shit over this because she didn't think of it first, but I know her—she's going to love it. I'm sure she'll want to talk with you about it. I'll also speak with Argo about getting approval for you to scan a *preformed* object with a consistent molecular structure, not just some dime-store trinket that, frankly, could've exploded the machine, by the way. This'll put you on the dev team, too—not just the advisory board. So prepare yourself for some long hours."

He managed a tight smile. "Thanks, Taraji."

"Thank *you*. We might just be able to turn this breach of protocol into something entirely new. And I think you just saved this project."

Aaron nodded gratefully, then stood to leave.

"One last thing, sweetie," she added, her tone softening even more as she appeared to return to her role of supportive friend. "Whoever this asshole is who's bothering you, if we see him on the street, just point him out and I'll kick his fucking ass."

Aaron chuckled with a tear-filled smile. "Thanks, T," he said. "Can I ask a favor?"

"Name it."

"I'd like that scan back. And the letter you got, and the envelope."

"You got it," she agreed cordially. "I'll need them for the meeting, but no one's going to want them in their files. I'll hand them off to you this afternoon. And *please* cut the watermark off anything else you have at home."

Relieved, Aaron turned and left the office.

That night, he told Drummer about the letter and the scan. He wanted to go further and confront Grant, but Drummer refused. They agreed that in principle, going on the offensive was not a bad idea, but in practice it would be a mistake. Aaron needed time to map out the coming months. He had to buy the condo that he'd occupy come Labor Day, and he had to construct a life inside that condo that contained no sign of Drummer or their shared history. He had to focus on the future, but he couldn't help worrying about what Grant might be up to on the sidelines.

UNIVERSAL CONSTANT

Once he saw it, he realized that it was everywhere.
It was in every atom in the room,
In every photograph,
In every moment,
And in every memory.

The needle's programming,
The basis of its function,
Was not merely found in the filament,
It *was* the filament.

The lattice constant of that twisting, microscopic thread—while uniform in two of its three axes—replicated a pattern in the third.

On one side of the singularity, the spaces between the atoms mimicked the unique vibration of the universe itself.

On the other side, the lattice constant served as programming, capable of being modified, with that modification reflected in the numbers on the needle—the "where" and the "when." The aged scientist concluded that passing gravitational energy through this lattice, with a living individual as a bridge, would connect that individual to the universe and take him whenever and wherever he programmed it to go.

As Drummer had once postulated, Aaron didn't need to know precisely how it worked. Only how to *make* it work.

CHAPTER 17
CONNECTING DOTS

DOZENS OF small-print documents covered the coffee table. Drummer looked over each one, and everything appeared in order. Aaron had done an excellent job negotiating for the condo. He even paid less for it this time around, having leveraged the aftereffects of the Great Recession.

Among the papers was a glossy sales brochure for the property. It lay open to a two-page spread showing an architectural floor plan of a corner unit and several photos of it staged and furnished. Drummer looked down at the brochure—briefly, for a time, then away, then back again—as he perused the legal paperwork.

Aaron returned from a trip to the gym. He set down his bag and sat beside Drummer. "You look… perturbed," Aaron said.

"Perturbed? That's a fancy word for you."

"I'm learning," he answered smugly. He looked down at the open brochure then back up at Drummer. "I bought the same unit as last time, didn't I?"

Drummer sat back. "Yeah, you did. I don't know why I'm surprised. I guess I should've expected it."

"I didn't do it on purpose, D. But you did insist on that building."

"Yeah, I know." Drummer took Aaron's hand and smiled. "I guess I thought you might end up on a different floor or in a different corner, or something. But it's comforting to know you'll be in the same place."

He picked up the brochure and flipped through it.

"There've been a lot of surreal moments over the past ten years," Drummer said, "but this one's unique. I look around this house and think about the things you're taking with you—things that I remember. A few weeks ago, this house was our life. Now it's like we're gutting our memories of it for use as props on a set over there."

"I hope you don't really feel that way," said Aaron.

Drummer answered with a wave of his hand. "I'm just being dramatic," he said. "Truth is, you're taking less with you than I thought you would. I appreciate that."

"Well, you said it… this house is our life," said Aaron. "And I hope you know that whatever happens out there in that building, this house will *always* be our life. And one day I'll come home, and I'll bring all that stuff back with me."

Drummer chuckled sweetly and gently caressed Aaron's cheek. "I love how sentimental you are."

"Just like you," said Aaron. He turned his head and kissed Drummer's hand. "Do you want to see it?"

"See it?" Drummer asked. "The condo? I don't know if that's such a good idea."

"Why not?"

"I just don't know how I'll feel walking into that place."

"Will you do it for me?" asked Aaron. "I want to see you there so I can burn the image into my mind—the image of you in that condo with me, as you are today. Besides—" Aaron took the brochure from Drummer and closed it. "—it bothers me to see you looking at these documents with that sad expression, like they're divorce papers."

Drummer revealed a shamed grin, for Aaron's assessment of him hit close to home. "Divorce papers. Now there's an analogy. Okay, fine. We can go."

Aaron perked up. "Really?"

"Why not?" Drummer said, relenting. "But let's go before I change my mind."

Drummer scooped up the paperwork and locked it in the safe. Since the loss of the needle, he and Aaron left nothing of any importance lying out while they were away. They'd also made several security upgrades to the house, including installing a long-overdue video surveillance system.

Once the place was locked up, Aaron drove them downtown.

From the passenger seat, Drummer watched as the city rolled by—old and new buildings, random people on the sidewalks, storefronts he vaguely recalled—all of it passing on and away in a dreamlike procession. He felt comfortably detached, but glimpses of the condo tower out of the corner of his eye fed him a slow, steady drip of anxiety.

They rounded a corner onto Mission Street. Directly ahead, seemingly risen from nowhere, stood that tall glass monolith.

Drummer stared at it. Every detail clawed at him. He could hardly believe it was real, but this idol from the past and portent of the future was no vestige of memory. He felt a sudden, oppressive incursion from within as his old life came rushing back, as if the building were alive and had noticed him approaching. It was no longer just a familiar profile against a distant skyline, or a photograph on his phone, or a reflection filtered through the lenses and mirrors of a telescope. It was real, and it was home, and it howled at him with accusations of neglect and abandonment, blaming him for deserting the man he'd loved and the life they'd once shared.

His gaze fell to his hands as Aaron pulled into the underground garage and parked. The ensuing silence was disturbingly perfect when the engine shut off, save for the cries of guilt in Drummer's mind. He didn't have to look up to know they were parked in one of the two spaces he himself had used years ago.

"D?" Aaron inquired cautiously.

"Just give me a minute," he asked in a soft appeal.

Drummer focused on his breath. He soon fell completely still. His guilt was loud, but he knew intellectually that it was irrational. There was no reason to blame himself for what had happened. His trip into the past had been an accident.

He chased the judgment away, then turned to Aaron and took his hand.

"I'm ready," he said quietly. "I'd like to see the courtyard first."

They left the car, crossed the gray concrete garage to the elevator, and rode up two floors to the lobby level. They exited through the back of the building into a park-like space half the size of the tower's footprint.

Standing in the courtyard, Drummer was amazed—it appeared exactly as he remembered. He and Aaron had spent many hours there for barbecues, birthday parties, and intimate conversations. He imagined himself with Aaron, sitting on a bench beneath a birch tree in the corner, the spot where Drummer once held him after a very public breakdown, when memories of Grant had swelled up from nowhere.

Drummer closed his eyes.

Visions came and went.

Eventually, his mind emptied and all that remained was the sound of the wind and the hope in his heart that his festive memories of the future would indeed recur—but that the painful ones would die.

He and Aaron returned to the building. As they entered the lobby, a man in his early twenties wearing a blue suit jacket passed them. He was the building's security officer. He greeted them with a kind nod that lacked recognition. Drummer recognized him immediately but said nothing, for there was nothing to say. They rode the elevator in silence, the floor numbers counting upward at a steady pace until coming to a stop at the twenty-fifth floor. The doors opened, and after only a few strides, the two men found themselves standing outside the unit itself—number 2550.

Aaron unlocked it. As he leaned on the door, the slight whooshing sound it made as it opened triggered a memory for Drummer, one both visceral and emotional. It was the soft, comforting signal of his partner returning home at night, the sound of Aaron opening the door, soon to greet him with a smile and a tender touch.

He held this memory close as he stepped inside.

The unit was filled with most of the same objects and furnishings he remembered from 2020, and all in the same places. The same table and chairs were in the kitchen, and the same bookshelf was standing by the far window. This was the home he remembered—everything he had lost—and now it was back, rebuilt piece by piece.

A gallery of a dozen framed photographs hung on the wall above the couch, much as they had at the house. There were several pictures of Aaron's skater friends—including one of Aaron with Willis—alongside other pictures of his family and close coworkers. A large photograph of Aaron standing with Lorraine and Francis on the cruise ship dominated the well-organized display.

"That's different," said Drummer, touching the frame. "You never had a cruise photo on the wall before I moved in."

"I'd never been on a cruise before," said Aaron. "And I'll always see you standing behind the camera taking that picture, D. I'm sure this place looks a lot like you remember it, but there are small pieces like that photo—pieces of our life—that I've put up all over the place. Items I can display without worry that I'll have to explain them. Those things will keep you with me so I don't forget."

Drummer stepped away from the photographs and crossed to the picture window that comprised most of the far wall. Many of the buildings he remembered outside had yet to be constructed, including the imposing Salesforce Tower that would eventually dominate their city view. He looked down at the streets below, curious to know the stage of the tower's construction, but the site was still occupied by an aging bus terminal that had yet to be demolished.

He went to the bedroom. Mounted above the headboard was Aaron's reproduction of *The Starry Night*. Drummer fell into his memories again. He relived the nightmares, the tears, the anguish, and the healing that had once taken place there. He imagined himself in the bed, holding Aaron in the dark, comforting him as he suffered the resurging traumas of his past. Drummer was glad to know that these events would not repeat, but part of him was sad to realize that such an intimate connection between Aaron and himself—as painful as it had been to experience—was gone forever.`

He heard a stirring in the master bathroom and turned toward it, peering through the open doorway. Aaron had gone in and now stood at the sink, facing the mirror. This vision was like a shiv in Drummer's déjà vu, reminding him of his last day living his old life. It drew him closer, and as he neared, Aaron smiled into the mirror at his approaching reflection. Drummer wrapped his tattooed arms around him from behind, and the two men beheld their reflected image together.

From the dreamy look in Aaron's eyes, Drummer could see that to him their reflection was a thing of pure beauty—a vision of the two of them that Aaron could commit to memory and hold close to his heart for the next ten years. But for Drummer, it was a painful reminder of another day. The last time he had stood there with his arms wrapped around Aaron this way, Aaron had been forty and Drummer forty-five. Now Aaron was thirty and Drummer was fifty-five. The greater difference in their ages didn't really bother him most days, but seeing it so visibly pronounced, and in this setting, laid bare every minute of their lost time.

Drummer lowered his head, hoping to chase away a sudden surge of grief that he couldn't hide.

Aaron turned around and held him. "I'm sorry, D," he said. "Maybe we shouldn't have come after all."

"No," Drummer answered. "I'm glad we're here. It's a lot, but I'm happy to see this place again." He glanced one last time at the pair of them in the mirror, then drew himself out of Aaron's embrace and left the room.

"This whole place is identical," he said as he and Aaron returned to the living room. "I don't know how it's possible for so many things to be the same, but I'm glad they are."

"Maybe I just copied the pictures," Aaron said in jest.

"No," Drummer replied with surety. "There are some new callouts, like the photo with Lorraine and Francis, but this place… it's destiny. We've been connecting dots for ten years, and those dots have led us right back here."

Drummer took a moment to study the beautiful contours of Aaron's face. In them he could still see the cocky twenty-year-old skater who had challenged him in 2000, and he could also see the wise and pragmatic forty-year-old man Aaron would become ten years from now. This thirty-year-old version standing with him in the condo was an amalgam of them both, the perfect bridge between two versions of the same man, from two different worlds.

"I'm sorry I haven't been the same lately," Drummer said, breaking the silence.

"I get it," said Aaron. "Losing the needle and knowing this day was coming—it hurts me too."

"But I've been distant, and I'm sorry. I've been telling myself that this life has always been our goal, and that this place is exactly where you need to be. *And it is*, but it shouldn't have been so calculated."

"I'm a scientist, remember? Calculations are what I do."

"But not me," Drummer said morosely. "I was in tech a long time ago, but I've always been more emotional than analytical."

"You've got a strong logical side, D," Aaron assured him. "And we're both romantics. We're well-matched."

Aaron sat on the couch and looked around the room. "It is a strange feeling, isn't it? Thinking back to the photos you showed me years ago. I was so blown away looking at that life. I thought, *will I really have something so wonderful*? Now here I am. But I'm realizing that it's actually the *past* ten years that have been wonderful. And I try to tell myself that the next ten won't just be a stale replay of those photos."

"They won't," said Drummer, sitting down beside him. "Everything you do here will be new. Lorraine and Francis'll be up there on the wall to remind you of that. And the best part—Grant won't be living in your head."

"Maybe."

"Definitely."

"But he's still out there."

"But he won't torment your dreams," Drummer said plainly. "You won't take those nightmares to work with you. You won't feel your heart pounding in meetings, forcing you to rush outside, desperate to find somewhere to cry. Grant's no longer a part of you, and that will make the next ten years something entirely new, even if you do follow in your own footsteps in other ways."

"But are you sure he won't get in the way?" Aaron asked.

"I am," said Drummer. "He's fixated on me at this point. I can tell. And I can handle him."

"Okay," said Aaron. "But I keep wondering if you *have* to. Like, do we need to go through any of this at all? What if it doesn't have to be like this?"

"What do you mean?"

"I mean… what if I stay? What if I don't move in here? What if I stay at the house with you instead, help you deal with Grant, and we keep living the life we already have? Lorraine and Francis—they *saw* us. They *envied* us. Those two perfect people saw something in us they'd never seen in anyone else. What we have is unique and glorious, so why end it? What if, instead, I don't reply to your younger self when he contacts me, and I don't go to him?"

"You have to," Drummer answered, though he felt the emotional undertow of Aaron's argument. "If you don't, then you and I will never meet—in either 2010 or 2000. You know that."

"I think we have doubts," said Aaron. "But if I don't go, would it really undo everything? Does cause and effect really work in a loop, like the grandfather paradox thought experiment? If we skip one thing now, would it really erase a decade? And what if your counterpart doesn't see the needle in the alley like you think? What if he doesn't pick it up? We don't really know any of these things."

"We know," said Drummer. "Look at this place. Look at the last ten years. Some things have been different, but everything has steered us back to this. We can't change it."

"But don't we have the right to try?"

"No, we don't," said Drummer, bluntly. "It isn't just about us, Aaron. It's also about *him*—the other Drummer. He needs you. He's alone. He's out there right now, thinking only of you, the undiscovered man of his dreams. He's at dinner with his friends and their partners, seeing them live their lives together, terrified he'll never meet you. And he's at home at night, playing video games by himself, wondering if you even exist. *He needs you, Aaron.* And you need him. You need him to give you the life that I can't."

"But you're the one I love, Drummer, not him," Aaron said with a firm voice. "And that other life with Grant—I've never known it. And I have a hard time believing that the universe is so invested in you and me specifically that it would sweep me back to that life if we made a different choice today."

Drummer looked off toward the bedroom and thought back to the nightmares, to waking up in the dark to the sound of Aaron's cries. "You might not know that life," he said, "but I do. And I can't take even the slightest chance that you'll have to go through that again."

Aaron sighed heavily. "Then… if I do go, we can still talk sometimes, right? I can call you, or text you?"

"No," Drummer said, firmly. "You have to live your life with him as if I'm not here."

"How am I supposed to do that, D?" Aaron retorted. "How do I not drive by the house every night after work? How do I not set up a telescope and look for you?"

"I don't know, babe, but you have to. And if you can't do it… then I'll have no choice but to make sure I'm not at the house for you to find."

Aaron looked at him with terror in his eyes. "You wouldn't really disappear on me like that."

Drummer peered back at him, stone-faced. The two of them had gone to great lengths to ensure their coming separation would work. They'd established a trust fund for Drummer and a property management plan for the house. They even paid shady third parties to scrub all online records of Aaron's name where it might be associated with the house's address. The work was done.

"Look," said Drummer, "I can't stop you from driving by, or doing whatever you need to do to get through this, but I'll do what I have to do so that we don't screw it up. This condo will be your home in a month, and that house will be a memory. And that's that."

Aaron searched his eyes for any sign of uncertainty.

"Be with him," Drummer said after a long silence, delivering his words softly and carefully. "Trust me. It won't be long before he becomes your entire world and you forget all about that house on the hill."

"I don't want to go," Aaron responded fiercely. "And I don't think I have to. And I don't think you're sure either."

"It doesn't matter what we think," said Drummer, "only what we do."

Aaron shook his head. "You're better with words than that, D. I'm disappointed."

Aaron's phone pinged. Visibly annoyed, he pulled it out and checked it. Then he dropped it on the coffee table like he'd been scalded.

On the screen, clearly visible to Drummer, was one new Facebook notification. It indicated a single message, containing a sweet, simple compliment:

"Beautiful."

PARADOXICAL LOGIC

Trial and error are the assessment of theory, the tuning instruments of science, and the progenitors of invention. They are also the stones that compose the road, the signs that show the way, and the footsteps in the dirt that hint at the paths taken by others. They connect dots, they eliminate doubt, and they bring light to darkness, clearing the gods from the night sky to reveal the daylight—and the truth.

Trial had sent him forward. Error had sent him back. And as a result, when he looked into the eyes of his duplicate self, he realized how he'd been wrong and where he'd been right.

Aaron had once believed that all of time was connected, and that human action worked in a loop. Forward and backward, then forward again. He'd seen it in the photographs, which had not visibly changed when their time came back around.

But looking into the eyes of his double told him that even though events had not appeared to change, neither had they looped. Instead they'd repeated, nearly identically, and that the photos, while indisputable, showed only what could be seen on the surface. Time may have worked in a loop, but cause and effect for anyone holding the needle did not.

Trial and error exposed Aaron's ignorance, and with that ignorance now pulled back, he beheld what he could not see before: the end of the road and the foot of a bridge.

CHAPTER 18
CROSSROADS

THE COURTSHIP was swift.

Aaron exchanged daily texts with Drummer's thirty-five-year-old counterpart. The two men also shared long, intimate emails, phone calls, and provocative photos. Through it all, Drummer watched. He saw Aaron's excitement blossom with the morning and wither beneath his guilt at night. The years Drummer had described as the best of his life were upon them, and it was clear that Aaron could see how different they'd be from those that had already come and gone.

His conflicted feelings were evident.

Drummer wished he could ease them, but he couldn't. He had his own conflict to contend with. His heart was breaking, and he knew these days signaled the end for him. Conversely, he also took comfort in the apparent surety that none of the roads he and Aaron had walked, or the digressions they'd made, had altered their trajectory toward this moment. Time was healing, and their future was finding its way.

On Sunday, September fifth, 2010, a brilliant sun rose above San Francisco, bringing with it a boundless blue sky and temperatures in the mid-seventies. The city had emptied for Labor Day weekend, as it did every year, and it felt like a paradise abandoned by all but the machines that turned its gears.

Drummer stood on the back deck of the house, looking out at downtown. The day was even more idyllic than he remembered. He thought about his younger self out there at that very moment—excited and nervous—hoping that this would be the day he met the man of his dreams.

This time he would be right.

Drummer took in the air, that first meeting lingering in his mind. He'd promised Aaron that he would go with him and stand by him as he crossed over from the life he knew to the life that waited. He wasn't afraid of being seen by anyone he knew, or even by his younger self. For today the world was empty, and Drummer's counterpart would have eyes for only one man.

But was *Drummer* prepared to witness that moment? Was he ready to watch as someone else took his place… even though that someone was himself? He felt as though he were about to give Aaron away, delivering him to the waiting arms of a groom in an arranged marriage.

Was it irony? Paradox?

No matter. He was ready.

He went back inside.

He found Aaron sitting at the kitchen table, visibly forlorn. A vase of fresh tulips sat beside him on the counter—a gift from Drummer. Aaron wore the blue Star Wars logo T-shirt Drummer remembered him wearing the first time he'd lived through this day. Aaron had also removed his wedding ring, which he held in his hand.

"I can't take this with me," Aaron said despondently. "If he finds it, I'll have a lot of explaining to do."

Drummer delicately took the ring from his hand. He got down on one knee and slipped it back onto Aaron's finger. "Will you marry me?" he asked, knowing the answer.

Aaron's dour expression took flight. "Of course I will."

Drummer smiled back. "Just tell him it's a family heirloom."

They held each other's gaze, sharing feelings of love and comfort, anticipation and loss. Drummer kissed Aaron's hand, then stood.

"Is there anything else you want to take with you?" he asked. "I noticed you left your tux in the closet."

"I don't think I could bear to look at it, let alone wear it again."

"You might want it for the cruise in five years."

"I'll buy another one," said Aaron. "Maybe a maroon jacket this time."

Drummer nodded. "So, there's nothing else here you want? Last chance. Tonight you go home to that condo for good."

Aaron looked away. "I got everything," he said with a heavy sigh, then added, "along with a million pictures from the last ten years, and everything of the next ten that I copied from your phone."

"You're not afraid he'll find those?"

"You're not the kind of man who looks through someone else's things, D." Aaron reached out to touch one of the tulip petals. "Can I have a little more time to myself?" he asked. "I'd like to say goodbye to this place."

"Of course."

Drummer peered toward the front door, down the hall. He was about to walk away, but his conscience wouldn't let him leave just yet. He had one last thing to share.

"Aaron," he said, "I know you told me you didn't want to know everything about the future, but you also said to prepare you for the big events. There's one more thing you need to know, a big thing. I've debated with myself for ten years whether I should say anything, but standing here now, I know I can't stay silent."

"What is it?"

Drummer conjured a tone as calm and reassuring as he could, but he knew that the nature of what he was about to say would be neither. "You know the swine flu from last year," he began, "and SARS from a few years ago?"

"Yeah."

"In late 2019, a new virus will appear. It'll start in Wuhan, China. It'll be more contagious and insidious than either swine flu or SARS. I don't want to be alarmist, but it'll be very serious. So take it seriously. By April 2020, entire cities will be in lockdown. Hospitals in Washington state and New York will be overwhelmed. All flights around the world will be grounded, and most international borders will be closed as countries try to slow the spread."

Even as Drummer was trying to lay his words down gently, he could see in Aaron's expression that they were landing hard regardless.

"By August, 2020," Drummer continued, "almost a million people worldwide will have died—almost 200,000 in the US alone. 2020 is a complete shit-show, baby, and it's going to feel like the entire world has lost its mind."

Aaron remained quiet, taking it in.

"And I left in August, so I don't know how it ends," Drummer admitted. "I wish I could tell you that it'll all be okay—and I think it will be, but I just don't know. Fortunately, San Francisco will be one of the safest places to live. You also have ample savings, no debt, and a solid career. Those things will protect you."

"D...," Aaron said haltingly. "It sounds really scary."

"Your good fortune will get you through it. You'll even be able to help others."

"My good fortune is because of you."

"Not all of it," said Drummer. "You're richer now than you would've been, but you never really had to worry about money. Just promise me this: don't let the virus dominate your thoughts between now and then. Put it on your calendar, put that calendar in a drawer, and live your life. In late 2019, take it out and pay attention."

"I will," Aaron said. "I have a question."

"Shoot."

"Do we get sick? You and me?"

"No. Not before August at least," Drummer said. "And your parents are fine, and mine are fine, so don't worry about them either. Most people who get it will have what feels like a miserable flu and recover. But the virus is unpredictable, so don't let your guard down."

"Okay," Aaron said through a long sigh.

"This isn't what I wanted to leave you with. I'm so sorry."

"It's okay. You're right, I need to know. Like you said, I'll put it in a calendar and put the calendar in a drawer."

Drummer nodded apologetically. He wanted to say more, to dull the impact of his foreknowledge, but he suspected that additional words would only amplify the dread. "I'll meet you out front," he said simply. He wrapped his arms around Aaron and held him tight, kissed him, then disappeared down the hall.

WHEN DRUMMER had gone, Aaron closed his eyes and thought about what he'd said. 2019—nine years away. A long time to keep a dire prediction to himself. But it was good to know about the calamity in advance. Without that foreknowledge, Aaron would've wondered if he'd somehow caused it himself.

He left the kitchen and walked through the house. Most of his personal items were gone, already moved to the condo. In the living room, however, almost everything remained. He stood in front of a bookshelf that contained souvenirs from his travels with Drummer, including photographs from their skydive and the cruise to Hawaii. He lamented the fact that he wouldn't be able to tell Drummer's counterpart about any of it, not without turning each story into a vague recollection about something he once did with someone he once knew.

He went to the side table that held the framed photograph of himself with Drummer on the cruise in 2005. He knelt beside it, tore a small piece of paper from a notepad, and on it he wrote, SEE YOU IN TEN YEARS. He removed his wedding ring and placed it on top, leaving it behind with the note as he left the house.

He found Drummer outside. They smiled sadly at one other, then walked down the hill to Castro Street Station, where they boarded a single-car subway train heading downtown. They stood at the front, close to the operator's cabin, where Aaron casually studied the people around him—all of them minding their own business, ignoring one another, and ignoring him. For the first time, he understood what Drummer had meant all those years ago, when he said that the people who filled this contemporary world seemed like ghosts. Aaron himself now had a life ahead of him that none of these people could guess at, but that he already knew all too well.

The view through the operator's window caught his eye. The dark subway tunnel extended straight ahead, white lights spaced equidistant along the north wall. He stared at those lights as they winked past, flashing in his eyes, one after the other in a steady rhythm, as if the train followed not the track but those lights, connecting the dots toward his ultimate destination.

He and Drummer exited at Powell Station, near Union Square, then walked to the nearby movie theater. Side by side, the two men approached the glass main doors. As they entered, Aaron's anxiety hit its ceiling.

This was the place. Once the doors closed behind them, there was no going back. A ten-year-long ticking clock was now counting down the final minutes and seconds.

Drummer took Aaron's hand as the doors eased shut. The gesture had always given the two men comfort, but now it served as a lifeline, confirming that neither of them were taking the moment lightly as they walked through the wide, brightly lit lobby together.

Aaron looked around as they went, studying the room. As he did, he imagined more than just the reflections of an iconic photograph. More than just an encroaching, pivotal meeting. He saw a time and place where all things converged, where all things started and ended. The great crossroads of his life.

"Do you see it?" he asked, his voice shaking.

Drummer glanced at him with obvious concern. "What is it?"

"Signposts," Aaron said almost breathlessly, enthralled by the visions in his mind. "They're all around us. Right here and right now, there are so many choices. So many ways this can go either right or wrong."

"There's only one way this can go, babe."

Aaron understood the imperative to stay focused, but he was still confused by his role and what he was *supposed to do*. His prescribed action was to fulfill the destiny he'd seen in the photographs and join the younger Drummer. But in his heart, he still believed that he could stay with the elder without repercussions. *Anything was possible*, he thought, and it all branched out from this very moment, each path represented by a signpost pointing the way.

But those signposts were mostly obscure and unreadable. Indeed, Aaron could read only one: the sign pointing to his future with Drummer's counterpart. It was the only definitive path he knew.

He wondered if it could be fate after all.

The two men stopped at a bench near a bank of tall windows at the back of the theater, overlooking a pedestrian parkway.

Drummer pointed across the room.

There, leaning against a large pillar near the ticket counter, stood a tattooed thirty-five-year-old man in a white A-shirt tank top.

Aaron stared at him.

He couldn't move.

It was the other Drummer, looking exactly as he had in the photo Drummer had shown him. A window on a transitional moment that Aaron had looked at hundreds of times from the outside.

That moment was now.

DRUMMER LOOKED away. Everything was progressing as he had expected, but it was still difficult to look at his younger self across the room.

"It's him," said Aaron, disbelief in his tone.

"I know," said Drummer. His voice cracked, along with his composure. "Aaron...."

"Oh, baby," Aaron said, reaching out. "You're supposed to be the stronger one today."

Drummer leaned against him, put his arms around him, and sobbed quietly into his shoulder.

"It's okay," Aaron assured him. "This is how it's supposed to be, right? That's what you've been telling me."

Gently, Drummer pulled away. "Yeah, it is." He took Aaron's hands in his. "Look, in a minute you're going to go over there, and his life is going to change completely… and so will yours. And in ten years, when you're at the peak of your happiness, he's going to disappear on you—*I'll* disappear on you—and I won't get to say to you what I wanted to say then. So let me tell you now: you gave me the best ten years of my life—no, *twenty*—and I am so, *so* sorry that I go away."

"I know, D," Aaron said, his own tears breaking the surface. "That's why I'm coming home to you. On that day, I'll come home to you. You don't have to try to save me anymore. Don't feel sad anymore. Ten years will go by, and then we'll have the rest of our lives together."

Drummer thought about the next ten years. He thought about the next few days. He thought about Grant. If he went after Grant as he planned—to shoot him dead and burn the place down around them—the consequences were clear. It would be the end. This moment—right here, right now—was his end.

Drummer shifted his gaze to his younger self. "He's waiting," he said, his voice gravelly.

"I don't want to go."

"You have to," Drummer insisted. "And you'll be glad you did."

Aaron and Drummer looked deep into one another's eyes, committing to memory every line, freckle, and curve of each other's faces. They kissed, deeply and passionately. It was a kiss filled with the love and joy of ten long, wonderful years, now coming to an end amid feelings of guilt, sorrow, and apology.

They released each other.

Drummer stepped back and wiped his eyes.

"I love you, Aaron," he said with longing and lament.

"Oh, Drummer, I love you too," said Aaron. "Ten years. I'll see you in ten years."

AARON TURNED and started away. He looked down at the floor as he went, trying to stay focused. More than anything in the world he wanted to run back to Drummer, but he was now mostly convinced that his future and his past were dependent on what stood ahead of him. If he wanted the entirety of that life to remain intact, and to see the elder Drummer in ten years as he planned, he could not turn back.

He greeted Drummer's counterpart with a forced smile, but his attempt at emotional control quickly crumbled as the younger Drummer's expression lit up. That smile was radiant. Pure. Gorgeous. Seeing it— seeing this younger man beam at him with unspoiled thrill and vigor— felt to Aaron like he was meeting Drummer for the first time all over again, in the parking lot of his suburban apartment. Only this time he knew exactly who Drummer was, how to make him happy, and how happy Aaron himself would be at his side.

ACROSS THE room, Drummer watched his memory unfold in real time.

History was repeating.

Dots were connecting.

Destiny and free will were colliding.

The younger Drummer pulled his phone from his pocket and took a selfie with Aaron.

At the sight of this, the elder let out a small, tearful sigh.

Drummer's counterpart put his phone away. Then he and Aaron began to walk off, toward the escalators to the theaters upstairs.

Aaron glanced over his shoulder as they went, locking eyes with the elder Drummer across the room, giving him one last loving, grateful smile.

The previous ten years, and all their glorious moments, flashed before the pair's eyes, exchanged between them in that final parting glance. Drummer wanted that look to last forever, but time moved quickly, and it was over in a blink. Aaron and Drummer's younger counterpart disappeared around a corner, to their waiting future.

Drummer's loss was immediate; he felt suddenly, profoundly alone. At fifty-five years old, surrounded by the world of 2010, he was still ten years displaced from his own reality. Though he'd been a man out of time for a decade, being with Aaron had given him a connection to the world. Now that connection was gone.

He found a long bench nearby and sat. His grief sat beside him as the people around him carried on.

A man used an ATM.

A woman crossed to the exit.

A couple chatted intimately in a corner.

For the first time in ten years, Drummer didn't see these people as ghosts.

For at that moment, the ghost was him.

ALL THINGS ended.

But it was not the end.

FIFTY YEARS away, another journey was reaching its own conclusion. It was the life of a scientist now eighty years old. An iteration of Aaron Hayes who'd lost everything in 2020, then toiled through time to build a bridge to his past and return to the crossroads where all things had come and gone, and all things started and ended.

As two gold lights bloomed.

THE BRIDGE

The lattice constant shifted as the filament reformed itself,
Building an architecture of gravity and relativity,
Around a singularity encased in crystal,
Connecting the abstract to the absolute.

The gate opened and the lattice sang its song,
As this bridge in glass extended a span to the past.
The old man crossed.

With him, he brought his message and the fulfillment of his purpose:
Knowledge to ignorance,
Health to sickness,
And justice to wickedness.

002.050.014.025.200 • • 236.000.000.139.851
[BACK 50 YEARS, 14 DAYS, 1 HOUR, 20 MINUTES • •
SOUTHWEST 86.9 MILES]
AUGUST 8, 2015

His first destination was a moment of distinct duality. He'd lived it twice before—each time with different feelings and motivations, but with the same outward expression captured in the photographs of the event. Now he viewed this moment from the outside, to confirm his theory that when time healed it may have done so identically, but imperfectly.

Before him, his thirty-five-year-old self, dressed in a maroon tuxedo jacket, crooned a country music classic.

But he did not sing Tammy Wynette, as he had years before. This time he sang Patsy Cline.

And he did not sing to the Drummer in the audience,

But over his head,

Backward through time,

To a similar man in a similar room on a similar ship,

Sailing on the same sea, ten years earlier:

"Why can't he be you?"

002.005.030.100.080 • • 055.000.000.148.601
[BACK 5 YEARS, 30 DAYS, 4 HOURS, 8 MINUTES • •
NORTHEAST 92.3 MILES]
SEPTEMBER 8, 2010

The gate opened and Aaron Hayes passed through a second time, crossing the bridge to a moment of sacrifice he felt compelled to witness. To verify its date, time, and location, and to confirm the imperative to prevent it.

Police lights flashed,
Firetrucks blocked the street,
And ambulances waited on standby,
As a small house on Potrero Hill raged with fire.

Two bodies would be found in the aftermath. One with a bullet hole in the front of his skull. The other with a self-inflicted wound through the temple. Both bodies would be burned beyond recognition, but Aaron had always known who they were.

002.000.003.400.000 • • 090.000.000.000.012
[BACK 3 DAYS, 16 HOURS • • EAST .0074 MILES]
SEPTEMBER 4, 2010

Another bridge formed.
Aaron crossed, to heal what had broken,
To break what had healed,
And prevent the deadly fire still to come.

Before him, sprawled out in a messy bed, Grant Zimmer slept. Clenched teeth, an angry brow, and hands balled into fists revealed Grant's hidden nature. The aged Aaron stood over him, holding, in a gloved hand, Grant's own gun.

He took aim.

At the same time,
In a small town,
At a large prison,
There was a riot.

001.000.000.275.000 • • 269.000.000.004.023
[FORWARD 11 HOURS • • WEST 2.5 MILES]
SEPTEMBER 5, 2010

The last bridge formed—to home.
He found flowers in the kitchen,
A black tuxedo hanging in an empty closet,
And a wedding ring resting on a note on a side table.

He saw ghosts on the street,
Lights in the subway,
And finally, a grieving man on a bench in a wide, bright lobby,
Alone with his sorrow at the site of a final farewell.

With measured steps, Aaron approached him.
And stopped a few feet away,
Unnoticed.

PART 3
SYNCHRONICITY

CHAPTER 19
AGAIN

In the theater lobby, not far from where he had said goodbye to Aaron just moments earlier, Drummer sat hunched over on a long bench, his face covered loosely by his hands. Though he knew his suffering was evident to anyone who passed him, he ignored any sign someone might be reaching out. He didn't need or want their attention or comfort. He'd done what he had to do—he had said goodbye to the man he loved, to preserve the future and the past. And it was time to turn his focus to his final task: eliminate Grant.

It would be a violent end, but Drummer had made peace with this. He'd lived a good life with Aaron, and he told himself that the twenty years they'd spent together would have to be enough. The decades might not have been consecutive, but the joy had been cumulative. He took solace in his belief that once he had dealt with Grant, Aaron would experience that same joy for himself, free from worry, as he should.

Drummer was proud. He'd saved Aaron and had devised a plan to deal with his lover's former abuser. But he was also angry, for he'd hoped to find a way to resolve the situation and still return home to 2020. Unfortunately, any such scheme would be too complicated to succeed. The fire he planned instead was a simple—even elegant—solution. It would destroy the crime scene and minimize the evidence left behind. It would also disguise Drummer's identity while leaving the remains of the obvious perpetrator, thus preventing his younger self from falling under suspicion. There was no alternative but to disappear into the ash.

Drummer's pride, grief, and anger took turns berating him as he sat on that bench. The discordant trio of emotions threatened to give him no peace. He'd made a promise he could not keep—to come home—but he was also intent on keeping the promise he'd made upon arriving in 2000. Now, as then, he was alone with his choices.

As he sat stewing in his grief, he heard his name spoken. It jolted him, like a cool wind on a hot day—his own name ringing in his ears in the form of Aaron's voice. He told himself that his mind had to be playing tricks on him. That just as Grant's voice had once whispered vile terrors into Aaron's head, now Aaron's was whispering sweet anguish into his.

He ignored it.

And he tried to chase the voice away.

But he heard it again, clearly, and he dared to ask himself if it could possibly be real.

He lifted his head. Cool air touched the tears drying on his cheeks as the bright lights of the room warped the view through his watering eyes. He blinked, clearing his vision, to find an old man of at least eighty years standing before him.

The elder looked down at Drummer with an expectant smile, one that conveyed sadness and empathy, but also quiet confidence and even a little cockiness. His lined face was unfamiliar, but that expression was unmistakable.

"Aaron?" he asked uncertainly.

The old man nodded. "It's me, D."

Drummer didn't know what to say, for the notion of an older Aaron coexisting with him had never entered his mind. But the aged figure was real, no figment of Drummer's memory nor product of his grief.

The elder Aaron reached into his pocket and—to Drummer's additional shock—pulled out the needle. It was luminescent and alive. Aaron peered at Drummer and said, with subtle vindication, "I found it."

Drummer was speechless. Tangled thoughts twisted in his head, and he could make no sense of them. But even as he fought with his mind, he could see that Aaron was also struggling with his emotions.

Aaron stammered into silence, then sat beside Drummer on the bench. He looked into Drummer's eyes, leaned against his shoulder, and cried.

Drummer held him as he wept, fighting back his own tears. This older Aaron seemed inconsolable.

"Oh, baby," Drummer said, his heart aching. He held Aaron with the same care that he had many years earlier, on many disquieting nights, to soothe the hard-edged remnants of his trauma. Though this Aaron's body was much older and frailer, it felt the same in his arms. He had the same quake of grief and the same rhythm in his cries. His clothes even smelled distinctly of the house. He was the same man, at any age.

Aaron calmed in Drummer's arms. He righted himself. "I'm sorry," he said, wiping his eyes.

"You never have to apologize to me," said Drummer.

"It must be a shock," Aaron added, "seeing me like this. Seeing me at all."

Drummer let out a short, fragmented chuckle. "Oh, babe, that's an understatement. What happened to you? You found the needle? I thought it was gone."

"So did I," said Aaron. "But in 2021 I went back to the house. I found it in the floor vent in the workroom."

"The vent?" Drummer asked. He vividly recalled searching the workroom and the vent himself after the house had been vandalized, finding nothing but broken glass.

"Don't blame yourself," Aaron said. "I searched the vent too, remember? It must've rolled around a bend in the duct."

The two men looked down at the brilliant device in Aaron's hand and regarded it with shared awe.

"It's beautiful," said Drummer. He hadn't seen it active since the first time he'd picked it up.

"It is," Aaron agreed. "It's quite the phone charger, don't you think?"

Drummer brightened at the quip. He studied Aaron's face. It had been weathered by time, but the younger man beneath was still there. In the older Aaron's voice, Drummer could still hear his once unapologetic cockiness, and in his eyes, he could see Aaron's unwavering determination. Even in the way he carried himself—just sitting there on the bench—his perfectly balanced pride and humility were apparent.

Drummer reached out and delicately touched his cheek.

Aaron shifted, clearly self-conscious about his age and appearance. But Drummer didn't care. He brought the older Aaron close and kissed him, then wrapped his arms around him and held him tight—this time not just to console him, but to show Aaron the purity of his love.

Aaron's tears came again, but this time they rode in on a broad sigh of relief.

The two men remained in each other's arms for quite some time before either spoke again.

"I'm sure you want to know why I'm here," Aaron said at last.

Drummer nodded. "You never do anything without a purpose."

Drummer hadn't even finished speaking when he realized that Aaron's purpose likely included more than just the desire to return to the past and see him again. But was Drummer ready to hear it? Was he prepared to do whatever Aaron might ask of him? And was he ready to learn what had happened to Aaron after Drummer disappeared on that day in August 2020, walking toward home on Dashiell Hammett?

Whether he was ready or not, he was about to find out.

"It was a beautiful life," Aaron said, leading him gently into his experience. "You said it right here in this room—that I'd be glad I went—and I was. We had ten amazing years, D."

Drummer was overjoyed to hear that all their planning hadn't been in vain, and that Aaron's life with him had indeed been prosperous and rewarding. But he also knew how it ended—in that alley, coming down from Nob Hill.

"That day came," said Aaron. "We went to Huntington Park, and on the way home we cut through Dashiell Hammett. I was terrified. I knew the needle was there. And I knew you'd find it and what would happen after."

"I'm so sorry," said Drummer, anticipating.

"No," said Aaron, softly. He paused for several seconds before finally adding… "It wasn't there."

"What?" Drummer asked, certain that he had misheard him.

"The needle wasn't there," Aaron repeated. "You didn't find it, you didn't disappear, and you didn't go back to the past."

Drummer stared at him in shock. "It wasn't there? Of course it was. Of course I went back. I remember everything, don't you?"

"I do," said Aaron. "But the needle wasn't in the alley that day."

"It had to be," said Drummer, louder. Confounded. "Didn't it?"

"I wish there was a simple explanation," Aaron said. "Yes, it had to be there, but it wasn't. We walked down the alley, turned onto Bush Street and… we went home."

Frantically, Drummer searched his thoughts for anything that could explain why things had changed so drastically, but none came to him. *They went home? They just left the alley, with neither a pause or a problem… and went home?*

"The next day," Aaron went on, "I went up to the house to look for you, but you weren't there. Everything was exactly the way we'd left it, though. The property management team had done its job—it was clean, bills and taxes paid, inspections up to date.

"I was glad to find I still owned the house, because it confirmed that you'd actually gone back to 2000 after all, and that everything we'd lived through had been real. But I was also confused, because your counterpart was still with me, and I had no idea how that could be. Worst of all, finding the house abandoned told me one more thing. That *you* were gone."

Drummer sank inside himself. If he hadn't been at the house, then his plan to eliminate Grant had gone ahead.

"Grant was killed in a fire in September 2010," Aaron said, as if reading his thoughts. "That was you, wasn't it? You're planning to go after him."

Drummer couldn't admit it aloud. Knowing what would come as a result of his actions shamed him.

"It's okay," Aaron said in a forgiving tone. "You might've gone after him then, but you don't need to do it now."

Drummer met his gaze once more, and this time, he saw Aaron's unmistakable, cocksure glint looking back.

"You did it yourself," Drummer concluded.

Aaron held up the needle as confirmation. "When you can go anywhere, and to any time, wouldn't you do the same? Take his gun from the future, use it in the past, leave no evidence but a bullet with no origin. It's poetry. And there's a certain cosmic justice in avenging myself, don't you think?"

Drummer smiled, impressed—again.

"Then, after I found the house abandoned," Aaron continued, "Covid-19 happened. It was easy on me, but not on you… on *him*. He died in a week."

Drummer didn't know what to say. So he said nothing.

"It's been forty years for me," Aaron added, "but I still relive that week every day. The night he was admitted to the ICU, the increasingly rare texts, and the sound of him on the phone, struggling to breathe. Then, a few days later, the call from a hospital nurse, saying he… he was gone."

"Oh, baby," said Drummer. To learn of his own death was disturbing, but to know that Aaron had gone through the ordeal alone troubled him even more.

"I'm sorry to give you the news," said Aaron.

"It's… strange to hear it," said Drummer, "but we can leave it at that."

Aaron nodded somberly. "I sold the condo and moved back to the house. In early fall of 2021, the furnace kicked on. I heard this strange rattling noise. That's when I found the needle in the vent."

"I can't imagine what that was like."

"Honestly? It was a relief."

"A relief?"

"Yes," said Aaron. "D, I'd lost both of you—forever, I thought—but finding the needle gave me back my purpose. I was able to make peace with my choices and start working on it again."

"And once you'd figured it out, you used it to bring you here."

"Yeah."

"I'm glad. But how could it have been in the vent? Why wasn't it in the alley?"

"It wasn't in the alley," Aaron said, "because that's not where we left it. The needle isn't like other objects we carry with us. It's more like… a celestial body. Like the Earth or the Sun. When we go back in time, we find the past versions of ourselves standing there; in a sense, we're duplicated, along with anything we've brought with us, like your phone. But the needle doesn't duplicate. It exists in and of itself, and there can only ever be one. It just happens to be small enough to be carried, while we're carried by the Earth.

"So to answer your question, the reason the needle wasn't in the alley in 2020 is because whoever left it or lost it there the first time, didn't have it in their possession when 2020 came back around. They couldn't leave it in the alley, because *we* had it. It was still in the vent."

Drummer struggled to understand. He thought he did, but Aaron's explanation went against everything he had long presumed to be true.

Unable to reconcile his confusion, he turned to the next question on his mind: "Then what about…?"

"The person who left it there?" Aaron shrugged. "It would've disappeared from their possession without warning or explanation. Wherever they were in October 2000 is where they would've found themselves stuck. Because once you appeared there with the needle in *your* hand, it would've disappeared from theirs."

Drummer turned it all over in his mind. "How did you ever figure this out?"

"Trial and error. As I got older, I watched elements of the needle being invented. The coordinate system. And the crystal containment cell that holds the singularity—you were right about that. I guessed at the rest, because you were also right that I didn't need to know exactly how the needle worked, just how to *make* it work. And once I figured out how to power it and operate it, the rest was, as I said, trial and error."

"Must've been frustrating."

"Very frustrating, but also exciting and *amazing*," Aaron said. "The first time it turned on, I nearly fell over. It was so beautiful. I'd never seen anything like it. I used an adaptive interface to program it and sent myself forward in time an hour. All I had to do was touch it. For the next experiment, I tried a full day. Then a week. I spent two years experimenting until I thought I had it perfected. Once, I jumped to a hilltop a mile away and a month in the future. *It was so easy*. So liberating. All of time and space in the palm of my hand."

Drummer felt chills, for Aaron's retelling was dramatic and riveting. In his old age, Aaron had not merely become good with words, he'd become great, describing his mastery of the needle with eloquence and passion.

"I didn't bother jumping back to my starting point when I was only going forward in time for short periods. But for the week and the month tests, I did. Nothing seemed to change. I realized later it was because I was jumping back to a point just *after* the moment I'd jumped forward. I wasn't going to find myself there because I'd already left. But, cocky as ever, I decided one day to go back in time without going forward first. I went back an hour. When I got there, I realized I'd made a terrible miscalculation."

"A miscalculation?" asked Drummer, afraid that the general statement concealed global repercussions. "What do you mean?"

"I hadn't yet realized that there could be only one needle at any given time. I jumped back, and suddenly there were two of me standing in the workroom. That part I'd guessed, but I also assumed there would be two needles—one in my hand and one on the table. But when I appeared with the needle in my hand, the one on the table *disappeared*.

"See, I had gone into the experiment thinking that an hour later my counterpart could use his own needle to jump back and close the loop.

But since there was only one needle in the room with us, we knew that he couldn't go back. Even if he took the needle from me and tried, he would just appear beside another version himself in the past and still have only one needle. It was a frustrating conundrum."

"I hate to laugh, but it sounds like something the Professor would do on *Futurama*."

Aaron smiled. "Doesn't it?"

"What did you do next?"

"I debated leaving it like that. Two of me might get the job done twice as fast. But it troubled me. I hypothesized that if I went back to a time when I knew I was in transit, conducting a test jumping forward, that it might fix things. It would eliminate my duplicate… as well as the version of me conducting that test. So I did it. And he was gone.

"But as I stood in that house, alone again, I felt sick. Like I'd murdered someone. But were we both individuals? Did he have a soul? Or if something like a soul exists at all, did we *share* one? Where did he go?"

Aaron's expression sank.

Drummer glanced across the room toward the ticket counter, where he'd just witnessed a younger Aaron and his own counterpart repeat everything that he remembered from his own past, beat for beat.

"What does all this mean for them?" he asked of the elder Aaron.

"They'll live the same life you remember," Aaron said. "There will be some differences, but in the ways that matter, their experiences will be identical to yours."

"Fate," Drummer said, musing aloud.

"No," Aaron replied. "Time loops, but our actions don't. Not really. They'll live the same lives not because they're fated to, but because they'll choose to."

"They'll choose to?"

"Yes," Aaron said, as if it were obvious. "Drummer, every day we make our choices based on who we are and on the state of the world around us at the time. But we also limit ourselves the same way. We have free will, but there are millions of things we'd *never* do, and that limits what we *would* do. So when we're presented with the same conditions, we make the same choices. Just like your counterpart took that selfie over there, exactly like you did.

"It might look like fate from the outside," Aaron went on, "but it isn't. It's like the stars in a constellation. We connect the same dots for ourselves every time we look up, not because they're the only ones in the sky, but because they're the brightest ones. They're the ones that call out to us, that paint a picture that's impossible to ignore. In that way we make the same choices, go to the same places, even take the same photos in the same settings."

Drummer pulled out his phone and opened the image gallery. He scrolled through the photographs of his life between 2010 and 2020.

Aaron smiled tenderly as he watched Drummer flip from image to image.

"All those things actually happened for you, D, and nothing will ever take that from you, even if the photos in your counterpart's phone end up looking slightly different. There's no grandfather effect. And there's no butterfly effect. You had your time with a younger Aaron, and now he'll have his."

Drummer stopped scrolling. He had landed on an image of himself with Aaron, both wearing maroon tuxedo jackets, on the cruise ship in 2015.

"And what about him?" he asked. "That version of you. Did I wipe him out?"

"No," Aaron answered. "I am him. The man in the theater upstairs… he's him too, just a little different. You'll be happy to know that he learned to sing after all. In the shower. And on that ship."

Drummer smiled, but sadly, as he came to a regrettable conclusion. "Then he was right after all, wasn't he?"

"About what?"

"He was right that I didn't have to send him away. Minutes ago, I didn't have to let Aaron walk away from me."

"No, you didn't," the elder Aaron said. "Your counterpart would've lived a different life without him, but the changes you made between 2000 and now were already said and done. Preventing Aaron from meeting your counterpart wouldn't have unraveled the past, and Aaron wouldn't have restarted a life with Grant."

Drummer sat in stunned silence. It was a lot to absorb. Should he feel glad, sad, or possess any feeling at all? He'd done what he thought was necessary—the right thing—but maybe there was no right or wrong to any of it.

"I have something for you," said Aaron, moving the conversation along. From a pocket, he produced a small metal box the size of a quarter.

Drummer took it and opened it. Inside were three tiny items: a micro-SD data storage card and two flat red pills.

"What's this?"

"Knowledge from ignorance," said Aaron with an air of satisfaction. "And health from sickness. The SD card contains passcodes and instructions on how to access three glass storage cubes that I've left at the house—five-dimensional storage on glass, D. There's also a compatible tablet interface. The cubes contain my journal entries beginning in 2021, and a detailed account of events to come for the next fifty years. Those two pills contain the vaccines for the coronavirus and all its variants, and every nasty bug to follow. Take one yourself, now."

Drummer placed one of the pills on his tongue and swallowed it. It left behind a faint bitter-sweetness. He closed the box. "Why are you giving me these things?" he asked. Though he had an idea, he dared not say it aloud.

"You know why I'm here, baby."

Aaron reached into his pocket again and took out the wedding ring his young counterpart had left at the house. He offered it to Drummer. "It's time to go home."

Feelings of guilt and fear welled up within Drummer as he stared at that ring. He hardly felt like he deserved such a gift—the gift of return. Returning to the man he had just sent away, presuming without evidence that it had been their only option.

He took the ring and clenched it tight.

His eyes filled with tears as he looked up at the elder Aaron. In his gaze—that satisfied, contented look—he saw the Aaron he knew from 2020 looking back at him. He wasn't gone or erased. He was here, now, and he was Drummer's salvation.

"Listen closely, baby," Aaron said. "I'm going to give you the needle, but you can't be careless with it. The gate is programmed to open only two more times, and then the needle will shut down. To use it, touch the gold lights with your ring finger and middle finger at the same time. This will create a circuit—a bridge to the filament and the singularity inside. You'll feel a slight shock, but it's not electrical, it's gravitational. Think of it as a tug, pulling you from here to there. It'll take you directly to Dashiell Hammett in 2020, while we're still at lunch.

"When you arrive, the numbers on the side of the needle will change as the filament reorders the lattice constant for its next use—I know that doesn't mean anything to you, so just trust me. Leave the needle on the sidewalk for your 2020 counterpart to find. He'll pick it up and trigger it again. And he'll disappear, just like you did. Do you understand what I'm telling you to do?"

"I do," said Drummer. "But you're sending him back to 2000? Based on what you just told me, won't that rewrite all of this and create a new future?"

"Did I say that?" Aaron asked.

"No, but…." Drummer stopped, confused. Had he heard Aaron wrong? Was he not putting the pieces together correctly? It was quite possible that the stress of this day was overwhelming Drummer's reasoning and messing with his ability to parse the complex details.

"There's more going on than you think, D," Aaron said. "Time doesn't loop, exactly. With the needle it does repeat, but eventually what we perceive as a loop reopens and time goes on. You and your counterpart are two different people now, so when he picks up the needle in 2020 and disappears from Dashiell Hammett, you'll remain in 2020 and carry on with Aaron at your side."

"But that…," Drummer started, still not understanding.

"In 2000, your counterpart will experience everything you did," Aaron said, with a tone that sounded even more insistent. "He'll follow the same road and live the same life. In *his* 2010, he'll meet another version of me, and this whole process will start over for his own counterpart."

"So it just keeps going?" Drummer asked, bewildered. "Time just keeps making copy after copy of me, forever?"

He searched his thoughts for anything that might confirm this conclusion, but he found nothing. For a moment Drummer wondered if Aaron could be lying to him about this. But why would he do that? Why deceive him? Drummer didn't think it was even possible.

"I'm sorry, babe," Drummer said. "This just doesn't sound right. It sounds like if he takes the needle and goes to 2000, it'll reset everything. Even if it doesn't—if this pattern *does* go on forever—it sounds like I never get out of it. Are you sure?"

He looked into Aaron's eyes, hoping to find answers in his expression, but the elder's features had hardened. Drummer couldn't read him.

"Baby," Aaron said, "you asked me once to trust you and your understanding of Grant. Now I'm asking you to trust me and my understanding of the needle." He raised his eyebrows slightly, peering at Drummer more intently, and added, "I know what I'm doing."

Drummer searched those beautiful blue eyes, this time looking for conviction if not an explanation. If he couldn't understand what Aaron was trying to say, he at least needed to know that Aaron *believed* he was sure.

"Of course I trust you," Drummer said, though he felt unsatisfied. Perhaps this was all merely beyond him. Maybe this was a case of not seeing the forest for the trees. Regardless, Drummer could only hope that Aaron was right, that the past would remain intact, and that the future for himself and for his counterpart would unfold properly.

Aaron put his hand on Drummer's leg.

"Don't worry," Aaron said. "I overcame my doubts about this a long time ago."

Drummer took in a long breath and exhaled, choosing to accept Aaron's words. Drummer gave him a quick nod.

"Good," Aaron said. "Because Aaron's waiting for you. That loyal young man in the theater upstairs might be having fun with your counterpart right now, but inside he's thinking only of you. He's also on that cruise in 2015, singing to the Drummer of 2005. And he's in that alley, after your counterpart has gone, wondering when *you* will return. He loves both Drummers dearly, *but you are the one he needs.*"

Drummer closed his eyes tight, choking back his regret. He'd hoped to give Aaron a better life, but it appeared that Aaron had suffered regardless. The elder version had found himself alone and had toiled for years, all so he could decipher the needle, return to this day, and send Drummer back to the life he'd lost. In the face of such sacrifice, did Drummer deserve a good future at all? He didn't know.

"I hurt you so badly," said Drummer through a resurgence of tears.

"Baby, no," Aaron countered. "You saved me. You saved *him*. And now—finally—I get to save you."

He offered Drummer the needle.

Drummer stared at it—that small glass key, swirling with energy, its golden lights flickering like sparklers.

He took it into his hands.

"What if my counterpart doesn't pick it up?"

"He will."

"But what if Aaron tries to stop him?"

"He won't. He feels too much doubt. As you probably guessed, Aaron will never tell your counterpart about you, because he doesn't know what'll happen if he does. And in that alley, he'll still feel doubt. He'll wonder if, by taking the needle from your counterpart, he'd undo the past, never meet you, and be destined to end up with Grant again.

"D, Aaron Hayes—in every time and place—is a skater and a scientist. If there's one thing that's fatal to his confidence, it's doubt. But if you remove that doubt, he'll charge straight ahead. He'll pursue his theories, even if they prove to be wrong. He'll take a perilous ride down a driveway on his skateboard and jump out of a plane at twelve thousand feet. He'll trust that you really are from the future, and he'll move to San Francisco with you. He'll trust that the tiny object you show him, without any demonstration or proof, really is a time machine.

"Aaron's not influenced by fear or worry—those things he can overcome. He's influenced by doubt. So, at that moment of truth, on Dashiell Hammett, when the needle's in your counterpart's hand, Aaron's doubt may waver as his fear of losing the other Drummer kicks in, but it won't buckle. And he won't interfere."

Drummer understood what the elder Aaron was telling him. It was logical and practical.

"What happens to you?" Drummer asked.

The elder Aaron's expression sobered. "I stay here. I'll go back to the house. Maybe I'll use that telescope to look down on them from time to time. And I'll make sure the glass data cubes I left are there for you when you arrive in 2020, even if I'm gone by then."

Drummer saw in this decision a sad irony. The elder Aaron would now be the one living a solitary existence as a man out of time, an aging ghost, riding out his days in that house on the hill, unseen by the world.

"You sacrificed your entire life for this," Drummer said, lamenting the loss he perceived.

"No," said the elder Aaron, "not a sacrifice. A choice. A fate of my own choosing. An intentional path leading me back to this day, where I was always meant to be. By your side."

He smiled contentedly and leaned in. "Give him the vaccine," he said. "Tell him about me. He'll want to know that he succeeded at saving you. And be with him… in every way possible. Give him the peaceful, joyful future you always wanted for him. But most of all, after ten years of isolation and lockdown… *live your life*.”

The elder Aaron reached out, took Drummer's hand, and stood, lifting him to his feet.

The two men embraced.

“I love you so much, Aaron,” Drummer said through tears. He was both nervous and thrilled, and at the same time heartbroken that he was leaving the older man behind.

“Oh, baby, I love you too,” said Aaron. “Don't forget me, Methuselah.”

“I never will.”

The elder Aaron took a step back.

Drummer positioned the needle in his hand. He scanned the room, making sure no one was watching, and then, with his loving gaze locked with Aaron's, he rolled the two gold lights over his fingers.

He was gone in an instant.

IN THE bright wide lobby, Aaron remained.

He wiped the last tears from his cheeks.

And sat back down on the bench.

He felt enormous satisfaction, but also a great deal of guilt. He had returned Drummer to the future, but to do so he had lied. Drummer was right; sending his counterpart to 2000 would have undone everything, wiping out Aaron and Drummer's earlier years and all they'd done together.

And if Drummer had known this truth, he would've faced the same decision upon returning to 2020 as he had in 2010: whether to preserve his counterpart's relationship with the younger Aaron or to prioritize his own. The elder Aaron already knew what Drummer's choice would be. The fire in Grant's house on Potrero Hill was all the evidence he needed. He also knew that compromise would not be acceptable, such as a three-way partnership between Aaron and the two Drummers coexisting in 2020. Even if the three of them were to somehow accept the reality of their situation, they wouldn't be able to share without guilt and jealousy eventually tearing them all apart.

So the lie, while manipulative, was necessary to convince Drummer that the best—only—option was to leave the needle in the alley. It also served a more personal purpose: it allowed the younger Aaron in 2020 to reunite with the elder Drummer—to come home—and live contented with the belief that a loop in time had been closed, with no loose ends remaining. Keeping the younger Aaron in the dark about the truth was the only way to give him a lasting peace.

As for Drummer's counterpart, his fate was more complicated. The elder Aaron had debated for years about what to do with him, because sending him back to 2000 would only have introduced more chaos to an already chaotic layering of time. So, he decided that when Drummer's counterpart picked up the needle in the alley, he would be delivered not backward to 2000 but forward to 2060 and a new life in the future. The elder Aaron felt a biting remorse for this decision, but he took comfort in knowing that it would spare that other Drummer from an untimely pandemic death and send him to a time with limitless potential. Aaron was hopeful—confident—that this version of Drummer would forgive him for his choice and find joy in that new world… a world deserving of his love and generosity in all the ways the elder Aaron believed he himself was not.

He glanced at the ticket counter, recalling his own meeting with the young Drummer, and indeed he felt undeserving. Though Aaron had enjoyed ten beautiful years with him and loved him unequivocally, he had not been fair to Drummer during those years. He'd believed that the needle was waiting for them on Dashiell Hammett in 2020, so he never seriously planned for their future. And he'd often been distracted by the past, most notably in 2015 on their birthday cruise to Hawaii. Aaron's love for Drummer's counterpart had been deep and genuine, but stunted and qualified. Drummer deserved far better than that.

Aaron cleared his mind. He stood and walked to the escalator, retracing the steps his thirty-year-old counterpart had taken just minutes before.

On the upper level, he approached the attendant at the door and flashed a ticket stub, one of the fifty-year-old mementos he'd taken from the framed photo at home. He entered the theater. The lights were dim, but the movie had not yet started.

He found his younger self seated beside Drummer, several rows back from the screen, where he knew they'd be.

He moved down the aisle behind them.

And he sat.

And he listened.

"It's not full of old people?" he heard the younger Drummer ask, joking.

"Course not," his younger self said, laughing. "Besides, older people are cool, come on. And like I said, in the middle of the Pacific the Milky Way is amazing. And there's this huge club at the back of the ship where you can sing karaoke—even 'Xanadu,' if you want to."

"That sounds pretty great," said the young Drummer. "You know the song 'All Over the World'?"

The young Aaron smiled. "I know it by heart."

"Then we should go. How about after the movie?"

"Thought we're playing video games tonight."

"Right. Hawaii another time, then."

"I'll mark my calendar."

The elder Aaron listened in silent serenity as the two men spoke. After all the years of planning and research, trial and error, he had succeeded. The tragedies of his life had been unwound and averted. Health had supplanted sickness. Knowledge had overcome ignorance. And justice had conquered wickedness. Time could now move on. And although an uncertain distant future awaited the Drummer seated in the dark before him, he knew that his next ten years would be exactly as joyful as they should be.

His only remaining regret was that he'd been unable to speak to his own young counterpart face-to-face. He wanted to tell the young Aaron not to look upon the next ten years as predestiny but as an unknown, and not to treat the man he thinks of as Drummer's *counterpart* as anything less than the version of Drummer he believes to be real. But the elder Aaron knew himself well enough to know that no matter how much he insisted or how much he begged, such a meeting with his younger self would be futile. Now, as then, as always, Aaron would experience these things on his own time and in his own way. The elder Aaron drifted into melancholy and allowed himself to sink into the younger men's voices. In their nervous laughter and shy glances, in their muted anxiousness and unspoken but shared hopes, he relived his own memory of falling in love with Drummer for the first time, the second time, and now, again, a third.

CHAPTER 20
HOME

ON SATURDAY, August eighth, 2020, Aaron and Drummer sat down to a picnic lunch in Huntington Park to celebrate Aaron's fortieth birthday. The sun cast a radiant glow upon San Francisco, with hues of blue and gold swirling through a vibrant midday sky.

It was the perfect setting for a celebration, but Aaron's thoughts were elsewhere.

For ten years, he had carried within him knowledge of the future and memories of a convoluted past, none of which he believed he could share with anyone. He'd seen predicted events unfold in unexpected ways, and he'd looked ahead to others—sometimes with anticipation, sometimes with reticence. He had a large circle of friends and a loving partner in the younger Drummer, but with the burdens of his knowledge, he was alone.

From the moment of their meeting in the theater in 2010, their relationship had blossomed quickly. And—as the elder Drummer had predicted—his younger counterpart indeed became Aaron's entire world, at times causing him to forget all about that house on the hill.

But such moments were rare.

Aaron loved the younger Drummer as much as life itself, but "life itself" had remained defined by the elder. The new roads the young men traveled were abundant with joy and adventure, but the tallest signposts had always pointed back to the previous decade, to a relationship filled with shared discovery and mutual purpose—the fundamentals of existence that Aaron had come to believe defined the best of times.

And just as he had looked backward, so too had he looked upward at that house on the hill, to see if the lights were on and if *he* were home. And to wonder if the elder Drummer might also be gazing down at him, curious about the same.

Until the day those lights had gone out.

And never went on again.

That was when he knew that the elder Drummer was gone. He would not be coming home, and Aaron could not go home to him. A few years earlier Grant had been found shot to death in his bed, but the person who'd done it had never been found—or identified. The only evidence was a single bullet. Nothing more. No weapon. No entry, forced or otherwise. Though Aaron had no proof, he was certain he knew who the perpetrator had been. Those lights had gone dark by necessity.

From that time forward, knowing that the elder Drummer was gone, he found himself cursed by recurring strokes of bitter déjà vu. They would manifest often, sometimes without warning. They were especially cruel at night, when his dreams would carry him back to the elder Drummer's loving arms, only to abandon him suddenly as he woke.

These moments were shocking, causing him to cry out in confusion, not knowing where he was or who lay beside him. The younger Drummer would then awaken, take him into his arms to comfort him and tenderly bring him back to himself. And all the while he believed a story Aaron once told him—that his trauma was the result of an abusive relationship, long passed, with a man named Grant Zimmer.

Ultimately the years between 2010 and 2020 had brought Aaron great happiness, but they'd also saddled him with an unshakable heartache. This duality proved particularly distressing when the coronavirus appeared. The world began to shut down in 2020, and a new clock started ticking for him, heralding the coming of both his greatest fear and his last remaining insight into the future: the knowledge that, on this day, minutes from this idyllic moment in Huntington Park, the man he loved would discover a small, strange device in a tree-lined alley and disappear from his life forever.

Unless Aaron chose to stop it.

"You've been distant today," said Drummer. "You okay, babe?"

Aaron studied him with both clarity and conflict of thought as they sat together on a blanket on the park lawn. In every aspect of Drummer's physical appearance, Aaron could see the past—in his blue polo shirt, the light jacket lying beside him, and in the full sleeve tattoos on both of his arms. On his left forearm the image of Cassandra and her forlorn expression spoke volumes. Aaron could confidently say that at this moment, Drummer looked exactly as he had when he'd first seen him in the suburbs twenty years earlier.

"I'm fine," he lied, hoping to dispel Drummer's worry. "I'm just thinking about that last spill off my skateboard."

"You didn't hurt yourself that bad."

"Maybe just my pride," said Aaron. "Coulda landed it fine a few years ago. Everyone out there's half my age now. Maybe it's time to hang it up."

"Those guys half your age can fuck themselves," Drummer said with a chuckle. "When they're forty, they'll be lucky to be half as young as you."

Aaron forced a smile. He surveyed the happy people around them and the ornate old hotels that encircled the park. This hilltop crown at the apex of a city on the edge of the world was as close to a utopia as he'd ever known.

"Would you do me a favor?" Aaron asked.

"Course," said Drummer.

"Take your phone out. I want to make a video."

Drummer obliged and offered him the device.

"No, I mean, you film me."

"Are you going to do a strip tease for me?" Drummer asked wryly as he brought the phone back. "I mean, it's my birthday too."

He began recording.

"Happy birthday, Methuselah," Drummer chirped.

Aaron grinned. "Careful what you say, old man…."

He'd barely finished speaking before he felt a resurgence of that overpowering déjà vu. He considered the words he had just said, and he wondered where and when he'd heard them before. Not in the past, as he first thought. Rather, they were a reflection of the present, seen twenty years earlier, replayed in a video on Drummer's phone in the Mowry Inn. How could he have forgotten? And how many other moments had played out in such a manner over the years? Too many to count.

"You turned forty-five last week, you know," Aaron added, hearing his voice echo through time. "But thank you. You're so good to me."

"And you to me."

The feeling of déjà vu persisted. Aaron forgot what else he wanted to say. He glanced about, hoping his thoughts would return to him, but they'd taken flight.

Drummer stopped recording and set the phone on the blanket.

"I think you have something on your shirt, babe," he said. "Stand up for a second."

"What, really?" Aaron climbed to his feet and looked down at himself, in search of whatever might've been stuck to him. He saw nothing, but he brushed his shirt anyway.

Drummer leaned forward, and in a single fluid movement he pulled a small box from the pocket of his coat, then lifted himself up onto one knee.

Aaron froze, his eyes locked on the box in Drummer's hand. He met Drummer's gaze and saw an expression overflowing with hope and anticipation.

"Aaron," Drummer began, visibly emotional, "we've been together a long time… ten years… the best years of my life. I know it feels like the world's falling apart around us sometimes, and the future can look bleak, but you've shown me that even now, in the middle of all this, there's still so much joy to be had."

He handed Aaron the box.

Aaron took it, his hands shaking.

Dread filled him.

This can't be how it ends, he thought.

He opened it and found a polished gold engagement ring inside. He held back his grief as he read the inscription, "To our next life."

Drummer continued with his marriage proposal, speaking tenderly and from the heart, but Aaron was sinking into despair. He thought about his own proposal to the elder Drummer fifteen years earlier. Though they hadn't been able to marry at the time, he'd always felt as though they had. Now, looking back, Aaron realized that he'd avoided the topic of marriage with the younger Drummer because he'd always believed that his own proposal to the older had been the real one.

The ring slid onto Aaron's finger. He cried at the sight of it. There was happiness in his watering eyes and in his aching heart, but also grief, for he knew that despite the promise of that ring, if Drummer picked up the needle, their next life would never come.

The picnic ended.

Aaron compelled himself to stand, though his body felt like stone.

He and Drummer left Huntington Park. They walked silently toward home, not saying a word until they reached Pine Street several blocks away.

"Are you sure you're okay?" Drummer asked.

"Thanks, baby. I'm fine." Aaron said, doing his best to hide the anxiety brewing within him.

They continued along Pine until they reached to corner of Dashiell Hammett, where Drummer suggested they cut through.

Aaron did not protest, but as they rounded the corner a voice in his mind began screaming at him to stop. It demanded that he turn around, go back up to Pine Street, and find another way home, but Aaron kept going regardless. He felt compelled to continue, almost forced down the hill against his will—but also in obedience to it.

He scanned the sidewalk with every step, believing that at any moment the needle would be there. They'd find it and Drummer would pick it up. Then everything would come to an end.

But did it have to?

Aaron had asked himself that very question every day for ten years. Did it all really have to end? Did he have to let Drummer leave the present to guarantee that they'd be together in the past? Did time really work that way?

He wanted to believe that it didn't. He wanted to snatch the needle from Drummer's hands when he found it, keep him at his side, move forward together into a shared unknown, and somehow retain the memories of a life that would—as a result of this intercession—no longer happen.

But even after ten years of this internal debate, Aaron's doubts remained. Despite his knowledge of the future and his insights into time and space, he still relied on the imperfect counsel of his own experiences and beliefs, just like everyone else. And when his moments of déjà vu would strike, like the one in Huntington Park, his doubt tightened its grip.

"Hey, check this out," Drummer said, indicating something on the sidewalk ahead. He moved forward to pick it up.

Aaron stopped.

This was it.

Every passing second felt like a minute. He felt a surge of fear. His doubt wavered.

When Drummer straightened, he had the needle in his hand. It was luminescent. The gold lights glimmered. It truly was a beautiful thing. For Aaron, seeing the universe come full circle like this was both awesome and horrifying.

Drummer paused as he met Aaron's eyes.

"Baby, I'm worried about you," Drummer said. "Are you sure you're all right?"

Aaron said nothing. He felt locked in, like a man physically paralyzed, unable to move or make a sound even as his mind ran in circles. He struggled to raise his arm, to swat the needle from Drummer's grip, but he couldn't budge.

The screaming in his mind grew louder.

Do it now or lose everything, you goddamn coward!

Drummer's eyes softened, and with the sweet concern Aaron had come to expect from him, he said, "Let's get you home." Drummer lowered the needle to his side, and as he slipped it into his pocket he turned it over in his hand, mindlessly rolling it across his fingertips.

The circuit connected.

The gate opened.

And in that instant, Drummer vanished.

Aaron jumped with a start. It had happened so suddenly.

His doubt and his fear evaporated, for they no longer served a purpose, but in their wake came rage. It wailed at him for not acting, for failing to decipher the needle's secrets when he'd had the chance, for obliging ten years of indecision and silence, and now, for letting Drummer disappear from his life for a second and final time.

He tried to tell himself that this was how it had to be. That he had to let Drummer go, to allow him to close the loop created when he had first gone back to 2000, or let the life they'd built unravel.

It was logical. Non-paradoxical.

But even in the face of this logic, Aaron's mental screams hammered him. They coalesced into a brutal, unforgiving voice that told him, in no uncertain terms, that he was to blame for his own pain, that each of his successes had actually been a failure, and that whenever he'd lost something he loved, he'd brought that loss upon himself.

His tears came quickly. He cried, but at the same time he scolded
himself for it. He felt undeserving. Unworthy. The angry, howling voice
inside him confirmed it.

AARON BELIEVED he had lived two lives, selfishly,
    And that he had sacrificed two Drummers.

AFTER EVERYTHING they'd given him,
    He had abandoned them both.

THE ELDER Drummer would not be coming home.
    Aaron could not go home to him.
    The dark windows in the house,
    And the voice in his head,
    Told him as much.

HE CLOSED his eyes, hoping to silence that voice, but it would not relent.
    The veins in his head pulsed, and his senses dulled as the world
disappeared into the blood-red rage of his wailing mind.

ALL THINGS ended.

IN THAT instant, Aaron imagined the future ahead of him—leaving
behind this life, growing old alone in that house on the hill, surrounded
by the trappings of a beautiful history but with nothing new to impress
on him but the sounds.
    The rain in the spring.
    The birds in the summer.
    And on cold, autumn nights, the echoes of his memory.

HE MOURNED, but his mourning was quickly cut short. He felt pressure,
warmth, and weight on his arm—real sensations he could not ignore.

He opened his eyes and looked down.

On the ring finger of his left hand, he now wore two gold bands. One was the ring he'd been given just minutes ago. The other was the ring he'd left at the house himself ten years earlier.

He looked up to find a fifty-five-year-old Drummer standing before him, appearing exactly as he had at the theater in 2010.

Drummer gazed back at him with a hesitant smile. He lifted his left hand to show the ring on his own finger, the ring with a shared promise inscribed inside.

Aaron stared at him, but he doubted his senses. He wanted to reach out and embrace Drummer, but he feared this image was a ghost, and that the second ring on his hand was little more than a relic of his déjà vu. Aaron could feel the breeze touch his tear-streaked face, contorted by grief, by ten years lived with knowledge of the future, and all the agony and isolation it had wrought.

Drummer reached out and caressed his cheek to wipe away his tears, and with that simple, loving touch, Aaron was brought home.

He fell into Drummer's arms.

His joy consumed him.

His guilt fled.

And the howling voice in his mind suddenly had nothing left to say.

DRUMMER HELD back tears as Aaron sobbed in his supportive embrace.

He held Aaron tight.

And took in the air.

He was home.

And everything he'd lost had been found again.

Only now did he see that this time and place—this tranquil afternoon on Dashiell Hammett—formed the great crossroads of his life. It was the point to which all pasts had led and from which all futures sprang. Where everything he loved had come and gone and everything he knew started and ended—and began again.

Back in the movie theater, Aaron had mentioned seeing signposts in his mind, pointing to a myriad of possible futures—one sign leading to a life once lived and the rest to others unrealized. Drummer could now see them for himself. Indeed, they'd always been there, but in his linear world view he too had been able to read only one.

Now he could read them all.

Keep reading for an excerpt from
Murder On Cabot's Landing
by Max Griffin

CHAPTER 1

Cabot's Star, NOMAD 129.683.365.120, is a class K star approximately 562 light years from the Immaculate Concourse. The Cabot system has six planets in conventional orbits ranging from .2AU to 86AU. The system was purchased in 2312 CE from the Grand Alliance by Cabot Industries Trust of Old Home Earth. The sole habitable world in the system is a satellite of the gas giant Kenebec (NOMAD 129.683.365.120.B). See the entry for Cabot's Landing (NOMAD 129.683.365.120.B.5).

—New Omnibus Mandaean Almagest and Dataset [NOMAD] 3172 CE

THE SHUTTLE shuddered, and Elam's seat belt bit into his shoulder. He tugged at the strap and fidgeted in his cramped faux-leather seat. The Syndicate's Auditor, Malcolm Bender, sprawled in the seat next to him, having settled there despite the fact that all the other thirty-eight seats on the *Zuiderkruis*'s shuttle were empty. Elam resisted the urge to squirm away. He'd managed to spend the forty-day passage from Elsinore in his stateroom, avoiding contact with people. Now, on the last few miles of a seventy-light-year voyage, he had to put up with this bean counter.

He sighed and tried to ignore Bender's cologne. Elam had no reason to take his past out on Bender. After all, Elam's past was Elam's fault, not Bender's or anyone else's. The poor guy was probably just lonely. Besides, before long, Elam would be alone on this Chaos-forsaken hole of a planet. It couldn't happen soon enough. Hermit-like solitude was exactly what he sought. What he deserved, too.

The craft shuddered, and Elam glanced out the window. Nothing but clouds. Bender straightened a crease on his gray slacks, smirked, and squeezed Elam's knee. "Don't worry, Mr. Vandreren. It's just the upper atmosphere buffeting the landing craft. The area around Cabot's Cove has a mild climate. Subtropical. Just like your briefing promised."

Elam eyed Bender's hand on his knee. So, that wasn't loneliness in his eyes after all. It was desire. That wasn't Bender's fault either. Elam had hidden his lean, battle-honed frame under a crumpled, shapeless orange jumpsuit, but he couldn't do anything about his face. Bewitching, some called it. Lean and hungry, Ivar had said. Elam squelched a surge of grief and self-loathing at the memory of Ivar. The kindest response to Bender would be to move his knee to one side. "I'll be fine, thank you."

Bender took the hint and withdrew his hand. "Sorry. I was just trying to be reassuring."

Elam read the micro-expressions that flashed on the other man's features. Bender wasn't sorry, he was hurt. Not for the first time, Elam regretted the training that let him read expressions most couldn't even see. Not that the training hadn't been useful in his prior life, but too much knowledge often proved hurtful. Like now.

Bender's expression also showed he thought Elam was a jerk. He was right on that too. Time to gloss things over and change the subject. "How long will the transfer take?" He kept his tone businesslike. Officious. "Isn't there an audit or something?"

"My team up on the *Zuiderkruis* has already processed the data we uploaded from the Cabot Cove AI. We've got Mr. Torrance's final report too. All that's left is the formal transfer from the current Resident to you. We can do that over lunch. It's my understanding Mr. Torrance and his spouse are eager to get back to civilization."

His spouse. Right. That meant Elam would have to find a way to tolerate two more people, not just one. "Over lunch, eh? Can't we just skip that?"

Bender frowned. "Really, Mr. Vandreren? Aren't you interested in the Torrances' experiences? He and his spouse have been here for nearly six years, after all. Mr. Torrance's final report was pretty terse. I've seen your briefing packet, and it's not like it was… comprehensive."

Elam shrugged and avoided looking at Bender. "It told me what I needed to know. I'll have this place to myself for the next ten years, right?"

Bender nodded. "Mostly right. But you won't be totally alone. There's the AI, of course, and the occasional ship that uses the port facilities. Plus, there will be the official quarterly inspections by the Margrave's representatives, to make sure you're still alive and in residence. That's the whole point, of course: to maintain the Syndicate's title to the system. Any break in human residency and ownership of the planet reverts to the Imperium."

"Yeah, yeah. I got all that." Elam could live with being around other people once every three months or so. Barely. He stretched his legs and tried to ignore his inner ears as the shuttle swerved while it made its approach.

The craft jittered, and a thump reverberated through the compartment. Bender smiled. "Ah, that will be the landing gear deploying. I do hope the Torrances meet us at the spaceport."

The shuttle bumped to a landing and taxied toward the terminal. Elam unfastened his seat belt and tried to relax. After what felt like hours, but that he knew were just a few short minutes, the shuttle ground to a stop. More clunking noises announced the stairway deploying, and then his ears popped as the shuttle doors opened.

He stood, stretched, and escaped to the outdoors.

He took a deep breath and wrinkled his nose at the stink. Kind of sick-sweet, not quite like vomit, but almost. He supposed that would be the genetically engineered wheat, *triticum cabitorum*, he'd read about. In the five hundred years since the Great Disintegration, it had time to spread over large areas of Cabot's Landing, apparently including the spaceport at Cabot's Cove.

The gas giant Kenebec with its spectacular rings hovered on the horizon, in half phase but still filling an eighth of the too-white sky. A warm breeze fluttered through his hair. The 0.87G gravity left him invigorated after the plus-G of the ghostship *Zuiderkruis*, but he knew better than to be fooled. It was just a moon, no longer of much economic value, with a single island chain in an otherwise world-encompassing ocean. True, he'd have to share the place with the native bandersnatchi, but if he stayed away from the deep sea, he'd be fine. They were mindless carnivores, in any case.

Bender stopped at the top of the stairs and muttered something into his phone before following Elam. He stood too close when he finally approached. Of course. Elam ignored him and continued surveying their surroundings. The runway stretched off in the distance, low mountains rimmed the valley, and a single-story concrete structure stood about fifty meters distant. An open-air, driverless vehicle puttered toward them and stopped a short distance away.

Bender sighed. "It appears the Torrances decided to just send transport instead of meeting us in person." He hesitated and then snapped in a commanding tone, "Cornwall."

A hologram flickered into existence, and Elam rolled his eyes. Just what he needed. Someone had programmed the AI to not only look like a person, but to look like a friggin' nineteenth-century butler. Give him ten minutes alone at the control console and he'd fix that.

The butler—Cornwall—bowed and spoke with a prim Oxford accent. "How may I serve you, sir?"

Bender answered, "Please let Mr. and Mrs. Torrance know we've arrived."

"Sir, Mrs. Torrance is presently in Lansbury. She's not answering her phone."

"What the devil is she doing there? Never mind. Just notify Mr. Torrance, then."

"Sir, I last saw him entering the lobby of the Lodge. My connection to the lobby has been disabled, so I am presently unable to comply with your request."

"Disabled, you say? A malfunction?"

"No, sir. I deduce Mr. Torrance has manually switched it off."

"Why would he do that?"

"That information isn't available to me, sir."

Bender shook his head and glanced at Elam. "Damned literal-minded AI. No bloody curiosity. But why switch off the connection? What if he needed Cornwall to do something?"

Elam shrugged. "Maybe he turned it off so he could have privacy." For damned sure, that's what Elam planned to do with the intrusive thing.

"Makes no sense. And why did Mrs. Torrance go gallivanting off to Lansbury? There's nothing there but the ruins of an old pre-Disintegration settlement. It's almost seven hundred kilometers north of here. Even by monorail, it's a ten-hour trip one way."

"If the village is in ruins, why keep the monorail connection running?" Elam regretted asking as soon as the words left his mouth.

"Got me. When the Syndicate rediscovered the planet seventy-odd years ago, they rebooted as much of the old technology as they could. Part of restarting the dysprosium mines. Now that the mines are closed and the place is abandoned again, I guess stuff is just running on inertia or something. Mau knows, we still don't know how most of the old tech really works."

Elam avoided snorting at the reference to a divinity. He understood the ancient technology well enough without appealing to superstition. Most of it, anyway. He even understood the ghost condensate drives that powered ships like the *Zuiderkruis*. That knowledge was one reason he wanted to hide on this moon. Not the only one, but surely a sufficient one.

Bender scowled at the AI, then turned back to Elam. "We may as well take the transport to the Lodge. It's a couple of clicks away. I'm damned well going to give Torrance a piece of my mind for this. I don't like disorder. No sir, I don't like it all."

Elam's lips twitched. The universe preferred Chaos. So did he. He climbed into the tram and settled in for the ride.

Bender couldn't seem to keep his mouth shut. "The smell is from the wheat, you know. The ancients engineered it specifically for the local conditions. The food processors use it to synthesize flavored proteins. They're amazingly good, actually. I rotate through here as an auditor, and have often shared meals with Mr. and Mrs. Torrance. Prime rib. Salmon. Lamb. Even shrimp. And bread, of course." He swept an arm at the golden waves of grain waving along the roadside, under the glow of Kenebec. "They were geniuses, back in the old days."

Elam quirked an eyebrow at his know-it-all companion. "They weren't smart enough to avoid the Great Disintegration. Besides, if the ancients were geniuses, why didn't they make the damned wheat smell better?"

Bender's features turned red. "Well, there is that. I'm told one gets used to it."

"No doubt." He hoped Bender would shut up for a while.

No such luck. The man perked up and pointed. "Look, there's the Lodge." A three-story structure of gray concrete and crystalline glass emerged as they crested a hilltop. In the distance, sunlight glinted off the waters of Cabot's Cove and the Central Sea.

Elam tried to not sneer when he said, "Looks like yet another revival of twentieth-century modernism. The ancients could build anything, and they chose that loathsome style. Chaos knows what they were thinking."

"It's true, the old Cabot Trust didn't spend anything on ornamentation. They were pretty utilitarian back then. But the facilities themselves are first-rate. They survived undamaged for nearly five centuries after they abandoned this place. Even the tech rebooted without a flaw. They built to last, rather than to be pretty."

Elam didn't correct him. He knew that the definition of working tech was one in which the bugs hadn't yet been found.

The little tram buzzed to a stop under a concrete canopy that protected the two-story, glassed-in lobby of the Lodge. Yellow plastic replaced one section of the glass, just to the left of the double doors. Elam pointed. "What happened there? Storm damage?"

"Actually, yes. The mountains on the west coast of Bountiful stop most storms from getting this far, but the audit data showed one got through three years ago. The Syndicate sent in a repair team."

"Hopefully, that won't be necessary during my term."

"You never know. A lot can happen in ten years. Some people can't take the solitude. Even with two of them here, the Torrances forfeited their bonus in order to leave before their term was up." He beamed at Elam. "I'm sure that won't happen with you. Shall we go in?"

Without speaking, Elam rose and strode through the entrance.

The foul smell of the wheat vanished, but the odor inside was worse.

A body lay crumpled at the base of the yellow plastic repair, visible only from the inside. Dark blood pooled underneath. The air conditioning wafted the coppery scent of death, mingled with the odor of feces and urine, toward Elam.

Bender shrieked, "In Mau's name, what's happened here?"

Elam knelt by the body and felt for a pulse. None. The flesh was still warm to the touch. "Is this Mr. Torrance?"

Bender held a handkerchief to his nose and edged forward. "Yes. Dear heaven, is he dead?"

"Yes. I'd say not more than an hour or so."

"This is horrible! What happened? Did he trip and fall?"

Elam snorted. "What, on a banana? There's nothing to trip on, nowhere to fall from. Look at his skull. It's all bashed in. Someone killed him."

Bender's voice shook. "You mean… he's been murdered?"

"That's what I said. His wife must have done it. They were the only people on the planet, right?"

"That's not possible. They loved each another. I had dinner with them."

"Then why has she run off to—what was it? Lancaster?"

"Lansbury. I still don't believe it."

Elam sighed. "Call the ship. We'll need the captain to organize an investigation. Whatever happened here, Mr. Torrance deserves justice." His fingers touched his shirt, just below the hollow of his neck. He caressed the pendant that hid there, a constant reminder of the fragility of justice, of love, and of life.

He stood and chewed his lower lip. An investigation meant people swarming over the planet. His planet. His refuge.

He'd have to be sure they didn't wind up investigating him.

Scan the QR code below to order

DEREK SOWERS was raised in California and has lived in San Francisco for over thirty-five years, where many of his stories take place. As a film school graduate focused on screenwriting and directing, his literary writing style evolved to be visually immersive and emotionally charged. He loves creating characters that experience the grand sweep of emotion strongly and deeply, with the hope that his readers feel the same.

Derek's work is often described as wistful but hopeful. He leans into themes close to his heart, particularly those involving self-sacrifice and the search for individual purpose. His characters grow within an evolving story and express their vulnerability as well as their strength. Even when a narrative turns dark, there's often a spark of light to be found. Derek believes in the Hopeful Romantic and the Reluctant Hero, and he enjoys crafting a compelling conflict arc and an emotionally satisfying resolution.

Derek is a fan of open-world videogames, time-travel stories, adult animation, and playtime with his cat, Cirrus. He considers himself an unqualified cat person, ready to make the sweetest (or sourest) kitty his cuddle buddy, even when the odds are against him. His employment history has run the gamut from film making to hospitality to customer service, exposing him to varied work environments and to people of unique and noteworthy backgrounds. If there's one thing he's learned from his time here on earth, it's that despite our differences, everyone's experience is worthy of story and song—you just gotta know how to tell it.

FOR **MORE**

OF THE

BEST

GAY

ROMANCE